THE DOG WHO TOOK HIS MAN FOR A WALK

THE DOG WHO TOOK HIS MAN FOR A WALK

Bob McCurdy

Prairie Viking Press
Westby, Wisconsin

The Dog Who Took His Man For A Walk

Published by
Prairie Viking Press
E7409 Sherpe Road
Westby, WI 54667

ISBN 978-0-9789332-7-2
ISBN 0-9789332-7-3

Printed in the U.S.A.

The Dog Who Took His Man For A Walk is distributed by:
Prairie Viking Press
www.sherpe.com

Cover Illustration by Jeanne Whilden

Also by Bob McCurdy:
Starting Over

ACKNOWLEDGEMENTS

I wish to extend immense gratitude to several people who have contributed generously to the editorial process of this book. Jeanne Whilden continues to offer grammatical advice and she courageously challenges my writing style offering terrific suggestions. My hope is that she doesn't run out of patience with me. She has also designed the covers for this and my previous book.

I am deeply grateful to my friend, Howard Sherpe, and publisher Prairie Viking Press. Howard is a PROUD Norwegian (Viking), who does not live on a prairie. I keep meaning to ask him about that.

My partner in life, Nancy Miller, amazes me with her eye for detail and rewording of awkward phrasing. My friend Billie Johnson, who contributed a great deal of time and effort to the editing and proofing process.

New on the scene, is a man I've known for years, Jim Ahlen, now a retired English teacher. His wife and he raise sheep and border collies. The third year after I came to Door County, I discovered that Jim sold self-composting toilets as a side business. I bought one from him, thus ending trips to the outhouse.

Jim went though this book with an eye toward teaching me grammar, and punctuation. What is heartening, is that he has had to do some research himself. It is a commentary on his quality ethos that he took the time to do so.

At this point, you're probably thinking, "Isn't having this many people involved in the editorial process kind of like 'over-kill'? Not when you're a dyslexic, hunt-and-peck typist, computer-challenged yutz like me.

A sincere thanks to Doug Smith, who manages our township office and is a computer whiz. I am always gratified when I bring an IT question to him, and he has to struggle with it for more than two minutes. He's got to be tired of seeing my face.

In my previous book, I gave homage to Door County. I am an avid sailor. Door County is a Mecca for fresh-water sailing. There is no place along the 250 plus miles of shoreline, that is not exquisite. It is never boring. It can sometimes be challenging.

DEDICATION

I wish to dedicate this book to a precious lady and dear friend, Jeanne Whilden. Like myself, Jeanne is a woodcarver. She does delightfully whimsical human figures. I met her several years ago when she asked me to do sharpening for her. It's only been in the past few years that a true friendship has emerged and developed. Jeanne is an uncommonly perceptive, sensitive, witty and sagacious lady, who has a well earned, and adoring circle of friends. I am honored that she has chosen to include me. I regret that it's taken so long to discover our friendship. I am grateful that it finally happened.

Anatomy of a typical sloop rigged sailboat

Many nautical term are used in this story. This diagram will help you understand where those parts are located.

1. jib (head sail)
2. mainsail
3. hull
4. shoal draught keel
5. coaming
6. jib sheet winch
7. rudder
8. stern rail
9. tiller
10. boom
11. mast
12. bow pulpit
13. forestay (also the jib luff)
14. back stay
15. side stay
16. main sheet
17. transom

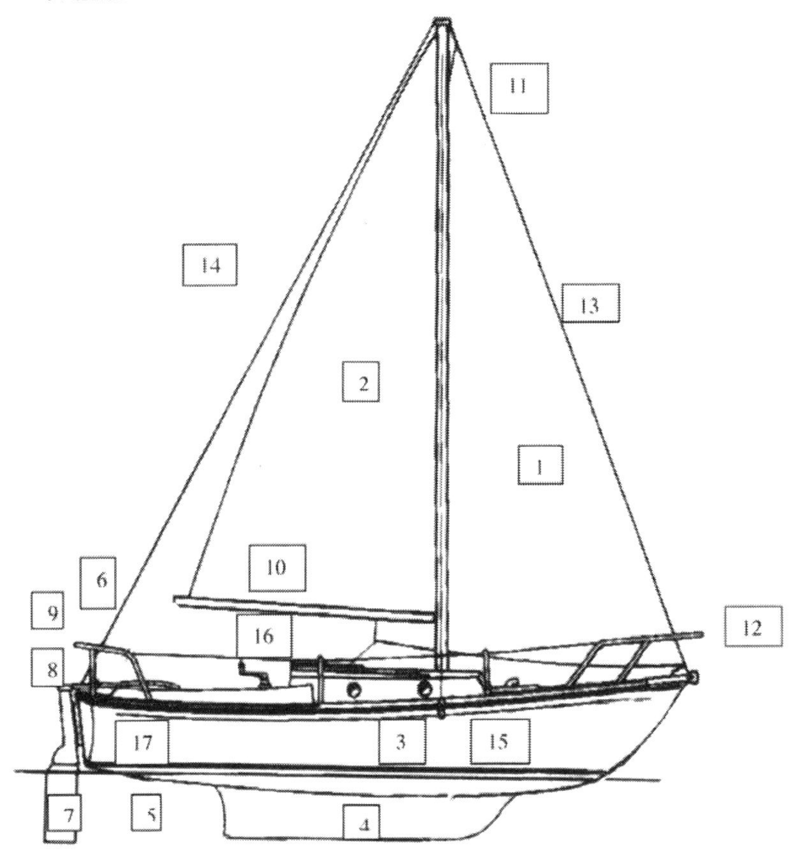

Chapter 1

Today was a special day. Andrew McLeod had no idea how special. He was about to embark on a life threatening, life changing adventure.

Andy awakened a little before 5:00. In the kitchen he turned on public radio, and let Cassidy, his fifteen year old border collie, out to do his business. He started the coffee brewing, dished up Cassidy's food and let him back in. Then he went to do his exercises, many of them aimed at working out arthritic aches and pains. His shoulders and legs bothered him the most in the morning. After showering Andy returned to the kitchen and poured the coffee into an insulated travel mug and his battered old thermos. He went through a mental checklist to think of what else needed doing before leaving. It was a given that there would be at least two or three things that he managed to overlook. Outside the tree tops were motionless. There was little if any breeze. The forecast predicted at least three more days of clear weather. He guessed the temperature to be somewhere in the low seventies; comfortable for mid-August. He went to his old 1981 pickup truck and opened the door on the passenger side allowing Cassidy to gingerly jump up onto the seat. Andy regarded the dog as a hero who had saved his life a few years back. The dog had warned him on two separate occasions about shooters. He felt certain that he would have been killed had it not been for the dog's alertness and warnings. He could not know that Cassidy would once again save his life. He stroked the old dog. "I'll miss you," he said to him. Cassidy gave him a lick, and then resumed looking out the windshield in anticipation. Andy went around to the driver's side, got in and started the engine.

Out on the road they had gone less than a mile before he saw his daughter-in-law jogging along the shoulder toward them. He stopped and she got in. "Morning, Mike." She was a tall, lean, attractive woman in her middle thirties who kept herself in good shape. She was barely winded though she had already run more than a mile. The two of them had great admiration for one another both as friends and as artists.

"Hi, Pops. You've got a perfect day for the start of your annual pilgrimage. I just wish you had someone going with you."

"We go through this same conversation every year, Mike. I'll be fine." She made no comment. It was one of the many things he liked about her. Reiterating old arguments was a waste. She had no new ones to make, nor did he.

"Not much wind to start out with," she commented.

"In the past I would have blamed that on Bush and the Republicans."

She put her arm around Cassidy and kneaded his left shoulder. "Well, now you have the Tea Party folks. You'd be lost without scapegoats." He glanced over at her and smiled. He saw her as both beautiful and smart. She had married his older son Brian sixteen years ago. The wedding had taken place under the old apple tree on his farm. "I was thinking about you as I was running this morning," Mike paused. "I was thinking that over the years you've become an institution in this town. Maybe a 'venerable character' would be a better description. I know you work hard to come across as a cynic and a curmudgeon. It's an act. The only people who you're able to convince are the outsiders who don't know you. The rest of us see right through you. How come you do that?" When he made no comment she went on, "sometimes I think you do it to test people. You seem to think it somehow separates out the phonies."

"The few friends I've got are genuine. I value my privacy. I'm not what you'd call *sociable* but I'm not a total recluse either." He gave her a slight smile. "You know what the definition of a cynic is?"

"Enlighten me."

"A disillusioned idealist. Maybe I do it to avoid disappointments."

"Disappointment is a part of life," Mike countered. "Artists probably suffer it more than most. You really are a nice guy and you give a damn. You've helped a lot of people and you're respected by a lot of folks in this community. I also think that underneath it all, you're still pretty idealistic."

He looked at his daughter-in-law for a brief moment. "I'd like to think I'm more of a realist." Then he added, "thanks, Mike. I appreciate the compliment."

They had come into town and were approaching the entrance to the marina where he docked his sailboat. "I know I'm wasting my breath telling you not to worry about me. I'll be okay. I've got a lot more to do before I face the big mystery. I do appreciate your concern." He turned in to the marina and parked close to the pier. He grabbed his backpack from the truck bed and handed that along with his coffee mug and thermos to her. He hoisted a medium sized cooler out. The two of them walked down the concrete pier with Cassidy following close behind. There was a hazy lemon mist hanging over the marina and the harbor beyond. Three fishermen in an aluminum boat were motoring toward the entrance. Another small fishing boat was being launched. The flags that lined the edge of the parking area hung limp.

At the boat they both climbed aboard. Andy opened the companionway and went below into the cabin to stow things. Mike immediately began taking the sail cover off the mainsail. When Andy emerged from the cabin he started the boat's engine letting it idle to warm up. Before casting off the two of them hugged. "I love you, Pops. Take good care."

"You know me, Mike. I'm nothing if I'm not prudent." He extracted the cell phone that Brian had bought for him from his jeans pocket. "I'll call you every evening. Don't panic if you don't hear from me. There may be some dead zones when I get way up north, or the battery may run low." Mike nodded. She knew Andy to be a skilled and competent seaman. She stepped off the boat and helped him cast off. He bid a farewell to Cassidy who stood on the concrete pier. In years past he had taken the dog along with him on these sojourns. He had given up that the practice two or three years ago. It was too much of a task getting Cassidy back into the boat after going ashore.

He engaged the engine in reverse and increased the throttle backing the 25 foot boat out of its slip. After putting the engine into forward, he looked back. He and Mike waved to one another again as the boat gathered forward momentum.

Outside of the breakwater there was only a slight ripple of wind on the water's surface. He opened the throttle to about two-thirds speed. As he stood holding the tiller, he leaned back against the stern rail. Steering toward the open waters of Lake Michigan he thought about Mike. There was a time when he had worried that his son Brian would make some of the same mistakes he had had made in choosing a partner. *What a gem Mike is,* he mused. It caused him a moment of melancholy that he had been so unsuccessful at finding a partner to share life with. He saw Brian and Mike as soul-mates.

Outside of the harbor, Andy headed the boat on a north-easterly course. There was a submerged rock ledge that extended out at least a quarter of a mile from shore. He needed to sail out a safe distance from that. He motored for more than an hour before a soft breeze began to pick up from out of the southeast. He saw increasingly larger patches of ripples on the flat surface of the water. The direction was perfect. However, for him to achieve his intended goal for the day, it would need to increase measurably. His preferred goal was Rock Island, which was just beyond Washington Island. He decided to raise the mainsail then unfurl the head sail fully. Without the engine, the boat slowed down. The haze was burning off. During the next hour the wind began to freshen and the boat picked up speed. He played with the sail trim to achieve increased efficiency. It was a steady breeze; he guessed it was now between ten to twelve knots. This boat was not built for performance. It was so slow in light air that he had often considered renaming it *The Barge*. However, in strong winds it was what was referred to as a 'stiff' boat. It did not heel (tip) easily or excessively and it stood up well in rough conditions. Andy attributed its stiffness to its long, heavy, shoal-draft keel and the shorter mast that reduced the amount of sail it presented to the loftier winds. Performance sailboats tended to have taller masts that exposed more sail to those higher, faster winds. They also had sleek, more hydrodynamic hulls and keels. He liked this boat specifically because it was designed for live-aboard comfort and manageability. He had the boat rigged so that he could manage almost everything from the cockpit. In strong winds and heavy seas that was an enormous safety factor. He was not out for speed. In his opinion, if a person wanted speed, a sailboat was an oxymoron.

By late morning, the boat was romping along at a brisk pace of over six knots, almost eight miles an hour. The haze had burned or blown off entirely. The sky was almost cloudless. He was well past the Cana Island lighthouse.

Andy had a device attached to the tiller that allowed him to lock the tiller into a fixed position. With a steady wind and fairly calm seas the boat was capable of holding a steady course for an hour or more. He would monitor it at intervals and tweak the setting if need be. Using his binoculars he identified landmarks along the shoreline to assess his progress. While Andy proclaimed that words like boredom or loneliness were not part of his vocabulary, it was moments like this during long passages that he wished he had someone to share the experience. Not just the joys that sailing provided, but also the tedious task of manning the tiller for hours, or to assist in managing the boat if a storm came up.

Andy thought back to how he had come to have this boat. He had been in the midst of a crisis situation. It had all started as the result of a relationship Andy had with a lady named Stephanie. She had come to live with him in Door County after giving up her job as a nurse in Chicago. He was living in a dilapidated old farm house at the time. Unbeknownst to him, Stephanie was a fugitive. Not from the law, but from a very wealthy and powerful man from whom she had stolen a huge amount of money. This man had hired operatives to find her with the goal of reclaiming the money, and most likely, to kill her. When it became apparent that Stephanie and, by association, Andy were in danger, they contacted the Sheriff's Department. A female Detective named Jan Miller was assigned to the case. As the Christmas holidays were approaching the situation escalated. Stephanie decided that she needed to orchestrate her own disappearance, thinking that would spare Andy. However, he continued to be scrutinized and attacked long after her departure. Stephanie's nemesis was convinced that Andy knew her whereabouts, and/or the location of the money. Stephanie had gambled with his life as well as her own. He had loved her, and for a long time after she left, he felt betrayed and angry. She had deceived him and put him in harm's way.

Andy checked the compass heading. The Sister Bay water tower and radio antennas were visible to the west. He returned to his recollections of that time in his life. Despite the involvement of three law enforcement agencies: the Sheriff's department, the State police, and the FBI, the situation had continued to drag on and escalate. An unusual relationship developed between Andy and Detective Miller. She was perhaps one of the most bizarre and eccentric people he had ever known. Her appearance, manner of dress and use of makeup were garish. She was a chain smoking, profane, closet-alcoholic. She was caustic to the point of seeming to be devoid of compassion. However, she ended up proving to be a shrewd, tenacious and talented detective. In time he discovered that she, also carried some terrible secrets from her previous life. Much like Stephanie, she had tried to flee her situation. Like Stephanie, she had ended up here, thinking she could start anew in this remote, out-of-the-way place. In the midst of her attempts at trying to help Andy, her past caught up with her as well. Again, by association, Andy came under attack from her antagonists. Hence the two of them became unlikely partners in trying to survive the threats posed by two separate entities. They shared an unorthodox relationship that excluded sex. Jan's traumatic past made it almost impossible for her to trust anyone, men especially. In retrospect, Andy was sure that she had allowed herself more emotional intimacy with him than she had with anyone else, possibly ever.

In a roundabout way they acquired this boat after Jan and he had fled Door County together. Fearing for their lives, they had crossed Lake Michigan to the town of Petoskey, where they were to be met by FBI agents. The plan was for them to be taken into protective custody. However, they became suspicious of the agents and decided they needed to flee them as well. In the process, they came across this boat that happened to be for sale. Jan contacted her boss, Sheriff Cummings. He arranged to lend them the money to buy it figuring they'd be safer wandering around northern Lake Michigan than anywhere else.

Andy snapped himself out of his retrospection realizing that it was early afternoon and he was well beyond the southern tip of North Bay. He had seen very few boats throughout the morning. There were two large freighters much further out from shore heading south, probably bound for the ports of Milwaukee, or maybe Chicago. The waves were increasing to a height of two feet. Because he was sailing on a broad reach going downwind, the wave action was not very noticeable. He spotted a small powerboat angling out into the open waters of the lake from the south end of North Bay. The boat was running at a 45° angle to the waves. There was visible spray as it crashed through them. It was hard to judge how fast the boat was traveling, but Andy thought its occupant was probably getting wet from the spray.

He did another visual sweep of the shoreline. Minutes later he began noticing the faint sound of the powerboat's engine. It seemed to be heading toward him. In a few more minutes it was close enough for him to see a lone occupant. It kept coming. *What's this about,* he thought. He checked the compass to confirm that he was still on course. As the powerboat drew even closer Andy began to feel uncomfortable. He wondered if the boater didn't see him. *Maybe I should use my air horn to signal my presence.* When the powerboat was about fifty feet away the driver began slowing down. It appeared that he was maneuvering to come alongside. He was a fairly muscular man who looked to be in his middle to late thirties. He was wearing a white polo shirt and cargo pants. He had blond hair and his face looked sunburned.

The man brought his boat about six feet abeam of Andy's boat. It was a tri-hull with an inboard/outboard engine, maybe fifteen or sixteen feet long. The guy yelled to Andy, "You got a cigarette?"

Andy raised his arms out to either side and shrugged while shaking his head. "No, I don't smoke." The guy shrugged, then to Andy's surprise he reached behind himself and pulled a black semi-automatic pistol from his waist band. He raised it and took aim at Andy who reflexively brought both of his hands forward as if to protect his face from a blow. The guy fired three shots in rapid succession. The first one missed him entirely. The second one grazed his right shoulder. The third one tore through his left hand and hit him in the forehead slamming him backward. He hit the safety line with the back of his neck dropping onto the cockpit seat in a half sitting/half lying position. Before speeding away, the man fired five more bullets into the sailboat's hull.

The impact of the bullet instantly knocked Andy unconscious. Andrew McLeod did not hear the other five shots aimed at wounding his boat, the roar of the powerboat's engine, or the man yelling, "Asshole!" as he sped away to the north. The sailboat continued plodding on. It maintained its course, but it was taking on water from three of the bullets fired into its hull at the water line.

Chapter 2

It was mid-afternoon when Andy's daughter-in-law, Mike returned from grocery shopping. She had left Cassidy at home not wanting him confined in the pickup truck while she was in the store. She took a first load of groceries into the house. On her way back to the truck to get a second, Cassidy suddenly began yelping and whining as if he were in terrible pain. He became extremely agitated running back and forth between the truck and Mike barking, whining, yowling and prancing frantically. Mike dropped to her knees startled by the dog's behavior not knowing what was wrong. Her first thought was that maybe he'd been stung by a wasp. His eyes were frantic. He looked panic stricken, running to her then spinning and running back to the truck. Mike immediately pulled her cell phone from her jeans pocket. She punched in her husband, Brian's number. After five rings she got the voice-mail message. "Goddamnit," she said as she punched the number for the school where Brian was principal. The school secretary answered on the third ring. "Elaine, this is Mike. Is Brian there?"

"Hi Mike, He's in a meeting with some parents." Elaine picked up on Mike's tone. "Is something wrong?" It would have been next to impossible for her not to hear Cassidy's tortured barking in the background.

"I don't know, I mean yes, please Elaine, I need to talk to Brian right away." She asked Mike to hold on. Mike could hear her practically run for Brian's office. She heard Elaine tell Brian that his wife was on line two, and that it sounded urgent. Brian picked up his phone immediately and asked what was happening. "I don't know, Brian. I just got home from shopping and Cassidy suddenly went into a panic. He's ballistic."

"Yeh, I hear him."

"Brian, this may sound crazy, but I think something has happened to Pops."

Before she could say anything more Brian told her that he

was leaving school immediately. "Call 911."

"And say what? That my father-in-law's dog is having a panic attack. Brian, I think something has happened to Pops. I don't know what else to think. You've just got to get home. I don't know what to do for Cassidy. We need to find out if Pops is all right, but I don't know where to start, or who to call. I'm really scared."

"Okay, you're right. Is Pop's truck there?" She said that it was. "Open the door. See if Cassidy will get in. See if that helps him to settle down. I'm leaving now."

Mike dropped to her knees, "Cassidy, come here, baby. I just called Brian. He's on his way. It's about Pops, isn't it?" Cassidy stopped and looked at her. His head was cocked. She summoned him over to her. Cassidy looked at her, and then at the truck two or three times. He reluctantly came to her. She extended her hand and touched the side of his face. "Brian is coming; we'll find Pop's, I promise." Cassidy gave a mournful whine. The second she withdrew her hand, he ran back to the truck, and again began pacing. She did as Brian had suggested opening the passenger door to Andy's truck. Cassidy immediately jumped into it. His yelps were more controlled, but he was still frantic.

Mike knew it would take Brian at least ten minutes to get home. She went back to her truck to get the remainder of the grocery bags. As soon as she had them gathered up, Cassidy jumped out of the truck and started running around her barking. She went directly into the house and began putting the items that needed refrigeration away. All the while she kept going over possibilities in her mind. Who should they call, the Coast Guard, the Sheriff's department? Who did they know who had a fast boat? What could have possibly happened out there? Did Andy fall overboard? Did he have a heart attack, or a stroke, what? Might something have happened to the boat? Mike realized that she had felt uneasy this morning at the dock. Had she ignored a vague premonition? She was certain that few people would buy the idea that a dog could sense that something terrible was happening to its human companion miles away. She had no doubt that Cassidy's behavior was linked to Andy and that the dog had sensed it at the very moment that it occurred.

She heard Brian's vehicle coming in the driveway. She heard Cassidy begin yelping frantically again. Cassidy ran to intercept Brian. He ran alongside of the jeep. Mike stepped down from the porch. Brian leapt out of the jeep as soon as it came to a halt. "I just got off the phone with the Sheriff's Department," he told Mike. "They're sending a deputy over. I'm going to call the marina and see if there's anybody around who has a fast boat. Pop's boat is anything but fast. I doubt seriously that he could be as far as Death's Door by now." The irony of that name for the passageway between the tip of the Door Peninsula and Washington Island sounded devastating at this moment. Brian was already unbuttoning his dress shirt. "I'm going to change into my grubbies."

"Wouldn't it be better to try to find someone with a boat up toward the tip of the peninsula?" Mike asked.

"That's a good idea. Maybe somebody on the Sheriff's Department will know of someone up there who can help out."

Mike followed Brian into the bedroom where he took his slacks off and put on a pair of faded jeans. "Brian, what if I've got this all wrong? What if Pops is okay? I'm going to feel pretty stupid."

"I don't think that's the case, love. Cassidy and Pops are linked to one another. I dread the day that Cassidy dies. I don't know what Pops will do without that dog." He dug in the closet for his deck shoes.

Cassidy began barking frantically again announcing the arrival of the Sheriff's deputy. On the way out of the house Brian asked what time their sons would be home. He looked at his watch. It was nearly three o'clock. She told him, "I need to pick them up at four. Dan is at work at the park. Shawn and Terry Nelson are there too. They're either canoeing, or playing volley ball."

Brian recognized the deputy. They had dealt with one another on many occasions concerning students at the high school. "Hi, Tom. This is my wife, Mike. Mike, this is Tom Jennings." They shook hands. Cassidy had already jumped back in the truck. He jumped back down to the ground and whined. He pranced impatiently as if demanding immediate action. Then he was back in the truck.

"What's going on?" Deputy Jennings asked. Mike

explained what had happened upon her arrival home from shopping. Jennings asked, "does your dad have a cell phone with him?" Brian said that he did but that he only turned it on to make calls. "Well, if he's in some kind of a fix, maybe he's got it on. It's worth a try." Brian tried calling his father only to get the voice-mail message.

"What about a marine radio? Has he got one of those aboard?"

"He's got a handheld VHF. Under perfect conditions it has a range of maybe five miles," Brian told him. "Again, the only times he ever has it on is to make calls or to check the NOAA weather."

"Let's see what we can do. Let's try contacting the Coast Guard. They've got an incredibly powerful antenna system. If he's got his radio on they might be able to pick up a signal." Brian led Deputy Jennings into the house to make the call. Jennings explained the situation to the Coast Guard Duty Officer in Sturgeon Bay. In the meantime Brian got out a detailed map of the county. He spread it out on the kitchen table. The Duty Officer asked if they could give him any kind of guess as to where they thought Andy might be right now.

Both Mike and Brian studied the map carefully. "He's got an almost perfect southerly wind. It's possible that he could be as far as Death's Door, maybe even somewhere along the east shore of Washington Island. Knowing him he'd be aiming to get to Rock Island. It's one of his favorite places." The Coast Guard officer asked what the name of the boat was. Brian said that it was called Desperado. The Officer told them that they hadn't received any distress calls. For the next several minutes, the Coast Guard tried without success to raise a response from the sailboat Desperado. Before hanging up, the Officer said that they would continue their effort.

"What about someone on Washington Island?" Brian asked. "Might someone up there be able to make a sweep of the east side to see if they can spot anything?"

"Let's give it a try," Deputy Jennings said as he tried calling the Island police to no avail. He went out to his squad car and radioed his headquarters. He asked the dispatcher to see if she could try to make contact with Officer Morris on Washington Island. He told her that he had tried to phone him without success. "If you're able to reach him, ask him to call me at this number." Brian gave Jennings his home phone number.

Three minutes later the dispatcher called back "There's no response from Officer Morris on the Island, 1022. I left a message for him to call you. I will keep trying from this end, sorry." Tom thanked her.

Cassidy jumped out of the truck. He lay down on the ground with his head on his paws. He whimpered looking pathetic. Brian went over to him and stooped down to pet him. "You've done a good job, Cassidy. I feel just as helpless as you right now." He stood up. "I can't sit here any longer. I'm taking Cassidy. We're going up to the Island. We'll find someone with a boat up there."

"Can I come along?" Mike asked. "I can call Sue Nelson to ask if she can pick the boys up."

"Would you mind staying here, Mike, just in case anything comes in that will be of help? The boys will be devastated if they find out anything has happened to their Grand Pops." Brian checked his cell phone. The battery was at half charge.

"Here, take mine," Mike offered. "It's fully charged. I'll recharge yours."

Brian gave Deputy Jennings the cell phone number. He went to get a windbreaker. He checked his wallet to make sure he had cash. "I'll stay in touch to let you know what's happening, love." Mike could no longer hold back her tears. They hugged.

Before leaving, Brian asked Tom what it would take to get the Coast Guard involved in a search. Tom shook his head, "A Mayday distress signal." Brian knew that meant lives were in jeopardy. "If it's an actual emergency, they'll scramble their Search and Rescue helicopter from Traverse City. It can be here within twenty minutes or so if they're not engaged in something else." The two men shook hands. Tom wished Brian good luck. "For what it's worth, you're doing what I'd do if it were me. Wish I could come along." Brian started for his jeep. Tom called to him, "if Morris calls, I'll fill him in about what's going on. I'll ask him to meet you at the ferry dock. He might be able to arrange to have someone with a boat there for you. At this point the enemy is time. It's going to take you a good hour-and-a-half to get from here to the Island. That won't give you a lot of time to conduct a search before nightfall. As you know, the waters up there are treacherous."

Brian nodded. He called Cassidy. The dog jumped into the jeep on the driver's side and then to the passenger seat. Mike ran back out of the house. She handed Brian a plastic bag with dog biscuits for Cassidy and a couple of apples for himself. "I love you," she said. He gave her a quick kiss, started the engine and left.

Brian made it just in time to catch the ferry from Northport pier. Once the ferry was underway he went up to the pilot house. He knocked on the door and asked the Captain if he could speak with him. The Captain waved him in. Brian explained the situation. The Captain got on his radio to call the island terminal. "Edna, see if you can get a hold of Dick Morris. I need to talk to him."

"What's the matter, Clarence? Is something happening on board?"

"No, everything's fine here. Just see if you can contact Dick. Do what you can," the Captain urged.

A few minutes later a man's voice came over the radio. "Clarence, this is Dick. What's up?"

"Dick, I got a fella here that's got a pretty serious situation. He's right here. I'll let you talk to him." The Captain handed the mic to Brian who introduced himself.

"Oh yeah, you're the guy that Tom Jennings called me about. I just got off the phone with him a few minutes ago," Officer Morris said. "Sorry I wasn't able to get back to ya before. Tom filled me in on the situation. I'm at the ferry dock right now. There's a marina over on the south end of the island. I've already called them to see if they've got someone who can help you out. They're good people. I'm sure they'll come up with somethin'. Do you need a ride?" Brian told him he had his jeep. "Well, I'll wait here for you, and lead the way." Brian thanked him.

After completing the conversation the Captain offered Brian a cup of coffee. He accepted gladly. Clarence asked if Brian's father was a good sailor. Brian told him that his father was an outstanding sailor. "I don't mean to say this to be scarin' you, son, but it's risky business to be out there in a sail-boat all by yerself. Things can happen pretty quick when ya least expect it. I wouldn't want to be out there by myself if say a storm came up." The Captain paused taking a couple of swallows of his own coffee. "It's been a nice day, a perfect day for sailin' north. He's had the wind to his back all day. Chances are that your dad is just fine. He's probably sittin' at anchor enjoyin' a cold beer right this very minute."

"I sure hope so," Brian said, but he was sure that was not the case. "I'd better get back to my car. I've got my Dad's dog with me." Brian thought about telling the Captain about how it was Cassidy's sudden panic reaction that had triggered their concern. He thought better of it, at least for now.

Brian got Cassidy some water and gave him some of the treats Mike had sent along. Cassidy ate two of them. He still seemed to be extremely nervous. Brian got in the jeep and talked to the dog explaining that they would soon be able to start looking for Pops. Cassidy kept looking ahead glancing over at Brian occasionally. He was panting rapidly.

It was exactly 4:30 when the ferry docked on Washington Island. Because Brian was the last car to be loaded at Northport, he was behind everyone else, and therefore the last to depart the ferry. Officer Dick Morris was there to meet him as promised and Brian followed him to the marina. When they arrived they were greeted by an athletic looking young man named Jason, the marina owner's son. Jason took Brian and Morris into the marina where there was a large framed chart of the north end of Lake Michigan on the wall. He asked several questions about when Brian's father had departed, the boat itself and the intended destination. Morris told them that he had already called both Rock Island and the person in charge of the marina at Jackson Harbor on the northeast corner of Washington Island. Brian's father was not at either place.

Jason pondered the chart. "Given everything you've told me, your Dad should be rounding Rock Island right now. He could still be somewhere along the east side of Washington Island." Jason touched the chart in both locations. "He wouldn't have decided to head somewhere else would he?" Jason suggested some other possibilities like Beaver Island or his trying to get all the way to Fayette State Park in Michigan's upper peninsula.

"He might have in his younger days. He's gotten wiser

with age," Brian said. "Especially about pushing himself that hard."

"Well then, let's start out by taking a drive up the east shore and seeing if we can spot any sailboats out there." Morris offered his car since it had communication equipment. Brian said that it was important for Cassidy to come along, so he and the dog would follow.

The road headed east along the south shore of the Island. As soon as it turned north, Cassidy began to bark and carry on. He jumped into the back of the jeep and faced south out the back. His whining became louder and more insistent. Brian immediately realized what the dog was trying to convey. He flashed his lights and slowed down hoping that he could catch Morris's attention. Moments later they came to a stop. "I know this is going to sound crazy," Brain said. "But just as soon as we started north, Cassidy went ballistic. My Dad is south of here somewhere." Morris and Jason looked at one another.

Morris shrugged, "okay, then let's try something else. I'll call a person I know on Detroit Island and ask them to see if they can spot a sailboat from there. Detroit is a pretty low-lying island so they're not going to be able to see out very far into the lake. I'll also contact the ferry and ask them to make a special effort to see if they can spot anything to the south and east."

He looked at both Brian and Jason. "I'm also going to call the airport and see if anybody is around. If there are any incoming or outgoing planes maybe they can spot something." He looked at his watch. "It's going to be dark in less than three hours." Brian nodded his agreement with the plan. "Let's go back to the marina. It's a waiting game at this point. I hope your dog is right."

Chapter 3

As Andy began to regain consciousness, the pain was excruciating. He almost plummeted back into unconsciousness again. He was disoriented. He had no idea where he was. He had no recollection about what had happened. It took him a while to realize that he was even on the boat. *What happened to me? Why am I in so much pain? Where am I? What time is it? How long have I been this way?* He had never experienced such severe pain, not ever. He could barely see anything out of his right eye. He could see nothing from the other. He had a terrible metallic taste in his mouth. As he gradually gained increasing consciousness, he came to realize that he was sitting in the cockpit of his boat. He wondered how he had gotten here. He asked himself again, *What happened to me?* Gradually the scene of the man in the powerboat, and of the man shooting at him emerged. It was surreal. The man in the boat, the gun. *He shot me. I've been shot. I'm hurt'.* The dreadful pain. *'I've been shot. How badly am I hurt? My head, is that where he shot me?* The pain was so intense it engulfed him like an inferno. He tried to focus on the source of the pain. He hurt all over, but the worst of it was his head. He sat there in a dazed state. He wanted to surrender. He couldn't. Not now. *Where do I hurt?* It was a tossup as to which hurt the most. Was it his head or his left hand? His neck, too. *Is my neck broken?* He wondered if he had been shot several times. *Did he only shoot me in the head?* He wondered how come he was still alive.

The guy asked me a question. What did he ask me? Who was he anyway? It had all happened so unexpectedly, so suddenly. Andy tried to focus his vision. What little he could see out of his right eye was blurry. He couldn't seem to open his left eye. He tried to look down but could only see his bare legs and the cuff of his shorts. Everything was red, dark red. It took moments more before it registered that it was blood; it was his blood. He remained stupefied. His brain was barely operating.

He couldn't get it to focus. It was processing so slowly. Nothing made any sense.

Was I shot in the head? Sitting there in this sticky redness with this terrible pain, a vision began to emerge. He whispered his younger son's name, "Corey". The image of Corey in his wheel chair emerged. He was reliving a terrible experience from the past. Corey had come home from the war. Corey was in the back yard. Andy was approaching his younger son who was sitting in his wheel chair. Corey's back was to him. Something was wrong. Something was wrong with Corey. Then he saw it; he saw the blood. He saw it and felt the dread, and an overwhelming anguish swept over him. Corey was sitting in his wheel chair at the edge of the garden. There was the blood. Corey was slumped in his wheel chair. There was a knife on the ground next to the wheel chair. Corey was slumped over, motionless in his wheel chair. *Corey is dead. My son is dead.* He was reliving that scene, those moments of abject agony; his scream of disbelief, the sense of the crushing futility, the paralysis, the utter helplessness, the senselessness. He remembered falling to his knees, *Oh, Corey, what have you done? Why? Why did you do this?* He had asked it aloud over and over. *It has come to this,* he thought. When he was finally able to move, to act, to realize; he got to his feet. He turned toward the house. Cassidy was lying several feet away watching him. *It has come to this.* He walked past the dog toward the house. Cassidy followed at a distance perhaps sensing his master's anguish, fearful about what would come next and at the same time watching over him.

There was a flapping sound coming from somewhere. It was insistent. It drew Andy's attention away from that terrible memory. He gradually returned to the brutal, searing, intense agony of the present. The sound was familiar, but he couldn't place it. He was in such pain. He was helpless to respond. In a few moments the sound stopped. He felt motion. The motion was tortuous. It went far beyond irritation. He begged it to stop. It exacerbated and intensified his pain. He wanted silence and stillness. *Is that too much to ask?* He heard the sound of water gurgling and faint splashing sounds. *Leave me alone. I'm fucking hurt. I'm in fucking pain'. Fucking leave me alone.* The flapping sound ceased, but the motion continued. A few minutes passed and then there was *that Goddamn flapping sound again.*

He was irate. He needed to find the source of the noise and the movement and make it stop. Strangely his anger helped him to focus. It even served to mollify the pain somewhat. He forced himself with determined effort into a sitting position. He raised his right hand to his right cheek. He touched his cheek. He felt a dry crustiness. He moved his fingers to his eye. It felt the same. He pressed his right eye and crust seemed to crack and crumble and fall away. He wiped at his eye with his wrist. He blinked and the caked blood loosened. He could see that he was in his boat. He could see the port bench seat across from him. He tried to look down, but moving his head forward sent megavolts of pain up and down his spine. He tottered on the brink. The brink of what: unconsciousness, death, what? It gradually began to subside. It seemed to take hours. The thought that maybe his neck was broken occurred to him again. He gave it another try in gradual increments. He was finally able to see his bare stomach and his shorts caked in crimson. His canvas shirt was open. He realized that there was a lot of blood. He wondered if he was still bleeding. *How close am I to bleeding out?* He felt less dazed now. Oddly, he felt no sense of panic or alarm. Nor did he feel calm. The pain was too intense to allow that. It was more like an acceptance. *It has come to this. Now what?*

When the flapping sound came again he was finally able to identify it. It was the jib sail luffing. The boat was clumsily sailing itself. When it came up too close to the wind, the headsail started flapping, and then the boat would fall off and sail on for a while. *How long had this been going on? What course is the boat on?* He had a vague, blurred recollection that the wind had been southerly. He had set the boat on a northerly course. Was it still the same? He couldn't see the sun. Judging from shadows he was able to deduce that it was behind him. It took several moments for him to reach the next logical conclusion; the boat was sailing in an easterly direction. Depressed, he concluded, *for God only knows how long, I've been heading out further into the lake.*

He tried turning his torso to see the compass. Even though he was sitting fairly close to it, he couldn't make out the numbers on the compass. *Maybe if I can clear my left eye I can see bet-*

ter. The slightest touch sent searing, stabbing pain down his cheek and up into his forehead. It was swollen badly. *Have I been stabbed by something? Has the bullet gone into my brain? Did it go through my eye*? He had a brief moment of bitter sardonic cynicism. *So, what's the good news, McLeod*? He had a second thought, *I can remember my name. That's something*. He moved his right hand onto the bulkhead next to the companionway, and slowly leaned himself closer to the compass. He was finally able to make out that the boat was on a course of one-hundred thirty degrees. He tried to force his brain to calculate the meaning of this information. With great effort he reached the conclusion that the boat was sailing in a southeasterly direction. *That means that the wind has shifted to the south. What can I do? How can I bring the boat about*? He knew WHAT to do, but how could HE do it in this condition?

After many minutes of deliberation, he decided that the only alternative was to try to jibe the boat. It meant he would need to change the boat's direction by bringing the boat stern-first in the opposite direction. It wouldn't be possible for him to try tacking the boat by turning it bow first into the wind. The mainsail (the large rear sail) would automatically switch violently from one side to the other on its own. Dealing with the jib (the front headsail) would be another matter entirely. He needed to release the jib sheet (the control rope attached to the jib) from the port (left) side where it was now. Realistically it was not going to be possible for him to haul the starboard (right side) jib sheet in tightly. He would do the best he could to secure the starboard jib sheet with the hope that it would catch enough wind to propel the boat forward. If all else failed he would just let it go. It could flap in the breeze. He would sail with the mainsail only. He would at least be heading westward toward shore however laboriously slow and clumsy that might be.

It took him a while to think through the steps he would need to take to execute the maneuver. Andy examined his left hand. It was mutilated. It was useless. *The bastard must have been using some kind of high impact ammo*. He considered that he may never be able to use his left hand again, or worse yet, it would need to be amputated. *Good, McLeod, you're thinking long term. That means you're expecting to get out of this alive. Always the fucking optimist*. What he was about to do was going to hurt. It might prove to be impossible.

The first thing was to slowly pivot his torso enough in order to reach the starboard jib sheet. He wrapped the sheet around the starboard jib winch (a ratcheting device used to haul the rope in). Taking in as much slack out of rope as he could, he tied it off on the nearby cleat. Raising his left arm, he draped his forearm on the tiller (the handle that is used to steer the boat). Using his right hand he loosened the tiller lock which allowed him to be able to pull the tiller toward him. The boat slowly began to come about stern to the wind. When the mainsail slammed from the port to the starboard side, he straightened the tiller. He could see the sun now. It was low enough in the sky that he judged it was late afternoon. Guessing, Andy adjusted the course to a northwesterly direction.

Now for the really painful part. Andy carefully moved himself to the edge of the seat. He took a deep breath before trying to maneuver himself off the seat and onto his knees. His head was throbbing. Keeping his back flagpole straight he got his right knee down and then the left one. He inched his way to the port side bench seat. After making contact with the seat he sat back on his heels for a few moments to gather himself. He was panting and sweating. He hoped it was sweat and not blood. Extending his right hand and slowly leaning forward he touched the port coaming (a boundary that keeps water from splashing in to the cockpit). His head throbbed so painfully he almost passed out. Something was trickling down his upper lip. He wiped his nose discovering it was bleeding. There was a sense of urgency. He'd come too far to give up at this point. The jib sheet had to be freed. He forced himself to push through the pain. By maneuvering his right hand slowly his fingers touched the port jib sheet. It took what seemed like several long minutes to finally free the rope from the cleat it was fastened to. The sheet was wrapped around the port winch three times. It wasn't going to run free unless it could be unwound at least two loops. Maybe this was more than he could or should ask of himself. *What if I end up passing out in the process*? Trembling, he felt a surge of anger. *Goddamnit, just do it, McLeod.* He wiped his bleeding nose again, and then reached for the rope. After the first loop was off the sheet slipped a few inches. *Come on Goddamn you, let go.* With the second loop off the rope began to pull loose. He mustered enough strength to free the line entirely. *That's it. Now I have to get back to the other side and see if I can take up any of the slack.*

As he turned himself to make the short journey back to the starboard bench seat he looked down into the cabin. The cabin sole (the floor) was underwater. At first it didn't register. He was focused on getting back to his starting position. His goal was to try to haul in as much of the jib as he possibly could. That was the plan. Perhaps it was a release of adrenalin. He moved less cautiously. The pain didn't seem quite as intense. *This must be what is meant by hitting the wall. Am I going to get past the pain?* He got back to the starboard bench. It took him several tormented minutes to retrieve some of the starboard jib sheet. He sensed that the sail was now catching wind. It was billowed out almost like a spinnaker sail used for sailing downwind. Unable to haul it in any further Andy studied the compass. The boat was holding a steady northwesterly course.

Back to what he'd seen in the cabin. *There is water in the cabin; ergo, there's a hole in the boat. Brilliant, McLeod.* With determined effort he managed to stand. Bracing himself with his right hand he got one leg, then the other over the lip of the companion-way. He finally managed get down the two steps to the cabin sole. Standing in about three inches of water, he tried to decide what to do about the problem.

Most boats with cabins experience interior condensation that collects in the lowest part of the boat referred to as the bilge. Andy had installed a low capacity electric bilge pump years before, to extract the condensed water. He seldom used the pump which only had a five-hundred gallons per hour capacity. He found the electrical control panel, but couldn't remember which switch the pump was connected to. He flipped the bottom switch and heard an immediate hum. He waited to see if the water was receding. After several minutes there was no perceptible change. *Just because there's the hum of a motor, that doesn't mean it's pumping, McLeod. Or maybe it's just keeping up with what's coming in. Or maybe it has lost its prime. If it's the latter, I'm screwed. Nothing I can do about that.* He scanned the cabin looking for any sign of holes. *If we're taking on water, the holes have to be at or below the waterline. Jesus, McLeod, You're a Goddamn genius.* In order to check that, he would have to access the storage compartments under the built-in berths on the port side. That was way beyond him. He would just have to wait to see if the pump was working. *Besides, the boat is heeling* (leaning) *to starboard now. That may mean that the holes are out of the water at least enough to slow down the leakage.* He was proud of that deduction. There was a renewed anger. *The monster who shot me also shot my boat.*

He located his cooler and fetched three very cold cans of beer which he set out in the cockpit. The handheld VHF marine radio was in a conveniently placed holder right next to the cabin entrance. He doubted that it would be of much use, but he would give it a try. Then he remembered his cell phone. His jeans were within reach draped on the port berth. The cuffs were submerged. He managed to get the phone out of the right front pocket only to drop it into the water. Andy tried bending forward but the pain made it impossible. It almost overwhelmed him. He stooped but was unable to locate it. *It probably won't work anyway after falling in the water.* It was time to get back to the cockpit. Andy hated the very notion of destiny, but at this moment he succumbed. Maybe it had come to this.

Several minutes later Andy was seated outside opening one of the beers. As thirsty as he was he could only take small sips. Beer was probably not the recommended beverage for a man in his condition. It didn't matter. Thirst and dehydration trumped sensibility. Finishing the first can, he opened another. He picked up the hand held radio. It was preset to the emergency channel 16. That and channel 9 are monitored by the Coast Guard. It stunned him to hear himself when he tried to speak aloud. His speech was garbled to the point that he thought it sounded like a stroke victim or a gagged man. Mayday! Mayday! (the message for a vessel in life- threatening distress) came out a muted, congested "Ma da, Ma da." This is the sailboat Desperado came out sounding, "Dih ah da sa bah de-pa-a da." *Jesus, is the speech part of my brain fucked-up?* He tried two more times with even worse results.

He thought that even if he had the cell phone, *I can't call Brian or Mike. It will scare the hell out of them.* Both of them and his grandsons knew how to text. But he'd ignored learning how. He vehemently disliked cell phones to begin with. Having one was a concession he'd made to his family. Andy wasn't just a curmudgeon, he was also a proud 'Luddite'. His attitude was, *where is the world going to be when (not if) the electrical grid fails?* He was sure that it eventually would. *Only we anachronistic troglodytes and the "uncivilized" peoples of the world will be able to survive. The rest of you will be SOL and up the famous creek.* He drank some more beer. *You should have grabbed half-a-dozen of these when you were down there, McLeod.* He moved so that he could see down into the cabin. He thought the water level seemed to have receded somewhat. *Wishful thinking, McLeod.* Did that qualify as a sign of optimism? *Christ, I hope not.*

Feeling an urge to pee, he tried to stand up to do so. The pain was too intense. Not having the will or the stamina to try he opted for the easy way, peeing himself. The sun was getting lower. *At least the weather's in your favor. Once the sun sets it's going to cool off, especially out here in the lake.* He needed to find the strength to go below for a jacket and some more beer. It would be a nice sunset. For some reason it hadn't occurred to him that the boat had a hand operated, high capacity bilge pump. It could be operated from the cockpit. He had to think for several minutes about where the handle for it was. He found it in a built-in storage compartment on the right side of the cockpit. He got to his knees and after fumbling he was finally able to insert it into the pump. As he began cranking it he experienced a sharp, stabbing pain specifically in his neck. He almost gave up, but after several strokes his neck muscles began to loosen up and the pain became less intense. The pain in his head was pervasive but slightly diminished. The pump was drawing water. He continued to work at it slowly and methodically. After ten minutes he checked the cabin again. There was no more standing water. He finish the second beer and opened the third feeling heartened. Maybe it was the exertion of manning the pump, or maybe it was the beer. His neck didn't hurt quite as much as it had.

Andy began thinking about what to do when he got close to land. Barely able to make out the silhouette of the county, he guessed he was several miles from shore. The thought entered his mind that the boat could have even backtracked. *What if I make landfall near North Bay. Will asshole be there*? He doubted the boat would reach landfall before dark. *Is there someplace I can run the boat aground to keep it from sinking?* Andy worried more about the possibility of it getting bashed all to hell on the rocks. He was almost certain there were no rock-free, safe places to beach the boat. Unless he was in the vicinity of Detroit Harbor or the narrow isthmus between Washington and Rock Island, there were no shallow soft bottoms. He would have to wait to see where he was. He was being overtaken by fatigue.

He decided to try starting the engine both to increase the boat's speed and to recharge the battery. The engine turned over, but did not start. It usually started instantly. *The electrical system must have gotten wet.* Running the bilge pump took precedence. Maybe he would try the engine again later. There was also the possibility that the engine might have suffered some damage from a bullet.

He tried talking aloud concentrating on trying to enunciate clearly. Speaking very slowly and deliberately his speech was almost intelligible. Trying to say Mayday still came out, "Mada." He tried to hum. That really hurt. The pain shot up into his forehead. *Maybe my damn nose is broken. That's the least of your worries, McLeod.*

The sun was getting lower. Andy decided to try to go below again while he still could. He would get some things out of the cooler. What else: a blanket, a jacket, a box of towelettes to clean some of the blood off himself. *Forget the jeans. I won't be able to get them on. Besides, they're soaked.* Checking the compass the boat was still holding a steady northwesterly course. Before going below he tried sheeting the jib some more, but was only able to bring it in a few inches.

Returning to the cockpit he heard the drone of an airplane. At first he couldn't spot it. *Damn, what's wrong with you, McLeod? You should have remembered to get your flare gun.* He tried to move quickly but he felt like he was in a state of torpor. He knew precisely where the canister with the flare gun was, but it meant lifting the port seat hatch where it was stowed. Under normal circumstance, it would be easily accessible. He was painfully able to raise the lid. When he bent forward to reach for the flare canister it was like someone had struck him in the forehead with an axe. The pain hit him like a bolt of high voltage electricity. It was blinding. His fingers touched the canister, but he had to pull back to an upright position. This was the most intense pain he had suffered thus far. He noticed something strange was happening. The plane he had heard a few minutes earlier was coming closer, and judging from the sound, it seemed to have dropped to lower altitude. He had to get to those flares. He bent sideways and reached down with his right hand. He got a hold of the top of the canister. He felt like his head was being crushed. He straightened. He had it in hand. It took critical moments for the pain to retreat enough so that he could take the next step of removing the lid and getting the flare gun in hand. The plane looked like it was banking. It was, and also changing direction. It looked like it was coming toward him. He fumbled to unscrew the canister top. Once he got it off, his vision was so blurry he couldn't see the flare gun. He groped inside the canister until his fingers found it. There wasn't time to determine if it was loaded. The plane was coming even closer. It looked like the pilot might be planning to circle him. He cocked the flare gun and fired it up at a steep angle off the stern. The bright orange flame of the flare streaked upward. He fumbled to get another flare out of the canister. He looked up at the plane to see its wings dip twice. *Does that mean that the pilot has seen me? Was that an acknowledgement of the distress signal* Andy began to cry. His sobs sounded not like a man, but like some grieving mournful beast. The plane circled him a second time dipping its wings, then it regained altitude and continued its journey south.

After the plane disappeared, he reloaded the flare gun. Checking the compass revealed that the boat was heading more northerly than before. Andy was able to alter the course back to the northwest. The sun was much lower. The time was probably somewhere between seven and seven thirty. He sipped some beer. There was a plastic jar with sunflower nuts in the starboard coaming compartment. He felt around and finally found it, along with small mirror. Upon seeing his face he was appalled. Most of his face was covered with caked blood. His forehead looked like some ferocious beast had dug claws into his left eye and then ripped upward tearing away the flesh. It looked like part of his skull was exposed. His left eye was swollen completely shut. It looked like his nose was indeed broken. The swelling in the left eye was forcing the nose to the right. He realized that he had been breathing through his mouth unable to breathe through his nose at all. After going through six towelettes he abandoned the effort to clean himself up. It was a futile waste of his dwindling energy.

He ate the nuts, dropping a lot of them, and opened the third beer. The sun was close to setting and it was getting noticeably cooler. He was near enough to land now to make out two important things. There was the gap between the tip of Door County and Plum Island. He was further north than he'd thought. The second thing was the flashing light of the buoy marking the entrance to the east end of Death's Door. That meant he was still two or three miles from the channel, maybe more. It felt like he was a long way from anywhere.

As the temperature was dropping, Andy began to shiver. After making several attempts to get his lined nylon windbreaker over his shoulders, he gave up on it. He managed to use the blanket as a shawl. He draped the jacket over his bare legs. After just a few minutes he felt the urge to pee again. He unwrapped himself, and managed to move himself to the edge of the seat. *The price for drinking those beers, McLeod.*

Chapter 4

While they waited at the marina for any word to come in about Andy, Jason had gone home and gotten some of his dog's food and a bowl for Cassidy. There was a restaurant next door to the marina. Al went to get them hamburgers. They ate in his office. It was close to 7:30 when a radio message came into the Washington Island airport from an airplane that had spotted what looked like a sailboat in distress. The plane was on its way south from Marquette, Michigan to Green Bay, Wisconsin. The woman pilot had dropped off a passenger/friend in Manistique, Michigan and she was proceeding south from there. She reported circling the boat twice at an altitude of two-hundred feet. A person on the boat fired a single distress flare. She gave an exact location of the boat and stated that it was moving in a northwesterly direction. She had added that while the boat was under sail it appeared that the head sail was not deployed properly. Officer Richard Morris was notified immediately. He drove directly to the marina to report the news to Brian.

Brian, Jason, and Jason's father Al were in the Marina office when Morris arrived. Cassidy had started pacing in a counterclockwise circle fifteen minutes before. The four men went to the chart. Al studied it and pointed to where the boat was. Brian, thinking out loud, said, "what the hell are you doing way out there, Pops?"

He turned to Al and Jason to ask how long it would take for them to get out there. Al rubbed his chin. "What do think Jase? Maybe an hour, give or take." Jason agreed. Al then said, "if your dad is hurt, it will take us even longer to get back here if we have to take his boat in tow. We can't just leave it out there."

Cassidy barked. Brian looked at him. "Is Pops hurt, Cassidy?" The dog barked again and twirled around several times. He was panting and shifting back and forth from one front paw to the other.

Jason spoke up. "I think we need to contact the Coast Guard. We don't know what the situation is." He gestured toward Cassidy. "I'm a believer." He turned to Brian, "that dog has already proven that he knows where your dad is. He seems to also sense that your dad is hurt, maybe badly enough that he's going to need immediate medical attention. I hope I'm wrong, but we can't take that chance. We need to get out there ourselves."

Al hesitated before speaking, "I agree Jase." He turned to Brian. "You're not going to like hearing this, Brian, but I think you need to stay here. If your dad is hurt badly, you're going to have to deal with that. He may need to be airlifted to a hospital. You need to be where you can respond in case this is serious." Al looked at his watch, then turned to Jason, "I'll call Jim. The last ferry leaves the Island in twenty minutes. Brian can stay here. If he needs to get back to the mainland, Jim's got a fast boat and he can take Brian to Gills Rock." He turned back to Brian. "Is there someone who can pick you up there?"

"I'll call my wife. She can meet me at the Ferry Dock."

Al got on the Marine radio. He contacted the Coast Guard. After reporting the situation, the CG radio operator consulted with the Duty Officer who came on the radio. "We're dispatching a helicopter immediately. Do you have an exact location? It will be dark by the time the chopper arrives at the target." Al gave the officer the information that the pilot had reported. "Our chopper will be lifting off in five minutes," the officer said. "It should be there in approximately forty minutes." Al told the officer that he and his son were leaving to intercept the boat in case it needed to be towed. He added that they would monitor the VHF emergency channel 9.

As badly as Brian wanted to accompany Al and Jason, he agreed with the decision for him to stay behind. Before leaving Al called his friend Jim. He explained the situation. Jim said he would come to the marina right away to make his boat ready just in case.

Brian, Cassidy and Officer Morris saw Al and Jason off. Their boat had a shallow draft and they were familiar with the waters. It allowed them to take a short cut. Instead of going the long way around that would have taken them out through the channel entrance to Detroit Harbor, they could exit the harbor via the shallow east side. That would cut close to twenty minutes off their travel time.

Before leaving Morris gave Brian his home phone number. "Call me if I can be of any further help." Brian expressed his gratitude for all that had been done in his father's behalf. "It's like that here on the Island," Morris said. "People look out for one another. We're pretty much in a world of our own."

Brian called home to explain the situation to Mike. In her sensible way she did not ask questions for which she knew there were no answers. "This is going to be the longest hour of our lives. I'll wait to hear from you." She added, "Cassidy is incredible. He's been right about everything so far. Let's just hope that whatever has happened to Pops isn't serious." Brian agreed, but he had a feeling it was very serious.

Brian would have liked to take Cassidy for a walk but he felt compelled to stay by the radio. Al had set the radio to Channel 9 so that Brian would be able to monitor whatever messages were sent. Close to forty-five minutes passed before the silence was broken. One of the Coast Guard helicopter crew reported, "We're approaching the location that was given to us about the sailboat in distress. So far we don't have a visual. We're not seeing any running lights." Brian knew that was not like his father. Moments later they reported that a commercial freighter was becoming visible at the west entrance to Porte de Morte, the French name for Death's Door.

Brian muttered, "Sweet Jesus."

The helicopter then reported, "a distress flare was just fired dead ahead."

A few minutes later they reported that they made visual contact using their search light. They radioed the freighter to either divert its course to the Rock Island passage, or reduce speed and be prepared to come to a temporary halt. The freighter captain chose the second option.

Moments later the helicopter reported, "the occupant appears to be incapacitated. We're lowering a crew member to assess the situation." Several very long minutes went by. Brian visualized the helicopter hovering and a crew member in a harness being lowered to the deck of his father's boat, which was exactly what was happening. When the pilot spoke again he reported, "we're lowering a second crew member with a stretcher. The boat's occupant has sustained severe injuries with major blood loss. We're requesting permission to transport to the nearest emergency medical facility."

The Duty Officer at the Traverse City Coast Guard station responded, "proceed with the rescue. Hold for further directions." A few moments later he came on the radio again. "Transport to Sturgeon Bay Memorial Hospital. They have been alerted. Sturgeon Bay FD and PD will provide you with ground lighting."

The first thing Al and Jason saw out ahead of them was the strobe lights from the oncoming helicopter. Next they saw an ascending orange streak of light from an emergency flare. Then they saw the bright search light from the helicopter capture the sailboat in its beam. They were approximately half-a-mile away, and on a direct course to the sailboat. They were at full speed. They arrived just as the Coast Guard crew members were about to begin lifting Andy up to the hovering helicopter. Al brought their boat alongside. Jason leapt onto the sailboat deck just ahead of the port side-stays. He secured a line from their boat to a bow cleat on the sailboat. One of the Coast Guard paramedics was ascending with the stretcher bearing Andy. It struck Jason as odd that the stretcher was being raised in a vertical position. The other paramedic gestured and yelled over the loud throb of the helicopter. "Head injured. Serious." When Jason saw the bloody condition of the cockpit he almost threw-up. The crew member moved next to him and asked if Jason knew how to lower the sails. Jason said that he would figure it out. A sling was lowered from the helicopter. The paramedic got into it and was quickly retrieved. As soon as he disappeared inside the helicopter, the engines revved and it rose up swiftly flying away in a southwesterly direction.

Jason experienced a sudden relief from the turbulence and the deafening noise of the helicopter. However, the gruesome scene of the cockpit made the task ahead almost overwhelming. He surveyed the configuration of the sheets and lines. He saw that Andy had rigged the boat so that he had access to all of the sail control lines from the cockpit. Jason cautiously stepped down into the cockpit. His first move was to dowse the head sail. He released the roller-furler line; then the jib sheet. He drew in on the furler line and rolled the head sail up.

It took a couple of minutes to figure out how to lower the mainsail. While Jason was at work lowering the sails Al was on the radio talking to Brian. "The Coast Guard dropped a rescue team on board your dad's boat, Brian. They put him in a stretcher and lifted him aboard the chopper. They just took off from here. It looks like they're headed to either Sturgeon Bay or Green Bay. We're going to take your dad's boat in tow. We might not get in until after midnight." Jason had the sails secured. Al waved for him to come back aboard their boat. "Here, Brian, I'm going let you talk to Jason. He's just finished lowering the sails on your dad's boat."

Al handed the radio to his son. Jason was hesitant to give Brian details of what he had seen. He simply said, "it's pretty serious, Brian. He's lost a lot of blood. I don't know if he was conscious or not when they lifted him off the boat. They sure weren't wasting any time once they had him onboard the chopper. I have a feeling that whatever happened must have occurred hours ago." Before the conversation ended Brian told Jason that Jim was there with him at the marina. They would leave immediately for the mainland. "I'll keep you posted about my dad." As an afterthought he gave Jason his cell phone number.

Al had towlines ready to attach to the sailboat. "We better take a look around before we get underway," he said. They soon discovered standing water in the cabin. Al flipped the switch for the cabin lights. They came on dimly. The battery was almost completely drained. He found another switch in the 'on' position. It was labeled 'BILGE'. Jason began operating the hand pump in the cockpit. His father went looking for the source of the leak. He found three jagged holes in the hull right at the waterline. They were in a storage compartment under the port bunk, and were about three quarters of an inch in diameter. He tore a couple of wide strips from a rag. Using a screw driver Al forced the strips into the holes. He also found three flattened bullets. He left the bullets right where they were.

The water level was going down quickly now that the holes were plugged. Al went to the companionway. "Come here," he said to his son. He showed Jason the three spent bullets he had discovered. "It looks like McLeod was shot, then he shot holes in the boat. He must have intended to sink it." He shook his head. "We need to take pictures of this in the morning. Christ, what kind of monster would do such a thing?"

Back out in the cockpit, Al used his flashlight to look around some more. When we get this boat back to the marina we'd better tie it up where nobody will bother it. For sure we need to cover the cockpit. The cops need to see this. "Looks like someone had a couple or three beers. I hope it was McLeod and not the shooter." Al went back down below to start the sailboat's engine in order to recharge its battery. Before returning to the cockpit he retrieved Andy's cooler and whatever personal items he could find. After they finished tying two heavy towlines from the bow of the sailboat to their boat, they started the long, slow journey back to the marina. The large freighter that had been waiting at the west end of the passage was underway again. As they were passing one another the freighter Captain radioed to ask about what had happened. Al told the Captain that the sailboat Captain was seriously injured and had to be airlifted by the CG. The freighter captain asked about what had caused the injury. Al had no idea. Jason got two beers out of Andy's cooler. He opened one for each of them.

"Have you ever seen anything like this, Dad?"

"Yeah, a long time ago in Nam. I hoped I'd never see such a sight again."

Neither of them said much more for the rest of the trip home.

Chapter 5

The two Coast Guard crew members who had boarded the sailboat to rescue Andy were experienced, highly trained paramedics. On a secured frequency they conferred with the emergency room physician on the way to the hospital. They explained that the patient was unable to tolerate being placed in a supine position. The ER physician said that it was probably due to severe intracranial swelling and that it was best to maintain him in an upright position. He advised them to administer morphine for pain. He asked if there appeared to be any cranial penetration. They couldn't tell. The skin of the forehead had been torn up and a part of the front of the skull was exposed. "The injury appears to have been sustained several hours ago. Most of the forehead is encrusted with dried blood. We can't tell if penetration has occurred through the left eye socket. The tissue surrounding the eye is badly swollen. It's completely closed." One of the crew members expressed an opinion. "Sir, it appears to me that the man was shot. Judging from the severe damage to the left hand I question whether it's even repairable. I suspect he may have reflexively tried to shield his face using his left hand."

"What are you saying?" The doctor asked. "Did someone try to kill the guy out in the middle of the lake?"

"It does appear that way, Sir."

"Duly noted," the doctor said. "He wouldn't have suffered such severe injuries from a fall or being struck by the boom."

The paramedic had one other thing to report. "We've taken his temperature three times. All three are ninety two degrees. The patient appears to be in the initial stages of hypothermia. His lowered body temperature may be what's kept him alive this long." The ER physician agreed. He decided to call the Sheriff's Department before the CG arrived. The authorities needed to be made aware of the situation.

Mike was waiting for Brian and Cassidy at the dock when

they arrived. It was a little after 10:00 P.M. Brian tried to give Jim some money to compensate him for his time and gas expense. Jim refused. "I'm glad I was able to be of help. I truly hope your dad will be okay." As soon as Brian was on the dock Jim departed for the return trip to the island.

As Brian and Mike walked quickly toward her pickup truck Mike said, "the situation doesn't sound good, does it." It was not a question. "I called Door County Memorial. Pops is there. They couldn't, or wouldn't tell me anything about his condition."

Brian told her about what Jason had told him via the radio. 'I can't imagine what happened. The only thing I can come up with is that somehow the boom tore loose and hit Pops in the head. He is always so careful. He's such a stickler about details. He used to drive Corey and me crazy with his compulsive concern with safety. Like most kids we thought we were invincible. We never thought about stuff like that. Pops is a risk-taker. But they're calculated risks, not foolhardy ones. He's not a careless person."

As they neared the truck, Mike said that she would drive. She opened the door and Cassidy jumped up on the seat placing himself in the middle. Before starting the engine she asked if Cassidy had eaten. Brian told her that they had both been well taken care of. "Where to?" she asked. "The hospital or home first?" He asked about the boys. "They're at the Nelson's. I told Sue we might not get home until very late. She said that the boys could stay overnight. They're going to camp out in the backyard." Mike added, "I got our copy of Pop's power of attorney out of the file. Just in case."

"Let's head for the hospital." Mike started the engine. She reached over first to give Cassidy a hug, then to take her husband's hand. Brian told her about how Cassidy had helped them to find his father. "We wouldn't have known anything was wrong at all, if it weren't for you, Cassidy." Brian scratched the dog's back, one of Cassidy's favorite things.

There were very few cars on the road, but it still took nearly an hour for them to reach the hospital. They reluctantly left Cassidy in the truck. At the front desk they were given directions to the ER. When they arrived there, they were told that the head nurse of the unit would be with them shortly. They had expected that Pops would have been admitted and situated in a room by now. A few minutes later the head nurse appeared. She led them directly to her office and invited them to be seated. Both Brian and Mike's anxiety levels were skyrocketing. This did not bode well. She bypassed all formality. "Mr. McLeod, your father is in critical condition. He is in emergency surgery as we speak. Three of our doctors are working to try to stabilize him. The Flight for Life helicopter is on standby. The doctors are debating whether to send him to the University Hospital in Madison or to a hospital in Milwaukee that has a team of doctors with experience in treating severe brain injuries." She paused to allow Mike and Brian to absorb this information. She cleared her throat. "It appears that your father was shot in the face several hours ago. There does not seem to be any other explanation for the severity of his injuries. It doesn't appear that the bullet actually penetrated his skull. However, it's possible that fragments may have entered the cranium through the left eye socket. We don't know for sure at this point." She paused again. "He's suffering from severe intracranial pressure. That's due to two things. The first is tissue-swelling. The second is fluid buildup. The doctors have literally cut a plug out of his skull in order to relieve the pressure on the brain. This would have probably been necessary even if he had received medical attention very soon after the incident. The problem is that it appears to have happened hours ago. We have no way of determining when the event occurred."

"I can tell you the exact time," Mike broke in. The nurse looked at her with a surprised expression. "My father-in-law's dog went into a hysterical frenzy early this afternoon. It was close to 1:30. I'd just gotten home from grocery shopping. I know this sounds crazy, but I believe Cassidy, that's the dog's name, sensed that something terrible had just happened to Pops at the moment it happened." Mike looked at the nurse intensely. She went on with a summary of how Cassidy helped to direct the efforts to find Andy.

The nurse looked at her watch. "If that's so, then it means it's been over nine hours between the time he was shot and when he arrived here." She shook her head. "That's amazing. I mean it's incredible that he has been able to survive that many hours having suffered such severe injuries and blood loss. He had to have been knocked unconscious initially. He may have been out for who knows how long." The nurse began taking notes. "The doctors will want this information. What else can you tell me?"

Brian told of his father having fired two distress flares. "The first was when a small plane circled him. That let everybody know that something was seriously wrong. In addition, it gave his actual location. He fired a second one when the Coast Guard rescue helicopter was approaching." The nurse asked if Andy had a radio on board or a cell phone. "He has both. I don't know why he didn't try to use them." Brian asked, "will we be able to see my father before he leaves here?"

"I'll see what the doctors have to say," the nurse told him.

"What about Cassidy?" Mike asked.

"I'm sure not," the nurse said, "I apologize for not telling you this in the beginning. The doctors have Mr. McLeod in an induced coma. It's standard procedure with serious brain injuries. Part of the reason for doing it is to spare the patient having to experience intense pain."

Brian commented, "who knows what an unconscious person is experiencing." The nurse agreed.

"Having Cassidy nearby might be the best thing for Pops right now," Mike said.

The nurse stood up. "I'll let you know what's happening. Your dad is in good hands. All three of the doctors are top notch. One of them was a combat surgeon in Iraq. He's seen it all many times over." Before departing she directed them to the waiting area, "There's coffee available. If not, ask one of the gals to make a fresh pot. Sorry, we don't have wine."

Brian said, "there is one more thing." The nurse looked at him. "If it's true that my dad was shot, then it's important that this be kept from the media. Whoever shot my dad is out there. If he finds out that Pops is still alive, it's likely that he's going to want to finish the job. Pops is the only one who can identify him."

"Good point," the nurse said. "I'll say something to the entire night staff. The rescue has already been reported to the Sheriff's Department."

The nurse left. Brian turned to Mike. "Let's get some coffee and see if we can find something to put water in for Cassidy."

One of the nurses got them a bed pan. She even filled it half full for them. They told her that they would be out in the parking lot if anyone needed them. At the truck Brian set the pan down for Cassidy. He looked at his watch. It was now after 11:30. The dog took a few laps from it. Brian asked Mike if she would take Cassidy over to a nearby grassy area. He tried calling the marina to see if Al and Jason were back yet. After several rings an answering machine clicked on. Brian left a message that they were at the hospital in Sturgeon Bay and that they would probably be there for the next few hours. He asked that one of them call him when they got this message.

Brian lowered the tailgate of the truck. He and Mike sat on it with Cassidy lying next to Brian. After a couple of sips of coffee Brian looked at the cup. "I wish this were a cold beer or a glass of wine instead."

"The grocery stores are still open." Mike told him. "I think they sell package alcohol until midnight. I'll run over and get a six pack. You and Cassidy can go for a walk. It's a nice evening. I'll be right back." Brian was hesitant. "Come on, sweet man. You need to stretch your legs and try to relax. This has been a hell-of-a-day."

After receiving the call from the ER doctor, the dispatcher called Sheriff Otis Peterson at home. It was after ten o'clock. If he was already in bed, she knew that he would not appreciate being awakened. She also knew that, under these circumstances, he would appreciate it even less if he were not called. When the Sheriff answered the phone he listened without comment until she had finished. He wondered to himself if this report was in any way related to the two others. Over the past three weeks the Sheriff's department had received two reports of missing sailors. "I thought you would want to know about this right away, Sheriff," The dispatcher said apologetically. "It sounds like it could be related to the two others."

"You did the right thing, Linda," he assured her.

Before ending the conversation the dispatcher told the Sheriff that the family was concerned about protecting the victim. "They're worried about what might happen if word gets out that the victim is still alive." It wasn't necessary to spell out the implications of that.

After hanging up, Sheriff Peterson called Detective Annette

Kline. He apologized for waking her up. He told her about the report that had just come in. She said, "it would appear that our suspicions about those other two guys who've gone missing may be warranted. I never did think they were accidental. No bodies, no bad weather." She asked, "how about the boat? Where's that?"

The Sheriff didn't know. He told her that he was going to go over to the hospital to talk to the family. "I don't think this should wait until morning."

Detective Kline asked what phone line the report had come in on. "The media monitors 9ll calls. They'd be all over this in a millisecond. It could screw things up. If there's some sicko out there popping people in sailboats, we need to find him." She said that she would meet him at the hospital in a half an hour. The Sheriff called the dispatcher to find out what line the call had come in on. She said it had been received on the non-emergency one. He relaxed a little.

Sheriff Peterson decided to go to the Justice Center before joining Detective Kline at the hospital. His presence there at this time of night was highly unusual and it piqued the curiosity of the night staff. He went to his office and placed a call to the Coast Guard search and rescue station in Traverse City, Michigan. He was turned over to the Duty Officer who shared the information that had been reported to him. "If you would like to talk to the response team paramedics, I'll have them call you, Sheriff. They're still on duty. They're at the station hanger." Sheriff Peterson did indeed wish to speak to them.

He received a call ten minutes later and spoke with one of the two paramedics. "It was a real mess, Sheriff. In my opinion the man was shot much earlier in the day. I suspect that the bullet entered his left hand initially. It tore his hand up badly, but that may be what saved his life. It may have slowed the bullet down, mushroomed it, and deflected it at a steep angle to his forehead. Otherwise it could have pierced the skull and lodged in the brain. His head was a real mess, but I don't think the bullet penetrated the skull. Fragments of it may have gone through the left eye socket into the brain. It was impossible for us to tell. I have to say, given his injuries and the amount of time that elapsed before our arrival, it is incredible that he was still alive when we got to him. He lost a lot of blood, and was on the brink of hypothermia. What's really amazing is that he was able to shoot a flare to guide the pilot as we approached the location of the boat." Sheriff Peterson asked what was done with the boat. "A father and son arrived very shortly after we got there. They're from a marina on Washington Island. They intended to tow the boat back to their facility. Sorry, didn't get the name of the marina. The Duty Officer may have that information." The Sheriff asked if the CG medic had shared his opinion that this was a shooting with anyone other than his colleagues and superiors. "Yes, Sir. I expressed that opinion to the ER doctor while we were en route. I thought it was important to give him a heads up so he could be prepared. He told me that he intended to report this to the police."

The Sheriff was puzzled by something and asked, "it was a warm summer day today. It's still warm. What's the hypothermia about?"

"It's much cooler out on the lake. The boat was headed in a northwesterly direction. That suggests that he may have been much further out in the lake than he was when we found him. He was probably unconscious for a lengthy period of time. The significant blood loss was a contributing factor. His shirt was open and he was wearing shorts."

Before hanging up Sheriff Peterson asked that a written report be faxed to him. "If anything else occurs to you that you think might be helpful, please call me." The medic promised to do both. He asked how the man was doing.

"I don't know, officer. I'm heading over to the hospital right now. On behalf of the family, I want to extend thanks for a job well done. I appreciate your time in talking to me tonight."

It was after 11:30 when Sheriff Peterson arrived at the hospital. He found Brian and Michelle McLeod in the visitors lounge along with Cassidy. They looked exhausted, and at the same time wired. He introduced himself. Sheriff Peterson was a big man at six-foot-four, and weighing close to two-hundred-fifteen pounds. He wore a pair of light brown slacks and a somewhat wrinkled, short-sleeve dress shirt without a t-shirt underneath. He asked how Brian's father was doing. "We don't know. The doctors are still working on him. The head nurse said that they requested a fourth doctor join them. That doctor is here now."

"We're going to do everything possible to keep the situation with your father quiet." Sheriff Peterson pulled a chair up close to them so he could talk in a hushed tone. "What I'm about to tell you is in strict confidence." They nodded. "Two other sail boaters have disappeared fairly recently. They went out sailing and weren't seen or heard from again. The boats were found, but not their bodies. I don't know if what happened to your father today is related or not. I was suspicious about the disappearance of the others. This has raised those suspicions to a much higher level."

The Sheriff asked about the boat. Brian told him Al and Jason Swenson went out to retrieve it. He explained the earlier radio conversation he'd had with Jason, and the awful scene Jason had encountered. "They were in the process of making the boat ready to tow back to their marina on Washington Island," Brian told him. "I left my jeep at the marina. The ferry was done running for the day. One of their friends brought me back to the mainland. I need to go up there tomorrow to get my car. Hopefully, they can give me more details."

"I'm going to the Island first thing in the morning," Sheriff Peterson told him. "I'm taking one of my detectives with me. She can bring it back. We'll drop it off at your place or here, whichever you prefer. You need to be here for your dad. We will probably impound the boat. I'm going to contact the state crime lab and request that a team be sent here to go over it. We need to try to piece together what happened out there. Your father isn't going to be of much help for a while. We might have a serial killer running around out there." Before he got up to leave Sheriff Peterson said, "what I've just told you is in strict confidence. We're going to do everything we can to find whoever did this to your father."

Chapter 6

At 4:00 A.M. two of the doctors who had been working on Andrew McLeod came into the visitor's lounge. Brian and Mike had fallen asleep. They were aroused by Cassidy even before the doctors arrived. The two physicians looked exhausted. The older of the two served as the spokesman. Brian figured him to be the ex-combat surgeon. He introduced himself and his colleague. "This is Doctor Kennedy, and I'm Doctor Johns." Brian introduced himself and Mike to them. "Do you mind if we sit? We've been on our feet all night?" They pulled chairs up so that the four of them were in a close circle. "I know that you're both anxious to know what your dad's condition is. He's suffered a severe concussion. He has a fractured skull." Doctor Johns pointed to his own forehead. "You know, of course, that someone shot him. The impact of the bullet was not direct. It hit his head at a fairly steep upward angle. We're not worried about the fracture. It's hairline and will mend on its own. Had the impact of the bullet been more direct it could have caused splintering and maybe even entered the cranium." He stopped for a moment. "We don't see any signs of either bone or metal fragments in the frontal lobes. The other good news is that there doesn't appear to be any major hemorrhaging. There was some, but not so serious as to cause paralysis. We're pretty certain that his hand both deflected and slowed the bullet's velocity. It was probably a reflex reaction that ended up saving his life. There is bruising, capillary damage, and swelling. We took an actual plug out of your father's skull to relieve pressure. It will be replaced once the swelling subsides. We have him in an induced coma to keep him from experiencing severe pain. It also serves to slow down brain activity which helps the healing process. At least that's the theory." Both doctors sipped some of their coffee. "I don't want to alarm either of you. I believe in letting people know what to expect. The next several hours are going to be critical. Things could go south at any time. We'd like to move your dad to a different hospital. He needs to be in a facility that has the sophisticated staff and equipment needed to deal with such severe traumatic brain injury. However, the risk of moving him right now is too great. Maybe in three or four days he'll be stable enough." They discussed the options. "We have two hospitals in mind. Both of them have outstanding reputations. He'll receive excellent care in either one of them." Milwaukee is one choice, and the other is Madison. The Milwaukee hospital was Brian's choice because of its proximity. "I'll go ahead then and contact that hospital to set things up."

Doctor Johns looked to his colleague who had been silent up until now. Doctor Kennedy cleared his throat before speaking. "Your father's left eye was injured by a couple of bullet fragments. It's badly swollen. We were concerned that the fragments may have entered his brain through the eye socket. Again, because of the sharp angle, the fragments entered the sinus that is located just above the left eye." Like Doctor Johns he pointed to his own forehead. "My specialty is in ear, nose and throat. I was able to remove the fragments. The sinus will eventually heal on its own."

Doctor Johns interrupted. "Oddly, the most complicated aspect of his injuries turned out to be the nasal passages and his sinuses. I happened to know that Doctor Kennedy was up here on vacation this week and he came over to help us out a couple of hours ago." Doctor Kennedy nodded. "It took the two of us almost two hours to clear out the impacted blood and mucus that had accumulated and was extending down almost into your father's throat. Had it extended much further it would have blocked off his breathing. We think the blockage prevented him from being able to speak intelligibly. Even if he had been able to contact anyone for help, he couldn't have made himself understood. The buildup was putting pressure on what, in lay terms is called, the voice box; he probably could only have made garbled sounds. When he does regain consciousness, he's going to have a very sore throat. His voice may end up somewhat raspy."

Mike asked about the left hand. "There is an excellent hand surgeon in Green Bay. I'm going to call him later this morning to see if he can come up here to examine the hand. It's pretty badly mangled. If anyone can repair it, he's the man. I've sent a couple of patients to him who suffered severe hand injuries in farm accidents. I was almost certain they were going to require amputations. I've seen both men since. They don't have full use of their hands, but I was amazed at how much they did have." Doctor Johns looked to Doctor Kennedy again. "Can you think of anything we've missed, Marty?"

"The left eye," Dr. Kennedy said. "There's no way of us knowing for sure if your father will have vision in that eye. It may take some time before the swelling goes down enough so that an ophthalmologist can determine that. The sclera, the white part of the eye, is filled with blood as a result of burst capillaries. It could remain that way, or it could clear up on its own. An ophthalmologist will know better."

At the conclusion of the conference, Doctor Johns said, "I sure hope they catch the guy that did this to him." They all four stood and shook hands with one another. "Why don't the two of you head on home and get some sleep. The hospital will call you if there are any changes. Your dad is going to be off in la-la land for the next couple of days at least." He added, "you know, one of the important things that's come out of the wars in Afghanistan and Iraq is a much better understanding of traumatic brain injury. Severe concussions can often mess a person's thought processes up for a long period of time. Your dad may not know who you are or where he is once he regains consciousness. He may not even remember the actual incident. That's pretty common. Hang in there. Eventually, he'll get a lot, if not most, of it back."

As they prepared to leave the waiting room Doctor Kennedy stooped down to pet Cassidy. "Is this a border collie?" he asked.

Brian said, "yes, he's my dad's dog. Let me tell you about Cassidy." As the four of them walked down the hall together Brian told the story about how Cassidy had contributed to his father's rescue. Both doctors were impressed.

Dr. Kennedy said, "my kids have been pestering us for a dog. We might look into getting them one like this. He's nice looking, not too big, and smart."

The sky was beginning to lighten as they drove out of the hospital parking lot. Brian was driving. Mike traded places with Cassidy so she could sit next to her husband. "How are you doing?" she asked.

"I guess I'm still incredulous. I'm having trouble wrapping my mind around what has happened. What kind of crazy bastard did such a thing? I can't begin to imagine what Pops went through. If it weren't for Cassidy, we wouldn't have known anything was wrong. What would have happened to Pops? I mean it's just amazing that he managed to survive and function at all. My guess is that the boat would have ended up either on the rocks or sinking." Mike slipped her arm under his. They were silent for a while. She reached down to pet Cassidy who was snuggled up against her butt. Brian checked his watch. "When we get home, I think I'll lie down and try to get some sleep. I've decided to go back up to the Island. I'll take the eight o'clock ferry over. I need to see the boat. Maybe it will help me to get a better idea about what happened."

"I want to go with you," Mike said. "I'll call Sue, and let her know that Pops is in the hospital. I'm sure she'll be willing to keep the boys. We can be back home by early afternoon, don't you think?" Brian agreed with her. He saw no reason why they would need to stay on the island for more than an hour or two.

At home Brian made sure Cassidy had water and food. He and Mike went to bed. Cassidy followed them into the bedroom where he curled up on the floor at the foot of the bed. It was close to 5:00 A.M. They were all asleep in moments.

Cassidy awakened Brian at 7:30 by nudging his arm gently. Brian got out of bed feeling groggy. He decided to let Mike sleep a bit longer. In the bathroom he whispered to Cassidy, "since when have you started providing wake-up calls?" Cassidy's wagging tail thumped against the clothes hamper. Brian went into the kitchen and started coffee before showering. Cassidy, who hadn't eaten much yesterday, ate all of his dog food. He let himself out the front screen door. Mike got up by the time Brian was finished dressing. "We're not going to be able to make the eight o'clock ferry. We can catch the next one at 8:30," Brian told her.

They took along some granola bars that Mike made herself. On the way, she used her mobile phone to call Sue Nelson who was willing to keep the boys. Sue asked about Andy. "He's hurt, Sue. It's pretty serious. I'll fill you in later." After she hung up she said, "don't worry; I'm not going to tell Sue about what actually happened. I trust her implicitly, but until this is all over, I don't think we should tell anyone."

At Brian's request, she called the school. Mike handed the phone to Brian. Elaine answered. "Elaine, I won't be in until early afternoon. We've had a family medical emergency. I'll tell you about it later." Then he listened. "Can you call her and let her know I won't be available until this afternoon? Tell her I'll call her when I get to school. I'll try to be there by one o'clock. Thanks, Elaine." He closed the phone. He told Mike that the school Superintendent, Gayle Krietlow, wanted to meet with him.

They arrived at the North Port pier a few minutes before the 8:30, the time that the next ferry was scheduled to leave. There were not as many people as Brian had expected. They were close to the front of the half full boat. Along with Cassidy they climbed up to the observation deck. It was another nice day. There was a fairly strong breeze out of the south which was barely noticeable as the ferry headed north toward Washington Island. They'd feel it more on the return trip. The Captain spotted Brian and recognized him from the day before. He invited them into the wheel house. "How'd things turn out with your dad?" Brian wasn't sure what to say. "Heard the Coast Guard was called out last evenin'. Was that about him?"

"Yeah," Brian admitted. "He's hurt. He needed to be taken off the boat." The Captain asked what had happened. "We don't know for sure. He's in the hospital down in Sturgeon Bay. I haven't been able to talk to him yet."

The Captain glanced at Brian with a slightly skeptical expression. "Must have been pretty serious. The Coast Guard don't get involved unless it's life threatening."

Brian told him a partial truth. "He was unconscious when they found him. He was still that way when we left the hospital a few hours ago."

"Christ, sounds to me like he got bonked hard in the head by the boom." The Captain turned the wheel to alter direction into the channel between the mainland and Plum Island. "Where's the boat?"

Brian was pretty sure the Captain knew exactly where the boat was. He probably knew nearly everything that happened on the island. "Al Swenson and Jason towed it in last night. It's at their marina."

"I went by there this mornin'," the Captain said. "That must be the boat that was all covered up. Al probably didn't want people nosin' around on it." He was pretending to be concentrating on his course. "Had somethin' unusual happen this mornin'," he went on. "The Sheriff and some lady detective came across on the 7:30 ferry. Can't remember the last time that happened." Brian said nothing. "Maybe he's here to check up on a few things for the Coast Guard."

You sly old fox, Brian thought. "I talked to the Sheriff last night. He came to see us at the hospital," Brian told the Captain. "He knew that a search had been on for my dad. He told me he might come up to the Island to look at the boat. My dad has a reputation for being an excellent sailor. The sheriff wanted to rule out the possibility of sabotage."

"You mean he thinks somebody might have cut a rope or loosened somethin'?" The Captain looked straight at Brian with a surprised expression. "Who'd do such a thing?"

"I think he wants to take a look at the boat to clear up any possible suspicions."

"Or to cast some. There're some weird people runnin' round out there these days," the Captain said.

"Amen to that," Brian said. *You have no idea how weird, Captain*. Brian changed the subject. "Captain, you met Cassidy yesterday. This is my wife Mike." She held her hand out to shake with the Captain.

He wiped his hand on his shirt before accepting hers. "I'm very pleased to meet you, Mrs. McLeod."

"Mike, please." She smiled at him, sure that he was unaccustomed to shaking hands with women.

Brian had called Officer Morris before getting on the ferry. Morris met them at the ferry dock and he accompanied them to the marina. Sheriff Peterson and Detective Kline were standing in the parking area talking with Al and Jason Swenson. The Sheriff looked somewhat displeased that they were here. "We're done here, Brian. I don't think you should see the boat. It's not a pretty sight. Besides, I don't want anything disturbed until after the State Investigation team has gone over it."

"I won't go on the boat, Sheriff. I won't touch anything. I

just want to see it." He quickly added, "we came over mainly to settle up with Al for towing my dad's boat last night and to get my jeep."

The Sheriff was insistent, "Al has it covered up. I'd prefer you not see it."

"Okay," Brian backed off. "Can you tell me anything? Have you discovered anything?"

Sheriff Peterson softened a little. "This is in strict confidence." Brian nodded. "The boat has five bullet holes in the left side of the hull. Three of them are at the waterline. Two more, probably the last two fired, are higher up and toward the front. We're just guessing, but the shooter may have suspected there was somebody else on board. One of the bullets was aimed into the toilet area. The other was aimed closer to the front of the boat into the sleeping area."

Brian said, "if I remember right, what you told us last night was that you found the boats from the two previous sailors that have gone missing, but not their bodies." The Sheriff confirmed that was correct. "So, why did he attempt to sink Pop's boat and not the other two?" The Sheriff had no explanation to offer.

Before leaving, the Sheriff reiterated that he didn't want Brian to look at the boat. As soon as the Sheriff and Detective Kline were gone, Brian turned to Al and Jason and introduced them to Mike. Al spoke up. "He's right, Brian. The cockpit is a real mess. You don't want to see it. I'm frankly surprised that your dad didn't bleed to death before the Coast Guard got to him." He looked down as if deciding what to say next. "One of the most amazing things about all of this is that your dad must have discovered the boat was taking on water. Somehow he managed to get himself down into the cabin and turn on the bilge pump. Jason and I figure that he also came to realize that he was on a course headed out into the lake. If the boat had gone down, it probably never would have been found. His VHF radio was on. His cell phone was on the cabin sole. It's not working. The circuitry must have gotten wet. It's impossible to know if he tried to send a May Day. The radio doesn't have much of a range." Brian told them what the doctors had said about his father not being able to speak. "Well, there you go then." Al went on. "Here's what amazed Jason and me the most. We know that the wind shifted yesterday afternoon from southeast to south-southwest. That probably caused the boat to change direction heading more easterly, further out into the lake. Here's where the facts end and our theory begins. Your dad was most likely unconscious for a period of time. When he regained consciousness, he was somehow able to figure out that the boat was going in the wrong direction. He was able to put two and two together figuring out that he had to turn it around. So here's this man who's had his head and his left hand damn near blown off. Somehow he figures out a way to get the boat turned in the right direction and bring the jib around to the starboard side. The mainsail took care of itself. That's freaking amazing, but that's not all. He discovers that the small volume electric bilge pump ain't doing the job. So he manages to work the high volume hand pump at least for awhile. We found the handle in the pump. How'd he manage to do that?"

"Did you tell the Sheriff these things?" Brian asked. "Yeah, but I don't think he knows squat about boats. He didn't seem the slightest bit impressed." Brian smiled. "How did you guys figure it out?"

"Brian, Jase and I were out there until one o'clock this morning towing the boat in. Even though I was able to stuff pieces of rag in the waterline holes, the boat was still taking on some water. When we got on the boat, the battery was so low the electric pump was barely working. I started the engine to recharge the battery. Jase worked the hand pump. On the long way back we managed to piece a few things together. It ain't exactly rocket science. I sure hope your dad pulls through. Both of us want to meet that man."

"Al, I can't thank the two of you enough for everything you've done. I won't ask you to uncover the boat, but can I take a look at the hull?" Al didn't see any harm in that. They had the boat tied to a dock where they could keep an eye on it. It was located where they kept boats that were seldom used by their owners. Jason left them. He had things to tend to. Al walked them to the dock. On the way Brian told him some of the things the ferry boat captain had said on the way over to the island.

Al laughed. "Ain't much goes on here that Clarence doesn't know about. He was probably listening to the Coast Guard channels. He doesn't always get his facts straight, though. It's amusing to hear some of the twists and turns his stories take. The Islanders, meaning the folks who live here year round and who've been here for generations, thrive on gossip. Clarence, God bless him, loves a good story. He must get pretty bored running back and forth between the Island and Northport day after day. He loves good stories and storms. A good storm makes for some good stories. Probably sooner than later he'll find out about what happened to your dad. He'll have a field day with that.

"I've got some concerns about that, Al. It could put Pops in serious jeopardy if it gets back to the shooter that my dad is still alive."

Al looked at Brian. "Christ, I hadn't thought about that."

Brian asked how well Al knew the captain. Al said they weren't close friends but they knew and liked one another. "Since I'm sure he knows that you and Jason towed the boat in, maybe you could talk to him. Maybe you could go so far as to tell him about my dad. Ask him to keep it quiet for the reason we just discussed."

Al thought about Brian's proposal. "I could do that, Brian, but it might be better coming from you directly. Maybe you can even offer to tell him the whole story if they catch the guy." Brian liked Al's suggestion.

Before leaving, Brian asked Al how much he owed Al for the towing. Al told him that two-hundred would cover everything. Brian wrote a check for three hundred. Al didn't even look at the check when Brian handed it to him. Brian thought, *good, let him be surprised later when he can't refuse it*. Before Brian got in his jeep, he told Mike that he was going to school to meet with Superintendent Gayle. "I'll go on down to the hospital from there." Mike insisted that he come by the house to pick her and Cassidy up on his way.

At the ferry dock, Brian learned that Captain Clarence was at Northport. He wouldn't be piloting their boat back to the mainland. Brian asked if there was some way he could get in touch with the captain. He had something he needed to discuss with him. The lady running the ticket counter took Brian into an office. She got the captain on the radio then left Brian to talk to him, closing the door behind her. Brian told the captain that his father was shot by someone yesterday. The captain didn't even try to feign surprise. "I figured somethin' bad had happened what with the Coast Guard getting involved last evenin', then the Sheriff this morning. Any idea who done it?"

Brian told him that no one had any idea and that was his reason for his calling.

He asked that it be kept a strict secret. The captain understood the reason and promised not to utter a word to anyone. "If they're able to catch the guy, and once everything is over, I promise to tell you the whole story."

He told Brian that he could be counted on not to say anything. "Things come my way every once-in-a-while. If I hear anything that will help catch the bastard, I'll be sure to let the Sheriff know. That's just about the worst thing I've ever heard anybody doin'." He paused a moment. "Put Edna back on the radio for me, will you?"

Brian summoned her. She talked to the captain very briefly. When she came back out of the office she went to her cash drawer. She counted out some money and handed it to Brian. "Clarence told me to give you this. He's not charging you for the ferry rides. He told me that from now on you won't be charged."

Brian tried to refuse. "He insisted," she told him. "I've never known him to do that before." Brian could tell that she would give just about anything to know what that was about.

Brian, Mike, and Cassidy went up to the observation deck on the way back to the mainland. It was a beautiful, sunny day. There weren't many passengers. Brian assumed that at this time of the day more people were coming to the island than leaving. It would be the opposite later in the day. He told Mike about them receiving free passage. "I'm blown away by the generosity we've received from everyone," he said. Mike agreed. She was getting chilled and said that she was going back to the truck to get a sweatshirt. "It slipped my mind to ask Al if they would be able to repair Pop's boat. I'm going to call him while you're doing that."

Al answered the phone. He recognized Brian's voice. "Brian, you cotton-picker. You way overpaid us for bringing your dad's boat in."

"Not at all, Al. You guys were there for me at a time when I needed help. I appreciate what you did." Al changed the subject. "Glad you called, Brian. I just got off the phone with the Sheriff. He called to tell me that the investigators from the state crime lab will be here tomorrow to go over the boat. Don't know what they hope to find, but what do I know? I'm surprised that things are happening so quickly."

"There's a reason for that, Al. I'll tell you about it later." Brian said. "My main reason for calling you is to ask if you guys are set up to do fiberglass repair." Al said that they were. "Good, then as soon as we get permission from the Sheriff and the insurance company, I'd like you to go ahead with the repairs. I'll get you the name of my dad's insurance agent and you can send an estimate to her." Al was agreeable to that. "One other thing, Al. I didn't get a chance to talk to Captain Clarence in person, but Edna let me talk to him by radio. He promised not to say anything to anybody about what happened. That was a good suggestion. Thanks." Brian decided that it would probably be best not to say anything about the captain refunding the fare and offering free passage in the future. He was sure it was an unprecedented overture of kindness.

Chapter 7

Brian arrived at school a few minutes before Supt. Gayle Krietlow. Elaine greeted him. Brian liked her and trusted her judgment and discretion. She handled students, and parents with ease and was well liked by the staff. She had been hired three years after Brian had become principal replacing a dour spinster lady who had been efficient but mirthless. Elaine hesitantly asked if everything was okay at home. He weighed how to answer her question. "No. As you know, my dad usually goes on an annual sailing adventure for two or three weeks. He's been doing that for years. He took off yesterday morning and was only gone a few hours when he had an accident. He was hurt badly and the Coast Guard had to rescue him. He's in the hospital."

She was genuinely shocked. "What happened?"

"We don't really know." Brian chose not to tell her what had actually happened or how serious his father's condition was. "Pops is kind of out of it and hasn't been able to tell us anything. He suffered a concussion and was unconscious for a period of time."

"Oh, my," Elaine said. "It sounds like he was hit in the head by the boom." Brian told her that was what everybody else thought, too. "I hope he recovers soon." Brian told her that he was going to the hospital as soon as his meeting with the superintendent was over. Elaine showed him a small stack of phone messages. "If you like, I can call some of these people to try and answer their questions."

"I'd appreciate that," he told her. "I'll sort through them first to see which ones I need to call." He asked if there was any coffee. She told him there was, but she had made it a couple of hours ago. It was probably pretty strong by now. "That's good. We didn't get a lot of sleep last night. Strong is good." He went to the teacher's lounge and poured a cup.

When he returned to the office, Supt. Krietlow had just

arrived. They went into his office. He asked her if she wanted the door closed. She told him he could leave it open. "I just have a couple of things to go over with you. It won't take long." She looked at him. "Pardon me for saying this, Brian, but you look like hell. You look exhausted. Is everything okay?" He gave her essentially the same version of the story he'd given Elaine a few minutes before. "Well, I won't keep you but a few minutes," she said.

There were two budget items she wanted to get his input on. She went over them with him in her usual concise, thorough way. He asked her to clarify one or two things about one of them. "That's one of the reasons I bring things to you, Brian. You're able to pick up on details that have either been overlooked or need correction. You would have made a good lawyer."

He smiled wryly and said, "that's an oxymoron." She laughed. They left together. On his way out Elaine asked him to let her know if he or Mike needed anything. He thanked her.

Their two sons, Dan, who had just turned fifteen, and Shawn, the thirteen year old, were at home when Brian arrived. Dan had Shawn's bike turned upside down and was working on it. He asked his father if he could help figure out what was wrong with the derailleur on Shawn's bike. Brian asked what the problem was and Shawn told him that it skipped gears when he shifted. Sometimes it even threw the chain off entirely. Brian looked at it. "I'm going to start turning the pedal, Dan. I want you to shift from one gear to another every time I say... 'now.'" Dan did as he was told and Brian was able to pinpoint the problem after a few turns. He showed both boys what the problem was and using a screw driver he showed them how to adjust the derailleur to correct it. He turned the bike to the upright position and asked Shawn to give it a try. Shawn rode the bike down the drive way and back. "How's that?" Brian asked.

"Good!" Shawn said.

Brian smiled and said. "That's amazing. I almost never get it right on the first try."

He had not seen Mike watching them. "Do you want some iced tea before we go?" She asked. He followed her into the house. In the kitchen he asked if she had said anything to the boys about Grand Pops yet. "No, I was waiting for you to get home. I'm not sure what we should tell them. Besides, I think it will be better coming from you." She put her arms around him. "I called the hospital. He's in intensive care. I talked to one of the nurses there. She had very little to report. He's still in an induced coma. His condition is regarded as serious but stable. She clarified that 'serious' was better than 'critical'. The chances of recovery are improved in the 'serious' condition. She said that serious patients require constant monitoring to make sure that they don't slip backwards." Mike, almost as tall as her husband, leaned forward and gave him a kiss. They held one another.

Dan came through the screen door. "Can Shawn and I go to the beach?"

"You can, but I need to talk to both of you first. Get your brother." Moments later both boys entered the kitchen. Brian pulled out a chair from the kitchen table and sat down. He invited the boys to do the same. "What's up, Dad?" Dan asked. "You look pretty serious."

"I'm very serious," Brian said as he traced invisible lines on the table top. "It's about Grand Pops. You know he left on his sailing trip yesterday." Both boys watched their father. "I want you to hear me out before you start asking questions. Okay?" Both boys nodded. "Grand Pops had a serious accident yesterday afternoon. Nobody seems to know what happened to him for sure. He was rescued by a Coast Guard helicopter last night. They flew him to the hospital in Sturgeon Bay. That's where he's at right now." Dan started to say something. Brian raised his hand. "Grand Pops has a serious injury to his head and his left hand. The doctors have made him unconscious so that he won't feel pain. As soon it's safe enough to move him, he's going to be taken to another hospital where he can get more specialized care. Your Mom and I are going to see him in just a few minutes. I know you'd like to come along. He's in very bad shape. Because he's unconscious, he isn't aware of anything that's going on around him." Dan asked what happened. "As I said, Dan, we don't really know. We probably won't know until Grand Pops is able to talk and can tell us."

"Is he going to be okay?" Shawn asked.

"Your Grand Pops is as tough as they come, Shawn.

Despite his injuries he battled hard to stay alive for several hours until help arrived. He got hurt early yesterday afternoon. He wasn't rescued until last night. In the meantime he lost a lot of blood. It's amazing that he was able to hang on that long."

"How do you know he got hurt early in the afternoon? Was he able to tell you that?" Dan asked.

Brian smiled weakly. He reached across the table and wiggled his fingers for Dan to take his hand. "I'm going to tell you an incredible story. Every word of it is true. It's something that happened with your Mom and Cassidy." He told the boys about Cassidy's sudden frantic behavior yesterday. Dan turned to his mother. "How did you know what Cassidy was trying to say to you, Mom?"

"I can't answer that, Dan," she said. "Cassidy started barking, and whining and running around. He was acting really upset. At first I thought he'd been stung by a wasp or something. It took me a couple of minutes to realize that it was something else. I can't explain it. I just realized that something had happened to Grand Pops. I called your dad. He came right home. On the way he called a Sheriff's Deputy he knows." She turned to Brian. "Tell the boys about what happened up on the island."

After Brian finished telling them the rest of the story he said. "I know it all sounds unbelievable. Most people would think we were making it all up. That's why I've decided it's probably not a good idea for any of us to go around telling anybody about it. The fact is, Grand Pops would not be alive if it weren't for Cassidy and your Mom. Nobody would have known he was hurt. Even if they had, they wouldn't have known where to begin looking for him. Cassidy saved him." Shawn asked how Cassidy could have possibly known those things. "I wish I could answer that, Shawn. Grand Pops and Cassidy have been together a long time. Cassidy goes everywhere with Grand Pops. He even sleeps with him. They can't talk with one another, but they seem to sense things about one another."

"That's not true, Dad." Shawn interrupted. "Grand Pops is always talking to Cassidy. Cassidy looks at Grand Pops like he knows what Grand Pops is saying. Maybe Cassidy has a code he uses to talk to Grand Pops. Maybe it's with his tail. I think he talks with his eyebrows and his ears a lot, too. Grand Pops seems to know what Cassidy is saying. Maybe Cassidy understands words and Grand Pops understands the other things."

"I've never thought about it that way, Shawn. I like that idea," Brian said. "After what has happened I realize that I need to revise my way of thinking. We need to give your Mom a lot of credit, too. After all, she was the one who figured out what Cassidy was trying to say. When she called me at school I could tell from the tone of her voice that whatever was going on was very serious."

Shawn turned to his mother. "Mom, maybe you and Grand Pops are dog whisperers."

Brian checked his watch. "Your mom and I are leaving now. We'll drop you guys off at the beach. We'll pick you up on our way home in a couple of hours." Dan asked if they could ride their bikes instead. "Nope, as Grand Pops would say, 'There are still too many summer weenies running around out there. It ain't safe. He's right."

Before the boys got out of the jeep, Brian said, "it's two o'clock. We'll see you around four. If we're a few minutes late, wait for us." There were several other kids at the beach. Some of them were vacationers. Others were locals that the McLeod boys knew from school. A volleyball net was set up on the beach and a game was in progress. Dan immediately joined in. Shawn had no interest in the game. He started for the water, but became distracted by some kids who were sculpting an elaborate dragon in the sand. He watched them for a few minutes. He eventually asked if he could join them.

Once they were on the road, Brian spoke. "So, dog whisperer, what's Cassidy got to say?"

Cassidy was on the seat next to Mike. She stroked his fur. "He's disappointed. He was hoping to go for a swim. He loves the water."

"I'm sorry. I didn't mean to sound like I was making fun of what Shawn said. He's the more sensitive of the two. I was impressed with his observations about what goes on between Pops and Cassidy. The kid doesn't miss much. He worships his Grand Pops."

"Both boys do. I do, too. I see so much of Pops in you," Mike said. "I know you're preoccupied with what's happening. Thanks for taking the time to help the boys fix the bike. You did more than just fix it. You showed them what to do. That's what Pops would have done. He does it all the time. Neither of you talk down to them or ignore their concerns. When you were telling them about what happened with Pops, you let them know that things were serious. I'm glad you left out the part about his being shot. That would have really scared them. Someday you can tell them the whole story, just not now. I'm struggling with it myself. It seems so utterly senseless and surreal." Cassidy gave a slight whine. He was sitting on the seat looking ahead. Mike asked, "What?" Cassidy gave her a quick glance and returned to looking ahead. He was panting. A slight amount of drool dripped to the floor.

Brian asked, "Is he okay? Cassidy, are you all right?"

"He's okay," Mike said. "He knows where we're going. He's probably hoping that he'll get to see Pops."

"I wish they would let Cassidy in," Brian said. "If Pops could just touch Cassidy, it would probably do more to help him than anything else."

At the hospital Mike and Brian took turns going in to see Andy while the other stayed with Cassidy. Mike went first. The staff of the intensive care, while sympathetic, were intractable about allowing a dog to enter the unit.

The head nurse approached Brian before he went into his father's room. "Before you leave, Mr. McLeod, I need a word or two with you. I'll wait for you in my office just down the hall." She pointed toward it.

When Brian entered the room, he was overwhelmed and shocked by the sight of his father. Tears welled up immediately. Andy's forehead was swaddled in bandaging. The left eye was exposed. It was bruised and badly swollen with a mixture of crimson and dark blue discoloration. His left hand was heavily bandaged. Brian spoke to his father in a faltering whisper. "It's me, Pops, Brian." There was no response. He had expected as much. Brian gently touched his father's bearded right cheek. It took several moments before he could get enough control over his emotions to say anything more. "Cassidy is here, Pops. He's out in the truck. They won't let him in to see you." Again he had to choke back tears. "He saved your life again, Pops. I'll tell you all about it when you get better. Actually, he and Mike worked together to save you." Brian took a hold of his father's callused, leathery right hand. "I know you're in there, Pops. I don't know if you can hear me or not. I love you. You're a great dad." There were more tears. "I kind of know what happened to you. What you did was incredible. I don't know how you were able to survive, nobody does." Brian let go of his father's hand to reach for some tissues. He wiped his cheeks and blew his nose. "The boat is okay. It's got some damage. The guy who shot you also shot some holes in the boat. The folks who own the marina on Washington Island towed it in. They're going to fix it for you. You'll be able to sail it again." Brian felt a terrible sense of sadness. He felt drained. He reached out to take his father's hand again. He sat with his father in silence for several minutes. Finally he stood. "I'll see you tomorrow, Pops. I love you."

Before he went to see the head nurse, he went to the drinking fountain and then to the bathroom to wash his face. He rapped lightly on her open office door. She appeared to have been waiting for him. She stood and invited him in. Her photo identification tag showed her name as Audrey Reye. Brian noticed that she also had a brass name plaque mounted on what looked like pink marble that sat close to the front of her impeccably well-ordered desk. He noted the initials after her name indicating that she held a Master's Degree in Nursing. She immediately launched into her agenda. "There are three things I need to discuss with you, Mr. McLeod." She started out. "First, Sheriff Peterson was here this morning. He has issued strict orders that no one other than you and your wife are permitted visitation with your father. He apparently has some concern about your father's safety. He did not go into details with me." She paused folding her hands on her desk. Brian suspected she was hoping for him to explain the reason behind the order. Brian said nothing. After a brief lapse she continued. "Next, Doctor Johns came in to examine your father. He plans to call you later today. He apparently has made arrangements for your father to be admitted to a hospital in Milwaukee. He did not divulge the name of the hospital to me. Your father will leave our facility as soon as he can be safely transported. I have no idea of when that might occur." Brian thought she seemed annoyed about information being withheld from her. Again, she paused. Brian told her that Dr. Johns had discussed that prospect with him last night. *Actually, at four o'clock this mornin.* "Finally, a Doctor Randolph from Green Bay plans to examine the damage to your father's left hand. We have been told to expect him early this evening. Doctor Randolph is considered to be a highly qualified hand surgeon. I'm not familiar with him. Apparently he was summoned by Doctor Johns." She unclasped her hands and glanced down. "Well, that's all I have, Mr. McLeod, unless you have some question or something you wish to share." Brian told her he couldn't think of a thing. He thanked her and left.

At the truck Brian asked Mike, "were you subjected to Dragon Lady?" She asked who he was referring to. Brian told Mike about his encounter with Audrey Reye.

"No, but from your description it sounds like I got off lucky." As Brian drove out of the parking lot, Mike said, "I couldn't help myself, Brian. I started to bawl like a baby when I saw Pops. It took everything I could muster to get myself under control. I said to myself, *Pops doesn't need me acting this way. Just stop it*. I'm glad we weren't allowed to see him last night. I would have been devastated."

Brian patted her shoulder, "I had the same reaction. I couldn't hold back the tears, but by the time I left him, something had changed within me. I found myself getting angry. There's a part of me that wants to get a couple of his guns. I'd like to borrow a sailboat and head up the coast. In my fantasy the sorry son-of-a-bitch comes out after me. I don't kill him outright. I make him suffer for awhile before making him disappear the way he had intended Pops to. It's a fantasy. I doubt seriously that I could actually do such a thing. I honestly don't know what I'd do if I ever had a chance to confront the guy. I don't have a great deal of faith in the criminal justice system, but I don't know that I could take the law into my own hands."

They drove in silence for awhile. Brian finally spoke. "Pops never talked much about the time he spent in Viet Nam. Once, after my brother Corey died, Pops said some things. He'd had too much to drink. I don't even remember how the subject came up. Pops told me about the first time he had killed someone in combat. I sensed that it still bothered him. After all those years he still wasn't able to put it behind him." Brian shook his head. "As I recall, he seemed to be trying to explain what had happened to Corey as well as to himself. Pops dismissed the idea entirely that Corey killed himself because of losing his legs. He implied that it was because of something else. I know that he and Corey talked about things that happened over there. Pops was the only person Corey seemed able to confide in. The two of them would occasionally get drunk together. When they were drunk their relationship went from being father and son to something more like brothers or buddies. I guess what I'm saying is that I've seen what war did to my dad and to my brother. I'm probably less capable of violent behavior than either of them."

Mike looked over at him. "Okay, then you find the guy and I'll shoot him." She looked dead serious.

That evening Doctor Johns called to give Brian an update on his father's condition. "I have some good news and some bad news," he said. "The good news is that the intracranial swelling is beginning to subside. If that continues we'll be able to gradually begin weaning your dad off the sedatives. Of course we won't be able to evaluate the extent, or even if there is brain injury until he's fully conscious. Another piece of good news is that the hand surgeon we talked about, Doctor Randolph, saw your father just a while ago. With your permission, he will arrange to bring his team up here from Green Bay the day after tomorrow to do an initial surgery. He said that it needed to be done soon. The hospital has granted him permission to use our facilities. If you give the go-ahead, they will reschedule elective surgeries in order to provide Doctor Randolph with an operating room. He says that it is going to take several hours due to the number of micro attachments involved. He made it clear that he doubts your father will ever have full use of the hand. At best he will be able to open and close it partially and have limited sensation or strength in it." Brian asked if his father could endure the surgery. "It shouldn't pose a problem, Brian. If we do nothing, the alternative is amputation and an eventual prosthesis." Brian asked Doctor Johns for his opinion. "I was afraid you were going to ask that." He weighed his response. "I don't know what to tell you, Brian. There have been some amazing breakthroughs in prostheses over the past few years. It's mostly due to the number of amputations of military personnel. Prostheses still have their limitations. It's the proverbial six of one, half-a-dozen of the other."

"If he has the surgery and it doesn't work out, can he elect to have an amputation later on?" Brian asked.

"Absolutely," Doctor Johns said.

"Then let's go for it. Let's do the surgery. If it works, great; if not, it will allow my dad the opportunity to make his own decision later on. If the tables were turned, I know that's what he'd do for me." Brian asked what the bad news was.

"Your dad is developing pneumonia. It's most likely what we call aspiration pneumonia. The fragmentation damage to the sinus caused a lot of blood and mucus to make its way down through the nasal passages and into the bronchial tube. When fluids enter the bronchus, the body's response is to cough in order to clear the air passages. Because your dad was unconscious for a period of time the coughing response didn't happen. We already have him on oxygen and antibiotics. I'm adding a different antibiotic to treat the pneumonia. We've elevated him even more. While he remains unconscious we're going to have to monitor his condition very carefully. We may have to abandon keeping him in a coma sooner than we would like to." Brian asked what would happen if the pneumonia got worse. "He could quite literally drown in his own body fluids," Dr. Johns told him. *What irony,* Brian thought. *Pops escapes drowning in the lake only to be faced with it in a hospital.* "We'll keep you informed," Dr. Johns said at the end of their conversation.

Chapter 8

Sheriff Peterson called Brian the next morning at school. He asked how his father was doing. Brian gave him a concise report. The Sheriff told Brian he didn't have much news. "I talked to the crime lab guys yesterday afternoon. They found all five of the rounds that were fired into the hull of your dad's boat. They couldn't tell much of anything from those. The bullets were too distorted. They guessed that they were 9mm. There's only about five-hundred bazillion of those around," he said sarcastically. "The techies admitted that their best attempt at formulating any kind scenario is speculative. They think the guy was most likely in a powerboat. Your dad was probably standing up at the time. That means the guy had to aim at an upward angle. That angle would vary depending on how close his boat was to your dad's boat. Their guess is that it was probably five or six feet off the left side. There is no evidence that the guy boarded the boat either before or after the shooting. So it wasn't a robbery. It was more like a senseless drive-by shooting. Your dad was probably caught completely off guard. I keep wondering if the guy even knew who he was targeting." Peterson asked, "Who knew that your father was taking off on his boat yesterday?"

"Probably less than a handful of people," Brian told him. "Nobody that would want to do him harm."

Peterson went on, "one of our theories is that the shooter may be targeting artists. The reason I say this is that the two other sail-boaters that have gone missing were artists. One was a potter and the other was a watercolorist. The boats that they were in were small daysailers. If he shot holes in those boats they probably would have sunk fairly quickly. According to the crime lab guys, your dad's boat is built like a battleship. It would have taken a long time for it to sink. I don't think the shooter knows much about boats. If I had been the shooter, I would have shot all sorts of holes in it and I would have made damn sure your dad was dead. I'm hoping your dad recovers for a lot of reasons, but one of them is that we need his help. We need to catch this guy before he strikes again."

Brian asked if the Sheriff had considered creating a ruse, setting up a decoy target. "Yeah, we've discussed that possibility, especially after what's happened to your dad. I don't know. If we're right about this guy, if he's targeting specific individuals, he's not going to rise to that kind of bait. I definitely don't think he's finished with his killing spree. Do you know how many artist types there are in this county, especially in the summer? I'd have a better chance at winning the lottery than I'd have figuring out who's next on his list. The first person who went missing was sailing out of Ellison Bay in Green Bay waters. The second one was on the Lake Michigan side. He was out of Rowleys Bay. We're trying to zero in on artists who own sailboats. We got a list of sailboat registrations from the Department of Natural Resources (DNR). Unfortunately, boats under fifteen feet don't have to be registered. Of the boats that are registered, seventeen are owned by people who we've been able to identify as 'artists'. Six of those boats haven't been in the water at all this year. We're kicking ourselves because no one thought to include your dad on our list. I'm embarrassed to say this, but no one on my staff regards woodcarving as an art form. We've interviewed all but two of the artists we have on our list. It's tricky. We don't want to scare the hell out of these people. We're not revealing the reason for our concern to any of them. We've recommended that they make sure someone knows when they go out and where they'll be. We ask that they let that person know when to expect them back. If they ask about why we're concerned, we tell them we've had a number of reports of power boaters harassing sail boaters this summer."

"It sounds like you've done just about everything possible to try to prevent any more of this kind of thing from happening," Brian told the Sheriff.

"I hope so, but I have a nagging feeling we're missing something. One of my fears is that maybe we're barking up the wrong tree. What if it isn't just artists he's targeting? What if it's broader than that? What if his list includes musicians and/or performers? That increases the list exponentially. Even worse, what if he's messing with our heads? What if he's leading us in one direction today and tomorrow he heads off in another? The guy's a terrorist, in the truest sense of the word, Brian."

"It's the essence of psychopathology, Sheriff," Brian said.

"They're one and the same to my way of thinking."

"I don't know if you know this about my dad. He wasn't always a woodcarver. Before he moved up here he was a psychiatric social worker for over twenty years. From what I've heard, he was considered very good at what he did. He said he left his profession because he was burned out. I'm of the opinion that, if he 'burned out', it was because of his sensitivity and his uncommon ability to empathize. He could read people. He could get into their heads better than many of his colleagues. Your predecessor, Sheriff Cummings, sometimes consulted with Pops as a kind of profiler. What I'm saying is, if Pops pulls through this, and his brain isn't all screwed up, he may be able to help you to find this guy."

"That's even more of a reason to pray that he makes it." Peterson thanked Brian for sharing that last bit of information with him.

After ending the conversation, Brian sat back in his office chair. He looked out the window. It was another bright, sunny day. He wondered where Pops would have gotten to today if none of this had happened. He thought about the Sheriff's parting comment about more of a reason to pray for his father to make it. *Pray to what? Pop's is an agnostic leaning toward atheism. He has no use for organized religion. He's one of the most spiritual people I know. Maybe that's why he's able to see into people. Maybe that's what he shares with Mike. They're more than kindred spirits. There are times when they seem tuned in to one another at some whole different level of understanding. I sense things about him, but I don't have that almost psychic ability. I'm not able to connect with people on that level, or plane, or whatever the hell it's called. Was Corey able to? Did Pops see it coming? Did he sense that Corey was going to end his life?'*

Elaine poked her head in the door to say something. It startled Brian. She apologized profusely. "I'm so sorry, Brian. I didn't mean to scare you. I should have knocked or something. Are you okay? I'm really sorry."

"It's okay. My mind was somewhere else. What's up,

Elaine?'

"There's a parent on the line. She wants to speak with you. Can you take the call or do you want me to tell her you'll get back to her?" Brian said he'd take it.

The woman's voice at the other end sounded strained and deliberate as if she were weighing her words and had no intention of mincing any of them. She introduced herself as Mrs. Pitts, Mrs. Penelope Pitts. She was calling about one of the male science teachers, a Mr. Darien Michaels. She asked, "how well do you know Mr. Michaels?" Brian sidestepped her question and asked the reason for her call. "What do you know about Mr. Michael's personal life?" There was an insistent tone. She was losing whatever patience she had started out with.

Brian composed himself. "Mrs. Pitts, do you have some specific concern about Mr. Michaels. If so, why don't you just come right out and tell me what it is?"

"Indeed, I do," she said enunciating as if speaking through clenched teeth. "Are you aware that Mr. Michaels lives with another man, AND that this man is a waiter at a restaurant called the *Fleur D'Amour*? Furthermore, your Mr. Michaels waits tables there as well." She paused as though waiting for some response. Brian sensed what was coming. He asked her what her point was. "I don't know if you are aware of it, Mr. McLeod, but that restaurant, *the Fleur D' Amour,* has a reputation of catering to homosexuals. It is my understanding that most, if not all of the staff there are of that persuasion. The owner himself makes no secret of his own homosexual preference. In fact he is outrageously blatant about it." The flood gate was open. Mrs. Penelope Pitts launched into a diatribe, ranting about how the county was becoming overrun with "those kinds of people." They were infiltrating the schools, the hospitals, the nursing homes, and on and on.

Supt. Gayle Krietlow appeared at Brian's office door. He gestured for her to come in. She already had a cup of coffee in hand. She sat down in front of his desk. He leaned forward and massaged his right temple. Finally he interrupted the woman. "Mrs. Pitts, you needn't go on. You've made your opinions exceedingly clear. I would like to respond to your comments. First of all, and probably most importantly, Mr. Michaels is considered to be one of our very best teachers. I have visited his classroom numerous times and have observed his teaching techniques. In my opinion he is a gifted teacher. He inspires his students to learn. He treats his students with absolute respect. If a student appears to be struggling with the material being presented, he goes out of his way to provide extra help to that student. On occasion he has reached into his own pocket to help students in need. I was a classroom teacher myself for several years and would like to think I was a good one. Mr. Michaels is in a league all by himself. I consider it an honor to have someone of his caliber on our staff. Certainly he could find a more lucrative position elsewhere." Mrs. Pitts was now on the brink of becoming irate. Brian kept control of the conversation. In a calm, soothing voice he said, "Mrs. Pitts, I have a meeting scheduled with our Superintendent of schools in just a few minutes. I will discuss this matter with her. With your permission, I will ask that she give you a call." Mrs. Pitts wanted to know what he intended to do about "this miscreant". "With your permission I will ask Superintendent Krietlow to get back to you after we have had a chance to discuss this. Do I have your permission?" She persisted with her question. "I am going to hang up, Mrs. Pitts. Expect a call from Superintendent Krietlow later today."

After hanging up, Brian folded his hands, brought them up to his lips, and looked directly at Gayle. "Trouble in paradise?" she asked. Brian explained the situation to her. When he finished she said, "I'm not familiar with Michaels. From what I just overheard he sounds like a candidate for canonization. Is he really that good?"

"Everything I said about him is true," Brian told her.

"Is he overtly gay? Does he admit to being homosexual?"

Brian told her this was the first time anyone had even intimated Michaels was not straight. Brian went on. "If he is, he's been extremely discreet about it. I can't imagine him ever crossing the line with a student. You heard what I said. He treats his students with utmost respect. He holds himself to the highest standards. For him to do anything that would be detrimental to any of our kids is impossible to imagine."

Gayle smiled. "You amaze me sometimes, Brian. You are one of the least cynical people I have ever known. That's a compliment. Let me ask you this." She sat more upright. "How would you handle a situation where one of your teachers stood accused of actual sexual misconduct?"

"Gayle, you've raised a completely different issue. You're comparing apples and rocks. Let's just assume for the sake of argument that Darien is gay and that he's living in a homosexual relationship. It's his business. He's not imposing his choices on anyone. That's the apples. The rocks are when a person, like Mrs. Penelope Pitts, seeks to impose her opinions on others. If I were to find out that one of my teachers was doing anything to harm any one of our students, I'd be on the horn to you and the cops in a blink. In my opinion, schools need to be sacrosanct. Every kid should feel safe and protected every second they're here." Brian relaxed and sat back in his chair. "I can be pretty cynical at times. Just ask Mike. I assure you, I am not Pollyanna. Naiveté can restrict sound judgment just as much an excessive cynicism. I learned that a long time ago from my father."

"I agree. I'm glad to hear you say that," she said. "Speaking of your father, how is he doing?" Brian told her what he knew. "I hope I get a chance to meet him, Brian."

Gayle had a few things she wanted to go over with him and before she left she got Mrs. Pitt's phone number. Brian asked how she planned to handle the matter. "I'm not entirely sure. I'll probably thank her for sharing her concerns with us. I'll let her know that we will keep our eyes and ears open. I'm hoping she's wrong. I'm not sure how we should handle it if she's right. Experience has taught me that zealots usually turn out to be a real pain in the ass. If she's one of those homophobic extremists, then this could turn into a very nasty situation." They both stood. Gayle started for the door.

"Gayle?" She stopped and turned to face Brian. "Darien really is an outstanding teacher. What he does in his personal life is his business. If he were to walk in here right now and admit to being gay, I couldn't care less. As long he continues to demonstrate teaching excellence, doesn't flaunt his sexual preference and doesn't step out of line with his students, I'll stand behind him."

Gayle took a couple of steps back toward Brian's desk. "I understand your position, and I agree with you. The thought crossed my mind that maybe we should have a discussion with him. We don't need to decide anything in the next ten minutes. Let's think about it. It brings up the whole 'don't ask, don't tell' thing. I've always regarded that as bullshit. I really hope this Pitts woman doesn't elect to go on a witch hunt. In a community as conservative and as small as this, it could end up ruining his reputation and his career. It could end up causing you and me some serious grief." She smiled wearily. "Have a better day," she said as she turned and left.

Brian smiled and shook his head. One of the things he liked about Gayle Krietlow was her willingness to call a spade a spade. He would never say that to her. He supposed it was partly out of deference to her position, but he, also felt a need to be somewhat cautious with her. It was one thing for her to banter with him. For him to engage in similar behavior might be misconstrued as his being flirtatious.

He finished what he needed to do at school by noon. He called Mike. "I'm heading for the hospital. Do you want to come along?" She did. "I'll swing by to get you. See you in a few minutes." On the way out he told Elaine where he was going. She stopped him.

"Brian, do you know who Mrs. Pitts is?" Sensing that Elaine had something she wanted to share with him, he asked her to enlighten him. Even though no one was around Elaine lowered her voice. "The Pitts's are very wealthy. They have a son and a daughter who attend school here. The son graduated from middle school last spring. He'll be a freshman this fall. His name is Jared. He and my son have gone all the way through school together. Jared has never been a very good student, not even in grade school. His teachers have always thought he was smart enough, but he refuses to apply himself. I get the impression that his mother is very controlling. I don't know if Jared knows he's got it made and doesn't have to work for anything, or if he's rebelling against his mother. Maybe a bit of both." Elaine looked around before continuing. "I know several of the lower grade teachers personally. They have told me that the mother's attitude is 'there is no such thing as a bad student, only bad teachers'. She blames the school entirely for Jared's poor performance. She's threatened on numerous occasions to send him to a private school. To several people's chagrin, that hasn't happened." Elaine looked uncomfortable. "I just thought you ought to know."

"Thanks, Elaine," Brian smiled. "Maybe I'll go have a talk with Joan (the middle school principal). See you in the morning."

"I hope your dad is doing better," she said as he departed.

At home Brian asked where the boys were. "Dan is mowing grass for the Phillips. Shawn met some kids at the beach yesterday. The family is vacationing here this week. They invited Shawn to go parasailing with them this afternoon. I met the family. They seem like very nice people, so I let him go.

When they went to get in the truck, Cassidy seemed reluctant to join them. He stood on the porch barely wagging his tail. Brian went back to the porch and sat down next to him. "What's the matter, Cassidy? Don't you want to go with us? Cassidy flopped down, and looked up with an almost forlorn expression. Brian laid a hand on the dog's back. "I know, you're missing Pops. I would give anything to let you see him." Brian got up. Cassidy raised his head but didn't get to his feet. He wasn't going anywhere.

Mike was already in the truck when Brian got there. "Poor old guy, I think he's depressed as hell." Mike said she was too. Brian motioned for her to sit close to him. When she slid toward him he could see she was crying. He gave her the bandana that he, like his father, always had in his rear jeans pocket. He started the engine. They drove for several miles in silence. Mike broke it by thanking Brian. He asked her "for what?" "For not trying to bolster my spirits. I'm in no mood for a pep talk." Moments later she said. "Brian, I am so Goddamned mad. I hate this. I feel utterly helpless. Who would do this to Pops?" Brian told her about his earlier conversation with Sheriff Peterson. Mike's response was, "the cops are looking for a needle in a mountain of hay." He agreed that it looked that way to him, too. They arrived at the hospital. Brian asked if she preferred not to go in with him. "I'm coming," she said. "Pops may not be able to respond to anyone, but I sense that he knows when we're there. The sad thing is that the thing he needs the most is not permitted."

Brian knew that she was referring to Cassidy. "It would probably help both of them," he said. Mike took his arm.

Brian and Mike stayed with Andy for close to an hour.

Before leaving the head nurse, Audrey Reye, asked to speak to them. In her office she informed them, "Mr. McLeod is scheduled to undergo surgery on his hand at 5:30 tomorrow morning." Brian told her that Doctor Johns had already contacted him about it. She asked if Doctor Johns had also discussed with him the option of amputation and prosthesis. Brian told her that he had. She asked what the reasoning was for electing to go with reconstructive surgery instead.

Brian looked down. Mike could see that he was becoming increasingly annoyed. He began almost pawing the floor with his right foot. She decided to intervene. "I'm sorry, is it me? I'm sensing that somehow you're feeling left out. Are you upset about not being included in the decision-making process?"

Nurse Reye seemed caught off guard. "That's not the case at all. That is a matter that is between the physician and the patient or the patient's proxy."

"That's absolutely right," Mike said resolutely. "Then is it that you feel like your authority is being usurped, that you're being dictated to?" Reye insisted that she was aware of and in charge of everything that was going on in this unit. "Then what is it? You seem to be pissed off about something." It was clear she was not used to being confronted and she had a hurt expression. Mike softened her tone a few notches. "I'm sorry. I didn't mean to snap at you like that." She reached out and touched Reye's arm. "I really am sorry." Reye's lips began to quiver, she looked like she was at the brink of tears. "What is it?" Mike asked gently. "Something is bothering you. Please tell us." Two or three tears trickled down her cheeks eroding her makeup. Brian got his bandana out again. He handed it to her. The nurse shook her head rejecting it; then she accepted it. "Please," Mike coaxed.

"It's worse than just being left out. I feel purposely ignored. I feel disliked by almost everyone; the doctors, my staff, the janitorial staff, even visitors to the unit." She began to sob.

Mike stepped alongside of her and put an arm around the woman's large rounded shoulder. She waited for the nurse to gain some control of herself. "How come?" She asked softly.

"I don't know." The nurse blew her nose.

"I think you do," Mike said. "I think most of us know what's going on when we feel we're being ignored or rejected."

Mike hugged the lady to her. "You don't have to answer that question, at least not to me. You do need to answer it for yourself. Just think about it will you?"

Mike waited for Reye to make eye contact. When she did she whispered, "Thank you." She tried to hand Brian's bandana back to him. He told her to keep it.

In the parking lot Brian said. "That was outstanding, Mike. You handled that beautifully." Mike thanked him. "I really mean that. I doubt that anyone has ever treated her more lovingly. She was being cranky and bitchy. You opened up the lonely little girl inside of her. She really is a lonely little girl who needs to put on a false front. It's her armor."

"If so, it's only working to exacerbate her loneliness," Mike said.

"Exactly, maybe you helped her to see that." Brian chuckled lightly. "I'm willing to bet you just made a friend for life. It will be interesting to see what happens next. I'll be disappointed if she continues to cling to her crap."

On the drive home, Brian brought up the subject of Penelope Pitts. He started to describe the phone conversation he'd had with her. Mike interrupted him to tell him that she knew the woman. "Their daughter is in the same grade as Shawn. I think the daughter's name is Alice."

"That's good," Brian said. "I was afraid you were going to tell me her name was Cherry or Peaches. Something like that. Get it? Cherry Pitts? Peach Pitt's? "

Mike nudged him in the ribs. "I keep hoping that someday you'll develop a sense of humor." She went on, "Alice is a very quiet, almost painfully shy girl. She's not very pretty. Once you see the mother you'll know why. Alice, unlike her mother, is kind of frail. Mrs. Pitts is anything but. She's a large lady. Imposing might be a more apt description. I haven't met the father. I think he's some kind of financial guru. He travels a lot. If I were married to someone like her, I would too. He apparently makes extremely good money."

"I take it that you don't like Mrs. Pitts," Brian said.

Mike was frowning, "You're absolutely right. Unlike Audrey Reye, I have no desire to try to crack that lady's suit of armor. I think she's a very angry person who enjoys bullying. In my opinion she's like a Nazi. Unfortunately she's rich and has a lot of time on her hands. Put those ingredients together and you have the makings of a very mean-spirited, busy-body meddler. There are merchants who want to lock their doors and close the blinds when they see her coming. She's rude and demanding. Nothing seems to please her. She finds fault with everybody and everything. She can probably afford to buy the entire county, but she's miserly. She acts like she's royalty, and at the same time she tries to give the impression that they're poverty stricken."

They were close to home. "What do you say to taking Cassidy to the beach? Maybe chasing a ball will help lift his spirits." Mike was all for it.

Dan was home from mowing grass. He wanted to go along. "It was so hot today I worked up a real sweat mowing. I'm going to bring a bar of soap along and take a bath in the lake."

Because it was late August, the volume of tourists was dwindling. School would be starting for a lot of kids before Labor Day. There were fewer families than the week before. Dan and Cassidy made straight for the water. Brian and Mike brought towels. They walked east along the beach until they were past the few people that were there. Dan was throwing a tennis ball out far enough into the lake that Cassidy had to swim to get it. "You'd never know Cassidy was as old as he is to see him now," Brian commented. "He's like a puppy. Look at him." Brian was wearing cutoff jeans. Mike had on a two piece swim suit. The two of them waded out into the water. The water remained shallow for the first fifty yards. Even then they were only in water up to their stomachs. They began swimming out into deeper cooler water. It was a nice day with a light breeze out of the southeast. With the wind in that direction it held the sun warmed water close to the beach. On days when the wind was northerly the water temperature was sometimes barely tolerable.

After Brian and Mike finished swimming they decided to wade further east.

Brian said, "I wish we'd thought to bring some beer." Mike smiled. She had four beers for them and a can of root beer for Dan in a plastic bag. The bag was buried in the towels. "Perfect," Brian said as he opened a can for each of them. "See, you really are psychic."

They began wading. Mike seemed almost pensive. "I wouldn't go so far as to say I had an epiphany today, but I did come to an important realization. I've been absolutely miserable the past two days. I have never felt so depressed in my life." She took a couple of sips of beer. "I finally made a conscious decision to try to get a hold of it. Being depressed is a waste of time. It accomplishes nothing. Pops is going to need a lot of help to get back on his feet. He's going to need for us to be strong for him. The last thing he's going to need is for any of us to be feeling sorry for him. That's the voice of reason." Brian put his arm over Mike's shoulder. She took hold of his hand. "I don't know, I kind of feel like I got in touch with the little girl within me this afternoon. I realized that she's very scared. You're right, Pops and I do have a very special relationship. I sensed it the very first time we met years ago. Rather than scold my little girl I tried to listen to her. She needed that." Mike stopped and turned to face Brian. "You've done that for me lots of times over the years, Brian. You and Pops are good listeners." She touched his chest. "This time I did it for myself. I listened to my little girl. It was almost like she was saying, *at last, you've finally heard me.*"

Brian smiled. "So, now what?"

"What do you mean?"

"Are you going to let her stick around? Are you going to be friends with her?"

Mike smiled, "Do you have a little boy inside of you?" Brian nodded. "Are you friends with him?"

"Yeah, I think so. He'd like for me to loosen up and play more than I do. I'm working on it. He gets pissed with me because I'm not more adventurous. I'm sure he thinks I'm a hopeless case at times."

"I love you, Brian." They were interrupted by Cassidy and Dan who were splashing toward them along the edge of the beach.

"Cassidy looks like he's smiling," Brian said.

Mike agreed. "He needed to come to the beach and play." As soon as Cassidy was next to them he shook himself spraying them with water and sand. Dan asked if they could stay at the beach for a while longer. Mike said, "I'll take a quick run home to see if Shawn's there. I'll be back in a few minutes." She asked if either of them needed anything from home. Dan asked her to bring him a root beer. "I brought one for you. It's with the towels."

After Mike was gone, Dan said to his father. "Mom's really been down. She seems a lot happier today."

"I've noticed that, too." Brian said. "The water feels really good. Let's swim some more."

Cassidy waded out with them a little ways, but decided not to swim. He went back to where the towels were piled and plopped down in the warm sand.

Chapter 9

Brian and Mike got up before six o'clock the next morning. They left Cassidy behind with the boys and drove to the beach. They went for a three mile run together. There was no one around when they arrived back at the beach. They bathed in the lake and went swimming. The boys were still sleeping when they arrived back home. Brian said, "I think I'll go over to Pop's house to check on things. I'll be back in a while." He took Cassidy with him. When they arrived at his father's house, Brian let Cassidy out. For years the dog had gone through the same ritual every morning. When Andy let him out, he would make a beeline for the meadow to the north barking the whole way. Then he'd stop to see if he'd been able to scare up any deer. He'd given up on chasing after them a while back. Andy would say to the dog, 'Well, Cassidy, have you finally wised up and realized you're never going to catch them or are you just feeling arthritic'? Cassidy would make a brief 'territory-marking tour' then come in the house to have his breakfast. After he ate, he would lap water. Andy had measured it out several times. Cassidy had, on a number of occasions drank almost a quart of water. *Loading your pencil for another boundary marking? I'm glad to see I'm not the only one around here who's making a career out of peeing.* This morning Cassidy plopped himself down on the front deck while Brian went to check the mail box out at the road. Ninety percent of it was solicitations for charitable donations. It hadn't occurred to Brian until now that his father's medical expenses were probably already astronomical. There were two issues of the local paper in with the mail as well. That triggered another even more urgent realization. After going through the house to make sure it was undisturbed, Brian went to the kitchen and placed a call to Sheriff Peterson. The Sheriff had just arrived in his office.

"What's up, Brian?" Peterson asked.

"Sheriff, nothing has been in either of the last two papers

about my dad. Our guy has to be wondering what's going on." Brian could almost hear Sheriff Peterson slapping his own forehead.

"Jesus, you're right, Brian. How could I be so stupid? I need to call the paper right away. I'll simply say that we're investigating another reported disappearance of a sail boater. We won't make mention of anything else. We'll just say that he left on a sailing venture three days ago and nobody has heard anything from or about him since. We'll say that according to the family he was planning on heading north to visit the islands. Knowing the media, they'll send a reporter to interview you. It means you're going to have to tell your kids to either say nothing or play along with our fabrication. I made sure the hospital didn't register him under his real name." He paused and then said, "I don't know how I could have been so stupid. I'm really sorry, Brian. Glad you caught it. I sure hope it hasn't set off an alarm with the bad guy." The Sheriff asked if there was anything else.

Brian couldn't think of anything; then, on second thought he said, "what about the Coast Guard? They are certain to have a report on record about what occurred."

"You're right. I'll contact them right away. I'm hoping I don't have to go all the way to the Supreme Court to get them to suppress that information. I'll emphasize that it entails an ongoing investigation that could be compromised if their report gets out." He apologized again before hanging up.

Brian told himself that he needed to start jotting things down. *The devil's in the details*, he reminded himself.

He went to his father's bedroom. He opened the drawer of the night stand next to the bed. He lifted Andy's 1911 Colt .45 out. The clip was in it. He drew the receiver back far enough to see that a round was chambered. There was another loaded clip in the drawer. He took that also. In the closet he found a half full box of forty-five caliber ammunition. In the den he went to the gun cabinet his father had built years ago. It held a 30-06 bolt action deer rifle, a twenty-two lever-action rifle and a twelve gage shotgun. He took the shotgun. There was a sliding door compartment below where Andy kept ammunition for all three guns. There were two boxes of 12 gage shotgun shells. One of them was a heavy assault load; the other was a lighter game load. He chose the assault shells. He checked the shotgun. It was loaded with a chambered round also. Brian was sure that the restrictor plug had been removed. Normally a shotgun holds three rounds. With the plug removed it could hold five. He knew his father's attitude about any weapon that was intended to be used for personal protection. It needed to be loaded and ready to shoot. *The bad guy's not going to excuse you while you get the gun ready to shoot his ass off'.*

Ignoring the law that forbids carrying loaded, uncased weapons in a vehicle, Brian put both guns on the floor of his jeep behind the front seat. Cassidy jumped into the jeep as soon as Brian opened the door. On the way home he noticed that Cassidy didn't seem to be depressed today. He thought that it wasn't so much the trip to the beach that had pulled Cassidy out of his funk. It probably had more to do with Mike. Cassidy was tuned into her as much as to his father. Maybe he had been reacting to her depressed feelings.

At home he brought the guns in the house. Mike asked why he had them. "Two reasons. One, in the event somebody were to get into Pop's house, I don't want these to go missing. The second is, I think we need to be prepared to take care of ourselves just in case." Mike was concerned about having loaded guns in the house. "I'll put them somewhere safe. I'll hide the pistol in your dresser drawer under your underwear. The shotgun can go in the back of your closet. The boys might go into my closet or dresser. They're likely to be squeamish about getting into your girly stuff."

He told her about the phone conversation with the Sheriff. "God, Brian, it didn't occur to any of us to cover that base."

"This is the first time I have ever been grateful that our paper only comes out twice-a-week." Brian said. "It was three days ago that Pops was attacked. We can say that none of us were concerned that something might have happened to him. It's not unusual not to hear from him for a couple of days when he takes off on one of his cruises. Now, after three days with no word from him, we are."

Dan appeared in the kitchen. Brian asked, "Is Shawn up yet?" Dan didn't know. "Would you please go get him? I've got something very important to talk to both of you about." When both boys entered the kitchen Brian asked them both to be seated. Mike had just poured coffee for herself and Brian. She joined them at the kitchen table. Shawn looked like he was not fully awake yet. Mike reached over and brushed his hair back out of his eyes and got up to pour juice for the boys.

"Guys, what I'm about to tell you is one of the most difficult things I've ever had to ask of you."

Dan looked almost panic stricken. "Did something happen to Grand Pops?"

Shawn was fully awake now. "Something did happen to Grand pops. First, I'm going to tell you what happened. After that I'll tell you why I've waited until now to tell you." Brian related the events of three days ago. He told them where their grandfather was. He told them that Grand Pops would most likely be transferred to another hospital in the next few days. The boys hung on his every word. "What I'm about to ask of both of you contradicts what your mom and I have insisted on, and that is honesty, no matter what. This thing that has happened to Grand Pops presents us with a whole different situation. If we tell the truth, the terrible person who tried to kill Grand Pops will know that he's still alive. He will try to finish the job to protect himself. That makes it necessary for all of us to lie. We don't have to say that Grand Pops is dead. What we have to say is that he's missing. We will say that we didn't know he was missing until now. We started to worry about him when we didn't hear from him after two or three days. It is really important that we stick together in dealing with this. I expect newspaper reporters will come here to ask questions. All we know is that he left for a trip on his sailboat and we haven't heard from him since and we're worried."

"I'm more worried knowing where he is," Dan said.

"Me, too," Brian said. He fought back tears. He reached over to touch his son's hand.

"Will we ever be able to tell the truth about Grand Pops?" Shawn asked.

"I hope so, Shawn," Brian said. "When they catch the man who did this to Grand Pops and if the man is put in jail for a long time, then maybe we can."

"What if people accuse us of being liars?" Shawn asked.

"If they do, we'll admit that we did and explain why. If they can't understand that and won't forgive us, that's too bad.

We did what we had to do in order to protect someone we love. I can live with that." Both of the boys agreed.

Even before he left for school that morning, Brian received a call from a reporter with the local newspaper. He told her that he would not be available for an interview until late in the afternoon. Mike said that she'd keep close tabs on the boys. "I think the boys and I should go over things together so that we have our story straight. I worry more about Shawn. I'm pretty sure he understands why we have to pretend, but he's so naïve he may mess things up unwittingly."

On his way to school it occurred to Brian that he needed to talk to Elaine and Gayle. They were the only other people he'd said anything to about his father being found alive. Brian called Elaine into his office as soon as he arrived. He told her about what had really happened to his father and because of that it was crucial that no one find out he is alive. Elaine became visibly upset. He asked her what was wrong. "Oh, Brian, I'm so sorry. Me and my big mouth, I've probably told three or four other people that your dad had a sailing accident and is in the hospital. I'm so very sorry. I don't know what to do." Brian thought about it. Rumors, like an infectious diseases, could spread at alarmingly fast rates, especially in a small community like this.

"Okay," He tried to remain calm and as accepting as possible. "See if you can remember who you talked to about my dad. Let's see if we can spread a rumor that counters what you told those people. Maybe you can tell them that you misunderstood the story about my dad. Brian suggested using the same story that he had just discussed with his sons. He realized that Elaine was taking down what he was saying as if he were dictating a memo. In a way he was. He was composing a press release. "You can say that it is not like my dad to not stay in contact with his family. Also add that Mr. McLeod has many years of sailing experience and is considered to be an accomplished seaman. That's why his family remains hopeful that he will be found safe." Brian asked Elaine to make a few copies of that statement for him.

Elaine apologized two more times. Brian held up his hand. "Elaine, I'm the one at fault here. I wasn't thinking clearly. I've been slow in coming to grips with what actually happened to my dad. Otherwise, I wouldn't have said anything to anybody other than the Sheriff."

Elaine looked at him. "Brian, now that I know about what really happened, I'm wondering how you've been able to function at all. I'm going to do as much as possible to undo the damage."

Half an hour later Gayle Krietlow came into Brian's office. She had large cups of coffee for both of them. She had brought a third cup for Elaine. She plopped herself down in the chair across from Brian's desk. "Well, I spent one of the most exasperating half-hours of my life on the phone with Mrs. Penelope Pitts yesterday. I thought I had prepared myself. I talked to Joan Hammond before I called Hitler's daughter. I had barely gotten my name out when she lit into me. What followed was a non-stop rogue wave of vitriol. The word bigot doesn't begin to describe her hatefulness toward homosexuals, but it doesn't stop there. It extends to liberals, anti-American, commie, fagot, pro-choice, tree-hugging, anti-capitalist, anti-corporate, fornicating, non-Aryan degenerates who are contaminating the gene pool each time they procreate."

"Well, at least the last part of that could be an argument in favor of homosexuality," Brian said.

"You're assuming rationality." Gayle scowled.

"So, how did you leave it with her?"

"I don't know," Gayle was still exasperated. "I honestly don't know. I offered to convene a special session of the school board to allow her the opportunity to make her views known to the district's governing body. I don't know if she heard anything I said. She was still ranting and raving when I politely hung up on her." Gayle sipped some coffee. "I'm no shrink, but I think the woman is certifiably nuts. I ended up calling our attorney. He agrees with allowing her an opportunity to meet with the board, but not in a special session. He said that if she's willing to meet with the board, he would attend the meeting himself. He is going to draft a letter of invitation and send it to her with both of our signatures. He recommends that from now on we restrict our communication with her to correspondence so that there's a paper trail. Either that or public forums where there are witnesses and minutes taken. He said if she makes any threats to anyone of us, he will petition the court for a restraining order." She asked Brian what he thought.

"My dad would say that she appears to be de-compensating. If that's true; my biggest concern is for her kids." He told Gayle about what Elaine and Mike had to say about her.

"Let's make a special effort to monitor her kids when school starts," Gayle said. "If there appears to be reason for concern we are obligated by law to make a referral to Family Services." They finished their coffees. Gayle asked, "are there any changes in your dad's condition?"

Brian produced the statement that Elaine had transcribed for him. "Before you read this I need to explain a few things to you first. The statement will make a lot more sense to you if you know the real story."

As Brian's unveiled the real story Gayle expressed shock and disbelief. "Sweet Jesus, Brian, this is terrible. I thought it was bad enough that he was hurt seriously, but that someone tried to kill him is God awful. It means there's a maniac running loose out there." He asked her to read the statement. When she was done, she handed it back to him saying, "I haven't said a word to anybody about your dad." She thought for a moment. "Brian, you need to focus as much of your energies as you can on his situation. Leave Pitts-bull to me."

"That's good, Gayle. I like Pitts-bull even better than Hitler's daughter."

After Gayle left, Brian called Mike to let her know that he was on his way to pick her up. She told him that she had called Sue Nelson to see if the boys could go over there for a couple of hours. "I don't want the boys here without one of us present in the event any nosy reporter types show up." He asked Mike if she had said anything to Sue yet about keeping the truth about Pops a secret. "I called her right after you left this morning. She assures me that she hasn't said anything to anybody except her husband. She said she would call him at work to explain the situation to him.

When Mike got in the jeep, she had a grocery bag with her. Brian asked what was in it. "I'm bringing Audrey a few things from our garden, some tomatoes, cucumbers and zucchinis." Brian made a remark about a 'peace offering'. "It's more a gesture of friendship. My guess is, nobody does anything nice for her. She strikes me as being a very lonely woman." After a while Mike said, "I guess I am feeling badly about yesterday. I came down on her pretty hard in the beginning. Maybe it is a peace offering." Brian repeated what he had said yesterday about how well he felt the encounter had ended. "Okay, let's call this positive reinforcement."

Brian told Mike about Gayle Krietlow's encounter with Mrs. Penelope 'Pitts-bull'. Mike laughed. "Gayle and Pops would get along well with one another. He has a great appreciation for rapier sarcasm. 'Pitts-Bull', that's good."

It was almost noon when they arrived at the hospital. When they came into the intensive care unit they were greeted by Audrey Reye. All but one other nurse was on lunch break. Brian was struck by how much softer she looked today. She was wearing noticeably less makeup. She told them that she thought Andy was still in surgery. She would let them know just as soon as she heard anything about him. She almost started to cry when Mike handed her the bag of vegetables. Mike told her they were picked from their garden this morning. She smiled somewhat timidly. "I don't care for store-bought tomatoes, but I love fresh ones. How nice of you." Brian excused himself to find the lavatory leaving the two women to talk. He was in the process of washing his hands when he heard a rather shrill beeping sound that was followed by an urgent intercom message repeating, "code blue, code blue, code blue."

When he exited the washroom, there were three people rushing toward one of the rooms. He quickly rejoined Mike asking what was happening. "I don't know for sure," Mike told him. "I think the patient in that room," she pointed, "just went into cardiac arrest. Audrey ran in there immediately."

Moments later they heard a female voice say, "Clear." After several seconds another voice said that there was still no pulse. The same voice they'd heard before repeated, "Again, Clear." After a few seconds delay someone reported that they had a pulse. Another voice said that there was respiration. A man who looked like a physician came through the entrance door to the unit. He was almost running and immediately went to the room where the other staff were.

Two nurses came out of the room a few minutes later. Mike asked them, "Is the patient going to be okay?"

"Yeah, he's going to make it. Reye got to him in time and

made all the right calls," one of the staff said with a slight tone of sarcasm. He licked a forefinger and made a gesture like he was marking something. "Chalk one up for Reye." Brian thought, *Audrey just saved someone's life and she's grudgingly being given credit for it. They really don't like her.*

When Audrey herself came out of the room, her face was wet with perspiration. Brian stepped toward her offering his bandana. "Thanks, I'll just grab a towel. I'll be back in a minute." She went into a room a short way down the hall. She came back out wiping her face and neck with a towel. "That was a close one." She said as she gestured for them to follow her to her office. She went behind her desk and invited them to be seated. "I feel so badly for that man. His wife died three days ago and he can't attend her funeral. I have a feeling that he just wants to follow her." This was a whole different side of Audrey Reye, Brian thought. "I'm going to call down to surgery and see if they're done with your father yet." She was still standing. She was on the phone very briefly. "Your father was just moved into recovery. They usually keep patients there for an hour to monitor them. If you've got some errands to run, why don't you? I don't know of anyone who enjoys hanging out in a hospital." She looked at her watch. "He should be back here and settled by one-thirty."

"Maybe we'll do that," Mike said. "Can we get you anything while we're out?" Audrey said she couldn't think of anything. She thanked them and they left.

Out in the parking lot Brian asked, "where to?"

"I read about a property that the Land Trust acquired fairly recently. It's not far from here. It's open to the public and it has some hiking trails. Let's go have a look."

They found the entrance to the preserve. The property was adjacent to the ship canal. At one time it was part of the isthmus that connected the Door Peninsula to the rest of Wisconsin. As Brian recalled the canal had been dug in the 1870's to make it easier for large ships to navigate between the Bay of Green Bay and Lake Michigan. Before the canal, ships had to sail north the length of the peninsula to go from one side to the other. The canal cut as much as two days off a ship's journey.

Brian and Mike hiked around the property for an hour. Brian talked about a sailing trip he and his brother Corey had taken with their father when they were in their early teens. "Pops decided that this might be the last chance we'd have to take a trip like this together. He was right. I started working full time the next summer. Pops hadn't moved up here yet. He had a sailboat that could be trailered. It was a twenty-two footer. It was a good boat but small for three people. We brought the boat here to Sturgeon Bay. After launching it we sailed through the canal and on across the Lake to Michigan's Manitou Islands. I remember leaving at the crack of dawn. It took us the entire day to make the crossing. It was mid-July." Brian laughed. "It was close to seven that evening when we spotted land. Both Corey and I thought we should steer towards it. Pops had charted a course and he insisted that we stay with the compass reading that he'd plotted. Keep in mind we'd been out of sight of land on either side for more than eight hours. As it turned out, Pops was right. An hour later we began to make out the Islands. It was after dark when we dropped anchor. I remember watching the moon rise over the lake. It was beautiful. The next day the wind picked up out of the north and blew like hell for three days. The boat had a swing keel, which means the keel could be raised up. With it raised we could anchor in two feet of water so we could easily wade ashore. We spent three days hiking all over South Manitou Island. It's a neat place, but I've never seen so many snakes in my life."

"Pops decided to leave on the fourth day and sail back across the lake. The original plan had been to sail north from the Manitou Islands to Beaver Island and cross back to Door County from there. He was afraid that we might end up getting stuck somewhere with bad weather. He only had another week of vacation time left. So we came back to Sturgeon Bay. We spent the rest of the time sailing around in Green Bay. It was a real adventure."

Mike took Brian's hand, "I love my dad," she said. "He's a very nice man, but he hasn't got an adventurous bone in his body. He is cautious to a fault. You've been lucky to have a father who isn't afraid to take some risks. It's one of the things I admire the most about him. It has helped to make you who you are. In your own way, you're adventurous, too."

"Not like Pops. I play it pretty safe," Brian said. "I feel like our boys are missing out on experiencing some of the real adventures that he exposed Corey and me to. I like Pop's definition of an adventure. 'It's not an adventure if there are not any risks'. In other words, it involves putting your butt on the line, and then figuring out how to save it."

"Well, Pops is experiencing the ultimate adventure," Mike said.

When they arrived back at the hospital Andy was back in the ICU. At Audrey Reyes' request, Dr. Martin, the hand surgeon, was there to explain what had been done. He was a tall, completely bald man with intense blue eyes. He was aware of what had happened to Andy. He explained the bullet had entered the palm of Andy's hand breaking, but not shattering two of the metacarpal bones. He pointed to the bones he was referring to in his own hand. That was the good news. The bad news was that it had severed nerves and muscles. The surgery he performed today was aimed at trying to reattach some of the nerves, and as many of the muscles and tendons as possible. "Because of his occupation, your father developed stronger, more defined hand muscles than most people have. In some ways that made it easier to locate, identify and rejoin them. Many of them were too damaged to be repaired. Your father will regain limited use of his hand. He might be able to achieve as much as thirty percent of his hand strength. I would be amazed at anything more than that. What I don't know at this point is whether he will be able to open and close his grip. He may have to resort to using his right hand to help his left hand perform that function." He demonstrated what he meant by that.

After the meeting with Dr. Martin, Brian and Mike went in to see Andy. He was still in an induced comma. It seemed like some of the swelling in his left eye had gone down. It was upsetting to both of them to see him this way. Audrey came into the room. She reported that Andy was showing signs of improvement. She cited two or three examples including the reduced swelling of the left eye and his being able breath more freely, meaning the pneumonia was beginning to subside.

Chapter 10

The next day Brian and Mike found themselves in the center of a media blitz. Television crews from all three of the Green Bay stations along with what seemed like a battalion of reporters descended on them. Mike called upon Sue Nelson to once again take the boys. Reporters followed both Mike and Brian everywhere. They ended up resorting to diversionary tactics in order to escape scrutiny long enough to visit Andy. They received help from friends and colleagues. Gayle Krietlow and Audrey Reye seemed to relish the opportunity to 'fool the vultures', Gayle's term for the media. Gayle had Brian dress as a maintenance man. She commandeered a toolbox and a district owned pickup truck. He would drive the pickup truck to the school bus maintenance garage. Using Gayle's car he would drive to Sturgeon Bay. When he returned a couple of hours later he would simply reverse the procedure. Audrey did something similar at her end for Mike. She supplied Mike with a casual uniform worn by most of the nursing staff at the hospital. Mike would drive to the Wal-Mart store in Sturgeon Bay. She would don the uniform, a blond wig, and sun-glasses in the washroom, then exit the store and be picked up by another hospital employee who would take her to the hospital.

By day five the doctors decided that Andy was ready to be transferred via ambulance to the hospital in Milwaukee. Doctor Johns met with Brian as Andy was being made ready for the trip. He gave Brian directions to the Milwaukee hospital and the names of two of the doctors that would be caring for Andy there. He told Brian that they wouldn't know for a while how successful the hand surgery had been. Andy was going to require additional surgeries on both his hand and face.

Brian and Audrey accompanied Andy as he was wheeled to the waiting ambulance. He was conscious but unable to talk because of a tube in his throat. Dr. Johns doubted that he could talk even without the tube. It would probably be extremely painful for him. His left eye was still swollen. He could only open it slightly. He was still on heavy pain medications and in and out of sleep. Brian was able to speak to him briefly. "Pops, it's me, Brian." Andy tried to utter something. The effort made him cough which set off a paroxysm of pain in his head. Brian took his father's good hand. He was struck by the strength of the man's grip. Andy didn't want to let go. "They're taking you to a different hospital, Pops. It's in Milwaukee. I will be there to see you tomorrow. I love you." As soon as the ambulance started on its way, tears started running down Brian's cheeks.

Audrey handed him a bandana. Brian found himself half blubbering and half laughing. They hugged one another. She told Brian, "your dad has come a long way in just these few days, Brian. He's got a long way to go, but he's going to make it. I'm certain."

Brian thanked her. "I know this is going to sound kind of schmaltzy, but I need to say it anyway. Every once in a while we meet up with someone special, someone we seem to click with. Mike and I feel that way about you, Audrey" He smiled at her. "We both regard you as a friend. We'll stay in touch."

He tried to offer her the bandana back. "Keep it," she insisted. "I still have the one you gave me. It's my talisman." She left to return to her unit.

The next morning Brian was up at 4:00 A.M. He went back over the things he intended to cover in his meeting with the faculty later that morning. He added a couple of reminder notes. At a quarter after five, he left the house to go for a three mile run at the beach. Cassidy followed him out to his jeep. "You want to go along for the ride?" Brian asked. Cassidy jumped up onto the passenger seat. "I know what you really want." Brian said as he started the engine. "You want to go for a swim?" Cassidy glanced over at him. "You're smiling, you good old dog. I just know it. You can't fool me." Brian mused as he drove, *I'll bet Pops talks to Cassidy like this all the time*. The image of his father being loaded into the ambulance the day before came back to him. It was followed by the image of Audrey handing him the bandana, and then of her refusal to take it back. He told himself that there were a few good things that had come out of all this. He was so lost in thought that he almost missed the turn that he needed to go to the beach.

When he arrived at the beach parking area he told Cassidy he'd be back in a while. Cassidy promptly curled up on the seat. He'd most likely sleep the entire time Brian was gone.

Brian started his run noting the stillness of the early morning. There were no traffic sounds, or people, just a few birds-cardinals, chickadees, mourning doves. In the distance he heard a Pileated woodpecker making its jungle-bird laughing sound. He got into his stride soon into the run. He felt good. He thought about the day's agenda. If all went well, his plan was to be able to adjourn the faculty meeting by eleven and leave for Milwaukee. He hoped to arrive at the hospital by mid-afternoon. He'd spend time with his father and then meet with one of the physicians who would be caring for Andy. He'd visit with his father until evening rush hour was about over, hoping to get home by 10:00.

When he completed the run, Brian stripped down to just his shorts. He got Cassidy out of the jeep and they went to the water's edge. The lake was flat calm and the water was cold. Brian had brought a bar of soup with him. He was standing about knee deep trying to gather the courage to move forward and make the plunge when he spotted something out of the corner of his eye. It was large and in shallow water further east along the beach. He studied it debating whether to go see what it was. Cassidy didn't seem to see it, but began sniffing the air. The dog began wading cautiously in the direction of the object. Brian followed him. As the two of them drew closer, Brian thought it looked like a partially deflated beach ball. Cassidy stopped and growled, sniffing some more then growling again. "Cassidy, what is it?" The hair was up on Cassidy's back as he stared directly at the object. Brian moved very slowly closing the distance until he was about ten feet from it. He caught the smell of decomposition and suddenly realized that it was a corpse. Rather than approach it, he carefully moved toward the edge of the sand. The corpse was lying face down with just the head and shoulders protruding from the water.

"Come on, Cassidy," Brian called to the dog as he sprinted toward his jeep. "Goddamnit to hell." Because he was running in soft sand he began panting. "I-don't-have-my-cell-phone-with-me." *What to do*? He thought. He was closer to the town marina than home. He knew that the harbor master opened the marina office early to accommodate fishermen. Cassidy, sensing Brian's urgency, leapt into the jeep as soon as the door was open. Brian started the engine, jammed it in gear and sped out of the parking lot. The harbor master had just arrived and was unlocking the door to the marina office when Brian screeched to a halt in front of the entrance. "Jim, I need to use your phone. It's an emergency." Jim quickly led the way into the office and showed Brian where the phone was. The 911 dispatcher answered on the second ring. "This is Brian McLeod. I just found a dead body at the county park beach." Brian told the dispatcher the beach's location. She asked him a few questions. "The body is in the water. I have no idea who it is. No, I have no idea how long it's been there." The dispatcher told him that her caller ID showed that he was calling from the marina."

"That's right," he told her. "This was the closest phone I could get to." Moments later she told him that a deputy was on his way. "I'm less than five minutes away from the beach," Brian told her. " I'll meet him there." He hung up.

Jim stood aghast at what he'd just heard. "Who is it?" he asked.

"I have no idea," Brian said as he bolted out the door. He drove less hastily back to the beach parking lot. The Town Constable came roaring into the parking area as Brian was getting out of the jeep. They greeted one another. The constable was a wiry man with a receding hairline, and a deceivingly boyish face. He had a handheld radio in his left hand. He had a semi-automatic pistol in a holster clipped to his belt. He spoke into the radio apparently communicating with the deputy who was en route. He told the deputy that he was at the beach along with the person who had reported the body. The deputy gave his location estimating that he was about ten minutes away.

"We're going to approach the body location." Brian chose to leave Cassidy in the jeep. He and the constable trudged across the loose, soft sand to the water's edge where the wet, impacted sand made for easier walking. Brian pointed to where the body bobbed gently in the dissipating wake of a fishing boat. It was some fifty or sixty feet from where they stood. They moved closer until the smell became too much for them.

A few minutes later the deputy arrived. He was a short stout man with a thick neck and very close cropped hair. The constable and he greeted one another. The constable introduced Brian telling the deputy that Brian was "the citizen who discovered and reported the body." Brian was beginning to think he and Cassidy had made a mistake. Maybe they should have just gone home.

Brian asked, "do you guys need me here for anything? If not I'm going home."

The deputy said, "Hold on. Can I ask why you're dressed that way?" Brian hadn't considered until this moment that all he had on was a pair of running shorts. He explained that he had gone for a run and was about to take a swim when he noticed something in the water. "When I discovered what it was, I immediately drove to marina, and called 911. That's it. That's all I know." The deputy and Brian stood looking at one another.

Brian was about to turn and leave when the deputy asked, "What's your name again?" Brian told him. The deputy asked, "you wouldn't by any chance be related to that sailor guy who's gone missing?" Brian told him that the missing 'sailor guy' was his father. The deputy pressed on. "Any chance this could be your father?"

Brian took a step toward the deputy and squinted. "There's no chance in hell."

The deputy seemed unconvinced. He asked, "how do you know that? You haven't seen the man's face, or have you?"

Brian decided he'd had enough. He turned and stalked away. The deputy started to say something. The constable stopped him.

Brian was still upset when he pulled into his drive way. Cassidy got out of the jeep and almost slinked toward the house. Mike was not up yet when they entered the house. Brian scooped some dry dog food into Cassidy's bowl. The dog was almost cowering several feet from him. He quickly realized that Cassidy was frightened by his obvious anger. Brian sat down on the floor leaning back against a cupboard. He spoke softly, "I'm sorry, Cassidy. I'm not angry with you." He held out his hand and tried coaxing the dog to come to him. Cassidy looked away, but finally got up and cautiously came to him. Brian put his face next to Cassidy's. He massaged the dog's neck and shoulders. It took a while for Cassidy to begin to relax.

"Brian, are you okay?" It was Mike. Her voice was concerned but soft. She was in a sheer summer night gown. He motioned for her to come sit next to him. She did. She asked, "what is it?" In the meantime Cassidy took a few bites of his food. He didn't seem particularly interested in eating. He lay down and curled up next to Mike. The three of them sat there in silence for a while. Mike finally got up and went over to the counter to make coffee. Brian got up and stood next to her. He told her about discovering the body at the beach. "Oh, Brian," she turned to him and held him.

He told her it was a man's body. "It was bloated and the smell was strong. It's obviously been in the water for several days." He told her about losing patience with the deputy who arrived at the scene. "I was still mad when I got to the jeep. Poor Cassidy must have thought I was mad at him. That's why he's acting so spooked."

Mike went over and knelt next to the dog. She spoke to him gently as she petted him. "Cassidy, Brian loves you. He misses Pops just as much as you do. He has to deal with a lot of stuff right now. Sometimes it just gets to be too much." She nuzzled him. "Hang in there, baby." Cassidy breathed in deeply and sighed.

Mike stood up and put her arms around her husband. "Thanks, love, I needed that," Brian said.

"That's not all you need, sailor." She took his hand and said, "Come on," as she led the way up the stairs to the bedroom.

Brian arrived at school twenty minutes before the faculty meeting. Gayle and he were in the faculty lounge. They had just poured some coffee when Elaine poked her head in the door. There's an important call for you, Brian. Brian went to his office to take it. "Brian, this is Sheriff Peterson. Are you free to talk?" Brian said that he was, but only briefly. "I'll get right to it. That body you found this morning. We're not positive, but we think it's a man who went missing a little over a week ago. He and another guy went out fishing together in the evening and never came back. They were up here with their wives vacationing. The other guy was an art teacher at a small college near Milwaukee. Both couples have been coming here together for years."

"So the other guy's body is still out there somewhere?"

"I'd bet on it," Sheriff Peterson said. He went on, "The guy you found was shot in the chest, right through the heart. The bullet probably killed him instantly. The clothes he had on match the description given to us by his wife. Also, he had a watch on that was given to him as a retirement present in June." There was a momentary hesitation. "I'm sorry you had to be the one to find the guy, Brian. I've been a cop for almost thirty years. I still find it hard to sleep for two or three nights after I see a murder victim. I've lost a lot of sleep over the years."

"Thanks, Sheriff. I appreciate that. In light of everything that's going on, I'm feeling kind of…," He couldn't come up with a word.

"Fragile," the Sheriff said using the word Brian most wanted to avoid.

"Yeah, I guess so. As unmanly as it sounds."

"Brian," Peterson cleared his throat, "feeling fragile, feeling vulnerable, those are not a sign of weakness. You're a sensitive man. That's a gift, as painful as it sometimes is, you give a damn. It's what allows you to reach out to others in a caring way. My profession has an over-abundance of macho-types. It's the ones who are sensitive, and able to empathize, that make the best cops. Unfortunately they bleed emotionally about the inhumanity they encounter. For many of them it gets to be too much." He stopped. Then in a soft voice he said, "you take care, Brian."

The faculty meeting went smoothly. Two or three teachers raised some concerns that Brian or Supt. Krietlow addressed. Close to the end of the meeting one of the teachers raised her hand. She was a young energetic third year teacher. "Mr. McLeod, where do things stand with your father? Is he still missing?"

Brian looked at Gayle before answering her question, "yes, he is." No one said anything. Brian went on. "I'm sure most of you have heard about my father's disappearance by now. We're into the second week and we've run out of possible answers as to his whereabouts. There's part of me that is refusing to accept that the worst has happened to him." He looked down as he weighed what he was about to say next. He looked up and scanned the somber faces before him. "I don't know that I should be sharing what I am about to say, I've decided to risk telling you. I'd like to ask that it stay among us." Gayle was about to interrupt and challenge him. She was sure he was about to spill the beans about his father. He looked at her. "It's not what you think, Gayle." He turned back to the faculty members. "I went for a run early this morning. I finished at the county beach park. I was about to go for a swim when I saw something in the water further up the beach. I went to see what it was." He paused. "It turned out to be a corpse." He added quickly. "It wasn't my father." There was a mixture of gasps and sighs of relief. "I reported it to the Sheriff's department immediately. It will probably be on all the news stations tonight, and in tomorrow's paper. My discovery this morning may be part of a bigger story. I spoke with Sheriff Peterson just before we started this meeting. The man that I found and his fishing partner went missing a couple of weeks ago. It was before my dad went missing. The Sheriff told me that this man was shot in the chest. It turns out that there have been similar kinds of disappearances over the summer."

One of the male teachers spoke up, "what are you saying, Brian? Is there a serial killer running around out there?" Brian told him that was what the authorities suspected.

Another teacher asked, "do you think this may be what has happened to your dad? Do you think your father has been shot"

Brian nodded. "My Dad is an accomplished sailor. He's had many years of experience. He introduced my younger brother and me to sailing years ago. In the past few years he's taken to sailing solo most of the time. Being out there by oneself has inherent risks. I won't deny that I worry when he takes off on one his extended cruises. While I have always had the utmost confidence in his abilities, I have also known that something could happen. To answer your question, yes. In light of what else is happening, it is possible that someone killed him." There were no other questions. Brian reiterated his appeal for confidentiality by emphasizing that an ongoing investigation was underway. "We don't want to compromise it."

After the meeting was over Gayle followed Brian into his office and closed the door. "Are you sure you did the right thing by telling all those people about what's going on?

"No, I'm not at all sure." Then he said, "Gayle, I have a lot of faith in my staff. I'm going through a lot right now. I think they have the right to know. I'm not looking for anyone's sympathy, just their understanding." He laid his legal pad and his pen on his desk. "The fact is, I'm considering either asking for a leave of absence or resigning. I've always tried to give one-hundred percent to whatever I'm involved in. I don't think I can manage to deliver that to this job under the present circumstances."

Gayle pursed her lips before speaking. "I don't think you can either, Brian. I don't think you should expect that of yourself." She began to walk back and forth. "I don't see any way that we can manage to grant you a leave of absence. We don't have anyone who can step in and fill your shoes, nor do we have the money in our budget to hire an interim principal. I don't want you to resign. I need to give this some thought." She paced some more. "I'm inclined toward trying to find some way of delegating some of your responsibilities. Hell, there are some things I can do to help out myself." She stopped pacing. "I know that you need to get on the road. Let's get together sometime tomorrow to discuss this." He agreed. Gayle accompanied him to his jeep. "See you tomorrow. You drive safely."

Brian stopped at a rest area south of Green Bay on 43 to make a pit stop. Before getting back on the road he called Mike. They talked briefly. He told her about his earlier conversation with Sheriff Peterson. "God, Brian, how many more are there? This guy's got to be stopped. I'm still worried for Pop's safety. He's the only one who has survived." Brian said that he thought maybe he should call Sheriff Peterson to ask if he had alerted the authorities in Milwaukee. Mike told him that she'd do it.

It was mid-afternoon when Brian entered his father's hospital room. Andy was asleep but he awakened shortly after Brian arrived. He was in an elevated almost upright sitting position in the bed. He tried to speak but began to cough which caused him to hack up some phlegm. Brian handed him some tissues from a box that was on the bed table. When he was finally able to speak, it was in a barely audible whisper. "Brian?"

"It's me, Pops." Brian was heartened that his father knew him.

"Where am I?"

"You're in a hospital in Milwaukee."

"Oh, that's nice," Andy looked like he was drifting off into sleep. Then his right eye reopened. "What day is it?"

Brian told him. "Pops, you were shot two weeks ago. You've been unconscious for almost that entire time."

"My Goddamn head hurts, Brian." He raised his left hand. "My hand hurts too. What the hell happened to me?"

"Somebody shot you, Pops. Do you remember anything about what happened?"

Andy coughed two or three times, which caused him to expectorate more phlegm. A young nurse named Georgia came into the room just as it was happening. She took a pillow and put it to Andy's chest. "Can you lean forward a little bit Mr. McLeod?" She assisted him in sitting forward. She patted his back rather firmly. Andy coughed up more phlegm. "That's great, we need to get as much of the nasty stuff out of you as we can." She turned to Brian. "The pillow helps to ease the chest pain when he coughs. It's good that he's finally able to."

She checked his IV drip, took his temperature, pulse and blood pressure, and entered the information into a computer. She asked if he wanted more water. He nodded. Brian said, "our last name is pronounced McCloud, like a cloud in the sky." The nurse repeated it correctly and thanked Brian for correcting her. She asked Andy if she could get anything else for him.

"A martini with two olives."

"I wish I could," she said smiling at him. "Right now, a martini would probably take the top of your head off."

"It's already off," Andy whispered.

The nurse looked at the top of his head. "By golly, you're right. I'll go see if I can find a cork to put in it." As she started for the door she said, "see you in a while. Don't go anywhere while I'm gone. I just hate having to run around trying to find my patients."

Brian raised his finger, "There is one thing. Pops is in a lot of pain. His head and his hand are hurting him a lot."

With a concerned frown she returned to the computer. She punched some keys. "Hmm, let me go talk to my supervisor. We may need to call the doctor to see what he says. Doctor Anderson saw your father this morning. He said that he'd be back later this afternoon. He wants to have a chance to talk with you." Brian could see that his father was experiencing increased pain. Georgia left and was back in ten minutes. She said that the doctor approved of an increase in pain medication. He wants to begin weaning your father off of it, but the trip down here was probably pretty hard on him. As she was injecting the medication into a port on the IV tube, she said, "he's going to get pretty drowsy in a few minutes." She was right. Andy was fast asleep in less than ten minutes.

Brian sat next to him for a while studying his father. Andy's tanned face contrasted with his white beard and longish hair. He had deeply creased frown lines in his forehead that seemed to contradict the lengthy smile lines in his cheeks. There was still some puffiness in his nose. The left eye was still somewhat swollen. In this deeply relaxed state it didn't look quite so gruesome. The stitches were still in place where the bullet fragments had entered the eye socket. Brian wondered if his father would ever have the use of his left hand or eye again. Brian felt relieved knowing that his father recognized him. He was under no illusions that the road back to normality was going to be an easy one. There were many questions that awaited answers. Had his father suffered serious brain damage and, if so, how much?

Brian felt worn out. He sat down, took his shoes off, and rested his legs on a second chair. He fell asleep in moments. He was awakened by the nurse who nudged him gently and told him that someone was here to see him. Brian sat up and looked at his watch. He had been asleep for over an hour. Standing just inside the door was a very tall, muscular and very black man dressed in light blue hospital scrubs. He stepped forward, extending his hand. He introduced himself as Clayton McMurray. Brian stood and they shook hands. Brian guessed McMurray was six-foot-five, and probably 210 pounds, most of it muscle. "I've been assigned to provide your father's security." McMurray enunciated clearly. "I understand that your father was shot by a possible serial killer and that he may be the only victim to have survived." Brian confirmed that was true. "Might not be a bad idea to let it be known that your father is still alive. I'd just love to catch me a serial killer." McMurray could see that his suggestion hadn't gone over very well. He apologized. "We're here to see to it that nothing happens to your father, Brian. We've admitted him under the name of Raymond Edwards. The records will show that he suffered a serious stroke. The team assigned to your father will be dressed like me. We want to blend in. Your father will be moved to a different room each day." He handed Brian a plastic card explaining, "there are three wings to each floor. When you present this ID card at the main desk, you will be escorted to an office where a member of the hospital's security staff will direct you to one of the three wings on this the third floor. It will not be the wing that your father is on. You will be monitored by security cameras from the moment this card is presented at the main desk. If we detect any anomaly you will be intercepted and detained until we are satisfied that no threat exists. Then, and only then, will you be taken to your father's room." McMurray studied Brian. "This may seem like cloak and dagger to the extreme. I need not tell you how dangerous this man is. Neither is he stupid. He is calculating, clever and ruthless. To him this is a game. We have no intention of letting him win it, not here, and not on our watch."

Brian asked if McMurray was with the police department. "We're a private security firm. We work under contract with various agencies and organizations and sometimes individuals. Most of us are former special ops. There are three of us assigned to your father. We'll be working eight on, sixteen off. I'm here noon to eight. The eight to four team member is Bill Clinton, I shit you not. That's his real name. He's a wiry little guy who I would not care to have as an enemy. Chances are you won't have the opportunity to meet four o'clock guy. Ted holds black belts in three different forms of martial arts, fifth degree in two of them. He's as deadly with a knife as I am with a gun. We will all act as orderlies. We will never be more than 20 feet from your father's room. None of the unit staff people have been told anything about our reason for being here. If at any time we feel your father's identity has been compromised we have the authority to switch to plan B." Brian had the feeling that he was being sized up the entire time that McMurray was speaking. McMurray concluded by saying, "I think that about covers it. Do you have any questions?"

"Just one for now," Brian said. "Who's paying for this? This has to be costing somebody a lot of money."

"I can't answer that," McMurray replied.

"You can't because you don't know, or you're not supposed to tell me?"

"Don't worry about it, Brian. The cost of our services is taken care of for as long as the threat exists."

"That might take a long time," Brian said.

"Maybe, maybe not; the person who did this to your father is probably very bright, but he is flawed. His pathology trumps his intelligence."

Brian decided to press McMurray. "Is there a suspect?"

"Let me end this conversation by saying that there is a team of very qualified people who are investigating this string of murders. The three of us assigned to guard your father are only a part of the bigger picture. The only way the killer won't be caught is if he decides to take a vacation from killing. I doubt that he can or will do that. He thinks he's invincible and in complete control. What he doesn't realize is that, he's actually out of control and losing more of it by the day. He can't stop himself."

As if on cue, Dr. Anderson entered the room. He greeted McMurray by his first name, "Hi Clayton, good to see you." They shook hands. The doctor turned to Brian extending his hand. He was a tall, slender man, dressed in a polo shirt, and brown khaki trousers. Brian guessed that they were close to one another in age. "I'm Russ Anderson. Steve Kim and I will be working with your dad." Brian introduced himself. "It turns out I've met your father on several occasions. We've been in his shop a number of times. We've purchased several things from him over the years. It's one of our favorite shops in Door County. So, I have an added incentive to get him back on his feet." McMurray excused himself. Russ, as he preferred to be called, invited Brian to have a seat. "Let me start things off. I'm sure you have a bunch of questions. Steve Kim and I have a policy of being up front with patients and their family. You can depend on both of us to give you straight answers. The other thing I want to say is that we view the recovery process as a joint team effort. We will do our very best to get your dad as close as possible to the way he was before this happened. I'm sure that your biggest question at this point is how much progress can we expect? I think we can expect quite a bit. I sense that your dad is a fighter. By all accounts he shouldn't even be alive."

Anderson leaned back in the chair, making himself more comfortable. "I once had a lady patient who had a serious brain tumor. She was just a bit of a thing. She reminded me of a small bird. She was aware that surgery to remove the tumor had some serious risks. She knew that she might not survive the surgery and, if she did, she might end up impaired. She'd been caring for her elderly mother at home. She didn't want to put her mother in a nursing home. I remember her saying to me in her very slow deliberate speech, 'Russell, you are going to find that I am a person of great determination.' She not only survived the surgery, she was able to resume caring for her mother despite a partial paralysis of her right side. I learned a lot from that lady. She was indeed 'a person of great determination'. I sense that your dad is, too."

Doctor Anderson leaned forward. "There's coffee in the staff lounge. Let's go get a cup." He continued the conversation enroute. "We want to get your dad off the pain meds ASAP, but we need to do it gradually. He's still experiencing a lot of pain. The sooner he's drug free, the more all of us can focus on the rebuilding process. By that I mean recovery of cognitive skills. He had a helluva blow to his head. There was serious bruising and fluid pressure in the area of the frontal lobes. The fact that he has retained so much speech ability and is able make out visual objects bodes well for him. He has no memory of the actual incident or anything afterwards. That's common. What's really amazing is that he apparently was able to do an incredible job of problem solving after he regained consciousness. He literally saved his own life."

Brian smiled, "I don't know if he was as concerned about trying to save himself as he was his boat."

"Same thing, no boat, no more Andy." Doctor Anderson poured coffee for both of them. "I guess what I'm saying is that in some ways your dad is atypical. We're seeing most of the symptoms one would expect from this type of severe head injury. It's just they don't appear to be as serious as what we would normally expect to see. It maybe that he was able to somehow escape the full impact of the bullet. That's one possibility." No one else was in the lounge; Brian and Russ sat down at a table. "There are some rare instances where people have been fortunate enough to recover completely unscathed. Nobody has an explanation for that. The picture your dad presents is atypical causing Steve and me some skepticism. This is a state-of-the-art facility, Brian. With your permission we would like to put him through a series of tests. If the test results prove to be negative, then we can all rest a lot easier. We'd rather err on the side of being overly cautious, than miss something that could prove to be serious, or even fatal."

Brian looked down at his almost empty cup. "I understand what you're saying, Russ, and I want you to go ahead. I have his power of attorney. I do, however, have a concern. My dad is not a rich man. He has insurance, but I don't know how close he is to reaching the limits of coverage."

"I see where you're headed," Anderson said. "There are some ways of navigating the system. There are some research grants available that sometimes pick up a portion of the costs. If your dad is a veteran, we might be able to get some VA assistance. If you give us the go ahead, we've got a team of people on the hospital staff who are experts at this kind of stuff. We'll figure the financial part of it out. Please don't worry about it."

On the trip home that evening, Brian felt more relief than he had in over two weeks. Andy was asleep when he left the hospital. He asked McMurray to let his father know that he would be back to see him on Friday.

Chapter 11

When Brian arrived at school the next morning he was surprised to discover Gayle Krietlow in his office at his desk. She was just finishing a telephone conversation and was hanging up. She immediately got up. "I'm really not taking over your job." She picked up her pen and a note pad along with her coffee. "How'd things go with your dad yesterday?"

"Better than I had expected. Pops is in pretty rough shape, but he was actually able to speak, although in a whisper. He knew who I was. Those are both great signs. I met one of his specialists. I like the guy. He was cautiously optimistic and straight talker. It's an impressive facility. Pops has better protection than the President. I don't think he could be in a better place."

"That's got to be a big relief," Gayle said. "I need some more coffee." They went to the teacher's lounge. Brian poured coffee for the two of them and they returned to his office. Gayle closed the door. "I had a brief phone conversation with Darien Michaels this morning. That's who I was talking with when you came in." She was frowning. She sipped some coffee. "He wants to meet with you in person this morning, if at all possible. He sounded really upset about something. He didn't say what it's about, but of course the first thing I thought was that Penelope Pitts-bull has launched an attack on him." Gayle handed Brian a piece of paper. "Here's his phone number."

Brian looked at his watch. "I'll call him right now." He punched in the number. The phone was answered on the second ring. Brian didn't recognize the voice and asked if he could speak to Darien Michaels.

"This is Darien," The voice he heard lacked Darien's usual ebullient confidence. He was almost speaking in a whisper as if he were trying to avoid disturbing someone or not be overheard.

"Brian, I need to talk to you. This can't wait. Can I come

over to school right now?"

Brian asked him to hold on while he checked his schedule. He covered the mouth-piece. He told Gayle that Darien wanted to come over right away. She nodded. "Sure, Darien, how soon can you get here?" Darien told him he would be there in twenty minutes or less. Brian hung up. "You're right, he sounds terrible." Gayle asked if he wanted her to stick around. "I'll leave it up to Darien whether he wants you included or not. We've got some other things to discuss. Do you want to try to tackle that later?"

"I haven't come up with any brilliant solutions for lightening your load. Not yet," Gayle said. "I was an elementary school principal for six years before I decided to get my doctorate in school administration. I know something about the ins and outs of running a school. How would you feel about the two of us teaming up as co-captains?"

"How would that work?" Brian asked. "I mean, we kind of operate that way already."

"We do," Gayle agreed. The difference would be that I would actually step into your position when you needed to be elsewhere. I'd arrange to be here physically in your absence. I'll do everything I can to avoid giving the impression that I am usurping your position. I'm not worried about the faculty. I'm more concerned about parents and people out in the community getting the wrong impression. We need to come up with a credible explanation for why I'm assuming this role."

Brian tilted back in his chair. "Gayle, I remember something my dad said to me a long time ago. The problem with fibs is that you have to keep track of them." Brian smiled. "In other words, and this is a Pops quote, 'Bullshit takes a lot of energy'. Let's just tell whoever asks that I'm dealing with a family medical situation, and your standing in on my behalf."

There was tap on the door; Elaine stuck her head in to say that Darien was here to see Brian. Brian waved his acknowledgement. "I like your plan, Gayle. We'll talk more later." He went to the door and invited Darien to come in. As they shook hands Brian noticed a bruise on Darien's left cheek, and prominent red mark on his neck and wrist. It looked like he had been in a scuffle with someone. In his office Brian was quick to explain, "Superintendent Krietlow is here on other business,

Darien. I'll leave it up to you whether you want her to stay or not. She and I can get back together later."

"If it's all right, I'd prefer talking with you privately, Brian."

Brian could see from the way Gayle gave Darien the once over that his injuries had not gone unnoticed by her either. "No problem," Gayle said as she got up, and gathered her things. "Give me a call when you're free, Brian."

As soon as the office door closed Brian turned to Darien, "what happened to you?" He gestured for Darien to sit.

"That's why I'm here, Brian. Something has come up. I'm in trouble."

Brian sat down. "What kind of trouble? Do you mean with the law?"

Darien was silent for a seemingly long time. Brian chose to wait him out. "It's not the law," he said when he finally spoke. "It's personal."

"Can you tell me about it?" Brian gently urged.

"I came here to let you know that I'm resigning. I have to leave here."

"Darien, that's not why you came here. You're scared about something." Darien's was wringing his hands. He looked down avoiding eye contact with Brian. "Darien, come on, what is it?"

Darien glanced up. "It's my roommate." Darien looked up at the ceiling. "You might as well know." He paused again before blurting out, "I'm gay." He looked at Brian who showed no sign of shock or disgust. Brian was leaning forward with his hands folded on his desk. "My roommate and I work together. We both wait tables at a restaurant that caters primarily to gays. That's how we met. I started working there a couple of evenings a week last year. Alex, that's my roommate's name, was unhappy with his living situation, so I invited him to stay with me until he could find something else. He ended up staying on through the whole summer." Darien shook his head as if trying to erase a thought or a memory. "At first things went well. We got along together. He was considerate. He carried his weight with the rent, groceries, all that kind of stuff. We don't share many of the same interests, but that didn't seem to pose any problem." Darien tensed up visibly. "We had sex with one another occasionally," he confessed as though admitting to some kind of heinous act. After school was out I started working at the restaurant full time. It was then that I discovered Alex was involved not only with the restaurant's owner, but two or three other guys that work there. The next time he approached me about having sex with him I refused. I told him that I thought he was playing Russian roulette with both of us, and I was not willing to risk getting AIDS." Darien fell silent looking down again.

"How did he react to that?" Brian asked.

Darien brought his hands up to his lips as if in prayer. His voice was barely audible, "He told me to suit myself, like he didn't care one way or the other. I also told him that I would prefer that he find somewhere else to live. He didn't say anything. He just walked out." Darien's expression hardened. "Late that night he showed up with a couple of guys I'd never seen before. One of them was a big guy, a biker type. All three of them had been drinking. They were drunk. I had already gone to bed and was asleep. They woke me up when they came in. They were loud and acting rowdy. I asked them to quiet down. Alex told me to fuck myself. He hit me in the stomach knocking the wind out of me. The next thing I knew they had me down on the floor and all three of them took turns raping me. They didn't leave until dawn."

"Sweet Jesus," Brian gasped as he sat back. "Did you call the police?"

"Alex told me that if I told anyone, he'd kill me. Then he showed me a gun. It was one of those semi-automatic pistols like what you see on TV all the time. I didn't know he owned a gun. I'd never seen it before."

"What did you do? You didn't stay there, did you?"

"I did a couple of things. I called the restaurant and told them I wasn't coming in anymore. Then I went to the hardware store and bought new locks. I replaced the old ones that same morning. I also bought a baseball bat. I boxed up all of Alex's stuff and put the boxes in the parking space that he usually used. I covered them with a plastic drop cloth and put bungee cords around the plastic."

"Jesus, Darien, I would've pitched all of his stuff in a dumpster. I'd have gotten completely the hell out of there. Weren't you afraid that they'd come back and do the same thing to you all over again?"

Darien touched his neck. He looked at his fingers to see if there was anything on them. "I know what you're thinking, Brian. This guy is a classic victim. You're absolutely right. I'm right out of psychology 101. I've been a victim my entire life. When I was ten years old I was sexually molested by our parish priest. It continued until I was fourteen and would have gone on longer if he hadn't been transferred to another diocese. I knew even back then that I was a queer. At first I was scared. I felt dirty and sinful and disgusted with myself. I frequently thought about suicide. In time I grew to enjoy the priest's attention. He was nice to me except when he'd had too much to drink. Even when he was drunk, he never hurt me, not really. He'd be kind of rough, but he'd be all apologetic the next time I saw him. The human mind can rationalize anything."

"Darien, when did this happen?" Brian gestured to his head.

"It started three nights ago. I moved up here at the beginning of this month. I was living in Sturgeon Bay until then. Even though I hadn't heard or seen anything of Alex, I was afraid that it was just a matter of time. I saw an ad for a cottage up here. It's one of three small efficiency units. The owner rents them out to tourists on a weekly basis. He had a family situation that required him to be out of town for several weeks. He agreed to give me half off the rent if I would manage the other two for him for the remainder of the season. I have no idea how Alex found out about where I'm living. I haven't gone to Sturgeon Bay for anything since I moved. I've practically been a hermit afraid I'd run into him or someone from the restaurant." At this point Darien's expression was one of utter defeat. "Alex showed up out of nowhere three nights ago at about 10:00. He barged right into my cabin. He had the gun. He made me get on my knees. The next thing I knew he was holding a rag over my nose and mouth. I knew immediately that it was soaked in ether. I tried to get away. He's strong. He stuck the gun to my head. I passed out. When I came to, I discovered he had bound my wrists and ankles. He had cut my clothes off. He had raped me while I was unconscious. He raped me repeatedly over the next two-and-a-half days. He'd tied a thin rope around my neck. Several times he pulled it so tight that I lost consciousness. I think I've got some cracked ribs. He'd go into these rages. He kicked me and hit me when he was in one of them." Darien stopped.

"How did you get free from him? Brian asked.

"I didn't. He choked me with the rope until I lost consciousness. When I came to he was gone. I was afraid to do anything. I was afraid that if he walked back into the cabin and saw that I was untying myself he'd kill me. After a while I decided that it didn't make any difference. He was going to kill me anyhow. It was only a matter of when." Darien looked at Brian with the most defeated pitiful expression Brian had ever seen on anyone. "Alex is crazy, Brian. He's out of control. He's dangerous."

Brian thought about what Clayton McMurray had said to him just yesterday. 'This guy thinks he's in complete control. He doesn't realize that he's out of control, and losing more of it by the day. He can't stop himself'. "I agree absolutely, Darien. As a matter of fact the only thing that amazes me is that he hasn't already killed you." Brian bit his upper lip. "This is going to sound like a strange question, Darien." He waited for Darien to look at him. "Does this Alex guy have a boat?"

Darien's face turned ashen. "Oh my God, Brian, you don't think Alex is the one?" Darien looked like he was scanning every nook of his brain. "No, he doesn't own a boat, but he borrows the boss's boat from time to time. The boss is the owner of the restaurant I worked at. He has a place somewhere over on the northeast side of the peninsula. He keeps the boat there."

"What's Alex's last name?"

"Kane, it's Alex Kane, with a K," Darien told him. Brian wrote it down.

"What's the restaurant owner's name?"

"Melvin Stark." Brian wrote that down.

"Darien, this has to be reported to the police. We've got to get you somewhere safe. You need medical attention." Darien was silent. "Darien, I think this Alex guy may be the serial killer." Brian picked up his phone and placed a call directly to Sheriff Peterson. He was told that Sheriff Peterson was in an important meeting and couldn't be interrupted. This is urgent. Tell him it's Brian McLeod calling. I need to speak to him immediately. The lady at the other end started to advise Brian to hang up and call 911. Brian practically shouted at her, "DO IT, GET SHERIFF PETERSON NOW!" She said meekly that she'd try. Sheriff Peterson was on the phone in less than a minute.

"Yes, Brian, what is it?"

"Sheriff, I'm almost positive I've got the name of the killer." He gave the Sheriff the name. "It's possible that he's going after somebody at this very minute." Brian told the Sheriff about Kane having access to a boat that belonged to his employer, a Melvin Stark who has a place somewhere on the north east side of the peninsula.

"I'm on it, Brian. You can give me the details later."

After hanging up with the Sheriff, Brian turned to Darien. "I'm going to call an agency in Sturgeon Bay, Darien. Their primary mission is to help domestic abuse victims. They have a network of safe houses. I doubt that they get many referrals for men. We've got to get you somewhere safe. You can't go back to the place you're living in now."

Darien raised his hand, "It's okay, Brian. I'll be all right. I've got someplace to go. I loaded the stuff I'll need in my car earlier." Brian told Darien that he wasn't comfortable with letting him leave here by himself. "Really, Brian, I'll be fine. Alex won't do anything during broad daylight. That's not his style."

"He might not do anything now, but what if he's following you?"

"Don't worry, Brian. I'll be careful." Brian wanted him to at least go to the emergency room to have his injuries attended to and to establish a paper trail. "I can't do that Brian. Any good ER doctor is going to figure out right away that I've been the victim of a sadistic maniac. I feel a horrible sense of humiliation and shame about what has happened." Brian started to say something, Darien again raised his hand. "Please, Brian, I made up my mind even before I called you this morning. I'm tendering my resignation, effective immediately. I know it doesn't give you enough time to find a replacement. I feel it's in everybody's best interests, including my students."

It was clear that Darien was resolute. A part of Brian wanted to continue to try to talk Darien into reconsidering. He was genuinely concerned about Darien's welfare. Another part him felt that maybe Darien was right. He needed to flee, to get as far away from the situation as possible. Then there was Mrs. Penelope Pitts. She'd had at least some of her facts straight. She was in a position to cause a lot of problems. "Where will you go from here?" Brian asked.

Darien shrugged, "I haven't given it much thought," he said. "The smart thing would be for me to just get out of Dodge." He stood up. He had a faint smile that Brian felt was incongruent. "I've enjoyed being here, Brian. I like this community, the kids and the school. You've been a terrific boss. I'll miss all of it." He stepped forward to extend his hand. They shook.

"If you decide to continue on with your teaching career, Darien, I'll give you a good reference. You've been a real asset. I'd like to hear from you."

After Darien departed, Brian called Sheriff Peterson. He gave the Sheriff a thorough accounting of the things that Darien had told him. It included mention of the apartment in Sturgeon Bay, the alleged rapes, his move to the cabin up north, the boat that Alex supposedly had access to and the restaurant that Alex and he worked at. He alluded to the history of sexual abuse Darien claimed to have suffered. Finally Brian described the injuries he had observed and Darien's account of having been enslaved for nearly three days. At the end of their conversation Sheriff Peterson said, "just when I think I've seen it all, a whole new train comes around the bend. What a sick situation."

Brian called Gayle Krietlow's office. When she answered her phone she asked. "What's up?" Brian said that they needed to talk. "Your place or mine?"

"I'll be over in a few minutes," he said. Gayle's office was just across campus. Brian told Elaine where he'd be. He chose to walk the short distance, in part to allow himself an opportunity to collect his thoughts. Gayle was waiting for him. It was a little after noon and her secretary was out running some errands. Gayle cocked an eyebrow as Brian sat down in front of her desk.

Brian told her, "Darien just resigned,"

"He looks like he just went through ten rounds with an enraged pit bull. What the hell happened?" Gayle asked.

"I won't go into all the details, Gayle. You don't need to hear them.

Suffice it to say, he admits to being gay. He's been in a relationship with an extremely sadistic guy. Judging from a lot of the stuff he told me, this guy might be the serial killer; maybe the guy who shot my dad."

"Holy shit, Brian, how come Darien's still alive?"

"That's a very good question. I talked to Sheriff Peterson just a few minutes ago. I shared everything Darien told me with him. I'm sure the Sheriff intends to move heaven and earth to find this Alex guy."

"God, I hope they catch up with him before he kills anybody else." She leaned forward. "What about Darien? Is he in danger?"

Brian told her about his effort to try to get Darien someplace safe. "He refused any help. He even refused to get any medical attention on the basis of being too humiliated."

"What are your guts telling you, Brian?"

"I don't know. I like Darien. He's been an excellent teacher. I'm concerned about what might happen to him. As a matter of fact, I feel like I'm more concerned about his welfare than he is."

"The classic victim?"

"From the things he told me about himself this morning, I'd say, yes. He even describes himself that way. Something doesn't fit, Gayle. As I've observed him over time and he has always impressed me as being confident and self-assured. He's commanded the respect of his colleagues and students alike. The 'classic victim' isn't able to operate that way. They find all sorts of ways to sabotage and defeat themselves."

"Isn't that what has just happened?"

"I guess so."

"But?" Gayle asked.

Brian searched for what to say. "I feel like I'm looking at two different people. There's Darien the personable, bright, likeable competent, young man. Then, this morning I saw a whole different person. A self-despising, defeated, empty loser. Something's missing. I can't quite put my finger on it."

"What does he intend to do?" Gayle asked. " School has already started in most places. He'll have trouble finding a teaching job at this point. Did he give any indication about what's next."

"No, and I asked. He seemed almost nonchalant about it."

"Well, maybe he's in a state of shock or denial. Reality hasn't set in yet." She studied Brian for a few moments. "He's not your responsibility, Brian. In my opinion you handled a very difficult situation admirably." She leaned back in her chair. "I have to be honest with you. I'm sorry that any of this happened, but at the same time I'm actually kind of relieved. I almost want to get on the phone to Mrs. Penelope Pitts to inform her that tranquility once again reigns in paradise. The evil forces have vanished. Sanctity and purity prevail once again." She smiled mischievously. "Naah, I'm going to let her stew for a while."

"Well, Superintendent, we have a position to fill and we've got less than three days to do it in. I'm open to suggestions."

"It just so happens that I keep a file of letters that I've received from applicants over the past year. Let's see if there's anyone among them that appeals to us. If there is, I'll call them to see if they're still available and interested. If that fails, I'll call around to some of my Superintendent colleagues. Maybe they can help."

Among the letters that had accompanying résumés they found two recent women graduates that appealed to both of them. Gayle called both. One had found a fulltime teaching position. The other was signed up as a substitute teacher in a district in central Wisconsin. She was also working part time as a waitress. She sounded thrilled, and asked if it would be possible for her to come in tomorrow even though it was Saturday. Gayle asked Brian if he could be available. "I'm planning on going to Milwaukee tomorrow. If she can come in early, say 9:00 o'clock. I'll arrange to be here." The young woman said she would be there, and Gayle gave her directions. "Let's keep our fingers crossed that she's a winner. It's a very tight job market. My guess is that there are a hell-of-a-lot of well qualified recent grads out there that haven't been able to score with finding a job."

When Brian got home that afternoon Mike told him that Sheriff Peterson had just called. "He tried to get you at school, but you had just left. He wants you to call him right away."

Brian went directly to the phone anticipating positive

news. Sheriff Peterson came on the line. "Brian, we've practically turned this county upside down since you called me this morning. We talked to this Melvin Stark guy who owns that restaurant called the *Fleur d'Amour*. He claims this Alex Kane hasn't shown up for work for over two weeks. He just quit coming in. No phone call, no nothing. Stark's got a place on Europe Lake. He's got a small aluminum fishing boat he keeps there. He says he hasn't loaned it to anybody and, even if he did, he doesn't have a trailer for it. No way somebody could transport it to the big lake without one. One of my deputies has verified that part of the story. We found the apartment in Sturgeon Bay that Darien Michaels rented. That part checks out. Michaels has lived there for the past two years. He moved out at the beginning of August. He left the place in good condition. Landlord says he was a good tenant. He always paid his rent on time. No complaints about him. The cabins that Michaels has supposedly been managing are out on Kangaroo Lake. They're part of what used to be an estate. After the owner died quite a few years ago; some of the guest cabins were sold off and moved to other locations. Three of them are still standing on the property. One of them appears to have been occupied recently. The other two don't look like anybody has been in them in years. Whoever stayed in the one, has been camping in it. There are no furnishings, nada, nothing. There are signs of recent fires in the fireplace. There's a filled in latrine out back in the woods. Maybe we can get some DNA samples from that. It looks like the occupant used the lake to bathe in. We didn't find anything else. There were no signs of violence. We're checking to see if any boats have been reported missing. Nobody rents boats on the Michigan side of the peninsula. This Kane guy could have a boat of his own. If he does, he could either have a trailer for it or he's keeping it at somebody else's dock. No boat is registered to an Alex Kane. In short, we haven't been able to come up with diddly squat. Can you think of anything else?"

An idea popped into Brian's head. "Sheriff what about any pictures of Kane? Can you see if anyone has taken a recent picture of the guy? If so, there's a possibility that my dad might recognize him."

"I'll see what we can come up with, Brian. What little I

know about brain trauma victims is that most of them suffer short-term memory loss. We're talking complete amnesia about what happened to him. In some instances it goes away. What the hell, it's worth a try. Even if your dad isn't able to identify the guy, it will help us to know what Kane looks like. That's a good suggestion." Before hanging up Sheriff Peterson asked. "One more thing, Brian. Do you suppose that it would be possible for our detectives to have a look at Michael's personnel records? If you'd prefer I can get a subpoena." Brian told him he thought it would be okay, but he'd check with Supt. Krietlow just to be sure. He agreed to call her right away.

Mike had been watching Brian throughout his conversation with Sheriff Peterson. When he hung up she came over to him and placed a forefinger just above his nose. "That's an Andy frown if I've ever seen one. I take it that Sheriff Peterson had some more bad news."

Brian told her about the earlier events of the day including his meeting with Darien Michaels, his calls to Sheriff Peterson and now this most recent conversation with the Sheriff. When he was finished he put his forefinger on the same spot on Mike's head. "It's contagious. You're frowning too."

"Brian, why would Darien lie to you? I'm sorry, but very little of his story seems to jive with the facts."

"I know. Let's talk about it in a minute. I need to call Gayle and get back to Peterson with her answer."

Gayle agreed that the detectives could see Darien's personnel folder with a caveat. "If the detectives find anything that they think may end up being used in court, then they will need to get a subpoena. We can't have Michaels coming back at us later on with a law suit."

Brian called the Sheriff back and relayed Supt Krietlow's proviso. The Sheriff asked if the Detectives could come to the school within the hour. Brian checked the time. "I'll meet them at school at 4:00."

After hanging up Brian asked where the boys were. Mike told him, "they went fishing with the Nelson boys at Kangaroo Lake. A friend of the Nelsons has a pontoon boat. She gave the boys permission to use it." He asked when they would be back. "They're going to camp-over at the same friend's place tonight and go fishing again early tomorrow morning. School starts

Monday. It's their last hurrah."

"I need to go over to school to get Darien's personnel records for the Sheriff's detectives. How about we take Cassidy with us and go to the beach afterwards." Mike liked the idea. They both put their swim suits on. Brian slipped his jeans on over his. Mike put four beers in a small cooler. Cassidy sensed where they were going and came to life.

On the way to school, Brian and Mike discussed Darien's story. Mike wanted to know what Brian made of the apparent lies Darien had told him. "At this point I'm wondering if any of what he told me was true." He told her about his conversation with Sheriff Peterson. "He sat there this morning and lied to me up one wall and down another. It's incredible. He's always come across as an honorable person. I was ready to defend him at almost any cost against Mrs. Pitts. His admission about being gay may be just the tip of the iceberg." Mike asked Brian why he thought Darien had lied so blatantly. Rather than answering her, he asked why she thought he had done so.

"I've got a theory, but I want to hear what you think first," she said.

"I don't know, maybe to buy some time. I have to give him credit; he's a hell-of-an-actor. I'm sure he was convinced by the time he left my office that I had completely fallen for his story. He had to know that as soon as Peterson started looking into his story the truth would be revealed Maybe he was just creating a diversion and putting up a smoke screen so he can make a clean getaway."

"I don't know, Brian. If he's a raving psychopath, he believes everything he says."

"Point taken," Brian said. "So, I've been had by an expert." She nodded in agreement. "Why? What's his objective?"

"He painted a pretty damning picture of this Alex Kane guy," Mike said. "He's done his level best to focus everybody's attention onto Kane. What if Darien is the actual killer?"

"Good point, Mike. I'm still puzzled though by the fact that he lied so blatantly. In so doing he's drawn our full attention on him. If he's the killer, you'd think he'd do everything in his power to avoid that kind of attention."

"You're having to revise everything you thought about Darien, aren't you?"

"Exactly, I just can't picture him as being a cold blooded, heartless killer. What I can picture him doing is manipulating someone else to act for him. If he is a raving psychopath, then he has serious issues with people in position of authority. I'm his boss. Maybe that's why he may have gone after my father knowing that he was inflicting terrible pain on me. He may be messing with the cops for the same reason."

"I can buy the manipulation part of what you are saying, Brian. Maybe he's a control freak. Let's not get carried away with the authority issues stuff."

They arrived at school ten minutes earlier than the appointed time. The detectives, a man and a woman were waiting for them. Mike said she'd stay with Cassidy while Brian went with the detectives. The outside doors of the school were locked. Brian had to run back to his jeep to get the key. In his office he quickly located Darien's personnel file. The detectives divided the paper work and started examining it. They asked if they could make copies of several things in the file. Noticing that there weren't any photographs in the folder, the woman detective asked if any were available. Brian remembered the year book. He found a faculty picture of Darien and three candid photos taken of him by students. He gave them a copy of the yearbook.

"Nice looking guy," the female detective commented. The two detectives thanked Brian and left.

On the way to the beach, he remembered that he and Gayle were scheduled to meet with the replacement candidate in the morning. He told Mike that he'd leave after the interview. "Depending on how Pops is doing and whether I need to meet with the doctors, I hope to be home by early evening."

There were just a few people at the beach when they arrived. They took the towels and the cooler with them to the water's edge. Dogs were required to be on leashes, but they didn't bother. Cassidy walked beside them uninterested in wandering or exploring. Brian and Mike took turns throwing a tennis ball for him. They went for a swim while Cassidy lay down next to the towels and promptly went to sleep. After their swim they opened a couple of beers and began wading with Cassidy a few feet ahead of them. They'd gone a short way when Brian stopped. Mike looked at him. "It was about here that I found that body," he told her.

When they resumed walking Mike asked, "how long do you think this killing has been going on?"

"I don't think anybody knows. I'm sure Sheriff Peterson is purposely trying to avoid telling the media anything. In part because he's probably trying to keep from stirring up a panic, which would just about kill the remainder of the tourist season. I also think he's playing it smart. If I were him I'd want to avoid giving the killer any publicity."

"You call him 'the killer'," Mike said. "Brian, is there a possibility that you're in danger yourself?"

"Why would he want to come after me?"

"Let's assume Darien is instrumental in these killings. He called you this morning and said he needed to see you right away. After feeding you an elaborate line of bullshit, he resigned. I worry that he was setting you up. He could have just disappeared, not called you, and not shown up next week. If he is the killer and he's on a spree he's not going to want anything or anybody to interfere with what he's doing. He's obsessed."

"What do you suggest I do?" Brian asked.

"I'd start by talking to Sheriff Peterson about it. Maybe you ought to get out your old briefcase and start carrying Pop's gun. You need to stop running by yourself in the morning. I'm even worried about you traveling to Milwaukee unescorted. You need to get super-paranoid until he's caught and this is over."

They turned around to start wading back. Brian called to Cassidy. They waited for him to catch up. Brian patted him before allowing Cassidy to take the sauntering lead again. He asked, "What about you and the boys? The worst thing he could do to me is to hurt you."

"That's a concern," Mike admitted. "School starts on Monday. The boys will be safe there. I'll be at the gallery during the day. The only time I think any of us are in jeopardy is when we're not in public. He avoids situations where there are witnesses." They finished their beers.

On the way home Brian asked, "do you know how to shoot a pistol?" Mike told him that she knew how to shoot a rifle and a shot gun, but not a pistol. "Let's go over to Pop's place. He's got a spot out in the woods where he goes to do target practice from time to time. We'll take his gun. I'll show you how."

Brian found a couple of pairs of hearing protectors in his father's workshop. They spent close to an hour in the woods practicing. Mike was nervous about it at first, but by the time they quit she was shooting fairly accurately at twenty-five feet. They had gone through all but one clip of bullets. Brian said he would pick up another box of ammo tomorrow on his way home from Milwaukee.

Chapter 12

The next morning, Brian left for school at eight. He was taking Mike's suggestion of not running the same route and not using the same roads to and from work each day. Today he ran on the track that encircled the football field. He showered at school. He was done just in time to meet with Gayle and Darien's prospective replacement. Both women were in Gayle's office when he arrived. He was taken aback by the young woman's appearance. She looked maybe five-foot-six, with an athletic build. Her hair was a mass of long, very tight curls. She was dressed nicely in a long full skirt and a short sleeved blouse. However, she had three diamond studs in her nose and silver rings in either eyebrow. She had at least six ear clips on either ear and as many rings on either hand. Even though she wore very little makeup, Brian thought she was an attractive young lady in spite of all the adornments. Her name was Samantha Riggs and she had a very nice smile.

The meeting lasted for a little more than an hour. Brian had to admit to himself that he liked her. She impressed him as bright and knowledgeable in her subject. She had excellent references from the middle school where she had done her student teaching. Her résumé showed that she had a 3.8 grade average despite working to put herself through school. It had taken her six years to achieve her degree.

At the end of the interview Gayle said that they would make their decision by the end of the day. Samantha said she preferred to be called Sam. She gave Gayle her cell phone number. When Sam got to the door, she turned to face them. "I'd like to say one other thing if I may." Gayle nodded. "I know you're kind of turned off by my appearance. I really do want this job, and I think I have what it takes to be a good teacher. I am who I am. What you see is what you get." She stopped herself. "No, that's not right. I have much more to offer than what most people see. I hope you'll give me the chance to prove that." She thanked them and left.

Gayle looked at Brian. "What do you think?"

"I like her. I think we should give her that chance."

Gayle smiled. "I do, too. Why don't you see if you can catch her before she's gone? I know you need to get going. I can show her around the school and her classroom."

She was already at her car, an older model Toyota when Brian spotted her. He called to her to wait up. When he got closer he saw that she was crying. "Welcome aboard, Sam. Why don't you go back inside? I have to leave, but Superintendent Krietlow wants to talk to you and show you around."

"Are you for real? She fumbled and dropped her car keys. "I can't believe this. I thought for sure I'd blown it. You won't be sorry, Mr. McLeod. I promise." She grabbed his hand and shook it vigorously.

"I'll call you when I get back in town this evening, Sam. We'll help you in every way we can to get things ready by Monday." She followed him to his jeep. She thanked him three more times before he got in. She waved to him as he drove out of the parking lot.

Brian felt a sense of relief. He anticipated that this little lady was going to need a lot of support in getting started. He was sure he could count on just about everybody to back her up. He checked his watch. It was 10:15. He estimated that he could be at the hospital in Milwaukee before two o'clock.

He was on County A, just outside of Jacksonport, when his cell chimed on the seat beside him. He picked it up to see that it was Mike. "Hi, love."

"Brian, where are you?" She sounded like she was on the brink of panic. He told her his location. "You've got to get back here right away. Not here, you've got to get to Kangaroo Lake." She gave him the address and directions.

He braked hard. "What happened?"

"Just get here. We're okay. Just get here."

He flipped the phone shut, made a U turn, and floored the gas pedal. He had only heard this kind of urgency in Mike's voice once before. It was the day his father was shot. He passed three cars. He was going close to 90. He was grateful that he was on such a long straight road. When he arrived at the address Mike had given him, there were numerous emergency vehicles, many of them parked in the yard. Some of them had their flashing emergency lights on. A Sheriff's deputy tried to stop him. He identified himself and said that his wife and sons were here. He found Mike and Sue Nelson with the boys gathered under a large maple tree in the yard. When Mike saw him, she said something to Sue, got up and quickly ran toward him.

Before Brian could say anything, she took his arm and swiftly led him away from the gathered throngs of emergency personnel and curious neighbors. In a low strained voice she said, "the boys were out fishing off that pontoon boat this morning. She pointed to it. Shawn snagged something. He couldn't reel it in. It was too heavy. The lake's so shallow Danny decided to dive in to see if he could free up the lure." Brian already knew what she was going to say next. "It was a body. It's in about ten feet of water. The boys got back to shore as quick as they could. They told Mrs. Martin, the lady who owns the pontoon boat, and she called 911. The police are out there right now trying to retrieve the body. Needless to say, all four boys are stunned and terrified. Hell, Sue and I are, too."

Brian held Mike for several long moments. "I'll talk to the boys," he said. The two of them walked back to where the boys and Sue were sitting. Brian sat down next to Sue. "Are you okay?".

"No, I'm not okay." Brian reached over to squeeze her hand.

"Who can tell me what happened out there?" Shawn spoke up repeating basically what Mike had told him and saying that Dan had decided to dive in to try to free up the lure. Brian asked Dan, "why didn't you just cut the line?"

Dan shrugged, "I don't know. It was an expensive lure. It's not deep. I figured it was probably tangled up on a log or something."

Dan looked at his father, "Are you mad at me, Dad?"

"No, I'm not mad at you. I'm upset that you had such a terrible, scary experience." He reached over and put a hand on Dan's shoulder. "Come on, you and I need to talk." They stood and Brian led Dan away from the others. When they were at a place where they could talk in privacy, Brian turned and faced his son. "Danny, I had a very similar experience myself a few days ago. I found a man's body down at the beach after I finished my morning run." Dan asked why he hadn't said anything about it. "I figured you didn't need to know. I was trying to protect you guys." Brian rubbed Dan's shoulder. "I was pretty freaked out by it."

"What happened to the guy? Did he fall out of his boat or something?" Dan asked.

Brian looked out at the scene on the lake. Deputies were on a pontoon boat. He guessed that it was the one the boys had been fishing from. They were probing the bottom with poles that looked like they had grappling hooks attached to the ends of them. Brian looked at his son. "The man was shot, Danny. He and another man were out fishing a few days before. The Sheriff thinks somebody shot both men, then sank their boat."

It took Dan a few moments to respond, "was it the same guy who shot Grand Pops?"

"It looks like it." Dan muttered what sounded like 'Jesus Christ'." Tell me about what happened out there, Dan."

"The first time I dove down I felt this big thing. I knew it wasn't a log. I didn't know what it was. I ran out of air and I had to come back up. The second time I dove I pulled myself down using the fishing line. I got a hold of the lure and I was trying to unhook it. I suddenly realized it was caught in somebody's leg. I came back up to the surface. I couldn't believe it. Then it finally dawned on me that it was a dead body. I had been touching it. I almost threw up." Dan looked up at his father. "Dad, I've never been so scared in my life." Dan's eyes were wide. He looked like he was close to having a panic attack. "I yelled at Scott to start the engine. I told him we had to get out of there. I climbed back on the boat. I took the fishing pole away from Shawn and threw it in the lake. Dad, I was so scared."

Brian pulled his son to him and put his arms around him. "I felt the same way, Danny. I'm a grown-up and I was terrified when I found that man's body on the beach. I was even more upset when the Sheriff called later on to tell me that the man had been shot."

"Do you think the man I found was shot too?" Dan asked.

"I don't know."

"If he was, it means there's a crazy bastard running around

out there killing all sorts of people." Dan said.

Brian was surprised to hear his son use that word. Brian tried to limit his own use of profanity. It was not a habit that would benefit him professionally. Mike, on the other hand, had few linguistic inhibitions. "This is just between you and me, Dan." Brian looked straight into his son's eyes. "The Sheriff thinks this guy is targeting specific people. He's not out there shooting just anybody. It looks like he's only killing adult men so far. There is no evidence that he has targeted any women or children."

"So far," Dan said. "You said 'so far' Dad."

"I did say that, Dan. You said something yourself a moment ago. You called him a crazy bastard. You're absolutely right, BUT there are crazy people and there are CRAZY people." Dan had a perplexed expression. "Let me try to explain. There are people who we call crazy who can't control their thoughts. They have something wrong with their brain chemistry. They hear things and see things that aren't really there. They act weird, but most of them are pretty harmless. Then there's this other group of people we call crazy who are very dangerous. They're able to act like normal people. They have something very wrong with them too, but they're able to hide it. Maybe it's their brain chemistry, also. No one seems to know for sure. This guy is one of those kinds. He not only knows exactly what he's doing, he likes doing it. There are people who are like him, but they choose to target women or children. This guy is just out to kill adult men."

"So, are you saying that he won't come after Mom, or Shawn, or me?" Brian nodded. "What about you, Dad?"

"Naw, he won't come after me." Dan asked why not. "I'm not his type." Dan didn't see any humor in his father's reply. "I'm sorry, Dan. That was a pretty dumb thing for me to say. He might, but I doubt it."

There was commotion among the crowd. Word spread swiftly that the body had been found. Brian could make out the three men on the pontoon boat working to lift and pull something out of the water. He guessed that the boat was maybe two-hundred feet from shore. "I think mom should take you and Shawn home." Brian said. He looked down at Dan who looked like he was struggling with something. "I don't think you need to see this, Dan. The body has probably been in the water for a few days. It will be all bloated, and it's going to smell bad. Go get in your mom's truck." Dan started for the truck. "Dad, what about Shawn's fishing pole?" Brian showed a weak smile. "We'll buy him a new one."

Brian caught Mike's eye. She saw Dan heading toward the truck and knew what to do. She told Sue Nelson that they were leaving. "Why don't you bring your boys over to our place, Sue? Maybe we can take the boys over to the park to go kayaking later on." Sue was in favor of the suggestion. Mike went to talk to Brian before leaving. She asked, "are you still going to go to Milwaukee?"

"Yeah, I think so. We hired that replacement teacher. Gayle's going to try to round up some people to help her get set up for the start of school on Monday. I thought about going to Milwaukee tomorrow, but I really think I need to be here on Sunday." Mike said nothing. "It will be a quick visit. I'll try to be home before nine." Mike nodded. If she disagreed with his decision, she said nothing. "I'm going to stick around here for a few minutes. I want to talk to Sheriff Peterson before I go."

They hugged one another. Mike held on to him tightly. "Be careful, Brian. I love you."

The deputies that found the body bagged it as soon as they had it aboard the pontoon boat. Sheriff Peterson along with an ambulance team were waiting when the pontoon boat arrived at the dock. Before the group of men lifted the bagged corpse onto a waiting wheeled stretcher, the Sheriff discussed a few things with the search team. The body was then taken to an ambulance to be transported to the morgue in Green Bay. The Door County morgue was not capable of handling autopsies. Except for two or three small groups of area neighbors, most of the onlookers dispersed. Deputies gathered and stowed equipment and before long the scene was down to a just three people. Sheriff Peterson approached Brian. Without preamble he said, "he was shot, just like the others, Brian. The back of the head this time. Can't tell much at this point. The body's been in the water for several days. Bloated big time. I hear that it was one of your son's that found the guy." Brian told him that it was. I suppose the boy's pretty shook up." Brian said that he was. "Would it be okay for me and Detective Kline to talk to him?"

"Sure, we've already talked to him about it some. I told him about my finding a body at the beach last week." Brian smiled slightly. "Dan's response was, "that means there's some crazy bastard running around out there."

The Sheriff gave a single laugh, "Roger that." He asked if Brian was going to be around today.

"I'm on my way to Milwaukee. I hope to be home later this evening. Why do you ask?"

Sheriff Peterson motioned for him to follow him. The Sheriff led the way to his unmarked car. He went to the passenger side and withdrew a brown paper bag from the glove compartment. He looked around to make sure they didn't have an audience. He reached into the bag and pulled out a semi-automatic pistol that was in a clip-on belt holster. "You know how to shoot one of these?"

"My dad has an old Colt model 1911. I just taught Mike how to shoot it yesterday."

"Well. this is similar to the 1911. It's a nine millimeter. It's easier to handle. You ought to give this to Mike and you carry the cannon. There are two fully loaded spare clips in the bag. The Sheriff pulled out a badge. I'm hereby deputizing you. He reached into his shirt pocket. This is a permit for you to carry a concealed weapon. Technically you're supposed to go through some training before being issued one of these. I won't tell if you don't." The Sheriff pulled the weapon out of the holster. "This is a nice gun. I carried it for years until the department decided to switch to forty calibers. That was a dumb move in my opinion." He showed Brian how to switch the safety on and off, and how to eject the clip. "With you making these regular trips to Milwaukee, I'll feel better knowing you can protect yourself if need be."

Brian thanked him. "I don't know if I could bring myself to shoot somebody or not, Sheriff."

"Let's hope you don't find yourself in that position. If push comes to shove, and it's you versus the bad guy, just freaking do it."

Brian had barely any memory of the trip to Milwaukee. His mind was completely occupied the whole time with trying to sort through and process everything that was happening. One of the few bright spots in all of it was Samantha Riggs. It was going to be interesting to see how students, colleagues, and parents responded to this funky, assertive, dynamo of a woman. He was willing to bet that the kids would take to her immediately. He wondered about how Mrs. Penelope Pitts would react. It remained to be seen how good a teacher Sam would be. Brian thought of himself as having good instincts about people. That is until yesterday. He was still struggling with having been so deceived by Darien Michaels. At this point he was convinced that Michaels was the bad guy. If that were true, then Darien truly was a full-blown psychopath who had been able to fly beneath everyone's radar. He hoped that Samantha Riggs would turn out to be the gem he sensed her to be. That might help to restore some of his self-confidence.

He arrived at the hospital a little after 3:00. After going through the intricate security procedures that had been put in place, he entered his father's room. He was pleased to see Pops sitting up and awake. His father's voice was raspy, but it sounded stronger. His smile was lopsided. The swelling on the left side of his face and the semi-closed eye prevented any sign of expression on that side of his face. They took a hold of each other's right hand and Brian leaned in to hug his father. "I can't believe how much better you look today, Pops."

"Yeah, I'm going to be released from here on Monday," Andy quipped. "Goddamn, my forehead itches something fierce. I can't scratch it. You ought to see my piss; it's bright orange. The doc says it's because of one of the antibiotics I'm on. Christ, I thought I was peeing blood the first time I saw it."

Brian laughed. "You are definitely on the mend, Pops. You're almost back to being your crusty old self."

"I'd give just about anything for a double martini, or two," Andy said.

"Pops, when you get back home, the two of us will sit down and get juiced together."

The two men turned to more serious conversation. Brian told his father about Cassidy's role in helping to save Andy. "God, I miss that old dog," Andy said. He wiped a trickle of tears from his right cheek. They talked about how the shooter had blown holes in the boat. Andy had no memory of anything that had happened, not the shooting incident, not his managing to turn the boat back toward land, not his shooting off distress flares nor the Coast Guard helicopter rescue, nothing. His first and only memory was of him being loaded into the ambulance to come here. He didn't even remember Brian being there while he was being put in the ambulance for the trip. He wanted to know if his boat was okay. He asked about Mike and the boys. Before Brian left Andy motioned for him to come close.

"I've got some money stashed in my kitchen, Brian. I've squirreled it away over the years. Probably close to forty thousand, all cash."

"Pops," Brian said in surprised tone. Andy shushed him. "Christ, what are you doing with that much money there? That money could have been earning interest for you all these years."

Andy gave a sarcastic laugh, "Ha, interest my ass. The little bit of interest the banks pay ain't worth the time and effort it takes to make the deposits. Besides when the electrical grid fails, and it will, the world is going to be screwed. Nothing's going to work. The entire financial world is going to grind to a complete freaking stand-still along with everything else."

"Pops, if it comes to that, money isn't going to work either. You won't even be able to buy gas. The pumps are run by electricity, remember?" He touched his father's hair. "You really are getting better, Pops. They're not going to release you on Monday; they're going to kick your scrawny butt out of here by tomorrow."

Andy insisted on telling Brian where he had stashed the money. He had it divided between two separate lock boxes. "I feel like a damn fool for not having told you before. What if I had bought the farm? Hell, you never would have found it."

As Brian was leaving his father's room he encountered Clayton McMurray. They shook hands, "your father is making great progress." Clayton said. "That man is a real piece of work." Brian agreed wholeheartedly. "Did you get a chance to meet Schaeffer? He's got the shift before me." Brian told him that no one had introduced themselves to him, and, besides he hadn't gotten here until 3:00 "I hope you get to meet him. He's kind of a spook. He's a master at invisibility. That's one of the things that makes him so deadly."

Leaving the hospital, Brian half wished he could bring

Schaeffer home with him.

By the time he reached Sheboygan dark clouds were rolling in from the west. He stopped at a Fleet Farm store on the north end of town to buy a box of forty-five caliber ammo. It was just starting to rain as he left the store.

He drove through some torrential rain between Manitowoc and Green Bay.

It was dark when Brian pulled into his driveway. There were lights on downstairs. Cassidy must have alerted Mike to his arrival. The dog ran to greet him. It was misting. Brian stretched, and then bent down to pet Cassidy. The dog sniffed him. "Do you smell Pops?" Mike was waiting for him on the porch. She asked if he had driven through much rain. She reported that it had come through here about five o'clock. The temperature dropped about ten degrees and the rain came down in buckets for close to an hour. She had treated the boys to pizza for supper and had saved some for him.

While Mike heated up slices of pizza in the microwave Brian excused himself. "I forgot something out in the car. I'll be right back. Brian had tucked the bag with the gun in it under the driver's side seat. He retrieved it and the box of ammo he had purchased. He was starting back toward the house when he heard the sound of a slow moving vehicle. It was approaching from the south. The slowness of it is what caught his attention. He took several fast steps toward a clump of large cedars that were to his left. He reached into the bag. He glanced back at the house. It looked to him like every light was on. He slipped the gun out of its holster and cocked the hammer. The car slowed even more as it came closer to the driveway entrance. It was too dark for Brian to make out anything. The driver had turned the headlights off. The car came to a complete stop at the end of the driveway. It just sat there idling. Brian raised the gun. He listened carefully. Only the faint sound of the TV inside the house and the car's engine could be heard. The car remained there for maybe two minutes. It finally moved off slowly, the headlights came on and it picked up speed.

Brian's heart was pounding. *You son-of-a-bitch,* he thought. He was angry. He remembered what Sheriff Peterson had said to him that morning. "If it's you versus the bad guy, and push comes to shove, just do it." Brian had absolutely no doubt about his ability to pull the trigger. If this was Michaels' scoping out his next victim, Brian McLeod was determined it was not going to be him or his family.

Chapter 13

Brian said nothing to Mike about the phantom car. They talked about the visit with his father. The boys went to bed shortly after nine exhausted from having camped out the night before and what had happened that morning. Mostly from what had happened at the lake. It seemed to Brian that Dan was depressed. He went upstairs to talk with Dan, but found him sound asleep. Before they went to bed he showed Mike the gun, deputy badge and concealed weapon permit that Sheriff Peterson had given him. "Is that what you went back out to the car for?" she asked. He told her it was. "How come you were out there for so long?" He told her he had to pee. "You must have had to pee like a racehorse," she said. "Didn't you stop anywhere along the way home?"

In bed they snuggled up with one another. Brian fell asleep in minutes. He awakened at midnight and after tossing and turning for nearly an hour, he got up and quietly made his way downstairs. He had left the gun on the coffee table. He found it thinking to himself, *brilliant, McLeod, a lot of good this will do you if the killer comes in and you have to go looking for it*. He made up his mind that he was simply going to need to exercise constant vigilance from now on. He went into the kitchen and got a beer from the refrigerator. The refrigerator light annoyed him. It made him a brief target. He twisted off the bottle cap and took a long swig.

He felt chilled. He'd taken his clothes off upstairs in the bedroom. He went to the laundry room and found a pair of his jeans and a hooded sweatshirt that were hanging on a coat rack just inside the backdoor. He almost tripped over Cassidy when he came back into the living room. The dog was lying on the rug facing the front door. Brian set the gun down on an end-table next to the couch. He stooped down to pet Cassidy and talk to him. He felt certain that Cassidy would warn him of an intruder.

He sat down in his old recliner. He had nearly fallen asleep when he heard movement upstairs. A light went on, and a few moments later he heard the toilet flush. Then there was the sound of creaking stairs. Mike asked, "Brian? Are you down here?"

"I'm here; I'm in the living room."

"Is something wrong? Why are you sitting here in the dark?"

"I woke up and couldn't get back to sleep."

"Something's wrong, Brian. What is it?"

"It would be easier for me to try and tell you what's right." She moved toward him and found his hand. She sat down on his lap. "Aren't you cold?" he asked.

"A little bit." He reached over his shoulder and drew an old quilt off the back of the recliner. He wrapped it over her shoulders. He asked if she wanted some of his beer. "Sure," she said. He handed it to her and she took a couple of swallows. "Tell me about the new teacher."

Brian knew this was one of Mike's tactics. She used it every time things had reached an impasse or things seemed impossibly bleak. She'd switch to a more pleasant or neutral subject. It usually served to diminish the magnitude of the problem.

Brian started by describing Samantha Riggs. "Oh, I like this girl already." Mike said.

He went on with a review of Sam's credentials and finished by telling Mike about the Sam's parting statement, quoting her almost verbatim. "I'm sure, at that point, she felt certain she wasn't going to get the job, and she had nothing to lose. It took Gayle and me less than two minutes to decide to offer her the job. I caught up with her in the parking lot. She was thrilled when I told her of our decision."

Mike put her arms around Brian's neck. "I love you so much, Brian." After a few moments she said, "I don't know how you're doing it. I get tired just watching you. It's beginning to catch up with you, isn't it?" They both knew that the 'it' she was referring to were the trips to Milwaukee, the beginning of a new school year and the emotional toll that the killings were having.

"At this point, I'm almost certain that Darien is the killer. When he's caught that will be a major relief."

Mike took another swallow of beer. "So, what happened out there tonight?" He told her about the car that had stopped at the end of their driveway. "Could you see who it was? Was it Darien's car?"

"It was too dark. I couldn't see a thing. It sounded like a high performance muscle car. Darien drives an older model Subaru. Maybe he bought a different car." Mike handed Brian the bottle. He finished it.

"Are you ready to go back to bed?" she asked. He was. They crept back up the stairs. He had the gun with him. In bed she told him to feel under her pillow. He did, and discovered his father's forty-five. He told her about what Sheriff Peterson had said about giving her the smaller nine-millimeter. He turned on the lamp and they traded weapons. Mike laughed at the absurdity of their exchange.

Mike let Brian sleep in a little later the next morning. She got him up at seven knowing that he needed to be at school to help set things up for the new teacher.

Dan came into the kitchen just as Brian was finishing his coffee. He asked Dan if he wanted to come along to help. Dan accepted the invitation. He still seemed down in the dumps. Mike announced that the tomatoes in their garden seemed to be ripening all at once. Her plan for much of the day was to put up jars of tomatoes. "Shawn can help me. He likes doing that kind of stuff." She had six cartons of canning jars stacked on one of the counters.

When Brian and Dan arrived at school, Gayle was already there. He had never seen her dressed casually before. He commented on her adjustable Milwaukee Brewers baseball hat. Brian introduced her to Dan. He was about to unlock the main entrance door when Samantha Riggs drove up. As she got out of her car she had a broad smile. She had a bag in hand. "I brought some donuts," she said opening the bag. They each took one. She asked Dan if he had any brothers or sisters. Dan told her that he had a brother. "Take one for him too, and take one for your mom." Dan looked to his father who nodded his permission. Dan thanked her. "I'm the one who should be thanking you. You're giving up part of your last day of freedom to help me. Let's see how fast we can get this done." Brian could see Dan warming to this teacher who was nothing like anyone he had ever met before. Not even his mother.

They went to the school office first where Brian gave Sam a key to the building. She was surprised. She didn't expect to be trusted with access to a whole school. He gave her class lists. "We're not a very big school, Sam. As a matter of fact we've been experiencing a reduction in enrollment over the past few years. A lot of young families can't afford to live here in Door County anymore. The cost of living is high and wages aren't. None of your classes will exceed twenty-five students." They went to her classroom. Gayle had shown it to her yesterday. A lot of things were already organized. There were cartons containing textbooks. The unopened ones were new books. "Sam, I want you to understand that no one is expecting you to walk in here tomorrow prepared to begin teaching your subject. You're going to be scrambling for a while to get on top of things. We'll help you in every way we can. Let us know if we're getting in the way. I'll be cruising by from time to time throughout the day tomorrow. Don't take it as a sign of any misgivings on my part. View it more as my being avuncular." She asked him what that meant. "Being like a friendly uncle."

"Hmm," she pondered. "I have two uncles. One of them is a Marine Corps drill sergeant. He lives in California. I've never met him. The other one is serving time for dealing dope. I like him, but he's a few cards shy of a full deck."

"I used a bad analogy," Brian said.

"No, I like it. It will be nice to experience a normal uncle."

Gayle said, "If I could choose an uncle, I couldn't pick a better one than Brian." Brian thanked her for such a nice compliment.

Sam asked Dan to help her bring in a couple of cartons from her car. One of them was filled with three dimensional puzzles. Dan asked her what those were for. "There are always some kids who finish their classroom assignments or tests ahead of the others. When they do, they get to choose a puzzle to work on. A lot of them are real brain sizzlers." She plucked one of them out of the box and handed it to Dan. "Here, see if you can figure this one out." She told him what the object of it was. Dan asked her if she could do all of them. "I can. I've got some more at home that I'm still working on. I'll bring them in next week. It will be fun to see if any of the kids can figure them out before I do."

Gayle left a while later. Brian showed Sam where supplies and the copy machines were. She seemed confident that she knew how to run the machines. He asked her if she had found a place to live. "I brought my tent. I found a private campground that's not far from here. I'll stay there until I find an apartment." Brian offered to call around to see if he could find someone who was looking for a roommate. He had two or three people in mind. Sam asked Dan if he wanted to come with her to help set up her tent, and maybe he could show her around. She would bring him home when they were done. Dan seemed eager to go with her. His depressed spirits were evaporating quickly. Brian said that would be fine.

On his way home Brian stopped at his father's house. He went into the kitchen and found the two lock boxes right where Andy said they'd be. He found the keys for both of them in Andy's desk. Andy had put a thousand dollars into each of forty envelopes, twenty envelopes per box. Brian relocked the boxes and returned them to their hiding places behind false backs in the cabinets. *Pops was right. I never would have found them.*

Brian looked around to make sure everything was all right. Andy's small office contained a computer that he seldom used, two large bookshelves with reference books, his gun cabinet, exercise equipment and two file cabinets. Brian opened the top drawer of one of the cabinets. It was well organized and labeled. One file contained checking account statements. Another had credit union statements. Brian looked at the most recent of those. He was surprised to see that his father had several CDs, and a savings account that totaled close to a hundred thousand dollars. *Pops, you old fox. For all of your complaining about the banking system, you've got a lot invested.* Brian knew, of course, that in his father's mind, credit unions were a whole different animal. The depositors were the owners. Andy saw banks as greedy corporations who were beholden to their 'elite bunch of stock holders'. Brian agreed with his father in principle. Andy loathed anybody or anything that took advantage of 'the little guy'.

Mike was just finishing up her canning, having filled thirty-two jars with tomatoes. She estimated that there were enough unripe tomatoes to produce another two dozen jars.

She asked where Dan was. Brian told her that he was with Sam helping her to set up her tent and that Dan was smitten with her. Mike was curious about why she was camping. "I suspect that she hasn't got enough money to take a motel room for even a few nights. I'm going to call a couple of people to see if they are looking for a roommate."

"Why don't you let her stay at Pop's house until she can find something? He's got a spare bedroom and I'm sure he wouldn't mind. Besides he's probably going to be in the hospital for several more weeks. It would be a relief knowing somebody was there to watch after his place."

Brian smacked his head. "You're absolutely right. I hadn't even thought about that. I don't think he'd mind at all. As a matter of fact she might even consider staying on after Pops comes home. He's probably going to need help, at least for a while."

Sam and Dan returned an hour later. Brian and Mike went out to greet them. Brian apologized for not having thought about it sooner. He explained the situation with his father, giving her the 'disappearance' version of the story. She was shocked by what had happened to him. He asked her if she would be willing to consider staying at his place. She seemed reluctant. Mike suggested that they take her to see Andy's house. She could decide after that. Once they had shown her the house and the property, she agreed to stay. "This is a sanctuary, Brian. It's so peaceful here."

Brian told her that it hadn't always been this nice. "Pops has worked hard over the past twenty-five years to transform this place into what it is today."

He gave her a brief description of how it had been when his father first came here. Sam wanted to know how much the rent would be. "It's not going to cost you a thing, Sam. You can move in here right now if you want." She was insistent that she pay something. "Here's the deal, Sam. Think of yourself as a care taker. Technically, we should be paying you to watch over the place." She finally relented with the understanding that she would do the yard work which included the mowing and she would maintain the house. She assured both Brian and Mike that she was a 'neat freak'.

Dan was eager to go back to the campground with her to

get her tent. The campground manager was nice enough to refund her fee. Sam introduced the word 'serendipity' to Dan on the way home. "My luck has changed, Daniel. This is serendipitous." She stopped at Wilson's to buy ice cream cones. As they drove she said, "I'm beginning to understand something your dad told me earlier. It really is expensive to live here. I could have this same ice cream cone at home for much less." She asked if prices came down after the tourist season was over.

Dan smiled at her, "Just about everybody that comes here thinks that. A couple of my friends have moved away. Their parents couldn't find jobs that paid enough for them to afford to live here. I hope that never happens to us. I love it here. I don't think I could be happy living anywhere else."

When Sam returned with Dan, Mike invited her to come back for supper. "Brian's making some of his famous spaghetti. It really is good, in part because he uses homegrown tomatoes from our garden." Mike told her that they usually ate around six or six-thirty. She asked if Sam drank beer or wine." Sam said she preferred wine. She wasn't much of a drinker. Mike smiled. "That's good. It means there's more for me. If you can make it back earlier that will give us a chance to relax and to visit before supper."

The next morning the Sheriff called Brian at school. Brian closed his office door. "I thought you'd want to know," he said. "We were able to ID the body we took out of Kangaroo Lake Saturday. It was Alex Kane. He was killed about ten days ago. The body was weighted down with rocks. If your sons hadn't snagged it, he might never have been found." He sighed. "It's looking more and more like this Darien Michaels is our killer. I've got everybody out looking for him. There's lots of nooks and crannies in this county assuming he's still here. I tell you, Brian, a part of me wishes he'd just leave. I know that, if he does, he's just going to continue killing people elsewhere. He's sure put a dent in our male population."

Brian told the Sheriff about the suspicious drive-by shortly after he'd arrived home Saturday evening. The Sheriff agreed with Brian that it probably wouldn't have done much good for him to have reported it, "It might mean that you're being scoped out. I'll have one of my deputies set up a surveillance camera near your driveway entrance. Meanwhile, I'll brief the deputies that are on that shift and ask them to make a special point of patrolling your area."

Later that morning Gayle called him. "How's our girl Sam, doing so far?"

"She's off to an exceptionally good start," Brian reported. She started right off by telling the kids that she was brand new to Door County. She'd only been here once before, and had camped at Potawatomi State Park. So she hadn't seen anything up here on the Peninsula. She had them each think of a place they thought she should see. They had to write it down, give her directions to the place, then tell why they thought she should see it. When they were done she collected them only to redistribute them so that each student had someone else's paper. She had them take turns reading the place aloud and then say why they either agreed or disagreed with the suggestion. They couldn't just say it was a dumb idea or a good one. They had to explain their position. It was a lesson in 'critical thinking'."

"How creative," Gayle said.

"I wanted to pull up a chair and stay the rest of the morning," Brian said. "I learned all sorts of things about the county I never knew before." He laughed. "Here's the best part. It was almost 10:00. She stops in the middle of everything and said, "you know what, these damn studs in my nose are really starting to bother me. I'm going to take them out right now. Has anybody got a Kleenex just in case they bleed a little?" She ended up asking one of the girls to help her. That led to a whole discussion about adornments." He went on to tell Gayle about the living arrangement that he and Mike had come up with for Sam.

"What a win, win situation," Gayle remarked. Brian had told Gayle about his sons finding a body in Kangaroo Lake Saturday morning. He told her about his conversation with Sheriff Peterson this morning. "So, Michaels really was lying through his teeth. He probably thought that by making this Alex guy disappear, everyone would assume that Alex is the killer and that he'd fled the county. My question is, do you think Michaels is going to be able to stop his killing spree? If he can't, he puts the spotlight back on himself. It's important that the discovery of a body be kept a secret." Brian admitted that thought hadn't occurred to him. A wave of panic quickly began to develop. *I wonder if any of the boys has talked to their friends about it?*

After hanging up with Gayle, Brian called the middle school principal. "Joan, can you have the Nelson brothers and my sons come to your office ASAP?" She said she'd go get them herself. She wanted to know what the problem was. "I'll explain it to you when I get there." He looked at his watch. Lunch break would be in less than twenty minutes. On his way out the door he told Elaine where he'd be.

All four boys were gathered and waiting in Principal Hammond's office when Brian arrived. He told her what had happened Saturday morning. He turned to the boys and explained why it was important that the discovery of the body be kept secret. Shawn said the one of the kids who lived close to the lake had asked him about it. He had told the kid what had happened. Joan said she would go get him. Brian told the boys that it was all right for them to talk about what happened with one another or with their parents. The lunch bell rang just as Principal Hammond re-entered her office with the other student in tow. The other boys were dismissed. Brian explained that the drowned man might be a man who has been missing for almost two weeks and the police have been trying to find him. If it turned out that the man who had drowned was not that man, then they had to continue looking for the other man. The kid looked confused by the story. He asked, "if the guy they found isn't the guy they're looking for, then who's this guy?"

Brian told him that was a good question. "I don't know. Maybe there are two missing guys. We'll just have to wait and see."

After the student was dismissed Joan said, "God, Brian, what a horrible thing for the boys to experience. Should I arrange for them to talk to a counselor?"

"Mike and I have talked to Dan about it extensively. We're keeping a close eye on both boys. We won't hesitate to get help if we see any signs that it's getting the best of either of them. I'm sure the Nelson's will handle their boys likewise."

"I won't say anything to any of their teachers, Brian, but I'll keep an eye on them myself." He thanked her for all her help. On his way back to his office he thought about Joan Hammond. He saw her as perceptive, trustworthy and an exceptionally good principal.

As always, at the beginning of a new school year there were a multitude of minor glitches. This year was no exception. Brian made sure both janitors were available to help kids with locker problems, mostly forgotten combinations. He assigned veteran students to the new ones to serve as guides and mentors. He did a similar thing for new teachers. He cruised the halls to trouble-shoot whenever he had a few free minutes. There were always a few parents who had specific concerns that he needed to be addressed. At the end of the day he had the teachers make sure the kids got on the right bus. There were always one or two who ended up on the wrong one.

After the last student departed, the entire staff gathered in the cafeteria. It had become a tradition that wine and cheese was served. The purpose of the gathering was for an informal debriefing. It was aimed at identifying problems and seeking solutions. It also provided an opportunity for new staff to be introduced and welcomed. There were two new teachers this year. Gayle Krietlow always made an appearance. A teacher raised her hand to ask what had happened to Darien Michaels. Brian said that he had resigned. Another wanted to know how come. "I ran into him a couple of weeks ago at the grocery store. He didn't say anything about not coming back."

"I know. Darien made that decision late last week." Brian avoided going into any details. "It came as a total surprise to us." Brian looked over to Gayle who nodded. He went on, "needless to say the Superintendent and I were in panic mode. We needed to come up with a replacement for him *post haste*. We lucked out. We met with Samantha on Saturday and immediately decided we needn't look any further. She's had zero time to prepare for the start of school today. If it had been me, I would have gone into a complete panic. I wasn't as worried about you, Adele. This is your fifth year of teaching." He turned to Sam. "I stopped by Sam's classroom a few times today just to make sure she hadn't fled the scene. I've got to tell you people, this lady has *ad lib* down to a science."

The faculty began clapping. Brian and Gayle welcomed both of the new teachers aboard.

Chapter 14

There were now six known and one suspected murder victims in the county. Out of desperation Sheriff Peterson asked for and received advice from the FBI. One of their profilers flew into Green Bay. Peterson and Detective Kline met with him in a conference room at the airport. After reviewing the cases the profiler recommended that Sheriff Peterson try to keep the media from reporting any further murders. The profiler explained that the murderer was a megalomaniac who derived immense pleasure and satisfaction from the attention he generated. It fed into his obsession with power over people's lives. Peterson didn't dispute the profiler's conclusions. He had hoped for something more concrete and definitive, rather than speculative and theoretical.

Upon his return to Sturgeon Bay, the Sheriff made an appeal to the managing editor of the local paper. The editor reluctantly agreed to suppress printing anything about the most recent discovery of the body found in Kangaroo Lake. He wouldn't commit beyond that. The problem was that the story had already spread due to number of onlookers at the scene that Saturday morning. Sheriff Peterson was now faced with a difficult decision. If the profiler was accurate, that meant he had to try to suppress any further information from getting to the media. He was desperate to stop the carnage. If depriving the killer from receiving media attention would stop the killing, then *to hell with the First Amendment*. Interestingly, the profiler was not convinced that Darien Michaels was the killer. He described Michaels as being more of a sociopath who enjoyed manipulating people, not torturing and killing them. Since Michaels was the Sheriff's only viable suspect, Peterson was unwilling to give up his search for Darien.

The week after Labor Day another body was found. This one was different from the others. The victim was naked and badly mutilated. He had not been shot, but savagely bludgeoned to death. The corpse was found in a streambed that emptied into Lake Michigan north of Sturgeon Bay. It was discovered by two college students who were doing a project for an ecology course. The surrounding area was made up of mostly expensive shoreline houses. Many of them were second and third homes. Their wealthy owners used them for a limited time each summer. Labor Day seemed to mark the end of the season for the majority of them. After the Labor Day exodus, the houses sat vacant the rest of the year. It was unlikely that the discovery would have been made had it not been for the two students.

Identification took three days. It was accomplished when a match was made to the DNA samples found at the site of the three cabins on Kangaroo Lake. It was Darien Michaels. Peterson met with Brian in person to tell him of what they both regarded as disturbing as well as disappointing news. They were back to square one. Someone else was the killer. They didn't know where to turn next.

The last two victims' deaths were different from the others in a couple of ways. One of the disquieting differences was the way in which the killer had disposed of their bodies. He had gone to great lengths to try to prevent anyone from finding them. They had both been discovered quite by accident. This contradicted the FBI profiler's theory about the killer seeking notoriety. Since neither Darien Michaels nor Alex Kane were artists that put the Sheriff's theory to rest. He had pretty much abandoned it anyway. The second major difference was that, instead of shooting the victim, this one was maimed. In a discussion with Brian he expressed a sense of bewilderment and frustration. "I don't know what to do at this point, Brian. I had the feeling that we were closing in on the killer. We were mistaken, and to make matters worse, the real one's gone off in a whole different direction."

"He might have done that deliberately," Brian suggested. "If he sensed that you were getting close, he may have decided to change his method in order to throw you off."

"If that's true, that scares me even more. He's not acting on impulse. He knows exactly what he's doing. That mean he's more in control of himself and the situation than we gave him credit for. Peterson said that he had asked for an analysis of blood samples from both Michaels and Kane. "The test results show that both of them were HIV positive. I don't know what that has to do with anything. The two of them knew one another. They had both worked as waiters at the same restaurant. It's unclear as to whether they had lived together, even briefly. They were both undoubtedly gay. What sticks out dramatically is how different Darien's murder is from all of the others. In all my years, I've never seen anyone so terribly maimed. The killer had to have been in a state of absolute rage. That's not consistent with a controlled, calculating cold blooded killer. Maybe the killer knew both of them. Maybe the killer's extremely homophobic? That might explain the shift in targets. That would explain the brutal nature of this last killing."

"I don't know, Otis," Brian said with some skepticism. "It would explain the change in targets, but why did he brutally beat Darien to death and not Kane. I'm more inclined to think that Darien may have done something to trigger a rage reaction."

"Maybe we're dealing with a schizoid personality," Peterson suggested. Brian was surprised to hear him use such a technical psychological term. "Maybe the killer's a Dr. Jekyll one minute and a Mr. Hyde the next. If he goes into these extreme temper outbursts from time to time, he's probably scaring the hell out of some of the people around him. If so, someone is eventually going to get scared enough to say something."

"Yeah, unless they end up face down themselves," Brian said. "Let's consider another possibility. What if the killer is gay? What if he and Darien were involved with one another? What if he began displaying temper outbursts toward Darien? If you remember, the day Darien came to my office to announce his resignation, he had suffered an obvious beating. If Darien was starting to feel seriously threatened, he might have tried to end the relationship. Rejection can trigger some very powerful emotions even in someone who is fairly stable." Peterson was listening intently. Brian continued, "what if Darien found out what this guy's been doing? The killer couldn't allow Darien to live. Combine that possibility with feeling betrayed and rejected. He probably went berserk."

"It makes sense, Brian," Peterson said. "If Darien confronted him and tried to break things off, that would be a double whammy, which could explain the extreme brutality." The Sheriff had some additional thoughts and questions. "I've been puzzling over several things concerning Michael's death. One of them is the location where the body was found. We're certain that Darien was killed somewhere else, and his body was dumped in that streambed naked. The autopsy results showed that the body had been refrigerated which made the time of death almost impossible to determine. The best guess is that he'd been dead for several days. There was little sign of decomposition. You'd expect that critters would have feasted on a corpse laying there for even a day or two. It was dumped there shortly before it was found. The body was discovered around ten in the morning. I keep coming back to the question of why he was dumped there? Does the guy live around there someplace? This time of the year the level of the stream it pretty low. If the guy carried the body by himself, he's got to be strong. He had to have waded to the spot where he dumped the body. No foot prints were found coming from either direction except for the two students that found the body. Wouldn't it have been a lot easier to have dumped the body out in the lake?"

Brian asked, "When you say refrigerated, do you mean the body was kept in a cooler, not a freezer?"

"Yes."

"So that means it had to have been a fairly large walk-in unit."

"Most likely," the Sheriff said. "I know what you're going to say next. Like the kind of walk-in refrigerators that larger restaurants or grocery stores have."

"I hadn't thought of grocery stores," Brian said.

"Yeah, well I'm maybe half-a-step ahead of you. We went over to the restaurant that Darien worked at. The owner wasn't there, but the manager let us have a look around. They've got a walk-in cooler that was spotless. The manager said that he hadn't seen Darien since mid-August. He said everyone at the restaurant liked Darien. He knew Darien was a teacher. He said that Darien had told him that he was planning to take a road trip before school started. He expected Darien to resume his part-time schedule after that. He apparently worked one night during the week and Saturday nights. We talked to the other staff. Everyone said that he had a great personality. He had a regular following of customers who would specifically ask for him when they came in. You know, of course, there's not a straight person in the place. My guess is that the majority of the clientele is also gay."

Brian asked, "have you met with the owner yet?"

"Not yet," Peterson told him. "His name is Melvin Stark. He's supposedly out of town. The manager says that he always takes off for a couple of weeks right after Labor Day. Business is slow then. He's supposed to be back on the fifteenth or sixteenth. We'll pay him a visit then."

"Where did he go?"

"To his favorite place, Key West. I verified that Stark's a guest at the Hilton there." Brian asked where the owner lived. "He has an apartment above the restaurant. If you recall, he's the guy with that small cabin up on Europe Lake."

"I wonder what the guy looks like," Brian mused. "I wonder if Pops could identify him."

By mid-September, Brian had an established routine for visiting his father. He'd take either Tuesday or Wednesday off, drive to Milwaukee, and return home that evening. He'd repeat the same trip on Saturdays. He wanted to have Sundays to relax at home.

Andy seemed to be reaching a plateau in his recovery. The doctors assured Brian that this was typical. They both felt that Andy was still much further along than most people who'd suffered his kind of injuries. Brian found himself becoming concerned about the impending winter months. Once the snow started to fly, there might be times when the trip would be impossible.

One of the principle reasons for Andy remaining in Milwaukee at this point was to undergo additional facial and hand surgeries. About fifty percent of the vision in his left eye had returned and the sclera was regaining its whiteness. The swelling was completely gone from that side of his face. His short-term memory was slowly improving. He could not move the fingers of his left hand. However, he could position them with his right hand and they'd hold their position. He couldn't throw a ball. The fingers wouldn't open to release it. How much more dexterity he'd be able to achieve was dubious.

Andy's ability to enunciate words had improved, but his voice remained raspy. Brian told him he sounded like on old blues singer who had spent too many years in smoke-filled bars. He had trouble with word retrieval. He found it frustrating. He'd start to say something and then not be able to find the word he wanted. He never had trouble with expletives.

The scarring on his forehead was quite noticeable. He was going to need additional surgeries to correct that. He was told that the scarring would be much less obvious, but it could never be completely erased. He would have to avoid exposing his head to direct sunlight. The place where they had cut a plug out of his skull to relieve intracranial pressure was almost entirely healed. Andy requested a buzz cut so that his hair could eventually grow back evenly. He kept his beard.

He still had frequent headaches. They'd start behind his right eye. He was told they were cluster headaches. Regular pain relievers brought no relief. He refused to take the more potent drugs that were prescribed for him. Instead, he had Brian buy him a jar of an ointment called Tiger Balm. He found that if he applied it to both temples when he first noticed a headache coming on, that would usually stop it or, at least, reduce the intensity. Doctor Kim was intrigued by this unorthodox approach. He recommended it to two or three of his other patients. They reported getting positive results. Andy told him, "now don't go telling everybody about this for Christ's sake. It'll get so expensive I won't be able to afford it anymore." Doctor Kim told him that he'd be very pleased if it worked with lots of people. If that drove the cost up, he'd personally buy Andy a case of the stuff.

Andy had been working diligently with his physical and occupational therapists. In the beginning, he pushed himself too hard and he often paid a painful price for it. It took him a while to accept that his recovery was going to be slow and gradual. He resisted the notion that a lot of things would never be the same for him ever again.

At the end of October, Andy underwent an extensive operation to correct his facial scarring. He was told that the goal of this surgery was to remove underlying scar tissue. He was in bandages for over a week. When the bandages were removed and he was handed a mirror, he was extremely disappointed.

The plastic surgeon, a diminutive Japanese man, apologized. He tried to reassure Andy that he would be much more encouraged with the next operation. That would involve the grafting process.

The third week in November Brian attended a meeting at the hospital. Andy was also present along with all of the staff who had been involved in his treatment. It was the unanimous consensus of the staff that Andy was ready to return home. He would need to return to Milwaukee for the additional plastic surgeries. Arrangements would be made for him to receive physical and occupational therapy close to home. He could leave the hospital on the Saturday prior to Thanksgiving. After the meeting Andy told Brian. "I finally did it. I wore the bastards down. I can't wait to get out of this place."

Brian put a hand on his father's shoulder and smilingly said, "hey, Pops, this wasn't a battle of attrition. You like all of the people here. I can't figure out for the life of me why they all like you, but they do This is going to be the best Thanksgiving all of us have ever had."

Mike was ecstatic when she heard the news that Andy would be coming home on Saturday. She wanted to accompany Brian, along with Cassidy. The problem was that they didn't have a comfortable, spacious-enough vehicle. They needed something that could accommodate the three of them, a dog, and Andy's belongings. During the three months he had been in the hospital, he had accumulated what he regarded as 'a shit-load of stuff'. Even though he planned to give most of it away, space was going to be a problem. That was solved the next day during the course of conversation with Gayle. Brian told her that his father was coming home this Saturday. He told her that Mike wanted to go with him, but couldn't because of the lack of space. Gayle, who drove a big Lexis SUV, insisted that Brian use her car. They'd trade vehicles on Friday.

That same day Brian asked Samantha to come in to see him after school. When she entered his office, he sensed that she was anxious. "Sam, this isn't about school. You're doing a fantastic job. I couldn't be more pleased. All of us feel that way." She still looked apprehensive. "I'm serious, I really mean it." She smiled as if to say, *Okay, then what?* "It's about my dad." Brian had given a good deal of thought about how to approach the subject with her. "I haven't been completely honest with you about him. I haven't been honest with anybody about him. I'll explain everything in a minute, but first I have to ask you to make a huge promise to me. I have to ask that you not say a word to anybody concerning what I'm about to tell you. When I'm done explaining, you'll understand why the need for absolute secrecy." He started out by telling her what had actually happened to his father and where Andy had been for the past few months. She was upset to learn the facts about his father. She was even more stunned to learn that his father's would-be assassin was the serial-killer who was still at large. "So now you know why this has to be kept a secret."

"This brings me to my reason for telling you all of this now." He explained that his father was being released from the hospital in Milwaukee on Saturday and would be returning that day. "Do you recall what I said to you when we first talked about you staying at his house?" She wasn't sure what he was referring to. "I told you that when and if he ever showed up, I was sure you would be welcome to stay on. Well, he's known all along that you've been living there. He's actually been relieved to know that the house is being lived in and cared for. I've told him all about you and he's looking forward to meeting you. When I first told him about you staying there he only had one question. He asked if you were beautiful. My dad's a piece of work. I hope you'll decide to stay. I think the two of you will hit it off."

Sam smiled, "So, how did you answer his question?"

"I told him you were drop-dead gorgeous, but that he'd be no match for you intellectually." Brian became more serious. "You need to know what you're getting yourself into if you decide to give this a try." Brian explained his father's injuries. "He's a fiercely independent man, Sam. He's had so much taken away from him by virtue of his injuries. I don't think anybody knows at this point how well he'll be able to function. He's ambulatory, but I don't know if he's going to be able to drive again. His left hand was badly damaged by the bullet. It's almost useless." He told her a few other things. "I guess what I'm really saying is, right now there are a lot of unknowns. We'll just have to see." He paused before asking. "So, what do you think?" Sam was willing to give it a try.

The Saturday before Thanksgiving, when Andy was to return home, was also the beginning of the traditional week-long gun-deer season in Wisconsin. Tom Nelson had taken his oldest son and Dan to a rifle range to teach them gun safety and to sight in their rifles. Andy had given permission for Dan to use his 30-06. This would be the boys first hunting experience. Sue offered for Dan and Shawn to stay with them that Friday night and Saturday.

Mike was sure that Cassidy knew Pops was coming home. When they got in the big SUV early on Saturday morning, Brian opened the rear door and Cassidy leapt onto the back seat. He slept most of the way to Milwaukee. When they reached the city, he awakened and sat up behind Mike looking out the windshield. As they drew nearer to the hospital, he began to pant and whine softly.

Andy had been walking for weeks now. He reluctantly used a cane to assist with balance. He could dress himself with some assistance. He had difficulty with buttons even using a device the occupational therapist had given him. He wore street clothing all of the time. That meant faded jeans and a flannel shirt. He'd lost twenty pounds which he couldn't seem to gain back. His clothes hung on him.

Brian had gotten permission to bring Cassidy into the main entrance. Andy was waiting for them there when they arrived. He dropped to his knees at the sight of Cassidy. Brian dropped the leash when Cassidy spotted Andy. The dog walked swiftly and directly to Andy, his fluffy tail wagging. He buried his head under Andy's chin. Andy was unable to hold back his tears as he held and rubbed Cassidy's face, talking to him as if to a dear friend. Brian looked at Mike who had tears streaming down her cheeks. They approached Andy and Cassidy. Mike knelt down. She and Andy embraced for several long moments. When they released from hugging, they both touched one another's faces. "Oh, Pops, I have missed you so much." Brian had come prepared. He handed both of them bandanas.

Andy told her he had missed her, too. "God, Mike, if anything, you've gotten even more beautiful." She thanked him as she studied him and touched his face again. "The same can't be said for me. I wasn't what you'd call Robert Redford before.

Now I'm downright butt-ugly."

"I didn't know what to expect, Pops. You look better than I thought you would." She put her hand to his cheek again. "That's not what's important anyhow." Mike got up and helped Andy to his feet. She looked him over. "You've lost a lot of weight, Pops."

"Yeah, chasing nurses all day for three months will do that."

"Come on, let's get you out of here." She picked up his suitcase and a box. Andy insisted on carrying a couple of shopping bags. Brian brought the rest. They loaded everything into the back cargo space.

Andy was curious about the car. "What, did the school district give you a corporate bonus? Where the hell did you get an ego-mobile like this?" Brian explained who it belonged to and that she had loaned it to them for the trip. "So how does a lowly school superintendent afford one of these? This has to be a fifty-thousand dollar vehicle, at least."

"It probably cost more than that, Pops. It's got so many whistles and bells you have to go though fighter pilot training to drive it." He explained that Gayle was single and lived in a condo. She could afford to indulge in a few luxuries. "More power to her."

Mike offered for Andy to sit up front. "Thanks, love, but Cassidy and I have some catching up to do." The dog sat next to Andy. He sniffed Andy's face, and studied the changes. Andy kneaded Cassidy's back and shoulders while speaking to him. He told Cassidy that he'd heard about what he'd done to save him this time. He told the dog about his injuries. Mike sat sideways in the front seat, mostly so that she could hear what Andy had to say. Andy showed Cassidy his left hand. "Look at this Goddamn thing. It's about as useful as a Republican at a homeless shelter." He demonstrated how little range of motion his fingers had. "And look at this," he said. Cassidy had his head cocked and looked back and forth between Andy's face and the hand. "I have to fold these three fingers down to be able to pick my nose." He extended his forefinger by folding the others down using his right hand. He folded that down and extended his middle finger using the same process, "or to use sign language."

Mike reached back and touched Andy's cheek. "Pops, I really have missed you. Whatever else you may have lost, your sardonic wit is as sharp as ever."

"My occupational therapist does standup comedy on weekends. I've gotten a bunch of tips from her. Do you know how important timing is to good delivery?" He took a hold of her hand. "Thanks, Mike."

She knelt in the seat to face him. She held on to his hand. "Pops, I know you're scared and feeling really self-conscious." They looked at one another. "I remember something I've heard you say to the boys a couple of times. 'It's not an adventure, if there isn't any risk'."

Andy looked down, then at Cassidy, then back to Mike. "You're right, love, I am scared as hell. Some of it is legitimate." Cassidy lay down with his head on Andy's leg. He sighed deeply. "One of the things that I'm scared about is how the boys are going to react when they see me this way." He gestured to his face.

"I expect they're going to be really upset, Pops," Mike said. "Not so much because of the way you look, but because someone did this to their Grand Pops. Dan was pretty upset when he discovered that body, but he was able to get over it fairly quickly. He may have a tougher time getting over what's happened to you."

Andy stroked Cassidy's side. "We've got our work cut out for us, old dog."

Brian kept glancing up at the rearview mirror to check on his father. About an hour into the trip, he saw his father applying something to his temples. "Do you want to stop and stretch your legs, Pops?"

"Naw, my legs are fine. I'm just getting another one of these damn headaches. Hopefully, this will get rid of it." He showed Mike the small jar of Tiger Balm.

"Whew," she commented. "That's strong stuff. It's clearing my sinuses." He awkwardly put the lid back on the jar and handed it to her. She read the label. "Does this work all of the time?"

"A lot of the time," he told her. "Not all of the time." She asked what he did when it didn't seem to be working. "I piss and moan a lot." Brian told him he did that anyway. Mike pressed him for an answer. "If it's really bad, and won't go away, I found that climbing several flights of stairs in the hospital seemed to help. My theory is that aerobic activity increases the blood flow to the brain. I don't know if that's valid or not." She thought it made sense. She asked him what seemed to trigger the headaches. He answered, "thinking." She told him she was serious. "I have no idea, Mike. They can occur anytime of the day or night." He told her that he could always tell when one was coming on. "If I get right on it, I can usually keep it from becoming a skull splitter." Mike asked if he'd had any MRIs or CT scans while he was in the hospital. "Once-a-day." He could see that she was tiring of his sarcastic humor. "I've had every test known to man. The docs don't have any answers. They are of the opinion that the headaches will gradually diminish in terms of severity and frequency and it is getting better." She asked if he had experienced these kinds of headaches before he was injured. "Years ago, after I left the city and moved up here. Back then, I blamed it on stress. It was tough going those first few years."

His headache began to gradually disappear as they drove further north. Brian successfully changed the subject to Sam. He told his father that she had agreed to stay on for the time being. "I think you're really going to like her, Pops. She's different. She's one of the neatest young ladies Mike and I have ever met. She's almost as neat as Mike."

"You almost didn't save your ass that time," Andy said.

Brian had kept his father informed about Sam, particularly about how well she was taking care of the house and the yard, and some of the creative things she did as a teacher. "Cassidy likes her a lot, Pops. I don't know how he figured out she was there. A couple of days after she moved in, he started going over to your place. It's spooky. He seems to know what time she arrives and he goes over there to greet her. I mean, she doesn't arrive home at the same time every day. He just seems to know when she's there."

Andy petted Cassidy's head. "Ya hear that, Cassidy. It's taken him all these years, but he's finally figured out that you're not a dog, you're a damn wizard."

"What do you want to do, Pops?" Brian asked. "Do you want to go to your place or ours? If you decide to go to your place, we want you and Sam to come over for supper. I put together a meatloaf that we can just pop in the oven."

"Don't be offended, Brian. I want to go home. I want to meet Sam, start a fire, put on my sweater, pour a martini, and relax, pretty much in that order. Mike raised some concern about his having alcohol. "Sweetheart, if it kills me, I will die a happy man. I haven't had a martini since the night before I got shot. The closest I've been to alcohol has been when the nurses wipe me with one of those preps before injecting me with something or extracting blood."

They arrived at Andy's house early that afternoon. It was a bright, sunny cold day with a stiff breeze from the north, a reminder that winter was not far off. Sam came out to greet them. Brian was surprised to see that she had removed the rings from her eye brows, and all of the ear clips. She was wearing a pair of large hooped earrings that looked good on her. She still had an abundance of rings on both hands. If Andy was surprised by her appearance, he didn't show any sign of it. They shook hands, and she helped to carry his things into the house. In the spacious open-ceiling living room Andy stood drinking in this cherished home. He looked like what he was, an old and weary refugee/soldier. He seemed relieved and at the same time incredulous that he had managed to return. The house was immaculate. Sam had a fire going in the wood burning stove. He turned to her and thanked her. "This is perfect. I have dreamed of this." He moved around the living room occasionally touching certain items.

Brian had disappeared into the kitchen. He returned with a martini, with a twist of lemon, and two large olives. "I bought you some good stuff, Pops. It's not the best gin in the world, but it's better than what you usually drink."

Andy took a sip. "This is looovely. It's the best martini I've ever tasted." He took another sip. "Isn't anyone going to join me?" Mike said she might have a beer. Brian and Sam opted for wine. They toasted Andy's homecoming. Cassidy waited for Andy to put on his old cardigan sweater and seat himself in his favorite chair. Then he lay down on the dog bed next to him.

Chapter 15

After Brian and Mike left, Andy sat and talked with Sam for a while. Early in their conversation Sam brought up the subject of her living here. "Andy, I love this place and being here. You've created a haven." He listened. "I just want you to know that I understand and respect that this is your world and that you value your privacy. If you want me to leave, just say so. I didn't know until Thursday afternoon what actually happened to you. I understand that you still have a lot of healing to do. I will do everything I can to help you. If my being here bothers you or interferes with your healing, I will leave as soon as I can find another place to stay."

Andy pursed his lips and leaned forward. "You're right, Sam. I do have a lot of healing to do. Probably more than I realize. Here's the thing. Even before all of this happened, I'd gotten to be a cantankerous old curmudgeon. I'm still dealing with a lot of physical pain. It can erode a person's disposition and ability to cope. I get frustrated as hell at times trying to find a word or do some simple task that I used to do with ease. I can't promise you that I won't bark at you. I swear too Goddamn much. I'm sarcastic as hell at times. I've lived by myself for quite a while. People who live that way aren't used to taking other people's needs into account." He sat back in his chair. "I like you, Sam. All I can promise is that I will try my very best to show you the respect you deserve. If I do something inconsiderate or say something hurtful, I want you to call me on it right then and there. I've let myself go over the past few years. A few things have happened in my life that were very painful and hard to bounce back from. I had a lot of time to think while I was in the hospital. I realize that I've let some of those events get the best of me. I owe it to those around me, you included, to get myself together. Self-pity gets in the way of letting people know that you love them." He looked at her and smiled. "I would be very pleased if you would consider staying."

"Thank you, Andy." Sam smiled. "I'd give you a big hug, but I don't want to hurt you."

"How about a little one then?"

Sam got up and went to him putting her cheek next to his. "Welcome home, Andy."

When it came time to go to Brian and Mike's house, Andy asked Sam if she knew how to drive a stick shift. She did. "Good, then let's take my truck, that is, if it will start. You can drive. I don't think I can manage that task just yet."

She assured him that it would start. "Brian asked me to drive it at least once a week. He changed the oil a couple of weeks ago." As they walked toward the garage, Andy remarked at how nice the yard looked. He asked if she had been doing the mowing. "I do the area close to the house. Danny does the rest. Brian changed the oil on the mower and sharpened the blades before putting it away for the season. He got your snow blower out last Sunday and showed me how to use it. We're all set for winter."

The truck started right up. Sam backed it out of the garage. Cassidy was sitting in the middle of the bench seat. "I like driving this old truck," she remarked. "I like sitting up higher. You can see more of the road ahead of you." Andy adjusted the heater controls. The truck's interior was as spotless as the house. He knew that he hadn't left it that way. Sam told him. "Dan cleaned your truck. He did it in exchange for some driving lessons." Andy asked whose idea that had been. She dodged the question by saying, "He's going to turn sixteen in less than a year. He's mature for his age. He's fifteen going on fifty. I like Dan." She shifted the gears flawlessly. "I wonder if Dan got a deer today. He probably would have called me to let me know if he had." It was dark and Sam had the headlights on the bright beam. As they rounded a curve three medium sized does crossed the road ahead of them. Cassidy was on full alert, but he refrained from barking. Sam slowed down just in case there was a straggler or two. "I remember the first time I went deer hunting. It was just barely light when I spotted a small buck. Even though my brother had warned me about buck-fever, man, my heart starting pounding like a kettle drum." Andy asked her if she got the deer. "I don't know. My brother and I shot at the same time. I don't know which one of us hit it. It was probably him."

Sam's expression changed. Andy waited for her to say something. "He was killed a couple of years ago." Her voice became flat, "He was an Army sergeant. He was into a second tour in Afghanistan. His unit was ambushed. He died trying to save two of his men." She glanced over at Andy. Her face bore an expression of stoic sadness. It made her look years older. "He was awarded the Bronze Star."

Rather than ask, Andy made a statement. "You were close to him."

"I was." She turned into Brian's driveway. "He wasn't just my brother. He was my best friend. We worked together as a team. We depended on one another." Sam stopped the truck close to the side porch. She turned the engine and the headlights off. "What a stupid war. What are we doing there? What do we hope to accomplish?"

"There are no intelligent wars, Sam. I felt the same as you many years ago." Andy said. "I've decided that, as a species, we're hard wired to keep repeating the same mistakes."

"Not all of us, Andy," she said.

"Point-taken."

Sam took Andy's arm to steady him as they climbed the porch steps. Andy stopped short before allowing Sam to open the front door. "I don't know if I'm ready for this." He said. Sam looked at him questioningly. "I hope the boys aren't going to be too shocked when they see me." He gestured to his face. Sam squeezed his arm, and gently led him inside. Cassidy followed.

Mike was the first to greet them. The boys were right behind her. Dan stepped forward. He was awkwardly trying to decide how to greet his Grand Pops. He held out his hand to shake. Andy took his hand and pulled him closer. They hugged one another. "Welcome home, Grand Pops."

"Thank you, Dan. It's good to be home." Shawn stepped forward to hug his Grand Pops, too. "God, I've only been gone three months, and you two galoots have grown a couple of inches at least."

Mike helped Andy off with his coat after which Shawn said, "Jeez, Grand Pops, you've lost a lot of weight."

Andy pulled both sides of his shirt out and looked down. "By God, you're right." He feigned surprise. "I hadn't noticed, I'll bet it was that hospital food. That stuff is tasteless." Dan took their coats and hung them on a coat rack just inside the door. They all went into the living room. Brian wanted his father to sit in his recliner. Andy went to the couch instead. He wanted his grandsons to join him. "So, Dan did you get a deer today?" Dan told him that he'd had a chance at a large doe, but he missed it. "It was buck fever, wasn't it." Dan nodded blushing slightly. "Danny, just about everybody gets buck fever. I did, your dad did. On the way over here Sam and me were talking about deer hunting. She said that the first time she went, she got buck fever, too." Dan showed surprise that this woman who he practically worshipped, knew how to hunt, and had experienced buck fever, too.

"How do you get over it, Grand Pops?"

"I don't know that you ever get over it completely, Dan. That may be the main reason why people continue to go out there year after year in all sorts of weather to hunt the critters. It's an emotional thing. First, you get that rush of anxious anticipation when you spot a deer. You have to somehow master those feelings in order to steady the gun and squeeeeze off the shot. If you hit the deer, there are a few moments of victory. For me, that's followed by a kind of solemn emotional experience. It's a kind of a sadness. Deer can be a nuisance, but they truly are beautiful creatures. I like what the American Indians do. They thank the animal for giving its life to them. After that, there's the messy task of field-gutting the animal. But even that has a reverent aspect to it. When you reach your bare arm deep inside of the beast to cut loose its lungs and heart you feel its warmth, you breathe in the smell of its interior. It makes you aware of the meaning of life and of death. You're in touch with the stuff of life, the stuff that drives all living creatures."

Shawn asked, "Do deer have souls, Grand Pops?" Andy told him that he had no idea. "If they do, where do you think it goes when the deer dies?"

"What are you really asking Shawn? Are you asking about what happens to all creatures when they die, including us?" Shawn supposed so. "Andy asked him what he thought happened.

"I don't know, Grand Pops. I don't think I believe in a place called heaven or that other place." He looked really uncomfortable. "Grand Pops, Dad said that you almost died when that man shot you. Is that true?"

Andy nodded. "I got pretty close to it."

"Did you see a white light, or hear harps or see your whole life flash before you? What was it like, Grand Pops?"

Andy held his hand out to Shawn. Shawn took it. "I don't remember much about it, Shawn. What I do remember is, I wasn't afraid. I didn't want to die, but I wasn't afraid. From what I've been told, I did what you'd expect me to do. I set about trying to stay alive."

Dan asked him, "How were you able to do that, Grand Pops? I mean, you were hurt really bad. How did you even know what to do? How were you able to make yourself do it?"

"I wish I could answer that, Dan. A lot of people would say that my 'survival instinct' kicked-in and took over. It would have been a lot easier to have done nothing and just let go. I don't know why some people try and others don't. I chalk it up to 'one of life's many mysteries'." With a tone of adjournment he said, "You've both asked some very good questions. People have probably been asking those kind of questions going all the way back to the very beginning of mankind. Nobody's come up with the answers yet. Let me know if you figure it out." Brian announced that supper was ready

After dinner was over Shawn asked, "Grand Pops, how were you hurt? I mean did the bullet go into your brain?"

Mike intervened. "Guys, Grand Pops has had a very long day. I'm sure he'll be glad to answer your questions, but not now, some other time."

"Your mom's right." Andy said. "I'm pretty wiped out, and do you know what?" He looked at both boys. "I get to sleep in my own bed tonight. I'm really looking forward to that." Shawn asked if Cassidy was going to sleep with him. "Absolutely."

When Sam and Andy left it was just starting to snow. Sam took her time driving the short distance, but not because of road conditions. The snow was melting as it hit the pavement. She finally broke the silence. "Your grandsons worship you, Andy."

"It's mutual," he said. "They're great kids. Mike and Brian are terrific parents."

"Andy, I know that we hardly know one another. I shouldn't ask this," She paused.

"Go ahead, Sam," She said nothing. Cassidy laid down resting his head on Sam's leg. "I know what you're wondering." She put her hand on Cassidy's shoulder. "You want to know about my other son." She remained silent. "His name was Corey. He was a couple of years younger than Brian." Andy paused. "He was in Afghanistan, too. He was blown up by an IED. He survived the blast, but he lost both legs above the knees." Andy turned his head away. In the dim light he saw his own reflection in glass. "Corey was in the hospital for a long time. He was at Walter Reed in Washington. I went to visit him there a few times. They fitted him with prostheses, and he got so he could get around pretty well. He'd use a wheel chair whenever his stumps or his back got to bothering him." Andy looked out the windshield. The snow was coming down harder. Sam turned into the driveway "When he finally came home, I began teaching him how to carve. I had fantasies of him eventually taking over my business. He was getting good. In many respects, he was better at it than me. He was more creative."

Sam stopped next to the porch steps. "I'll put the truck away in a while. Go on, Andy. Tell me what happened." She left the engine running. The heater was just beginning to produce warm air.

"Well, what he wasn't good at was dealing with people. He'd always been friendly, outgoing as a kid. When he came home he was a changed man. He had lots of patience when it came to carving. He had almost none when it came to dealing with people. Whenever he was at the shop, if someone pissed him off, he'd either tell them to bugger off or he'd walk out on them. He'd go over to the Pub and start drinking. He'd just blow everything off. I finally told the owner to call me whenever Corey showed up angry. I'd either see if Mike could come down to run the shop or I'd close it up and bring him home. We never fought. He'd refuse to talk to me, sometimes for two or three days." Andy ran his hand through his hair. "I took him to three different VA centers. The psychiatrists would prescribe medications, and he'd take the pills for a while then quit." Andy petted Cassidy. "The strange thing is, that towards the end, things were improving. He cut back on his drinking. He'd limit himself to a couple of beers in the evening. If someone pissed him off, he might turn his back on the person, but he didn't express his anger. He started exercising. He was getting himself back in shape. I thought the worm was finally turning. He went sailing with me a few times. Things improved between the two of us. I'd had a tiger by the tail for almost two years. I felt like I could finally begin to relax my grip." Andy reached to his back pocket and pulled out a bandana. He blew his nose.

"This is the hard part." His voice faltered. "I came home one evening. Corey was in his wheel chair. He was over there." Andy motioned toward the garden area. "I sensed something was wrong as soon as I got out of the truck. I called to him. He didn't respond. When I got closer I saw the blood. When I got to him I discovered that he had cut both of his femoral arteries. He had bled out. He was dead." Andy had both of his hands between his knees. He was leaning forward. They sat in silence. He wiped the tears streaming down his right cheek. Sam reached to lower the temperature setting on the heater. "I've never stopped wondering if there was something more I could have done. I've never forgiven myself for not being able to see it coming. There have been a few times when I felt so Goddamn angry at him for blind-siding me, us, like that." He blew his nose again and wiped his eye. "I still have the note that he wrote me. He asked for my forgiveness. He told me that I was a great father. He thanked me for all I tried to do for him. Finally, he apologized for giving up. He told me that he loves me. I don't know, Sam. How can you tell someone you love them, then turn around and rip their heart out?"

Sam reached over and took Andy's damaged hand. "I don't know, Andy." She spoke in a soft whisper. "I can't imagine the agony that he must have felt." She stroked Cassidy. "I was devastated when I found out my brother had been killed. I wasn't sure I could go on. Life lost all meaning for me for quite a while." Andy asked her how she had gotten past that; what had made her want to go on from there. Without hesitation she said, "I didn't want to be like my mother. She gave up on everyone around her. I couldn't let that happen to me, or my sisters." She squeezed his feelingless hand. "Come on, Andy. I'll put the truck away after I get you into the house." Cassidy stayed in the truck.

When she and Cassidy came into the house, Andy had just finished shoveling some of the ash out of the wood burning stove. He was placing a log on top of a bed of glowing embers. He still had his coat on. She helped him off with it. She hung both of their coats up. "What can I get for you, Andy?" He asked if she would join him in having a glass of wine. She poured two glasses and got him his sweater.

Andy checked the weather instruments that were mounted on the wall next to the kitchen. He reported that the thermometer read sixty-six degrees. "I'm on blood thinners. I feel cold most of the time." He complained. "This is going to be a long winter."

"I'm looking forward to this winter," she told him. "I'll bet it's really beautiful up here." He agreed that it was. "Andy, I know it was really painful for you, but I appreciate you telling me about Corey."

The two of them sat in silence for a while. Cassidy was lying on the couch next to Sam. She finally spoke, "My dad killed himself when I was ten years old. He shot himself in the heart. We were told that he didn't die right away. The bullet must not have hit his heart directly. My brother, who was three years older than me, found him." Andy asked if her brother was her only sibling. "No, there's a gap between me and my two younger sisters of nine and eleven years. After dad died, my mother started drinking and running around. I ended up raising my sisters. When my brother turned eighteen he joined the Army. He was kind of lost and he needed the structure. I encouraged his decision. The Army was exactly what he needed. He became a dedicated soldier." Cassidy nudged Sam's hand wanting her to pet him. "Shortly after my brother left for basic training, my mother took off with a boyfriend for California. It was just before Thanksgiving. My brother arranged to have most of his paycheck sent to me to help us out. Just before Christmas of that year, I got a call from an aunt who lives in Arizona and I had never met her before. She offered to fly the three of us girls out there to visit she and her husband. It turned out that the two of them are very successful realtors. They're very wealthy. At the end of the stay, they invited us to come live with them. I was in my senior year of high school. I didn't want to have to change schools. I had already been accepted at one of the state universities in Illinois. My sisters jumped at the chance. It has turned out to be the best thing that could have ever happened to them. They have a loving, stable home. I was afraid my aunt would end up spoiling them. She hasn't at all. She and her husband have worked hard for what they have. They've raised my sisters with those same values. It was a big relief for me not to have to take care of the girls anymore. It meant that I could go on to college. My brother continued to send me some money which helped pay some of my school expenses. He died when I was in my junior year in college. I was the beneficiary of his life insurance. I used the money to pay off my student loans and to put a down payment on my car."

"What about your mother? Is she still alive?" Andy asked.

"I have no idea. After she left for California, I never heard from her again. I don't know if she's alive or dead."

"Do you even care?"

"If you're asking, am I angry with her, the answer is, I'm indifferent. When she was still with us, I worried about her constantly. I was the adult. She was an incorrigible brat. It took me a long time to realize that I was fighting a losing battle. No matter what I did, no matter how hard I tried, she'd screw things up." Sam had a fierce expression on her face. "I don't ever want to go back to living that way ever again. If she's still alive, I hope she's gotten herself straightened out for her own sake. If I never see her again, that will be fine by me."

Andy decided to change the direction of this conversation. "You've done well, Sam. I'm just sorry that you didn't have a childhood. You've been a caregiver most of your life. Now you've ended up here. I'll try not to be too much of a burden to you. You really like being here, don't you?"

Sam had been frowning. Her expression brightened. "I love it here, Andy. Has Brian told you the story about how he ended up hiring me?" He told her that he had. "It's the best thing that has happened to me, ever. I love my job. I love the people I work with and the kids. I love the county. Most of all I love this place. This is Camelot."

"You were right before when you called this place a haven." Andy said. "I'm beginning to feel better already. My head doesn't hurt as much. I can breathe more easily. I feel relaxed for the first time in months." He smiled, "Of course, the martini didn't hurt the cause."

"Andy," Sam said, "when Brian told me that you were coming home, I was scared. I didn't know what to expect." She smiled at him. "You're a very nice man."

He shushed her. "I don't want anybody to know. I've worked too hard to build a reputation of being a Grinch." He finished the rest of his wine. "I'm sorry, Sam. I'm exhausted. This has been a very long day for me." He got up from his chair. "I'll see you in the morning." Cassidy got down from the couch and stretched. "Come on, you old dog. You need to go out and pee." After he let Cassidy out he said to Sam, "The snow is really coming down. We might have to crank up the snow blower in the morning. He flipped on an outside flood light. The falling snow looked like hundreds of thousands of down feathers being dumped on the landscape. He went to the kitchen window to check the outside thermometer. He reported twenty degrees. "That's good; the cold temperature will make for a drier, lighter snow. That's easier to deal with." He found an old towel in the laundry room. Cassidy was sure to need the snow wiped off his back when he came back in.

Sam volunteered to do it. "Bending over must really hurt your head." He told her that it did. That's why he avoided bending over, and got to his knees instead. "No shoveling for you in the morning, Andy. I'll start the snow blower and you can run that. I'll take care of the shoveling."

In his own bed, in his home, with Cassidy lying next to him, Andrew McLeod felt a sense of peace for the first time in months, maybe even years. It had helped to talk about Corey. He regarded Samantha Riggs as a gift, a kindred soul. He was very happy she was here.

Chapter 16

After an uninterrupted, restful sleep, something hospitals do not provide, Andy awakened at 6:30. It was light enough that he could recognize objects in his bedroom. Cassidy lay by his side. He reached over to touch the dog. Cassidy took in a deep breath. He felt the dog's rib cage expand. He lay there for a few minutes enjoying the familiarity. Finally he said, "I gotta pee, Cassidy." He slid his legs over the side of the bed. He knew that he needed to raise his upper body slowly. To do otherwise guaranteed that he would suffer high voltage jolts of pain inside his skull. Getting to an upright position was always painful. All he could do was to control the degree of it. Andy didn't own pajamas. In the summer he slept naked. In the winter he slept in underwear shorts and a T-shirt. If it was really cold he'd put on a sweat shirt in place of the T. He went into the bathroom, peed, and slipped into a hooded sweat shirt and jeans. His slippers were an old pair of deck shoes. Cassidy followed him into the kitchen. He opened the front door to let him out, noting the amount of snow on the deck railing. It looked like at least six inches. The snow had stopped during the night. It looked like it would be a sunny day. The thermometer read twelve degrees, unusually cold for this time of the year, he thought. He put dry food in Cassidy's bowl. Opening a can of moist dog food, he spooned out a portion and mixed it in with the dry. He stooped down slowly to set the bowl on the floor. After letting Cassidy back in, he set about making coffee. There was a coffee cup in the dish drainer indicating that Sam was a coffee drinker. He measured out six scoops instead of his usual three, enough to make twelve cups.

Standing in the middle of the kitchen, he tried to think of what needed doing next. It finally came to him. He went to the wood burning stove. Normally he'd get up half way through the night to add logs to the stove. He'd slept so soundly he hadn't awakened to perform that task. There were just a few embers left. He stirred them, put in some kindling and a couple of smaller logs on top. Using bellows he forced the kindling to ignite. He left the stove door open just a crack to encourage the fire to come back to life more quickly. He found his sweater and with effort managed to put it on. The inside temperature read fifty-six. It would take an hour or more to bring the temperature up to a comfortable sixty-six or seven. He had a backup furnace. He went to the thermostat and turned it up to sixty-five. The furnace ignited and in few minutes warm air began to pour into the house. Andy had failed to notice Cassidy's disappearance up the stairs. He was going through a stack of unopened mail that was piled neatly on the counter that divided the kitchen from the living room area. He heard the clicking sound of Cassidy's nails as the dog led Sam down the stairs. She was wearing flannel pajamas, a thick fleece robe and big red fluffy slippers. She greeted Andy cheerfully. He smiled at her appearance. He had quite forgotten what it was like to have anyone else living under the same roof with him. He'd not had an overnight guest, since long before Corey's death.

"Did Cassidy wake you up?" he asked.

"I was awake. I heard him sniffing at the bottom of the door. I let him in, and we snuggled for a few minutes." She asked if he had slept well.

"I slept too well," he said. "That's why it's so cold in here. I didn't get up to tend the fire."

Sam went to the large front window to see how much snow had fallen. She was surprised and pleased. "God, Andy, it's beautiful." Because there had been very little wind that night, the tree branches were laden with snow. He had to admit that it really was beautiful. He started for the stove to add wood. "I'll do it," she told him. She added a couple of larger logs. "The fire's going pretty good. Should I close the door tightly?" He nodded. Andy had built a large storage rack for firewood on the east wall. It was about half full. "I'll fill up the rack after we finish clearing snow," she told him. She offered to make breakfast, but instead the two of them worked on it together. Sam insisted on doing the cleanup afterwards. Andy took the opportunity to take a shower and dress for being outside. He told Sam how cold it was and advised that she dress warmly.

"I assume that a bikini and sandals will not be appropriate," she said.

While Sam was getting dressed, Andy and Cassidy went out. Andy took a broom and was clearing a path from the door to the stairs. The scar on his forehead began throbbing from exposure to the cold. He tried pulling his hood up and drawing it tightly. That hurt his head almost as much, plus it impaired his already limited peripheral vision. What to do' he thought. What I need is one of those..., he couldn't think of the word. He went back into the house. He found a knit earwarmer. He tried putting that on but it was too tight and hurt his scarring. Sam came down the stairs and saw his exasperated expression. She asked him what was wrong and he told her. She thought for a minute. "I've got an idea." She went back upstairs. When she returned she went to the kitchen and got a pair of scissors. She took a clean dish towel out of a drawer. She had a pair of pantyhose. She cut a leg off near the crotch. She cut twelve inches off that. She had him sit down. "This will work for now," she said. She put the band she had cut from the pantyhose leg over his forehead. She gently tucked the soft dish towel under the band so that it protected his forehead. Finally she put his watch hat on over that. She smiled at him. "I won't tell if you don't."

The two of them went outside. She went with him to the barn and pulled the sliding door open. She surprised him by starting the snow blower without any instruction from him. By the time he had the driveway cleared of snow, Sam had the side porch and the front deck cleaned off. She was in the process of filling the wood rack. He saw that she was doing it by carrying an armload at a time. "Let me show you something." He beckoned for her to follow him. In the barn he pointed to a two wheeled cart that looked like a dolly except that it had wide bicycle tires and sides. "I use this for hauling wood. The wide tires let you pull it up the steps. You can carry about six armloads at a time with this thing." He apologized for not telling her about it before. "The woodshed was too full to put it in there. So I stuck it out here in the barn. Since you've moved some wood already, there ought to be enough room in the shed for it now." It only took three loads to fill the inside rack. Sam asked Andy where he had gotten the carrier. "I made it. A friend of mine did the welding part of it. Pretty slick, don't you think?"

"Damn slick, McLeod," she said.

She asked how the pantyhose protector was working. "Damn slick, Riggs." He asked her if she knew the name for the kind of hat that covered everything but the eyes. "It's called a balaclava." She pronounced the word for him three times until he got it right. "I'll write it down for you when we get inside." She asked if he was game for a walk.

"Sure, I'd like that. Cassidy and I go for walks every day. I have almost two miles of trails that I kept mowed," he told her.

"Danny kept them mowed, Andy. He's helped out a lot around here."

They walked the entire length of the trail system as well as some of the mature hardwoods. He was surprised at how many of the trees she was able to identify. She told him that she had made it a point of learning about them after she had moved here. He admired that kind of curiosity in anyone. He had sought to foster it in his sons and now his grandsons.

Sam told Andy that Dan had shown her the big plastic garbage can that he kept sunflower seed in. He had told her that Grand Pops feeds the birds all year long. He had shown her where the feeders were located. He taught her the names of the different kinds of birds that frequented the feeders. She had continued the feeding routine. With the new snow there were fresh animal tracks. Andy showed her the difference between the doe and the buck deer tracks. They found fox, and rabbit, and turkey tracks as well. He gave her his bandana to blow her nose. He insisted that she keep it. He had some paper towel in his coat pocket for himself.

As they were nearing the end of the walk, Andy told Sam to go on ahead. He wanted to check on something. She started for the house. She stopped and turned. She patted her leg and called for Cassidy to come. Cassidy glanced at her, but opted to go with Andy instead. As soon as Sam had rounded the corner of Andy's studio, he started trudging through the powdery snow toward the back side of his studio which faced north. He had noticed something that didn't look right. As he got closer, he saw that there were large human foot prints coming from the woods to the west of the studio. They came to a stop at the northeast corner of his studio. Whoever it was had apparently stood there observing the house. They were recent, meaning that it had stopped snowing by the time the person had been here. Whoever it was wore heavily cleated boots and had about the same shoe size as Andy. Andy began walking parallel to the tracks so as not to disturb them. He noted that the person had walked a fairly straight path through the woods. He deduced that he was not wandering. The intruder knew where he was going. He also knew the woods well enough to go directly from point A to point B. It was less than fifty yards from the studio to the road. At the road Andy could barely see where the person had parked on the shoulder. The county snow plow had already made an initial pass covering most of the tire tracks. Andy had heard the plow rumble by shortly before he had started blowing snow. This meant that the intruder had been here before 7:30. Maybe it's the guy who tried to kill me? Is he looking to see if I'm back? What about Sam? Could this be some kook who's stalking her? His speculative imagination was off and running. Instead of returning through the woods, he walked the thirty yards or so to his driveway entrance. He and Cassidy had just started up the driveway when the southbound snowplow came by for its second pass. Andy turned and waved to the driver who waved back. I wonder if he might have seen the car'?

Andy was almost back to the house when Brian drove in. Andy went through a moment of panic until he saw that it was his son's jeep. Brian and Dan greeted Andy as they got out of the jeep. "I see you've already cleared the drive. Who did what?"

Andy had made a decision a while back to make a real effort toward trying to curb his sarcasm. Therefore he bit back the urge to say something like 'I did it all myself. Sam was too busy painting her toenails to help out.' "Sam did the Lion's share," he told them. He turned to Dan, "Danny, why don't you go on in the house. I need to show your dad something." Dan left without hesitation. Andy turned to Brian and gestured, "come with me." Brian wanted to know what it was. "You'll see." Andy led the way to where he had discovered the tracks. When they arrived at the spot Andy pointed. "I just discovered these a few minutes ago. Somebody was here earlier this morning." Andy pointed toward the woods. "Whoever the asshole is, he parked down on the road and walked straight up here. My guess is that he's been here before. He seems to know his way around." Brian stooped down to examine the tracks. Again Andy fought back his sarcastic urge to say something like, 'What is it, Tonto? Were we visited by the Abominable Snowman?'

When Brian stood back up, he told his father about the suspicious car experience he had back in September. "For all I know, Pops, this has been happening on a regular basis. The guy is on a mission."

"I'm not going to waste my energy trying to speculate about him," Andy replied. "I'm calling the Sheriff."

"I've got your 45 pistol and your twelve gauge at my house. I'll go get them. I'll call Sheriff Peterson from there. I agree with you, it looks like the guy's been here before. What about Sam? Are you going to say anything to her about this?" Andy needed to think about that.

When they got back to the jeep, Brian said. "I'll be back in a few minutes, Pops."

Andy went into the house. It was comfortably warm now. Sam and Dan were in the kitchen. "We're making a batch of chocolate chip cookies." He unzipped his coat. Dan came over to help him off with it. "What's that on your head Grand Pops?"

Andy pulled it off. He smiled despite the grim mood he was in. "This, my dear boy, is a modified version of, Sam…, what's the name of that thing again?"

"A balaclava," she replied. She wrote it down and came over to give it to him. On his third try Andy was able to pronounce it correctly. Dan wanted to know what a balaclava was. Andy explained it.

"Oh, yeah," Dan said. "Mr. Nelson and Steve have those. I wished I'd had one when we were out hunting yesterday. I could barely see because my eyes were watering so much. That might have helped." Andy went searching for a pen. He'd been thinking ahead to Christmas. He would put that down as a present for Dan. Meanwhile he needed to put the modified version away. He decided to put it in his coat sleeve. That way he wouldn't have to go hunting for it the next time he went out. All that occupational therapy has not been for naught.

When Brian returned he took the weapons to Andy's studio before coming in. Sam had another pot of coffee brewing. Andy was sitting in his recliner next to the stove with Cassidy on his cushion by his side. When Brian entered the house he commented on the aroma of the baking cookies. Dan addressed his grandfather saying, "Sam plays guitar, Grand pops. She's been teaching me how to play it." He asked Sam if he could go upstairs to get her guitar. She nodded her permission.

Andy stopped Dan. "I have a beautiful old Gibson guitar in my bedroom closet, Dan. I used to play guitar quite a bit. I've kind of gotten away from it these past few years." He avoided saying that he had given up music altogether ever since Corey's death. "See if you can find it." Dan returned a few minutes later carrying the guitar. He sat down on the couch and began tuning it. Sam commented on the nice rich tone it had. "It's an old one," Andy told her. "I bought it back in the early sixties when Gibson was making quality instruments. Folk music was really popular for a period of time back then."

Sam poured three cups of coffee. She asked Dan if he wanted one. The boy asked his father if it would be okay. "If you're old enough to go hunting, you're old enough to drink coffee," Brian said. Sam poured the remainder of the pot in a cup and added some milk. Dan went over to the counter to get it. Sam warned him that it was hot. He took a sip. It was hot. Brian told him to let it cool for a few minutes. Either that or get an ice cube to put in it. Brian brought a cup to his father.

Dan set the cup down on the counter. Seemingly out of nowhere he said, "I haven't heard of any more bodies being found, Dad. Do you think the guy has gone somewhere else?"

Andy had been reading the local newspaper. He was leaning forward with it lying across his lap. His almost useless left hand prevented him from being able to hold it up using both hands. He leaned back in his chair, and moved his reading glasses to the top of his head. He looked directly at Brian waiting to hear his response. It was true; it had been a while since any bodies had been found.

"I don't know, Dan," Brian said. "What made you bring that up?"

Dan shrugged. He seemed uncomfortable, as if he was

sorry that he had. He realized that all eyes were on him. "I don't know. If the guy is still around, I guess I'm just worried that he might find out that Grand Pops is home again."

Brian said, "I am too, Danny. I've been thinking about that a lot." He turned to Andy. "Pops, I'm really uncomfortable with you being here all by yourself during the day. How would you feel about spending days with Mike at our place?"

"I appreciate your concern, Brian. The glib thing for me to say is, 'Naah, don't worry about it. I'll be okay'. If the bastard IS still around, and if he DOES know that I'm back, he's going to want to do something about it. He'll try to do that whether I'm here or at your place. I don't want Mike jeopardized. It worries me having Sam in harm's way." Brian started to say something. Andy put his hand up. "Hear me out. Remember those guys that were assigned to protect me while I was in the hospital?" Brian nodded. "Well, Clayton and I had a lengthy discussion before I left. He said that if I had any concern about my safety that I should call him. There is nothing they would like better than to be the ones to bring this monster down." Andy dug in his shirt pocket. He pulled out Clayton's business card. "I was going to wait until you left to call Clayton. I can do it right now if it will make you feel any better." Dan went over to help his grandfather out of the chair. Andy handed the card to Brian. Brian lifted the receiver off the wall mount and poked in the number from the card. Clayton wasn't available. Andy left a message.

"I'm not leaving until we hear back from him, Pops."

Dan picked up his coffee cup and took a sip, then another. He asked what coffee tasted like without the milk. Brian handed him his cup. Dan took a sip and made a disapproving face. "What do people like about this stuff?"

"It's an acquired taste," Sam told him. "I thought the same thing the first time I tried it."

The phone rang two minutes later. Brian picked it up. It was Clayton. He handed the phone to Andy. "Clayton, it's good to hear your voice." Clayton asked a question. "Affirmative," Andy said. "Early this morning." Clayton asked another question. "We had snow last night. I found footprints a while ago." Clayton asked another question. "It looks to me like it was a recon run," Andy told him. "Thanks, Clayton. See you later." Andy was about to tell the others what had just transpired. The phone rang again. Andy got it himself. It was Clayton. He had one more question. "That's a distinct possibility. We can discuss that when you get here." Andy hung up the phone. "The cavalry is on the way," Andy said.

Brian had questions. He decided that they could wait until there was less of an audience. The oven timer dinged. Sam opened the oven door to check the cookies. "They're done," she announced using a hot-pad she extracted two sheets of cookies from the oven. She slid two more sheets in and reset the timer. Using a spatula she loosened the cookies from the pan. "We'll wait a couple of minutes for them to cool. I just love cookies fresh from the oven." They proved to be outstanding.

Sam asked if the grocery store was open on Sunday. Brian looked at his watch before telling her that it would be open until 4:00. "We need a few things. Dan, do you want to go with me?" Dan was all for it. Andy reached in his pocket and withdrew a small wad of bills. He asked Sam how much she needed. She told him she could take care of it herself. He handed her forty dollars asking if that was enough. She reluctantly took the money. Brian told her to take his jeep. As soon as she and Dan departed, Brian called home to talk to Mike. He told her that he would be at Pop's for a while. When he hung up Andy said, "That's nice, Brian. I mean that. It's nice that you're so considerate. I like that the two of you don't take each other for granted." Brian thanked his father for the compliment. Brian started to put his coat on, "I'm going to your studio to get your guns. I used up some of your forty-five ammo teaching Mike how to shoot. I got you a box of fifty to replace it."

When he returned, Andy was finishing his third cookie. "Damn, these are really good. That girl is going to make some guy one hell of a wife. That is, if she's ever able to find someone who can keep up with her."

"You really like her, don't you, Pops?" Brian said as he hung his coat back up.

"I do. Makes me wish I was thirty years younger," Andy said. "Of course that's being awfully presumptuous of me." He had a wry smile. "Did you ever hear the story about the man who was searching for years for the perfect woman? When he finally found her, he asked her to marry him. She declined because she was looking for the perfect man."

Brian laughed. "Pops, everyone has flaws."

"True enough, it's just that some of us have more than others." Brian asked Andy why he was so self-critical. Andy thought about it a moment. "Self-deprecation gives one an air of humility."

Brian changed the subject. He asked, "what did Clayton have to say?"

"Clayton suspected something might happen. Before I left the hospital, he told me to watch my back and call him if anything out of the ordinary occurred. Finding those foot prints qualifies. I was hoping this son-of-bitch had either gone somewhere else or figured me for dead. My heart just sank, Brian. My worst fear is that he might show up when Sam is here. If I don't get the best of him, he'll kill her, too."

"You're not thinking of exiting the scene are you, Pops." He quickly added. "I don't mean suicide. I mean taking off."

"I know what you mean." Andy was irritated by the question as well as the situation. "The answer is, no. If the bastard knows I'm alive, he's going to try to get me. He screwed up. He wants me dead. I'm the only one who can identify him. The fact is, I don't know if I can or not. I have little or no memory of the attack. I don't know if I'd recognize him if he came up to me and gave me a great big kiss. He can't take that chance. I'm not running away. Someone's got to stop him. Hell, I've even thought about putting a front page story in the paper. The head line would read McLEOD'S BACK. Then I'd tell the story of my survival to really piss him off and challenge his arrogance. His conceit and arrogance are the only reason I'm still alive. He's a sick, cocky terrorist bastard who left the scene without making sure I was dead. Terrorists are insane tyrants. The tyranny of the ill, Brian. The tyranny of the Goddamn ill. I hope it leads to his downfall. He thinks he's infallible and invincible. I wish I could be the one to end his career. I'd like to make him suffer." Andy was fuming. "Helplessness, Brian. We all hate feeling helpless. I'd make him wallow in it." Andy had raised his voice to the point that it was upsetting Cassidy.

"Pops," Brian said softly. "You're all worked up. Calm down."

"Damn right I am," Andy fumed. He worked to regain control taking a few deep breaths. "I realize that if I could make him suffer even half of what I've been through, I'd end up being no better than him."

"When is Clayton going to be here?" Brian asked.

"He said they'd be on their way within the hour. When he called back he wanted to know if your family was in jeopardy, too. I told him that I thought that was a possibility. I think he's planning to bring a second team along to provide protection for you guys." Andy shook his head. He looked at Brian. "Knowing how Clayton's people operate, they'll be discreet. You probably won't even know they're around. They are experts at blending in. It's up to you as to whether you want Mike to know or not."

Brian asked his father what he would do if it were him. Andy smiled at him. "Mike's one tough lady. If she finds out that this bastard is out there intending to do any of us harm, she'll probably find him and rip him a new asshole."

Brian replied. "Trust me, if she was capable of finding him, she would have done it a long time ago, Pops."

Andy removed his pistol from the bag. He took the clip out to check that it was fully loaded. He made sure a round was chambered. "There have been a couple of times when I didn't go anywhere without this being within easy reach. It's come around again. If three's a charm, and I survive this one, maybe I'll never have need of it again." Andy tucked the gun between the cushion and the right arm of his chair.

When Sam and Dan returned from shopping, Brian left with Dan. Andy helped her put the groceries away. They worked in silence, but Andy could see that Sam was upset. She finally broke the silence by asking what was going on. He leaned against the counter. "I found some foot prints on the north side of my studio when we got back from our walk." She asked who he thought had made them. "I don't know. My fear is that they were made by the guy who shot me." She asked if he planned to tell her about this discovery or not. "I've been debating it, Sam. I didn't want to say anything in front of Danny." She asked what he planned to do about it. He told her about the protection he had received while he was hospitalized. "That was who I called, Clayton McMurray. They will be here in a couple of hours. They will probably be bringing some extra people along to protect Mike and Brian and the boys." Sam made no comment. She busied herself putting the cookies into a couple of large plastic bowls. Andy watched waiting for her to say something. He finally broke the silence. "I'm sorry, Sam. It was stupid and naïve of me to think this wasn't going to happen."

She looked at him with an austere expression. "I can move out after school tomorrow. If you prefer, I can stay in a motel tonight."

Andy looked down at the floor. Cassidy came over to Sam. She was standing with her arms crossed almost defiantly. Cassidy nudged her twice before she relented and leaned down to pet him. Andy cleared his throat. "I don't want you to go, Sam." The refrigerator started up just as he began speaking, drowning out the sound of his words. Sam told him she hadn't heard what he said. He looked directly at her and increased his volume. "I don't want you to go."

Her expression shifted from one of indignation to concern. "I don't want to go, Andy. I know you're in serious danger." She took a couple of steps toward him. "I won't lie to you. I'm scared. I'm scared more for you than for me. You're the one he's after." She dropped down to her knees and held Cassidy's head looking into his eyes. "We were all hoping they'd catch this guy before you came home. Brian and Mike and I talked about it several times." She got back to her feet. "Don't you have some way of protecting yourself, Andy?" He told her about the pistol. She wanted to know where he kept it. He told her where it was at the moment. He told her about the shotgun. "The only thing I've ever shot is a deer rifle. How hard would it be for me to learn to shoot a pistol?" she asked.

"Not very," he told her. "You'd be better off with the shot gun though. You'd have a better chance of hitting the target with it than you would with the pistol."

She asked him if he'd teach her how to use the shot gun. He said that he would. "Good, let's do it right now," Sam said.

He smiled at her. "You don't mess around, girl." They put on their coats. Sam arranged the towel and the panty hose on Andy's head. He put a handful of shotgun shells in his coat pocket. Out in the barn he found an empty tomato juice can in the recycling container. Andy led the way to an open area on the south side of the barn. "When I first came to live here this was all open meadow." A dense forest of red pines now stood south of the open area. "I had it fenced in and I grazed a couple of beef cattle, and a few sheep. I did that the first five years I lived here. I finally gave up on raising critters and planted those trees." He brushed snow from a pine stump and set the can on it. "Damn, I forgot to bring some hearing protectors." Sam asked where they were. He told her and she went off to find them. The sun was shining; there was hardly any breeze. Checking his watch, it was almost 2:00. The sun was already more than two-thirds the way across the sky. It would be dark by 4:30 he reckoned. Sam returned a couple of minutes later with two sets of the protectors. Andy ejected three shells from the gun. He started by showing her the safety mechanism, then how to load the weapon. He had her do what he'd showed her. He explained, "The beauty of a shotgun is that you don't have to aim carefully. At twenty-five to thirty feet the shot is spreading out, but it's still got enough velocity to penetrate and knock a person down."

"What's the bad news?" She asked.

"A big shotgun, like this one, has a hell-of-a-kick. You'll soon see." He showed her how to shoulder the weapon and cautioned her against getting her face too close to the back of the receiver. He explained the consequence of failing to do both. "You'll look like you got into a bar room brawl. It'll bruise your shoulder and give you a black eye." He handed her the gun. "Normally I'd demonstrate, but I'm afraid that the kick will be too much for me." He touched his head. They put on the hearing protectors. He had her go down the checklist out loud: safety off, shoulder the weapon, face back from the receiver. The large shotgun was unwieldy. "Line up the front and rear sights on the target. Squeeze the trigger." The roar of the gun going off was followed by the can flying up and off to the right. "Beautiful, Sam. See what I mean. It's hard to miss using a shot gun." Sam immediately switched the safety back on. He complimented her for doing so.

She retrieved the can and after examining the damage, she put it back on the stump. She shot it four more times not missing once. Cassidy was lying thirty yards from where they were shooting. "Cassidy's not afraid of guns," Andy explained. "He just doesn't like the loud noise. Probably hurts his ears." As they walked back to the house Andy said that he'd look into seeing if he could find a smaller gauge shotgun for her tomorrow. "This old twelve gauge is a damn howitzer. A smaller gauge will be easier for you to handle."

"But will a smaller gun be as effective?" she asked. He told her that it would be a little less so, but it would still do the job. "If you find one, I'll pay for it," Sam told him. As they neared the house, she asked him to show her the footprints he'd discovered that morning. He took her to see them. On her own she followed them into the woods a short distance. When she returned she said, "It does look like he's been here before. He knew right where to go." She looked at Andy. "What if he's got a high power rifle with a scope? You'd be an easy target at night."

Andy agreed. "It's one of things I plan to discuss with Clayton when he shows up." Andy checked his watch. "They ought to be here pretty soon."

Chapter 17

Clayton, along with five colleagues, arrived a little before three in the afternoon. They came in two large white Chevy Suburbans. Andy wanted them to meet Sam. He explained that she was a teacher at the high school where his son was the principal and that she was living here. Clayton invited her to accompany them on the tour of the premises. When the tour was complete, all of them gathered in Andy's living room. Sam brewed a pot of coffee. Each man on Clayton's team had something to contribute to the surveillance strategy. They had a number of questions for Andy. It was decided that a man would be stationed in Andy's heated studio/workshop. A number of monitoring devices were to be deployed around the house and even in the woods and along the road. Andy asked how they were going to be able to do that without making it look like an Army had been marching around the place. Clayton said, "It complicates things a bit, but we have our ways." He gave Andy one of his broad smiles. He looked at his watch. "Well, gentlemen, we have miles to go before we sleep. Let's get started."

Andy asked if Clayton needed directions to his son's house. "Nope, the magic of satellite imaging guides the world. If you want to call him and give him a heads up that will be fine. Tell him we'll be there in about half-an-hour." Clayton motioned to the shotgun propped against the wood rack. "You got any other fire power besides that?" Andy produced his forty-five. "Sweet," Clayton remarked. "It's one of my personal favorites." He looked at Andy, "You carried one of these in Nam."

"I carried this one in Nam," Andy told him.

Before leaving the house, all six men entered Andy's cell phone number into their mobiles. Clayton entered his into Andy's. "Don't bother calling 911, if the bird lands." Clayton told him. "We'll take care of that ourselves, afterwards." Andy asked about having lights turned off in the house. "Nope," Clayton said. "We want things to look normal. The only way anyone is going to get in here without our knowing is by tunnel."

Andy watched the men deploying various devices from his front window. Each man had specific tasks to perform which they did with precision and efficiency. He found it almost ironic that many of these highly sophisticated devices being deployed were done so using crossbows. They actually shot crossbow bolts that had micro-cameras attached to them into strategically chosen trees. Two or three were shot into his old barn. As Clayton had promised, there was barely any indication they had been here. It took the team of men less than twenty minutes to deploy their surveillance equipment. One man was left behind to set up and begin monitoring from the studio/workshop. The rest got into the Suburbans and left for Brian's house. The sun was setting as they drove away.

After the men were gone, Sam commented, "this is scary. I hope the things those guys have deployed around here work as well as Clayton claims." She shrugged. "So much for privacy. It's a thing of the past." Andy asked her if she felt less afraid now. "I guess so. I'm skeptical. It may sound strange coming from someone of my generation, but I don't completely trust technology."

"I'm so glad to hear you say that," Andy told her. "I not only don't trust it, but for the most part I dislike it."

They had an early supper, and then Sam went upstairs to work on school stuff. Andy read for a while before falling asleep in his recliner. He was awakened at 10:30 by Sam who had come downstairs to tend the stove. She apologized for waking him up. She asked him if he needed anything. He said that the skin on his forehead felt really tight. "The plastic surgeon gave me a jar of ointment to put on my head. It's got all sorts of good stuff mixed into it. It's probably in my toilet kit." She said that she'd get it for him. She returned with the jar. He was in the kitchen taking a pain pill. She asked if he was hurting. "Yeah, I overdid it with the snow blowing this morning. I'm really out of shape." She watched him apply the ointment to his forehead. She asked if it hurt him to touch his head like that. "Yeah, but it feels good when I stop."

"Andy, I wish you'd let me take care of the snow blowing, and strenuous things like that. I can take care of the stove at night. You don't have to get up. You need to be able to get a good night's sleep." Before he could mount a rebuttal she went on. "And as for groceries, I can handle that, too. You don't need to be giving me money. You're paying the utilities, and all the other expenses of this place. I have a decent income now and I'm almost debt free. I want to be able to carry my own weight. It's important to me."

"Fair enough Sam, with a couple of exceptions." She wanted to know what they were. "I pay for the dog food and the alcohol." She agreed to that.

Before leaving to go back upstairs she said, "Andy, I was really scared that you were going to ask me to leave today. I think we're off to a good start with one another, don't you?"

He smiled at her. "We're off to a very good start, Sam. I'm glad you're here." He refrained from telling her that he didn't know how he'd manage without her, but he thought it.

The next morning, Monday, the phone rang at 6:45. Andy was already up. He had just fed Cassidy and was in the process of starting coffee. "Andy, it's Clayton. What time does Sam leave for school?" She came into the kitchen at that very moment. Andy asked her. He told Clayton that she left at 7:30. "Tell her not to get spooked by a white Suburban following her." Clayton said, "Man, you sure have a lot of deer running around your place at night. We counted well over a dozen. All but one camera is operational. Somebody will drop by in a while to install a new one and to relieve Stewart who's been on surveillance duty." The phone clicked. Clayton hung up before Andy could say anything.

He told Sam that she would have an escort as he finished measuring out the coffee and turned the maker on. She asked how he was feeling this morning. He told her that he felt better than he had expected to. She was dressed casually wearing khaki slacks, a plaid shirt with a red V-neck sweater over it. She was in her stocking feet. "You look nice," he told her. She thanked him and asked what he planned to do today. "I think I'll play around in my studio. I have to figure out a way to manage carving with one hand. While I was in the hospital, I had plenty of time to design some devices in my head. Now I need to see if my ideas will actually work."

They each had bowl of cereal and some toast for breakfast. "School lets out at noon on Wednesday," she told him. "I plan to come home and bake a couple of pies for Thanksgiving that afternoon." He asked her what time she usually got home from school. "I usually go for a run after school. I guess with snow on the ground I'm going to have to start running in the gym from now on." He asked if she would be able to do that now that basketball season was underway. "Jeez, I forgot all about that."

"I've got a treadmill in my office/den," he told her. "You can use that." He took both of their empty bowls to the sink. "Before this happened," he waved his right hand at his face, "I was running nine or ten miles a week. I'm going to see if I can handle walking any distance."

Before going back upstairs to brush her teeth, Sam said that she'd probably be home sometime after 4:00. When she returned, she put on her coat, and boots. She had a large woven bag that was spacious enough to serve both as a purse and as a brief case. It looked like it was full to capacity with papers she had brought home to grade. She bent over to say goodbye to Cassidy. She surprised Andy by coming over to him and giving him a quick hug. "See you later," she said. "Have fun today."

Sam had brushed the snow off her car the day before. Andy watched her out the window. Her car groaned a few revolutions before starting up. She got back out and scraped frost off the windshield. He'd give priority to rearranging things in the garage so that Sam could put her car in out of the weather. He also wondered if she might be in need of a new battery. He felt good despite the threat hanging over their heads. He thought about what Sam had said last night about their being off to a good start.

A white Suburban came up the driveway. One of Clayton's men got out and went directly into Andy's studio. He came back out, went to the Suburban and withdrew a cross bow. He walked swiftly toward the barn. He disappeared from view briefly. When he reappeared, he went back to the studio. The man who had been on duty through the night came out and got into the Suburban. He turned the vehicle around and followed Sam out the driveway. The phone rang fifteen minutes later. It was Clayton, "Sam's at school. Is your cell phone fully charged?" Andy told him he didn't know. "Check it, leave it turned on, and keep it with you." There was no urgency to his voice. Andy doubted that he knew anyone who was as self-assured as Clayton. Andy spent ten minutes trying to find the cell phone. It had sat unused since even before he had been shot. It took him a few more minutes to locate the charger. Amazingly the phone's battery was fully charged. Brian had probably recharged it.

Andy struggled into his coat. After he put his head protector on and slipped his pistol into the right-hand pocket of the coat, he and Cassidy went to garage to see about making room for Sam's car. His studio/workshop was on the backside of the two-and-a-half-car, thirty-two foot wide garage. He decided that it would be easier to move things around if he backed his truck out first. He opened the garage door and started toward his truck. Before he even touched the handle to the driver's side door the man on watch opened the studio door wanting to know where Andy was going. Andy apologized. "I'm sorry, I wasn't thinking. I'm not going anywhere." He told the guard. "I'm just going to move my truck outside for a while. I want to make room in the garage so that Sam can put her car away." The man nodded. "That's probably a smart thing to do. The bad guy may be more apt to make his move if he thinks no one else is here." That idea hadn't occurred to Andy. His next thought was, *That probably won't stop the arrogant prick. He thinks he can do whatever the hell he pleases.*

It took Andy almost two full hours to clear out space from the east side of the garage. He did some rearranging. There were a lot of things he decided could be stored in the barn. He loaded the stuff into the back of his pickup. He would enlist Sam's help unloading the truck when she got home. Andy noticed that high clouds were starting to move in. Snow was predicted for Tuesday night into Wednesday. He managed to back the truck up to the service door on the side of the barn. It had been the entrance to his old studio that he worked in the first several years he had lived here. He took a couple of manageable items from the back of the truck and went into barn. Everything appeared to be exactly as he had left it. There was a set of stairs on the west side of the studio area that went up to the loft area of the barn. The loft ran the full fifty foot length of the barn, where Andy had a considerable amount of wood stored. There was also a lot of accumulated odds and ends. *Mostly junk I ought to get rid of,* he thought. *Maybe I'll have a big yard sale come Spring.* He'd been threatening to do that for years and had never gotten around to it.

He climbed the stairs carefully. When he got to the third stair from the top, he set the items he was carrying on the floor of the loft. He turned to flip the lights on. He was wearing a pair of lined leather gloves. The fingers of his right hand were starting to hurt from the cold. He immediately noticed two large cardboard cartons lying on the floor of the loft. They were about three feet from where he stood in the stair well. He climbed the last three stairs and went over to the boxes. They were both taped shut. He wondered if Brian had brought them here to store some things. He debated whether to open one of them or not. He got out his pocket knife and knelt down next to the closer carton and ran the blade down the taped seam. He pulled one side open. He didn't realize what he was seeing at first. There in the carton was a clear heavy-duty plastic bag. Inside the bag sitting on top of the rest of its contents was a human head. Andy groaned, "Oh, Jesus, NO!" The rest of the bag was filled with the dismembered body parts, presumably belonging to the head. He dropped his knife. He felt faint. He managed to get to his feet. He fumbled in his coat pocket for his cell phone. He was breathing heavily. His heart was pounding. He grabbed a nearby support beam. As cold as he was, he began to perspire. It took him three tries before he was able to hit Clayton's number. He put the phone to his ear but heard nothing. Puzzled, he looked at the phone and realized that he had not pressed the send button. On the second ring Clayton answered asking Andy what was wrong. "Clayton," Andy could hardly speak. "Clayton, I need you to get here quick. Please Clayton, I'm in the barn."

"Five minutes, Andy. Five minutes."

Andy turned to look for the stairs. He shuffled towards the stairwell. He wasn't sure he could manage descending the steps. He needed to get away from here. He needed to get down the stairs. He put his hands against the barn wall to steady himself. He stepped down one step. He stepped down a second step. His head was throbbing with pain. The pain was causing his vision to blur. He slowly lowered himself to a sitting position. He couldn't go any further. Cassidy had stayed downstairs. Despite his dislike for stairs, he climbed them to stand in front of Andy. An emotional numbness was taking over. It was a numbness that had taken control of him years before. It had happened in an alien place half a world away. A place of insanity. It had served to protect him from going crazy back then. Now it felt like something evil, not something protective. He had thought that, once he had finally been able to rid himself of it, it would never return. He was wrong. Cassidy gave a slight whine. He nudged Andy's good hand. Andy made a weak effort to acknowledge the dog.

Less than five minutes later, Clayton and two of his men arrived. They leapt through the entrance door, guns drawn. "Andy, Andy, Where are you, man?" Clayton scanned the room his weapon ready. He looked up to see Andy sitting at the top of the stairs. He charged up the stairs. Cassidy backed away from Andy. He managed to turn and make his way down the stairs. The other two men immediately took up defensive positions. Clayton stopped in front of Andy. Judging from Andy's expression something was terribly wrong. He cautiously took another step up allowing himself to see the two boxes. He touched Andy's shoulder. He said nothing. He moved past him and went to the opened box. Using the barrel of his gun he moved the lid fully open. "Sweet Jesus," he exclaimed. "Come on, man, we've got to get you out of here." He called to one of the two other men, "Ted, come on up here. Give me a hand." The man called Ted holstered his gun and quickly ascended the stairs. Clayton helped Andy to his feet. He hooked his hands under Andy's arms, and Ted lifted his legs. The two of them carried him down the stairs. When they got him outside, they helped him to stand. Clayton told Andy, "Take some deep breaths." The first few attempts were shallow. "Deeper." Andy was starting to shiver almost uncontrollably. Clayton told the two men to get Andy to the house. "Get his coat off. Sit him close to the stove in the living room. I'll be with you in a few minutes." The men said nothing. They began escorting Andy to the house.

Clayton got his cell phone out and placed a call. "I need to speak with Sheriff Peterson. Tell him Clayton McMurray is calling."

A squad arrived within five minutes followed by another a few minutes later. Neither officer had been told what they were responding to. Clayton introduced himself to the officers. Without giving any details, he informed them that two bodies had just been discovered on the premises. Sheriff Peterson was on his way here. The officers asked what they needed to do. Clayton told them to just sit tight until the Sheriff gets here. Peterson accompanied by his two detectives arrived fifteen minutes later. The medical examiner arrived right behind the ambulance. None of the vehicles had their sirens or their flashing lights on. Peterson oversaw the brief investigation that ensued. He ordered his detectives to have a look around the barn. One of the deputies began taking photographs of the loft before and after the boxes were removed. They were loaded into the ambulance to be transported to the morgue. As soon as the ambulance departed, the Sheriff dismissed the deputies. Then he, Clayton, and the detectives went to the house to talk with Andy.

Andy was in his chair. He had his sweater on. Someone had added wood to the stove and it was burning vigorously. Cassidy stood near the front door. His tail was not wagging. Peterson sat down across from Andy. He had his wide brim hat in his hands and was turning it clockwise. "Andy, I can't tell you how sorry I am that you had this happen. I should have thought to have a couple of my men come up here and check the place out before you got home." Andy said nothing. Peterson looked around the room at each of the people present. "I guess we all know what this is about. We're ninety percent sure about the victims' identities. One of them appears to be Hispanic. The other guy was a handyman; that is, when he was sober. They were both reported missing about three weeks ago. The Hispanic guy was reported two or three days before the other one. The killer's message is clear. He knows you're alive, Andy. He's waiting for you. He's messing with everybody's head."

Andy cleared his throat. "He's doing a real good job of it, Sheriff."

"He's screwing with all of us, Andy." The Sheriff said. "He's got his thumb to his nose and he's wiggling his fingers. He's taunting us, saying 'catch me if you can'."

"It looks to me like he's holding most of the cards, Sheriff."

"It does appear that way." Peterson was looking down. He stopped turning his hat. He looked up, "Andy, I've had this gut feeling for a long time that we've been missing something. I think I may have figured at least part of it out. I don't know how, but this guy has probably known you were still alive for a while now. Furthermore, it would appear that someone tipped him off about when you were coming home."

Clayton interrupted by asking, "so, where's the leak?"

"I don't know. From what Andy's son Brian told me, your people devised an air-tight security system at the hospital." Clayton nodded and asked the Sheriff to continue.

The Sheriff turned back to Andy, "Okay, so he knows you're alive. He couldn't get to you while you were in Milwaukee. He must have decided to bide his time. He learned that you were coming home and when. The Medical examiner thinks that both of these bodies were butchered and refrigerated right after the men were killed. He said there is little or no sign of decomposition or putrefaction. He also thinks they were brought here as recently as Friday or Saturday. That's when that cold front came through. If they'd been here before that, it would have gotten warm enough in the upstairs of the barn for them to start decomposing. It probably gets downright balmy up there on sunny days. I think the guy has finally screwed up. He has to be getting some inside information from somewhere." The Sheriff turned to Clayton. "What are the chances of it being someone on the hospital staff in Milwaukee?"

Clayton shrugged. "That's always a possibility. It would mean that the killer had to know what hospital Andy was at. Knowing that, he'd then either have had to recruit a spy or plant one." Then Clayton said, "There's another possibility, perhaps a more probable one. What if the killer's informant is someone who's on the staff of the hospital here?"

It was Sheriff Peterson's turn to shrug. "That would account for the killer finding out that Andy survived the shooting and where he had been transferred to. What about finding out when he was going to be released?"

Clayton said, "I'll have one of our techies scan the hospital phone records focusing specifically on calls received from the Sturgeon Bay area. Then we'll focus on the quantity of calls from specific numbers. It may take a few hours. If we're lucky we might be able to find the needle that way." Clayton flipped his cell open as he headed outside.

Sheriff Peterson turned to Andy. "Again, I am really sorry about all of this, Andy. The sight of those two bodies today was almost more than I could handle. I thought I'd seen it all." The two men sat in silence for a while. "I'm going to call Brian. I don't think you should be here by yourself for the rest of the afternoon." Andy didn't refuse.

The Sheriff was put through to Brian immediately. "Brian, something's happened at your Dad's place. He's okay. He hasn't been hurt, not physically. Can you break free?"

"I've got a situation I need to deal with here, Sheriff. I'll call Mike. She's close by. I'll get there as soon as I can."

A few more minutes went by before Andy finally spoke, "Sheriff, those two people would still be alive if it weren't for me."

"Goddamnit, Andy," Sheriff Peterson barked at him. "Those two people and several others are dead, but not because of you. They're dead because there's a maniac running around out there who gets his rocks off playing God. If we don't stop him, he's going to add more to his list. Find something else to feel guilty about. It hasn't got anything to do with you." The Sheriff quickly got a hold of himself. "You got any coffee?" Andy scooted himself to edge of his chair to get up. Sheriff Peterson extended his hand to help him stand. "I'm sorry for yelling at you like that, Andy. I'm pissed. I'd give anything to get that bastard in my sights."

The men stood with their hands still clasped. Andy tightened his grip.

"Thanks, Sheriff." They went into the kitchen. There were a couple of cups of now cold coffee left in the carafe. Andy poured it and put the cups in the microwave.

They heard Mike's truck and moments later she came rushing into the house. She seemed surprised to see the two men standing in the kitchen drinking coffee. "What happened?"

She was slightly winded. Andy motioned to Sheriff Peterson. He told her about what Andy had discovered in the barn. "Oh, no," she looked horrified. "Oh, Pops, how awful." She turned to Peterson, "Do you have any idea about who they were?"

The Sheriff gave her a few details. "Here's the thing, Mike." He explained what they had been able to put together thus far. "The message is pretty obvious."

"It means the killer knows Pops is alive." Mike said. "And he had a pretty good idea about when Pops was coming home. He waited until just before to put the bodies there."

"Exactly, Mike." Sheriff Peterson said. "Now for the important question?"

Mike beat him to it. "Somebody has been keeping the killer informed. Maybe going back as far as when Pops was first transferred to Milwaukee."

Sheriff Peterson finished his coffee. "Maybe even before that, Mike."

Mike looked at him with surprise. "Are you saying that someone from the hospital here has been feeding information to the killer?"

The Sheriff set his cup down. "Maybe, it's a possibility."

"But how would that person have access to that kind of information? I mean Pops wasn't registered under his real name. It's not like the person could call the Milwaukee hospital to find out how Andy McLeod was doing."

"That's true." The Sheriff said. "The only people who knew that beside Clayton and his team were you and Brian. You didn't mistakenly tell anyone else, did you?" He looked at Mike.

Mike suddenly looked almost ashen. "Oh shit, how goddamn stupid of me. There is someone, Audrey Reye. She's the nurse in charge of the intensive care unit." Andy and Sheriff Peterson were stunned by her revelation.

Mike gave them a brief description of her altercation with Nurse Reye. "In the end I thought all was forgiven. I felt like we were on our way to becoming friends. About a week after Pops was transferred to Milwaukee, she called me. She seemed genuinely concerned about him. She called me just about every week after that. I gave her progress reports. She seemed to know a lot about brain trauma. She explained a number of things to me about Pop's condition. When I think about it, she often asked about whether he was recovering any of his short term memory."

The Sheriff asked Mike, "When's the last time you talked to Ms. Reye?"

"Last week sometime," Mike said. She searched her memory. "It had to be after the staff meeting Brian attended. We didn't know that Pops was going to be released until then. The meeting was on Tuesday. So it would have had to have been either Wednesday or Thursday of last week."

"Good, Mike. That's a big help." Peterson said. "I need to get next to Clayton before we do anything. If I have her picked up right away, it could end up tipping the killer off. We could lose him altogether."

"I'd be worried about her safety, Sheriff," Andy said. The Sheriff looked at him. "This guy is not stupid. He's sent his message. If she's his source of information, he's probably done with her. She's a liability. He may have already killed her. If she's still alive, she needs immediate protection."

Sheriff Peterson went directly to the phone. He punched in Clayton's number. He told Clayton what he had just learned. He told Clayton what Andy had just said about Ms. Reye being in imminent danger.

Clayton told the Sheriff, "I'm at least twenty-five minutes away from Sturgeon Bay. Call the hospital administrator. Tell him that this is a matter of urgency and that he must not say anything to anyone. He needs to find out if Reye is on duty. If she is, have the local police detain her at the hospital. And make sure that she is not allowed to contact anyone. If she's not on duty, have the cops go to her address. Let's hope she's still alive. Let me know what you find out."

After hanging up Sheriff Peterson told the three of them what Clayton said. He left for Sturgeon Bay himself. Sam almost collided with him as she was about to turn into the driveway. She was alarmed at seeing the Sheriff barreling out of the driveway. Seeing Mike's truck parked close to the house only added to her fears. Cassidy, who was normally there to greet her, was missing. She was nearly panic stricken when she came barging into the house. What she saw was Andy and Mike standing in the kitchen. Cassidy came toward her, his tail sweeping back and forth causing his butt to wiggle. "What's happening?" She asked, unable to get a hold of her panic. Brian arrived and pulled up behind Sam's car. He rushed into the house behind her.

Andy saw the alarm on both of their faces. He set his coffee cup down and went to Sam. "It's okay, Sam. Something happened here today. I'm still pretty shaken by it. The cops may be very close to catching the killer. Hopefully, we'll know before long." He smiled weakly.

The two of them stood looking at one another. Finally Sam asked, "Are you okay, Andy? You don't look okay."

"I kind of had the rug pulled out from underneath me for a while today. I'm having a bit of trouble getting back up," he replied. "The end of this nightmare may be in sight."

Mike said, "I need to get back home." She looked at her watch. "The boys are probably there already."

Brian told her he would be right along. He turned to his father. "Pop's, what happened?" He saw something he had never seen before. His father looked worn out, like he couldn't take much more. Brian reached out to touch his father's shoulder.

"I'm pretty exhausted, Brian. Let's talk later." He looked at his son, "Okay?"

Brian nodded and looked at Sam. She still looked worried. "I've got stuff to do tonight," she told him. "I'll probably be up till ten or so." He took that as an invitation to call her later on.

After Brian left, Sam started to take her boots off. Andy said, "I cleaned out the east side of the garage this morning, Sam. There should be plenty of room for your car. You can park it in there from now on. That way you won't have to scrape frost off your windshield in the morning."

She thanked him. "I'll go do it right now." She re-buttoned her coat. Andy asked her if she would put his truck back in the garage, too. Cassidy followed her out the door.

Chapter 18

After driving less than a mile, Sheriff Peterson turned his flashing lights and siren on. He sped up having decided he needed to get to Sturgeon Bay with alacrity. The hands-free phone chimed. He pressed the button to receive the call. It was Clayton. "Sheriff, the hospital administrator just called. He said Nurse Reye had the day off today. She's single and lives by herself. He gave me her address and phone number." Sheriff Peterson started to give Clayton directions to Nurse Reye's apartment complex. "We put the address in our GPS, Sheriff. We're probably ten minutes away. See if you can get a couple of City Police squads to meet us there. Tell them, no lights or sirens. Tell them what we're driving."

Peterson placed a call to directly to the Sturgeon Bay Police Chief. He gave the Chief a summary of the situation. Two squads were immediately dispatched to the apartment address. He grabbed his coat and all but ran out of the building toward his own car. When he arrived at the apartment complex, Clayton had already deployed the city cops to the rear of the building. He and two of his men were about to enter the building. A civilian was standing close to one of the squads. He called to the Chief. "I'm the manager. I gave them a master key." It was already dark. It was beginning to snow. The temperature was falling. The Chief unsnapped the security strap on his holster, but did not draw his weapon.

Nurse Reye's apartment had an inside entrance on the second floor. Clayton tested the lock on the door handle. It was locked. He carefully slipped the master key into it and turned it slowly until it clicked. He quickly put the key into the deadbolt and turned it. He and his two men stormed into the apartment followed by the Chief. The apartment was dark except for a nightlight in the bathroom and a soft vent hood light over the stove. One of the officers found a light switch next to the door that turned on two living room lamps. The apartment was compulsively neat. They advanced to the bathroom, then the bedroom. Clayton flipped the switch next to the door to discover a woman on the bed. She was fully clothed, and her hands were folded on her abdomen. Clayton went to the bed and touched her neck for a pulse. "She's alive, just barely. Call for an ambulance." Three prescription bottles sat on the night stand. None of them bore labels. Two of them were open. One was empty, the other half full. Clayton took a pill out of the half-full bottle. "Anybody?" He held the pill so that all could see it. "What's this look like?" No one knew the answer. "This lady's an experienced nurse. My guess is that it's a sedative." He rechecked her pulse. "No way of telling when she started taking this stuff." He lifted one of her eye lids, then the other. "She's in a very deep coma." He stood up and put his pistol back into his shoulder holster. "Look around the apartment for two things. No make that three. A cell phone, a suicide note and any signs that someone else has been in here." Clayton opened the third bottle. It contained the same kind of pills as the half full bottle. "The lady wasn't messing around. She knew what she was doing," he said to the Chief. One of Clayton's men came into the bedroom. He was holding a purse in one hand and a cell phone in the other. "Where'd you find those things?" Clayton asked.

"Just where you'd expect, in a large cast iron pot buried under a couple of nested pans in the cabinet next to the stove." Clayton asked if they had found anything else.

The third man came into the bedroom. The ambulance siren could be heard approaching. "I think you need to take a look at something," he said to Clayton.

As they started from the bedroom Clayton said, "Come on, let's all of us get out of the way. The paramedics need to get this lady to the hospital ASAP. Ted, let the medics know that she overdosed, possibly on sedatives. Make sure they take one of the bottles with them to identify the pills. Bag the other two for prints. Tell them that we have no idea when she started to make her exit."

Clayton was taken to a small desk in the living room. It had a drop lid that served as the writing surface. A writing pad lay on the open desk lid. "It looks like she had written a letter to somebody. There are impressions on the paper." Clayton told him to go get 'the kit'. Moments later the ambulance team came through the door. The man called Ted led them into the bedroom. After checking Audrey's pulse with a stethoscope, they lifted her onto their stretcher and swiftly wheeled her out to the waiting ambulance. The hospital was only a few blocks away.

When the third man returned to the apartment, he opened a large plastic box. He withdrew a bottle and sprinkled a black powder on the pad of paper. He carefully tapped the dust off the pad into a plastic bag. The impression left by the previous correspondence was visible. It read:

Dear Mike,

I'm so ashamed of myself. I have betrayed you. The man who shot your father-in-law threatened to kill me if I didn't do as he told me to. I know that he's done using me. He's an extremely cruel person. I can't go on living in such fear. I swear to you I don't know who the man is or anything about him. I'm certain that he's the man who has killed all those other people. Please forgive me.

Audrey

Clayton turned to the Chief. "If our boy finds out Reye is still alive, he's probably going to come after her. Can you provide her with protection?"

"We're stretched pretty thin." The Chief said. "We'll do what we can." He asked Clayton what he thought her chances were.

"Honest answer? Less than fifty-fifty. She's barely alive." The Chief asked who Mike was. "It's a long story, Chief. Sheriff Peterson will tell you all about it when this is over. The Chief said that he had just one more question. He had deduced that the man she referred to in the letter was the serial killer. He wanted to know how nurse Reye was connected to this man. "The guy's a fifth degree psychopath. He's been using her to track the only victim who has survived. It appears that she was coerced into keeping him informed." The Chief asked who the survivor was. Clayton smiled at him. "I'm supposed to be protecting him. If I told you that, I wouldn't be doing my job."

Sheriff Peterson came into the apartment. He greeted the police chief then turned to Clayton. "The Chief can fill you in on the situation here, Sheriff. We need to get back up north without delay. I think our boy is about to make a move. It might be wise to set up squads on highway 42 and 57 and maybe another one where the two converge. He may try to make a run for it." The Chief said that he would set up the squads just north of town. That freed the Sheriff up to man the other two positions. "Gentlemen, tell your men, shoot to kill. This guy is going to go for broke."

The Sheriff asked, "Do we have any idea who he is?"

"I hope to have that information for you in a very short while. One of my men is working on the nurse's cell phone as we speak. Hopefully we'll be able to identify him based on calls made to her. I'll let you know if we come up with a name." Clayton and his two associates left.

Sam asked Andy to show her how to make a martini. They went to the kitchen. Andy got out the ingredients. "They're one of the easiest drinks there is to make. However, there is great controversy concerning the methods used," he said in mock seriousness. "One school, we'll call them the Goths, advocate shaking the ingredients to blend them. The more refined and civilized school prefers gently stirring the ingredients so as not to bruise the gin. Then there's the issue of serving the martini over ice. That is opposed by those who shun diluting the mixture. They might allow the drink to be mixed using ice to chill the ingredients before pouring it into a glass, minus the ice. There are those who see no need for a twist of lemon. There's another group who are fussy about the size and/or the quantity of olives. Finally there are those who prefer a dash of the olive juice be added." Andy demonstrated his straight forward method. He preferred mixing rather than shaking. Otherwise there was no measuring, easy on the Vermouth, no less than two olives, and a twist of lemon if he had one around and with ice.

When it was mixed, Sam asked for a taste. She scrunched up her face after swallowing it. "Yuck, how can you stand to drink such a horrid thing?"

Andy smiled. "That is precisely how I reacted the first time I tasted one." He told her. "I gradually developed a taste for them."

Her only question was, "Why?" She started up the stairs, then stopped. "That was really nice of you to make space for my car, Andy. It's never been in a garage before. I almost couldn't get it started this morning."

Andy had already decided to ask Brian pick up a new battery for Sam's car. He didn't think he should dare to drive anywhere yet. Brian and he could install it on Friday, the day after Thanksgiving. He had a second thought. 'Sam's pretty independent. Let her do it. I'll act as a consultant'. Andy set his drink down on the table next to his chair, opened the door to the stove and stirred the hot coals. He fetched a couple of split logs from the rack and, one at a time, placing them in the stove. Suddenly there were two sharp popping sounds outside. Cassidy sprang to his feet and began growling viciously at the door. The hair on his back stood up. Andy knew instantly that something was wrong, and moved quickly to his chair. He fumbled for his gun. His fingers found it. He was pulling it from between the chair's arm and the cushion when the front door crashed open. A man took three steps into the living room holding a pistol in his right hand. Andy recognized him. The man aimed the pistol at Andy and was about to pull the trigger when Cassidy, who had been standing half way to the door rushed forward and leapt at the man sinking his teeth into the man's left calf. The man swung the pistol down to shoot Cassidy. Sam was standing at the top of the stairs. "NO!" she screamed "NO!" Andy raised his pistol and fired at the man. The man's gun went off an instant after Andy fired. Sam started down the stairs. She lost her footing in her stocking feet and fell tumbling down the last several stairs. Because the man had twisted to his left to try to shoot Cassidy, Andy's shot grazed the back of his right shoulder. The man was panting. He raised his eyes to look at Andy. He was bent slightly forward. He turned as if in slow motion to face Andy. He seemed oblivious to Cassidy or Sam or anything else. He was entirely focused on Andy. He raised his gun aiming it straight at Andy. His mouth was open. He seemed consumed with rage and almost frothing at the mouth. Andy fired again. The bullet struck the man in the center of his neck just above the sternum. The impact of the bullet drove him backward and, at the same time it straightened him. His arms splayed out and the gun fired wildly. The bullet hit the corner of a painting that hung on the east wall. He toppled backward a distance of two feet or more from where he had been standing. He was still holding his weapon as he hit the floor flatly. Cassidy lay on the floor. He was struggling to get his feet under him. The man still had an enraged expression. His breathing was deep. There was a bubbling sound, and then blood began pumping up from inside his chest and flowing out the gaping hole in his neck. Andy was standing ten feet from him. He quickly stepped toward the man and pointed the forty-five at the man's chest. Just as he pulled the trigger the man's eyes rolled back, his head lolled to one side. The impact of the forty-five bullet made the body jump as if hit with a jolt of electricity. His grip on the pistol loosened. Andy lowered his gun slightly. He glanced over at Cassidy. Cassidy was bleeding. He was panting. He looked at Andy almost pleadingly.

Andy kicked the gun free from the man's hand. He shot one more round into the lifeless body hitting it in the left side of the chest. He turned to Cassidy. Sam was already down on her knees at the dog's side. Andy dropped to his knees. Blood was oozing out of Cassidy's right flank. Andy located the wound. "Sam, get the bandana out of my left back pocket. An end of it was protruding. She pulled the bandana out. Andy took it from her, and pressed it firmly on the wound.

"Doc Bitner's number is on the refrigerator. Call him. Tell him Cassidy's been shot. Ask him if he can get here right away."

Sam ran to the refrigerator. She found the number. She placed the call and was just starting to tell him about Cassidy when Andy heard a sound from outside. He heard footsteps on the stairs, then on the deck. He groped for his pistol while looking at the door. Sam had her back to the living room. She was engrossed in her conversation with Doc. Andy got a hold of the gun just as another man came through the door. Andy raised his pistol. The man had a gun. His left hand was pressed to his chest. "Thank God," the man gasped. "You're alive." He gasped. The man was one of Clayton's security team.

Sam turned to see this second man holding a gun. It didn't matter that the gun was not aimed at Andy. She dropped the phone and grabbed one of Andy's butcher knives from a block on the counter. She started around the end of the counter, unable to gain much traction in her stocking feet. Andy saw her coming. He yelled, "NO, SAM! NO! IT'S OKAY!" Sam almost lost her balance trying to stop her momentum. "He's one of Clayton's men." She continued to hold the knife ready to attack. "He's been hurt, Sam." She slowly abandoned her fighting stance.

"The guy shot me," the man gasped. "In the chest." He gasped again. "Twice." He half stumbled to the body. The security man looked at the dead man, then at Andy. "I'm wearing," gasp, "a vest." gasp. "Broken ribs." He winced "Knocked the wind," gasp, "out of me." Sam suddenly remembered the phone. She turned and rushed back to it.

Doc was still on the line. "What the hell's going on over there?" He asked gruffly. Sam apologized and told him that someone else had just come in. She was afraid that it was another attacker causing her to drop the phone. "Christ, I thought it was something I said." Sam was in no mood for humor. "I'll be right over." Click.

When Sam returned to the living room, she saw that the door was standing open. It was getting cold in the house. She went to close it. She gave the body a wide berth when she returned to where Cassidy lay. She looked at the security man and saw that he was in terrible pain. She told Andy that Doc was on his way. She went to the Security man to lead him to the couch. "No," gasp, "over there," he motioned to the counter. "Can't sit. Need to stand." He reached into his shirt pocket and pulled out his cell phone. He handed it to Sam. "Call Clayton, First number."

Sam placed the call. Clayton answered. There was a moment of silence. Clayton was taken aback to hear her voice. "Clayton, this is Sam. One of your men has been shot." Her voice began to quaver. "Andy got the...," She started to cry. She was unable to fight back her tears. "The killer's dead," she sobbed.

She heard Clayton sigh. "We got the alarm. We were already on our way. We should arrive there in a few minutes. Is Adam alive?"

"Yes,"

"Is he hurt badly?" Andy motioned for Sam to come to him.

"Here, Clayton, talk to Andy." She handed the phone to Andy. She got back down on her knees and put her hand on the bandana compress that Andy was applying to Cassidy's flank.

"Clayton, it's over. It's the guy who shot me." Andy got up and began walking in a tight circle. "Your man has some broken ribs. His vest stopped the bullets. He got the wind knocked out of him. He's having trouble catching his breath." Clayton asked about Sam and him. "We're okay." Andy assured him. "Cassidy is wounded." Clayton asked how seriously. "I don't know. The vet's on his way. There doesn't seem to be any arterial bleeding." Clayton asked if Andy wanted him to call Brian. "I'll do it, not just yet. Call Peterson." They hung up. Andy went over to his chair. He set the gun on the table, and picked up his drink. He took some of the martini into his mouth. He held it for several moments before swallowing it. *Brian is right. This quality gin is much smoother and more flavorful. Think I'll buy a case of it.* He wondered if a better vermouth would enhance it even further.

Andy heard a vehicle pull up the driveway. He picked up his gun and went to the door. He flipped on the outside light and stepped outside. It was Doc Bitner. Doc had been responsible for bringing Andy and Cassidy together years before. The vet parked close to the porch steps. He went to the back of his truck and pulled out a large box. It looked heavy. Andy stuck his gun in the back of the waistband of his jeans and went to see if he could help Doc with anything. "How bad is it?" Doc asked. Andy didn't know. He told Doc the same thing he told Clayton, about there not being any sign of arterial bleeding. "It looks like the bullet went clean through the right flank." He stopped the vet before they climbed the stair. "Uh Doc, there's a dead guy in there. I'm pretty sure it's the guy that's killed all those people. He's the one who shot me."

Doc Bitner looked at Andy. "He shot Cassidy? I'm glad you killed the bastard." When they got inside, the vet stopped for a moment to look at the corpse. "Good work, McLeod. Remind me not to piss you off." Doc went to Cassidy. He had trouble getting down on his knees. He unlatched the top of his box. He got out his stethoscope. He touched Cassidy's head. "You're older than me in dog years, Cassidy." He applied the stethoscope to several places on Cassidy. He looked at Sam. "Who are you?" Sam introduced herself and added that she was rooming here. "Pleased to meet you, Sam, I'm Joe Bitner. Let me have a look at the wound." Sam took her hand away from the bandana. "I see you still carry your all-purpose snot rags around with you, McLeod." He slowly and gently lifted the bandana from the wound. "Yep, the bullet went clean through. It might have nicked the intestine. You're right, no arterial bleeding. Won't know how serious his insides are until I can scope and X-ray him. Don't think the bullet fragmented. That's good." He Looked at Sam. "There's a board just inside the back of my truck. It's got straps attached to it. Can you get it for me?" He reached in his coat pocket and pulled out a flashlight. Sam took it and left to get the animal stretcher. Another vehicle was coming up the driveway. When it got close enough she could see that it was a white Suburban. Clayton parked behind Doc Bitner's truck. He got out and two of his men got out. Another vehicle came up the driveway. It was Sheriff Peterson. He had one of his detectives with him.

Sam found the animal stretcher. Clayton and his men followed her into the house. She brought the stretcher to where Cassidy lay. She got down on the floor and helped to carefully slip it under Cassidy. Doc fastened straps around the dog. Then he closed up his case. Sam got to her feet and helped Doc get to his. Two of Clayton's men lifted the stretcher board and carried it out to Doc's truck. "You want to come along, Missy? I'll need some assistance when we get to the office."

Sam looked to Andy. "Go ahead, Sam. I'll be there in a while."

After she put her coat on she took the heavy box away from Doc and carried it out to his truck. The truck had a passenger cab behind the front seat. Doc had converted it to a spacious platform for carrying animal patients. Cassidy had been placed there. The vet had fashioned a means of easily securing the four corners of stretcher to the platform using shock cord. He checked to make sure Cassidy was ready for transport, then he and Sam got into the truck and departed.

Doc Bitner had a reputation for being a loquacious raconteur. He regaled Sam with some of his favorite Andy McLeod tales on the way to his clinic, and all the while he tended to Cassidy. Sam listened intently. Having met Andy only three days before, she was interested in learning about him, even if some of it bordered on legend and myth. She had already begun to form some opinions of her own about her enigmatic landlord. She had seen him at several extremes. There had been moments of fragility and weakness. There had been other moments of sensitivity and kindness. This evening she had seen a driven, determined man. He had shown no fear when faced with the devil-incarnate. He had not hesitated in shooting the man. He had made doubly sure that the man was dead. He had not shown anger. That didn't mean he hadn't felt angry. Maybe he just hadn't let it get in the way of what had to be done. She remembered her father's temper outbursts. She remembered how terrified she and her brother had felt as small children. She remembered waking up to the yelling and the sounds of things being thrown and broken. Her brother was a bed-wetter until his early teens, something she blamed on her father. This man was the complete opposite of him. Even though she had only just met Andy, she hoped that their relationship would continue and grow.

An ambulance arrived. Sheriff Peterson's detective was photographing the scene in the living room. Adam, the security man who had been shot, had his jacket, bullet proof vest, and shirt off. The whole left side of his chest area was already showing signs of serious bruising. The bullets were lodged in the vest. Clayton commented that, had they not been hollow points that mushroomed upon impact, Adam would probably be dead. He had detected an intruder approaching through the woods to the west of the studio/workshop. The person was moving swiftly. Adam had sent out an alarm signal, and then moved to try to intercept the intruder. He had just opened the sliding door of the studio and stepped out onto the deck when the man came around the corner of the garage. "He had to have known I was in there. He stepped out from the building and shot me before I could take aim. The impact of the bullets knocked me back inside. I really thought I was dead. It took two or three minutes for me to be able to draw in anything more than shallow breaths. I had all I could do to get enough air to be able to make it to the house. I was sure I was too late." He stopped. "I expected to find Andy and Sam dead. I focused on trying to take out the killer. I didn't want him to get away."

Sheriff Peterson asked the paramedics to tape Adam up while they were waiting to remove the body. His detective finished photographing the body. One of Clayton's men unbuttoned the dead man's shirt. He summoned Clayton over. Clayton stooped down. "Look at this, Andy." Sheriff Peterson came over to have a look, too. "Stark was wearing a vest."

Andy asked. "Is that his name?"

"Melvin Stark," Clayton told him. "The owner of *Fleur d' Amour* restaurant. The place where Darien Michaels and Alex Kane, and the little Hispanic guy you found, worked.

"Good shooting, Andy. Your bullet struck him just above the vest. If it had hit the vest instead it would probably have only knocked him down. My guess is that, after it went through his neck, it hit his spine. It probably splattered into a thousand fragments that tore him up inside. He died almost instantly."

"It wasn't a matter of good shooting," Andy said. "It was dumb luck. I missed him with my first shot. I was aiming for his face with my second shot."

Clayton lifted up Stark's right arm. "There's blood here." He rolled the corpse a little onto its left side. "Look here," He said. "You didn't miss your first shot." He showed Andy, the Sheriff and the detective where Stark had been grazed by the first bullet. "That may have stunned him just enough to let you get the second shot."

Clayton stood up. Andy asked him how they had discovered Stark's name. "You were here when your daughter-in-law Mike told us about Nurse Reye. We went to Reye's apartment after we left here. We found her in a coma. She attempted suicide by overdosing. Reye is the head nurse of the intensive care unit at the hospital you were first taken to. Stark must have had some doubts about whether he had actually killed you or not. We don't know how he ended up zeroing in on her. He managed to coerce her into giving him information about you. She must have confirmed that you were still alive. We're guessing that he forced her to keep him informed." Andy wanted to know what Clayton meant by 'forced her to'. "Exactly that, he threatened to kill her if she didn't do as he said." Clayton told Andy that Reye was in a very serious coma at this very moment. "We found a note she wrote to your daughter-in-law. She told Mike, in so many words, that she was a dead woman walking. She decided to punch her own ticket rather than wait for him to do it." Andy wanted to know if she was going to make it. "Don't know. It doesn't look very promising." Clayton then said. "Your daughter-in-law is feeling terribly guilty,

Andy. Apparently she befriended Reye while you were in the hospital here. She very innocently supplied Reye with information about you. I'm sure she had no idea that her trust was being violated." Clayton rubbed the back of his neck. "I'm not much of a believer in coincidence, Andy, but I don't think it was an accident that Mike was here during our discussion this morning. It suddenly dawned on her that she had innocently told Reye about you coming home on Saturday. We were certain something was about to come down when you found those two bodies upstairs in your barn this morning. To answer your question about how we found Stark's name, we found Reye's cell phone in her apartment. We were able to trace numerous calls made to her by him. She made none to him. It was a one-way street. He knew who she was. I doubt that she knew who he was."

Clayton looked at Sheriff Peterson then back to Andy. "I'm feeling pretty guilty myself, right now, Andy. I should have stationed at least three of my men here armed with automatic weapons. Stark got the drop on Adam. After that he had you and Sam in the palm of his hand, or so he thought. We had just discovered who he was at the same time he was launching his attack here. We probably would have caught up with him eventually, but only after the fact."

Sheriff Peterson hadn't said anything up till now. He cleared his throat before speaking. "Well, gentlemen, I don't know about you, but the longer I stick around, the more I'm coming to believe in destiny. I've been beating myself over the head about this guy being able to get away with all these killings for so long on my watch. All of a sudden everything fell into place today. I am glad he's dead. I'm incredibly relieved that he didn't kill you or Sam, or your dog, Andy. It could have gone the other way. Destiny, or dumb luck or whatever it is showed itself in favor of the good-guys this evening." He looked at his watch and turned to his detective. "Are you about done here, detective?" He was. "Let's hit the trail then. We'll write up our reports in the morning." Before leaving he said to Andy and Clayton, "Imagine the circus his trial would have ended up being. You saved the tax payers a bunch of money, Andy."

The paramedics had the body bagged. They wheeled it out

to the ambulance. Two of Clayton's men volunteered to clean up the living room. They rolled up the blood stained rug. It would be put it in storage for the time being. One of them found a plastic bucket and filled it with soapy water to clean up the spattered blood. Clayton asked to borrow a screw driver and some pliers. He used the tools to remove the bullet that had gone through Cassidy into the floor. He presented it to Andy. The other man cleaned up the broken glass from the picture that had been shot. Adam and Clayton went out to the studio to begin gathering up the surveillance equipment to be loaded into the Suburban. Andy decided to refresh his martini before calling Brian.

With drink in hand he stood at the end of the kitchen counter surveying the living room. He was uncertain about how he felt at this moment. There was a degree of relief that the ordeal was over. It occurred to him that something had happened that hadn't registered until now. He had recognized Stark as the man who had shot him months before. The encounter he'd had with Stark last summer lasted a very few seconds. Andy had come to accept that the memory of that moment was lost to eternity. He found it incredible that he had recognized the man tonight. This feeling of uncertainty hung on. *I should be feeling triumphant. I should be feeling grateful that we're alive. I should be feeling a sense of satisfaction that I was able to reap vengeance for what this bastard did to me.* His mind went back to an earlier time. He remembered having survived a shooting incident that had occurred at a place called Thorsen Point. He remembered how he and his friend Jan had been badly shaken by it. He remembered that they had just held one another. He wanted to hold somebody right now. He felt profoundly vulnerable standing there alone. He noticed the distorted bullet that Clayton had dug out of the floor lying next to him on the counter.

Before calling Brian, he thought about what he was going to say. He placed the call. Mike answered. "Hi, love. Is Brian there?"

Mike heard something in his tone. "Are you all right, Pops?"

"He's dead," Andy's voice started to waver and he suddenly felt like he was about to burst into tears.

"Oh, Pops," Mike said. She called Brian to the phone. He wanted to know what was happening. Andy asked him to come over.

"Sure, Pops, We'll be right there. Are you okay?"

"Uh, it might be better if you came by yourself." Things are kind of up-for-grabs here at the moment." There was silence. Andy felt compelled to offer a partial explanation. "Cassidy's been shot. I think he's going to be okay. He's up at Doc Bitner's clinic. Sam's with him. I need you to take me up there."

"What about you, Pops? Are you okay?"

"Yeah, I'm okay. It's nothing that three or four martinis won't cure."

"You're not okay."

"Just get here." Andy hung up.

Clayton's men were finished with the cleanup. They told Andy they were going to the studio to help Clayton and Adam load equipment. Andy thanked them for all that they had done. They were sorry that they hadn't been able to prevent Stark from coming so close to killing him. "You guys take care of yourselves and thanks again."

Brian drove up shortly after they left the house. Andy was adding wood to the stove when he came in. Brian had a worried expression. He looked around the living room, then at his father. "I smell cordite."

"I'm sure you do. Get yourself a beer." Andy flopped down in his chair.

Brian went to the refrigerator and got a beer. "So what happened?" He asked returning to the living room.

"The guy's name was Stark. Melvin Stark." Andy told him that Stark owned the restaurant that Darien had worked at. "He got past the security guy who was on duty in the studio by shooting him in the chest. The guy's vest saved him but the impact knocked him on his ass and knocked the wind out of him. He's got some broken ribs. Stark came running in here and Cassidy nailed him right off. If it hadn't been for Cassidy I wouldn't have had time to respond. I shot him. I caught him right in the throat." Andy pointed to his own throat. "I tell you, Brian, nothing beats a forty-five for stopping power. It knocked him back and down. It was all over in seconds." Brian wanted to know how Cassidy had gotten shot. Andy explained it to him.

"I can't believe it, Pops. He must have had it all planned out. He obviously knew about the security, and who was where. How about Sam? Where was she while this was all going on? You're lucky to be alive, Pops. Where's the body? How long ago did all of this happen? Where was Clayton? I mean, the place is all cleaned up. I assume the cops were here. Clayton's packing up, and you're on you're what, second or third martini?"

"One and-a-half." Andy lifted his glass.

There was a knock on the door. Clayton came in. "We're set to go, Andy. We're leaving the micro cameras. No point in trying to climb all over the place in the dark to remove them. No one will ever notice them anyhow. We're out of here."

Both Andy and Brian got up and went over to him. "Thanks for everything, Clayton." Andy said. They shook hands.

"You want to know what I'm the most sorry about?" Clayton asked. "I wanted to be the one to snuff that guy's candle."

"Next time, Clayton. I promise to save the next one for you."

"Let's hope there never is a next time, Andy. You take care of yourself." Clayton shook hands with Brian. "Look after this man, Brian. He's getting too old for this kind of stuff."

"Come on, let's go to Doc's. He ought to be about done patching Cassidy up by now." They put their coats on. "I hope that old dog can come home with me tonight. God, I missed him when I was in the hospital."

They talked on the way to the clinic. Andy answered all of Brian's questions. When they got to the clinic, Doc Bitner and Sam were sitting in his office chatting. "I was just telling Sam about how you came to have Cassidy," he said as he led the way back to the recovery area. Cassidy was lying down when they entered the room. His tail started wagging. Doc opened the door to the stainless steel cage. Andy got down on one knee to pet him. "Cassidy was lucky. No sign of internal injury. The bullet went right straight through him. It's probably stuck in your floor. What's amazing is that it scratched his intestine, but it didn't penetrate the intestinal wall. I've started him on an antibiotic as a precaution against infection. He can go home with you. I want to see him again on Friday, that is unless something doesn't seem right. I don't think I missed anything, but you never know." Andy asked what he owed. "Don't worry about it, McLeod. We'll settle up later."

Andy insisted on riding in the back of Brian's jeep to be with Cassidy on the way home. When they got to Andy's house, Brian let them out. "I'm heading on home. Mike's probably frantic by now. I'll fill her in on what all happened."

In the house Cassidy went over to his water bowl and began lapping. Sam looked around. She noticed the missing rug. She was surprised to see the place restored to such order. She asked if Andy was hungry for anything. "How about we just have some cheese and crackers?" She said that she would get them. He retrieved his drink from the counter adding a bit more gin and a single ice cube to it. "Tomorrow is Wednesday," Andy said reminding himself of what day it was. "You're going to be home early tomorrow?" Sam said that she would be. "Good, let's take a walk before it gets dark. We haven't been able to do that for a couple of days." Sam said nothing. Andy was leaning against the counter. She was slicing cheese. Her back was to him. "Sam?" He said. She turned to face him. "I'm really sorry that you had to see that." He gestured toward the living room.

She bit her upper lip. She set the knife down. Tears welled up in her big dark eyes. She clenched her fists. "Andy, I almost got all of us killed." She squeezed her eyes shut. "I acted so stupidly."

Andy was caught off guard by her sudden display of self-recrimination. "How did you act stupidly?"

"I stood up there at the top of the stairs and just screamed at him."

"What do you think you should have done?"

"I should have thrown something at him."

"Like what? What did you have to throw?"

"I should have found something, anything."

"Sam, there wasn't time for that. Everything happened in an instant."

She fumed unable to let go of her frustration. "Then, when I finally started down the stairs, I fell. When I landed at the bottom of the stairs, I heard shots. The first thing I saw was

Cassidy." She stopped there.

"What else did you see, Sam?"

"I saw that man falling backwards."

"What else?"

"I saw you go up to him and kick his gun away." Andy continued to look at her. "I saw you shoot him again." She shook her head and wrapped her arms around herself. She sobbed, "oh, Andy, I've never seen a person die before." She shook her head again. "That's not what I mean. What I mean is, I've never seen someone killed. Andy set his drink down and went over to her and put his arms around her. She buried her face in his chest and cried. He rubbed her back. Her sobbing gradually subsided.

"Guess what?" he said.

"What?" she asked.

"I'm all out of bandanas. I used my last one on Cassidy." Sam tried to laugh through her congested tears. She turned away from him and got herself a paper towel to blow her nose. Andy reached for his drink. He held it and looked at it before taking a sip. He picked an olive out of it and handed it to Sam. "There's nothing like an olive that's been soaked in gin. Try it." She looked at the olive with uncertainly. She ate it reluctantly.

He asked her what she thought of it. She shrugged, "I'm not a big fan of olives."

He chuckled. It felt good knowing that he still could. He asked her how she was, realizing immediately that the question needed clarification, "I mean, did you hurt yourself when you fell down the stairs?"

"My shoulder, my right glut and my ego are bruised. Otherwise, I'm okay."

He didn't know what to say to her. They stood in awkward silence. Andy wanted to tell her how glad he was to have her in his life and to resume holding her. He finished his drink and rinsed his glass out. "Come on, Cassidy let's take you out before we hit the sack." He glanced up at Sam, "Sleep tight, Sammy. See you in the morning." He patted her shoulder. She nodded. Andy thought he detected a slight expression of disappointment.

Chapter 19

Andy put on his coat and went out with Cassidy. There was a light snow falling and the thermometer read eighteen degrees. When he came back in he added wood to the stove. He noticed that the shotgun that had been propped next to the wood rack was missing. Sam must have taken it upstairs with her.

In his bedroom Andy was afraid of lifting the wounded, bandaged Cassidy onto the bed. Using a laundry basket turned upside-down and a throw rug on top, he provided Cassidy with a step to get up onto the bed by himself.

Before getting into bed, Andy made sure the doors were locked and that his pistol was nearby on the night stand. He still felt an uneasy need for vigilance. Everyone seemed convinced that Stark was the killer including himself, but he still felt apprehensive. What if Stark had an accomplice?

His neck and shoulders were tight. He hadn't realized until now how much tension he was carrying. After several minutes he got back up and went to the kitchen to take a muscle relaxant.

When he climbed into bed, he reached over to touch Cassidy. The dog usually curled up toward the bottom right side of the bed. Tonight he was stretched out next to Andy on his left side. He was facing toward Andy with his head just shy of the pillow.

Andy was almost asleep when he heard a light tap on his bedroom door. "Andy, are you still awake?" He said that he was. Because he was clad only in a t-shirt and jockey shorts he was reluctant about going to the door. Sam asked if she could come in. She opened the bedroom door. "Andy, I can't sleep. I don't want to be alone. Is it all right if I get into bed with you?" He surprised himself by agreeing to allow her to join him.

"Uh, Cassidy is stretched out next to me. Can you help me slide him over to make more room?"

After Cassidy was repositioned, she slipped into bed positioning herself with her back up to him. "Andy, I want you to hold me." He put his arm over her and she took a hold of his hand. After a few moments, she asked him to put his leg over her, too. Her hair smelled good. She kissed his hand. "I don't think either of us should be alone tonight." He agreed entirely. After several minutes she said, "I'm too warm with my robe on." She got out of bed, took the thick robe off and got back into bed, this time facing him.

"Andy? There's something I want to say. It's not about tonight. Well, maybe some of it is. I want you to know that I am glad to be here, and to be with you." She rubbed his shoulder. "I know from talking with Brian that you don't believe in destiny. I'm not sure I do either, but things have happened that I can't explain any other way. Like my getting this teaching job and my coming here to live. As for the two of us; I knew the minute we met a few days ago that we had something special. I don't know what it is. I just know it feels good." She scooted up to touch his face and she kissed his cheek. She whispered, "Good night." She rolled over and they resumed their previous position.

"Sam?"

She squeezed his hand. "Andy, you don't have to say anything. Just hold me."

When they got up the next morning, a light dusting of fluffy snow had fallen. It was ten degrees outside. Andy again went out with Cassidy. Sam went upstairs to shower and get dressed. When he came back in, he turned on public radio, fed the stove, and began making coffee. Sam came down the stairs. She squatted to snuggle Cassidy as part of a morning ritual they had established now that Andy was home. She picked up his food bowl and measured out his dog food. She added one of the antibiotic pills Doc Bitner had given them. Cassidy ate slowly and ended up leaving a third of the food. He drank some water, and then went over to lie down near the stove. Sam asked if Cassidy was okay.

Andy was occupied with scrambling eggs. He looked over at the dog. "I'll keep an eye on him today. He's probably in pain. I gave him a pain pill before taking him out." He asked how she was feeling this morning.

"Not as bad as I thought I would." She touched her back side. "I won't be sitting much today." She came over and snuggled up to his back. She thanked him for last night. "I want to believe that it's over, Andy, but a part of me doesn't trust that it is." He understood. She asked him why that was.

"I don't really know, Sam, but for whatever it's worth, I'm feeling the same way. A little paranoia isn't necessarily a bad thing."

They ate breakfast at the counter. Sam asked. "You said last night that you recognized Stark as the man who shot you. How sure are you?"

"I've come a long way from where I was, but I still don't trust my brain completely. I was astounded that I recognized Stark last night, but I didn't realize it until afterward. It must have been the shock of being eye-to-eye with him again. I'm absolutely certain that he was the guy who shot me last summer."

After breakfast Sam went back upstairs to brush her teeth. Andy took a broom and went outside to sweep the snow off the deck and the steps. It caused him some pain, but he was determined to not give into it. A few snowflakes were still drifting down. When Sam came out of the house, she came over to give him a quick hug. "See you this afternoon." She opened the garage door. After several tries she was finally able to get her car to start. Andy was sure she needed a new battery. He would call Brian to ask him to pick one up for her.

Andy and Cassidy went to the studio. After turning the space heater up he went back out to finish clearing snow. It wasn't until later in the morning that Andy discovered one of Clayton's business cards on his work bench. There was a brief note on the back of it. "Good job, Andy. Sorry I wasn't there when you needed me. Best regards, Clayton." Andy taped it to one of the storage cabinet doors. "Christ, Cassidy, I'm beginning to think that you and me are the only two who aren't feeling guilty about yesterday." He got a treat for Cassidy. Andy looked around the shop. There were no signs that it had served as a command center.

He called Brian's school. Elaine recognized his voice and the two of them chatted briefly. She told him that Brian had called a brief faculty meeting this morning and told everybody the "real" story about what happened to you. She said that everyone understood why Brian had needed to present a different version. She told him how glad everyone was that you are alive and that the killer had been caught.

Hm, he thought. That's an interesting way of putting it. Brian must have avoided telling people that his father killed the son-of-a-bitch. It's probably just as well. Elaine put Andy through to Brian.

"Hi, Pops, how are you doing this morning?"

Andy told him that things were back to normal, whatever the hell that was. "I called to ask a favor. Sam's car battery is on its last leg. Would you pick up a new one for her? We can install it on Friday. I'll pay you back then." Brian said he would. He asked how Cassidy was doing. "We're here in the studio. He's doing okay. He's experiencing some pain. You know, Brian, I'm really looking forward to this Thanksgiving. I feel like one of the luckiest people on the planet. I haven't felt this grateful in years."

"We feel the exact same way, Pops. We came close to losing three of the nicest people there are yesterday."

"Thanks, Brian. Thanks for including, Cassidy. I almost never think of him as being a dog anymore."

After hanging up, Andy called Mike. She started to cry as soon as she heard his voice. "Oh, Pops, I'm so sorry about what happened. I feel like most of it is my fault. That monster never would have come after you if it weren't for me."

He interrupted her. "Mike, listen to me. That monster knew I was alive. I don't know how he found out, but he did. He was going to come after me sooner or later. I don't blame either you or that nurse. He was one clever, sick, son-of-a-bitch. It's over with. The good guys won. Stop beating yourself up about it."

"It's just that the three of you came so close to being killed." Mike couldn't stop crying.

"That's true. It was a very close call. I ended up having to change my underwear after it was over." Mike gave a stifled little laugh. "Come on, Mike, let go of it. I just got off the phone with Brian. One of the things I said to him was how much I'm looking forward to sharing Thanksgiving with you tomorrow. I love you dearly, Mike. I am so glad that we're in one another's lives."

"Thanks, Pops. I feel exactly the same." Then she added,

"Most of the time." They both laughed.

Andy called Sheriff Peterson next. "How are you this morning, Andy?"

"Glad to be able to have a conversation with you, Otis."

The Sheriff laughed. "Hardly anybody ever calls me that, Andy. As a kid everybody called me Pete. What can I do for you?"

"A couple of things. First off, how's that nurse doing."

"She's hanging in there. She's not out of the woods yet, but there's a better than fifty-fifty chance that she's going to make it. That's a damn sight better than they thought yesterday. I'm hoping we'll get a chance to interview her in the next few days. We'd like to be able to fill some of the gaps about how Stark found out you were alive, and how he manipulated her. Maybe she can shed some light on the subject." The Sheriff's voice took on a tone of secrecy. "Just between you and me, I'm sure hoping it doesn't turn out that Stark had an accomplice. My gut tells me that he was a lone wolf."

"I found myself thinking the same thing lying in bed last night. I had my gun next to me." Andy asked, "What if it proves to be that she or somebody else was in cahoots with Stark?"

"Good question, Andy. I haven't ever heard of case of a serial killer conspiring. They're not exactly what you'd call 'team-players'." Andy reminded him of Charles Manson. Peterson had forgotten about him. "If Stark had an accomplice, and I were that person, I'd vamoose. I'd get the hell out of here and never come back." Andy told him that he intended to remain vigilant. Peterson didn't discourage him from doing so. "Call me if anything seems suspicious, Andy." He asked, "What's the other thing you wanted? You said you had a couple of things."

Andy couldn't remember what the other thing was. "I'll call you back if it turns out to be anything important." He hung up. He was annoyed. He guessed that he had been hoping Peterson would be able to allay his lingering fears. He realized that he was expecting the impossible. He asked himself what he'd do if he were in Peterson's shoes. He decided to give Otis credit for at least leveling with him when confronted. Andy had started the day in a fairly good mood. He decided not to allow this anxiety to ruin it.

He and Cassidy went back up to the house. He went into his bedroom and got his pistol. If having it readily available would serve to reduce this sense of unease, then so be it. He called Brian a second time. Brian was unavailable, but called him back a few minutes later. "I have a second favor to ask. See if any of the gun dealers in town have a small gauge shotgun in stock. I want something like a 20 gauge or a 410. I don't want a single shot or a bolt action. I'd like either a pump action or a semi-auto. If you can find one, pick up a couple of boxes of ammo for it also." Brian wondered why his father wanted a gun like that. "I have a plethora of red squirrels running around the place. They're destructive little devils. I need to thin their ranks."

After hanging up he turned to Cassidy and said, "There, that feels better." He went into the kitchen, poured the remaining coffee and sat down at the counter. He tried to remember something else he had thought about doing earlier. It came to him when he saw a pair of Sam's shoes by the door. He wanted to add her to his Christmas list. For years Andy had made a special handcrafted item for each member of the family. He regarded her as family even though they had met less than five days ago. Until last night he had been entertaining fantasies about adopting her. Now he was confused. I'm her landlord, for Chrisake. For some reason he remembered a line from a song from the musical Les Miserables. 'I'm the master of the house, the keeper of the zoo'. He thought, Hell, she might move out at the end of the school year. Who says she'll even decide to stay up here in Door County. She's an intelligent, attractive, outgoing young woman.

He remembered that he hadn't gotten yesterday's mail. After draining his coffee cup, and washing it out, he put his coat on. A few feather-like flakes of snow drifted downward as he and Cassidy walked to the end of the driveway to fetch the mail. There were a couple of bills, four appeals for donations, three Christmas catalogs and the local newspaper. Back in the studio Andy perused the paper. There wouldn't be anything about yesterday's incident. He did wonder what would be reported in the Friday edition. Was the media even aware that a serial killer had been in their midst? Would he be identified as the person responsible for 'bringing down' the serial killer?

That thought brought on a wave of concern. If there was a co-conspirator out there, Andy would be thrown into the limelight, increasing the likelihood of being targeted. He picked up the phone and called Sheriff Peterson again.

He was put through to the Sheriff moments later. "Otis, McLeod here. I've been thinking about what you said, the possibility of Stark having an accomplice. How is what happened yesterday going to be handled by the media?"

"Interesting how things sometimes work, Andy," the Sheriff said. "Detective Kline came to me with what is turning out to be a brilliant theory. We picked up the manager of the *Fleur d'Amour* restaurant just a while ago. It turns out he has a place over on Rowleys Bay. He also owns an eighteen foot tri-hull power boat with an inboard-outboard engine. Detective Kline and the D.A. are having a discussion with him at this very moment. His name is Randall Sweet. Mr. Sweet has admitted that Stark had unlimited use of his boat throughout the summer. He doesn't know what Stark used the boat for. He says, and I quote, 'Poor Melvin is under such incredible stress running the restaurant during the summer months.' He let Stark use the boat a few times to get away from the rat-race and blow off some steam. Hell, who isn't stressed out during the summer around here? When we asked how often Stark borrowed the boat, he couldn't remember exactly. The D.A. is discussing the implications of aiding and abetting, as well as being an accessory to felony crimes. He's decided that he wants his attorney. The D.A. is offering the possibility of a plea bargain, but only if he gives us a straight and complete story. While we're waiting for his attorney, who is from Green Bay, we're exercising a search warrant of Sweet's place."

Andy heard a voice in the background. The Sheriff said he'd be there in a few minutes. "Sorry for the interruption, Andy. Let's see, where was I?" He remembered. "I'm pretty sure that Melvin and Randy were lovers. We haven't told Randy what happened to Stark yesterday. All we've said to him is that we're looking for him as a person of interest. We've told Randy that if we find out he's been withholding important information, he's going to find himself in serious trouble. I can't tell, what, if anything, Randy knows about Stark's activities. The good news is that we may have a possible accomplice in custody." Peterson promised to let Andy know what came of this most recent turn of events. To Andy, this all seemed too easy. As much as he wanted to, he wasn't ready to let his guard down.

He spent the rest of the morning in his studio trying to come up with one or two quick-release, vice-type of devices that would serve to take the place of his almost useless left hand. They had to hold things tightly enough that he could work on them. They also had to allow him to be able to change the positions of the objects easily. His occupational therapist had given him some good suggestions. The problem for him now was being able to construct the things he needed without having the use of both hands. Maybe he could enlist Sam or Mike to help him.

He was absorbed in thought when he heard a car come up the driveway. Cassidy got to his feet. Andy quickly went to his work bench and pulled the forty-five out of his coat pocket. Whoever it was, parked in front of the garage. Andy only had two ways of being able to determine who was there. He had to either go outside and go to the front of the garage, or open one of the garage doors from inside. Either way he was vulnerable to attack if the visitor was unfriendly. His only other alternative was to wait to see who came through the garage service door, or the east side sliding door. He took a position where he could see both entrances and still have some cover. He was greatly relieved when he saw Doc Bitner approaching the side door. He quickly hid the gun under his coat.

Andy opened the sliding door and invited Doc in. After stomping the snow off his boots Doc entered. "I was in the neighborhood and thought I might as well drop by to see how Cassidy is doing today." Cassidy approached and sniffed Doc before allowing Doc to pet him. Doc got down on one knee and Cassidy obliged him by laying down and turning on his left side to allow Doc to examine him. He carefully lifted the bandaging from the wound talking to Cassidy. "You're a good old puppy, Cassidy. I wish more people were half as smart as you." With the bandages off Doc took a close look at the wound area. "It doesn't look like there's any infection. It usually happens within the first twelve to twenty-four hours. Keep him on the antibiotics though. I gave you enough to last seven days."

Andy asked if Doc would like some coffee. He glanced up at him. "When you get to be my age, you learn to go easy on coffee. Otherwise, by late morning it doesn't pay to zip my pants back up." Doc patted Cassidy's head. He reached into his coat pocket and drew out a tube of antibiotic ointment. He applied some to the wound. Then he pulled out some gauze pads and tape. He re-bandaged Cassidy's side. Andy helped Doc get back up to his feet.

"How old are you now, Doc?" he asked.

"I'm twenty-five, but I've had a hard life." He looked around Andy's work shop. "I'll be eighty come March. Millie's wanted me to retire for the last fifteen years. There are days when I think I should, but I like what I'm doing. I'm not one of those of guys who enjoys fishing or golf. I'm not good at makin' things. The one thing I do enjoy, and have gotten pretty good at, is playin' the saw. Have you ever seen a saw played before?" Andy confessed that he hadn't. He thought Doc was up to some shenanigans. Doc said he'd be right back. He went out to his truck and came back with a carpenter's saw, and a violin bow. After rosining the bow, he set the handle of the saw on one of the stools. He sat on the handle. The saw produced an almost eerie melodic sound by his flexing the blade and drawing the bow back and forth across back-side of it. He proceeded to play a couple of familiar folk tunes.

"God, Doc, that's just beautiful," Andy told him.

"Here, you try it." Doc got up and had Andy take the seat. "I'll work the bow, you flex the blade." Doc showed him the technique of flexing the blade, and before long Andy was able to manipulate the blade to produce a somewhat recognizable melody. "It's all by ear, McLeod. It takes practice to get the feel for it. You've got the idea, though." Doc asked if Andy had a carpenter's saw. He did. He showed Doc three saws that he never used anymore. "Perfect," Doc said. He asked if Andy had any use of his left hand. Andy showed Doc how he could hold things by moving the fingers of his left hand into place with the right hand. Doc laid the bow down on the stool. Andy was able to pick it up using the method he'd just demonstrated. "Wonderful," Doc said. "I've got an old bow I don't use any more. I'll give it to you when you come by the clinic on Friday.

You'll need to get you some rosin. You can get that at the music store in Sturgeon Bay." Doc looked at his watch. "I promised Millie I'd be home for lunch. I better get going. See you and Cassidy on Friday."

Andy went to the phone to call Brian for the third time. "Brian, I need for you to stop by the music store and get me some rosin. You know, the kind of stuff that's used on violin bows."

"I'm not even going to ask what you need that for, Pops. Can you think of anything else. School's out in twenty minutes. I'll be leaving shortly after."

"Nope, that should about do it for today."

Andy decided to go up to the house to feed the stove. He thought about Doc. "That old fox came by here as much to check on me as he did you, Cassidy." As he and Cassidy strode to the house he noticed that the clouds were becoming thinner. There were some faint patches of blue and vague shadows. He guessed that there would be a visible sunset by late afternoon. His spirits were improving.

Chapter 20

Sam arrived home shortly before 1:00. Andy had held off heating up some soup for the two of them until she arrived. When she came in the house, she apologized for being a little late in getting home. "I've got something for the house, Andy. I need your help to bring it in." He followed her out to her car. She opened the trunk to reveal a large opaque plastic bag. She lifted it into a position where Andy could get a hold of the puckered top of the bag. Sam took the bottom of it. It was fairly heavy. When they got the bag in the house, they put it down on the floor of the living room near the door. She borrowed his pocket knife to cut the twine that held the bag closed. She wrestled the bag off the contents revealing a folded rug.

As she began to spread it out, Andy could see it had an abstract design done in vivid crimsons, blues and dark green. "Wow, Sam, this is stunning. It's a work of art." She was smiling, pleased that Andy liked it so much. "It's magnificent, Sam. Where did you find this?"

"I went to that department/furniture store in downtown Sturgeon Bay. I just knew when I saw it, that this would be perfect in the living room, but I wasn't sure if you'd like it."

"It's beautiful."

"Here's the best part, Andy. It was on sale. I would have bought it even if it hadn't been. But I saved forty percent." Andy looked at Sam. She looked like a little girl who had just won a prize. "This is the first time I've ever purchased something brand new for a place I live in."

"The old rug was okay, but this makes a bold statement. I can't wait for Mike and Brian to see it. You have outstanding taste, Sam."

She moved the coffee table and pushed the couch back far enough to locate the rug in the center of the room. The new rug was a few inches longer and wider than the previous one. She repositioned the furniture, then stood and admired it. "I'm so glad you like it, Andy." Finally she said, "well, we can either go for a walk now, or we can wait until I get the pies made and put in the oven."

"Let's have a bowl of soup, and then you can make the pies. If we wait until later, I think we'll be able to catch a nice sunset." As they ate their soup, Andy told her about Doc Bitner's earlier visit and the concert that Doc had treated him to using a carpenter's saw. Andy commented about what a character Doc was.

She smiled. "Doc says the same thing about you, Andy." She set her spoon down and reached across the counter to take his hand. "Serendipity, Andy. Coming here has turned out to be the very best thing that has ever happened to me."

Andy wanted to tell her that he felt the same way about her being here. Instead, he said that he was glad that she felt that way. He almost added, *"although, I doubt that you were feeling that way last night." Why spoil this pleasant moment by bringing up that subject* .

It was a little after three o'clock when they went for their walk. Even though the snow was deep, it was light and easy to hike through. The sky had cleared. The sun was low in the sky and the light that filtered through the trees seemed to make them glow. Cassidy led the way. When they reached the meadow, Cassidy came to an abrupt halt looking toward the north corner of the open space. He barked and there was a sudden flash of white flags as four deer bounded off toward the forest beyond. "He used to chase after them," Andy told Sam. "He's gotten wiser in his old age." Andy told her how both Cassidy and Lucy had the habit of barking when he'd let them out at night. "Then they'd stop and listen for the hoof beats of the fleeing deer. Because of the bedrock, it sounded like a herd of fifty of them. "If dogs had hands, I'm sure both of them would have pounded their chests in triumph. It must make them feel pretty powerful."

Sam looked at Andy. "You're still missing Lucy, aren't you?" Andy admitted that he was. "Doc told me the story about how you lost her. He said that it broke his heart almost as much as it did yours. It made him angry enough that he wanted to find the bastards and shoot them himself."

"She was a precious dog." Andy looked at Cassidy. "Did

Doc also tell you the story about how Cassidy came to be with me?"

"He did. He also said that matching the two of you up with one another is one of the best memories he has of his entire veterinary career. He thinks that it saved both of you." Andy wondered what else Doc had told her about him.

It was almost dark when they finished their walk. The phone was ringing when they entered the house. It was Sheriff Peterson. "Andy, you got a few minutes?" He did. "Here's where things stand with Randall Sweet. Turns out he and Melvin have been lovers for the past six years. It's an almost classic story of escalating domestic abuse. When the relationship started out, Stark was verbally abusive. After purchasing the restaurant four years ago, things began to go to hell. Stark started playing around with staff and with some of the restaurant's customers. He began drinking heavily. Sweet was pretty sure that Stark also used a cornucopia of drugs. Sweet admits that he felt jilted, but he was afraid to confront Stark. The few times that he did, he says Stark went into rages and beat the hell out of him a couple of times. Sweet says he finally got to a point where he didn't think he could take anymore. He says he was afraid to try to end the relationship for fear that Stark would kill him. Tell me if this doesn't sound like a textbook example of a domestic abuse situation." The Sheriff paused. "It was only after Darien Michaels and Alex Kane were found murdered that he suspected Stark of being the serial killer."

Andy asked, "do you buy that part of his story?"

"Not entirely. I think he's trying to cover his own ass. I think he probably knew that Stark was behind the killings that took place prior to Michaels and Kane. I think he knows more than he's willing to admit, but I have no way of proving it. I do buy the part about him being afraid to leave Stark. A part of me was tempted to let him know that his fears are over, that Stark is dead. For now, I want him to think that his safety depends on his cooperation with us. I made it crystal clear to him and his lawyer that all bets are off if we find out that he assisted Stark in any way."

"What did your people find at Sweet's place?"

"We found the boat. We found drug paraphernalia. We found a bunch of kinky sex toys. Damned if I know what most of them are used for. We didn't find anything that would suggest that Sweet was Stark's accomplice other than lending him a boat and letting Stark use his cottage. We did find three boxes of nine millimeter hollow points. The place is remote, Andy. A person would have to make a deliberate effort to see what was going on there. It's not very likely that neighbors witnessed anything. Almost all of the surrounding places are closed up for the winter. We interviewed the four people who live in the nearby area year around. They didn't know squat. You'd be surprised at how many little nooks and crannies there are like that throughout the county. But I digress."

"So where do things stand?" Andy was feeling a headache coming on.

"Nowhere, at the present. Sweet's lawyer says that unless we arrest his client and bring specific charges, there's nothing to discuss. That's why I don't want Sweet to know that Stark is dead. I told both Sweet and his attorney that as long as Stark was still at large, Sweet was running the risk that Stark might come after him. I told him he was on his own. If Stark shows up at his door, he'll have to call 911 and hope we can get there in time."

"I take it Sweet opted for leaving."

"He did. I wouldn't be at all surprised if he's is on his way out of the county as we speak. Even if he does decide to stick around, I don't see him as being any kind of threat to anyone. He's a classic victim."

"Are you sure about that, Otis?"

"Andy, the only threat he poses is in his selection of partners. My biggest fear about him is that he'll stick around and attract another Melvin Stark or someone even worse. People like him are working their way down the ladder. The only thing that surprises me is that Stark didn't kill him. There is no record of Sweet ever having called 911. That means that either he's feeding us a line about Stark abusing him, or he thrives on having his ass kicked."

"Or he was too terrified to try to do anything about his situation."

"I suppose," Peterson conceded. Andy asked if Audrey Reye was showing any more signs of improvement. "I'm told that she's still comatose but that she's breathing on her own and that her vital signs are improving."

Andy thanked the Sheriff for calling. As soon as he hung up the phone he went on a quest for his jar of Tiger Balm. While he had been on the phone with Peterson, Sam had taken the pies out of the oven. She was in the process of cleaning up the kitchen.

"Are you okay, Andy?" she asked. He told her that he was getting one of his headaches. He finally found the Tiger Balm in a drawer in his night stand. He applied it to his temples. He sat down and eased his recliner all the way back. A few minutes later Sam came into the living room. She went to the stove and shoveled out a buildup of ashes into the ash bucket. She added wood. "Are you warm enough, Andy?" She went to check the room temperature reporting that it was sixty-five degrees. She got a decorative quilt from the back of the couch and draped it over him. He thanked her. "I worry about you," she told him. "These headaches don't seem to be getting any better."

"They are, but not very quickly." He was asleep in minutes.

Brian called. Sam told him that Andy was taking a nap. He sounded surprised and concerned. "He must be in pain." She told him that Andy had another one of his headaches. "I think I'll see if I can schedule an appointment to talk with the neurologist next week when I take Pops back to the hospital." He went on to tell her, "Pops asked me to pick up some things for him today. I put them on the work bench in his studio. You guys must have been out for a walk when I stopped by."

Sam fed Cassidy. She locked the doors and checked the outside thermometer. It was falling. After a brief debate with herself, Sam decided to go to her room. She went to the wood rack and picked up the shotgun to take with her. In her room she propped the gun in the corner next to the door and left it ajar. She took her shoes off, slipped under the comforter and lay there mulling over the events of the previous night. She was still feeling uneasy thinking that this must be what it is like to be paranoid. She considered calling Brian. *And say what, that you think the boogie man is lurking outside the front door?*

She eventually drifted off to sleep only to experience a vivid dream. A pack of wolves had Andy, Cassidy and herself surrounded in the woods. It was winter. There was deep snow.

The wolves kept circling the three of them. Andy gave her his pocket knife. He pointed to one of the wolves telling her that it was the alpha male. "I'm going to grab him, and try to get him down. Try to stab him in the heart. If we can kill him, the others will flee." In the dream Andy lunged at the wolf. The whole pack began attacking trying to get him off the alpha. Sam threw herself into the mêlée only to drop the knife in the snow. She was on her knees in the snow. The wolves were attacking all of them. She woke up. In the dream she had been screaming "No!" over and over again. She was breathing hard and sweating. She didn't know if she had actually been screaming, or if it was just a part of the dream.

Sam got out of bed and went to the top of the stairs looking down to see Andy still asleep in his chair. She went into her bathroom to wash her hands and face before quietly making her way down the stairs. It was after ten according to the clock on the living room wall. She went to the refrigerator, poured a glass of milk and picked out a few slices of cheese left over from the night before. She crept over to the stove and quietly started to add more wood. Just as she closed the stove door, Andy awoke. His right hand shot down to his side feeling for his pistol. Then he realized it was Sam. His gun wasn't in the chair anyway. He remembered that he had left it in his coat pocket.

Sam apologized for startling him awake. She asked if his headache was gone. He told her that it was. She asked if Andy wanted anything to eat. He didn't know. He looked at the clock before getting up from his chair. He ruled out having a martini afraid that it might trigger another headache. He went to the refrigerator and got a beer. She helped him put his sweater on. He went to the coat rack to retrieve his gun from his coat pocket noticing that the deadbolt was locked. Returning to his chair he also noticed that the shotgun was not propped next to the wood rack. He looked at Sam who had been watching him. "I took it upstairs with me," she said matter-of-factly.

He smiled at her knowingly. "It would appear that we're both still pretty spooked." He told her about both of his conversations with Sheriff Peterson today. She asked him if he thought this Randy Sweet posed a threat. "I don't know, Sam. Peterson doesn't seem to think so."

"So what are we supposed to do, just sit here and wait to see what happens?"

"Look, Sam, there is no one who dislikes inaction more than me. For the moment I don't see any opportunity to become proactive. Peterson hasn't told Sweet that Stark is dead. He's holding his feet to the fire. The nurse that Mike confided in is still in a coma. I don't see any other options besides waiting. I'm not willing to go into hiding." He took a swig of his beer and sat forward. "Look, Sam, you didn't ask for any of this. If you would feel more comfortable being somewhere else, I understand completely. I'll even help you out by paying half of your living expenses."

"Andy, I don't want to live anywhere else. I love it here. Yes, I'm scared." To illustrate just how scared she was, she told him about her dream.

When she finished describing the dream Andy shook his head, "wow, it wouldn't take Sigmund Freud to interpret that one. No hidden symbolic meanings." He got up from his chair and started for the door. She asked where he was going. Cassidy and I are going out to pee. She told him that Brian had called earlier to say that he had left some things for him in the workshop. Andy asked her help to put his coat on. Before opening the door he said, "you know what? I've got a taste for some popcorn."

"Sure, I'll make some," she said.

When Andy and Cassidy returned, he had a long slender carton and a bag. "Damn, it is really cold out there. I've only seen it this cold this early in the year once before." Sam was still in the kitchen waiting for the corn to finish popping. He set the carton and the bag on the counter. "This is an early Christmas present, Sam." The carton lid was taped. She broke the tape with a paring knife and lifted the lid to see a shotgun. "It's a 410," Andy told her. "It's a smaller gauge than that 12 gauge cannon of mine. He lifted the gun out of the carton. This is a pump action. You have to pull the fore-stock back and then forward to eject the spent shell and chamber a live one." He demonstrated before handing it to her. She agreed that it was much lighter and easier for her to handle.

"You didn't need to do this, Andy. I can get along with the other one."

"I know," he said. "I didn't get it strictly for self-defense. It's still rabbit season. We could go out hunting. I told Brian I wanted it for shooting red squirrels. They are destructive little rodents. We can both use it for shooting them as well."

Sam smiled at him, "you're such a romantic. I was hoping I'd get a shotgun for Christmas. You really know how to win a girl's heart."

For one of the first times in his life, Andrew McLeod had no comeback. He almost blushed. With Cassidy happily ensconced next to Sam on the couch, the two of them ate pop-corn, drank beer and talked until one in the morning.

Chapter 21

Andy slept until the unprecedented time of 7:15 on this Thanksgiving morning. The house was cold. Neither he nor Sam had gotten up to feed the stove. Andy put on his ancient terry cloth robe and went to the living room. The outside temperature showed eight degrees. He let Cassidy out, then turned the thermostat up. The backup furnace clicked on. There were so few live embers left in the stove he decided to clean out all of the ashes and start from scratch. Sam came down the stairs. After greeting one another, she commented on how cold the house was. She was wearing her pajamas and thick robe. She went to the coat rack, put on her coat, checked the outside thermometer, let Cassidy back in and went into the kitchen to make coffee. Her new 410 shotgun lay in the carton on the counter. Sam greeted Cassidy by stooping down and snuggling him. She told him what a good fellow he was. Cassidy rewarded her by giving her cheek two licks, and then sat to wait for her to put food in his bowl.

Somewhere in the process of going through the morning routine, Andy became aware of something he hadn't noticed before. During the course of the past few days, he and Sam had divided up the tasks of daily living between one another. They had done this without speaking a word about who was in charge of doing what. *There are things that I simply can't do. She does those without being asked. There are things that I am perfectly capable of doing, but she's decided to do those things herself.* He wondered what this whole thing was all about. He suggested making scrambled eggs for breakfast. With this new awareness, he watched what happened. She got out the eggs and broke them into a bowl while he got out the skillet and started heating it. He got out the bread and stuck a couple of slices into the toaster, while she added some milk and scrambled the eggs. He got out a jar salsa and the bacon bits suggesting that she add them to the eggs.

When they sat down at the counter to eat, Sam took the same stool she always did, the one closest to the end that allowed her easy access to the kitchen in case they needed anything else. Andy wondered if Sam and her brother had operated this way. Quite aside he asked her, "when is your birthday?"

"In two weeks," she told him. "I was born on December seventh, the day of infamy. I've spent my whole life trying to avoid the curse of that day."

"There's another way to look at it," Andy said taking a sip of coffee. She wanted to know what that was. "It was the day that the struggle to defeat evil began."

"You know Andy, for a guy who claims to be a cynic, you sure can come up with some Pollyanna beauties at times." He asked her how old she was going to be. "Twenty-nine," she told him. "When is yours?"

"George Bernard Shaw's birthday, July 27th,"

"You're kidding me." She started laughing. "Honest to God?" She touched his arm. "That's perfect. That's rich." She patted his shoulder. "I might have known." She swallowed a piece of toast the wrong way and began coughing. When she was able to get enough control, she went to the sink to drink some water. "That explains all sorts of things, McLeod. I should have guessed that. You and Shaw could be twins and you are a perfect example of a Leo. She recited some of the typical traits of his astrological sign."

After breakfast Andy cleaned up the kitchen while Sam went to shower. They went out to the meadow mid-morning so that Sam could practice using her new shotgun. She liked this one much better. Andy suggested they walk back along a trail that wove through the forest of conifers he had planted years before. "We might spot a red squirrel or two."

The day was sunny. The temperature had risen into the low thirties. In a short time, Andy heard the scolding chatter of a red squirrel. He spotted it and pointed to where it was. They moved closer. The squirrel scurried to the other side of the tree. In a low voice Andy said, "you stay here. I'll go over there." He pointed. "The little devil will think I'm after him and he'll come around to your side of the tree. You can pop him when he does." The squirrel did as Andy had predicted. Sam took aim and shot. The squirrel dropped to the ground. It twitched a few times before it went still. Andy pulled out his pocket knife and cut the squirrel's tail off. He handed it to her asking if she had remembered to put the safety back on.

"Oops, sorry, I forgot." She switched it on and looked at Andy like she was expecting a scolding. Instead, he complimented her on her shooting ability. As they continued on toward the house, she asked what to do if she were hunting by herself. "I mean, I assume all squirrels do that. They go to the opposite side of the tree so you can't see them."

He told her they often did that, but not always. "You can try to wait them out. If you stay still long enough, curiosity usually gets the best of them. Sometimes you can walk up to the tree and try circling it. Sometimes they'll go out on a limb. They're acrobats. They can travel easily from tree to tree and make their escape that way. You have to shoot quickly before they take off."

"It sounds like it's all but impossible to get them once they're on the move."

He told her that was true. "When that happens, it wasn't the squirrel's time."

She looked at him askance. "You don't believe that. As far as I can tell, the word 'destiny' isn't even in your vocabulary." He agreed that it wasn't, but he thought, as excuses go, it sounded good.

Chapter 22

The three of them arrived at Brian and Mike's house mid-afternoon. Brian and the boys were unloading firewood from the back of Mike's pickup. They had already stacked four truckloads on the concrete patio outside the back door. After greeting Mike, Andy went out "to supervise the men folk." Cassidy accompanied him. Despite their age difference, Mike and Sam enjoyed one another's company. They had become like sisters and dear friends.

Andy wanted to help out with the unloading but found that he could only manage one log at a time because of his crippled left hand. When the very back of the truck bed was clear of wood, he got up into the bed and tossed wood back to the others. Brian didn't attempt to discourage his father from helping out. The man's sense of dignity depended on his being useful. He watched his father feeling a sense of respect. This man had done more than survive a major trauma. He had also conquered the insane predator who had inflicted these severe injuries on him. Most of all, his father was determined to recover as much of what he had lost as possible.

When they finished stacking that load, Brian declared that was enough for one day. "A couple more loads should do it. We can finish up moving wood on Saturday or Sunday." Dan asked if he and Shawn could take their dad's twenty-two rifle to target shoot. They had a place back in the woods where they could shoot safely. Brian told them they could, but they were limited to using one box of cartridges each. The boys went in the house to get the gun.

Andy had tallied up the receipts from the things Brian had gotten for him yesterday. He handed Brian a check for a bit more than the total. Brian didn't even look at the check. He stuck it in his vest pocket. "Pops, what do you think of the idea of going up to Washington Island tomorrow? I'd like for you to meet Al Swenson and his son Jason. Al called me yesterday to tell me they've finished repairing your boat. They're going to store it for the winter."

Andy considered the question. Brian had told him about the damage done to the boat. He had also explained the theories about how Andy must have forced himself to do several things to keep the boat from sinking. Andy remembered none of those events. "Yeah, I'd like that. If we don't do it pretty soon, we won't be able to see it until next spring."

"Pops, I get the feeling that you're not sure about wanting anything more to do with the boat, or with sailing." Andy asked why he thought that. "You haven't asked about the boat, not once. I've kept you informed about what's been going on with it. You just haven't shown much concern or interest."

Andy responded a bit defensively, "Well, I've had a lot more important things to concern myself with."

"Its okay, Pops. I understand. I'm merely making an observation, that's all."

"I know, Brian. I'm sorry. Let's do it. Maybe Sam might like to accompany us. I'm sure she's never seen the Island." They heard some shots. Brian said he was going to go check on the boys. Andy decided to tag along. They started for the woods. "You're right, Brian. I do feel less enthusiastic about sailing. I'm not sure I'm going to be able to handle the boat single-handedly anymore. Maybe it's kind of like falling off a horse. If you don't get back on it, you get stuck with the fear. I admit to being scared. I'm not sure I want to get back on the horse again or not."

They had just entered the woods when Cassidy gave a bark. They saw Shawn running in their direction. Both Brian and Andy reacted with alarm. "Dad," Shawn called out. "A wounded deer, there's a wounded deer. Dan is trying to follow it."

Brian told Shawn to go the house. "Ask your mom for a bunch of paper towels. See if you can find some rope. Not string, rope. There's a hunting knife in the glove compartment of my jeep. Bring all that stuff back. Cassidy will go with you. Call him." Shawn started toward the house. He called to Cassidy. Andy motioned for Cassidy to follow Shawn which he did.

Brian and Andy began walking swiftly. "I don't know about you, Pops, but I almost hit the panic button. I was terrified that something terrible had just happened." Andy agreed. When they got to the opening where the boys had been shooting, no one was there. Brian called to Dan. There was no response. Andy was already searching for clues about which way Dan had gone. Brian began looking, too. Brian called out, "over here, Pops." He'd found Dan's footprints in the snow and the scattered trail of blood from the deer. Brian kept calling Dan's name every so often. When Andy finally caught up with Brian, he was somewhat winded. "Best thing," working to catch his breath, "for Dan to do." He took a couple of deep breaths. "Sit down." Two more deep breaths; "Let the deer bleed out." The two men moved further into the woods. Brian continued calling Dan's name. At one point Brian stopped and asked how was Shawn going to find them. "Cassidy will lead him."

A few minutes later, they heard Dan call back to them. "Over here, Dad. I'm over here." The trail of blood had gradually diminished. There were occasional droplets. They were in the midst of a dense cedar swamp. They were less than twenty feet from Dan before they actually saw him. Dan was not moving. "The deer is over here. I think it's still alive. Should I shoot it?"

Andy told him to wait. When they reached Dan, Andy stooped down holding his right hand close to the deer's nostrils. It was a medium size doe. "It's barely alive." Andy touched his hand to the deer's chest. "Shoot her right here, Dan." The boy took reluctant aim and shot the deer. Seconds later its eyes grew dim and glassy. The boy bit his upper lip. Andy looked at his grandson, then back at the deer. He pointed to a bullet hole in the deer's lower midsection. "She was gut shot. If you hadn't found her the coyotes would have feasted on her tonight." There was no sign of Cassidy and Shawn yet. Brian helped Andy to his feet. "You need to field gut her," Andy said looking straight at Dan. "Are you up to giving it a try?" Dan nodded. Brian took the rifle. Andy opened his pocket knife. "The knife is sharp, Dan. You need to cut her open from her brisket to her crotch. Dan looked uncertain.

Brian stooped down and showed his son where to start. "You don't need to make a deep cut, Dan. You just want to cut through her skin in order to open up the intestinal cavity."

Dan started, and then stopped. "I don't know if I can do this, Dad."

Brian studied his son for a moment. "I felt the same way the first time I shot a deer, Danny. Grand Pops probably did, too. It's a part of the taking of a creature's life. In a sense, it's a way of honoring the animal. You're keeping your end of the bargain. You didn't kill it just for the sake of killing." Dan returned to the task. Shawn arrived on the scene led by Cassidy just as Dan finished making the long incision. Brian and Andy walked Dan through the process of removing the deer's entrails. When it came time to clean out the heart and lungs, Andy explained about how the thoracic cavity was divided from the abdominal cavity. Dan would need to cut through the diaphragm to gain access to the heart and lungs. Andy told him to take off his jacket and roll up his shirt sleeve. Dan gritted his teeth and forced himself to do it.

When the task was completed Dan stood up. "Whoa, dude, gross. Look at you," Shawn said. "Your whole arm is covered with blood."

"That's why I told you to bring plenty of paper towels," Brian said.

"Oh shit, I knew I forgot something." Shawn said. All four of them contributed their bandanas to Dan's cleanup. Brian used the rope to tie the deer's back legs together. He tied a large loop in the rope. The boys then began dragging the carcass toward home.

It was close to sunset when they reached the house. Andy had them load the deer into the bed of his pickup. "I'll hang her up in my barn for two or three days, to let the meat cool down and the rigor dissipate. Maybe we can butcher her on Sunday."

A part of the conversation at the Thanksgiving table was taken up by Dan's experience of finding, tracking and field dressing the deer. Andy and Sam were sitting next to one another at the table. Two or three times during the course of the meal, Sam touched his shoulder and gave him a squeeze.

Whenever Sam spoke, Andy looked at her attentively. Mike noticed it and smiled. They avoided any mention of Melvin Stark. Shawn was aware that Cassidy had been shot two nights ago. After dinner he got down on the floor and lay next to Cassidy. He petted Cassidy's head and neck and talked to him.

He knew second hand that Cassidy had probably saved his Grand Pop's and Sam's life. He told Cassidy what a hero he was. Sam joined him on the floor. "It's true, Shawn. Cassidy really did save our lives. I'll tell you all about it someday, but not today. I'm not ready to talk about it yet."

"Sam?" Shawn hesitated. "You really like Grand Pops, don't you?"

"I do. He's a very special man."

Chapter 23

On their way north to catch the ferry to Washington Island Andy, Brian and Cassidy stopped at Doc Bitner's clinic. Doc was pleased with how Cassidy's wound was healing and he redressed it. They went on to Northport to board the ferry. Sam and Mike had plans to go shopping together. Both of the boys had basketball practice at school. The day was cloudy with strong winds out of the northwest. It made for a rough ride across the waters of Death's Door. At the marina, Brian introduced Andy to Al and Jason Swenson. Jason greeted Cassidy as Wonder Dog. The boat was still in their spacious workshop. The Swensons showed Andy pictures of the boat prior to the repairs. Al gave Andy a theoretical explanation of how they thought he had somehow been able to save himself and the boat that fateful day. Al explained that the wind had shifted by noon causing the boat to change course. "You were heading further out into the lake. Because the holes were on the portside, they were submerged and taking on a lot of water. By turning the boat to a northwesterly course it listed to the starboard side slowing, maybe even stopping the leakage. If you hadn't managed to do that, the boat probably would have sunk in another few hours."

In the workshop, Al showed Andy where the bullet holes had been. It was impossible to tell now because of the expert workmanship in repairing the hull. They all climbed a ladder to look at the boat's interior. It was completely restored. Andy thought it looked better than it had before. He was very pleased with the work they had done. Back in Al's office, Al produced a large brown envelope. "I don't know if you want to see these or not, Andy. They're photos taken of the cockpit area, and the cabin's interior the next day. They're pretty gross." Andy asked to see them. Al pulled them from the envelope. "You lost a lot of blood. I mean a lot of blood. Much more and you would have died for sure." The pictures were indeed gross. Brian hadn't seen them either.

"God," Brian exclaimed. "What an unbelievable mess."

Andy said, "I was out of it. I don't remember a thing that happened that day except for the guy pulling up close to my portside. I don't remember him shooting me or anything that happened after that."

Al smiled at him. "Well, you apparently had a couple of beers sometime after it happened. You still had your priorities, badly wounded as you were."

Al told Andy that all of the costs of repair had been paid by the insurance company except for the five-hundred dollar deductible. "I tacked three hundred dollars onto the estimate I submitted to your insurance company, for winter storage." Andy had his checkbook with him and he paid Al the deductible. "We're all square, Andy. Let me know when you want us to launch the boat come spring. We'll have it ready for you." Al thought of one other thing. "Jason went over your engine. We had trouble starting it. He ended up replacing the fuel filter. He pulled the carburetor and blew it out. It's running good now. That one's on us." He extended his hand. "Welcome home, Andy."

The ride back on the ferry was much smoother with the wind to their back. When Brian dropped his father off at his house Andy thanked him. "I appreciate all that you've done for me over the past few months, Brian. You've done a tremendous job." Andy smiled. "I'll be sure to remember you in my will." He pointed a finger at Brian. "A little comic relief."

"Very little," Brian chuckled. He put his father's truck back in the garage, got in his jeep and honked on his way out the driveway. As Andy and Cassidy mounted the stairs to the deck, Andy thought about Brian's reaction to the pictures they had been shown. He had been visibly shaken. Andy thought about how he would have reacted if this had happened to Brian. He doubted that he could survive losing him, too.

He was feeling out of sorts. Seeing those photographs this morning had been upsetting. Andy had long ago come to accept that there were evil people in the world. Stark represented the sadistic extreme. For the past three months, he had tried to make sense of what had happened to him. It defied reason. It had been a senseless random act. Even if there were answers to people like Stark, he doubted it could change anything. There would always be conscienceless, feelingless people like him. They were unsalvageable. They either had to be locked away for good or destroyed.

Sam wasn't home yet. He was about to go out to the barn to check on the deer the boys had found yesterday when the phone rang. It was Sheriff Peterson. "Andy, I thought you'd want to know. That nurse, Audrey Reye has regained consciousness. Detective Kline and I were able to talk to her briefly. You'd have thought we had handed her the winning lottery ticket when we told her Stark was dead. I think the woman was desperate. She was terrified of the man. She outright admitted that she'd gotten to the point where suicide seemed like her only option. She's feeling guilty as hell about having used Mike to point Stark in your direction. She's never heard of anyone by the name of Randy Sweet. She had no idea that Stark was gay. My gut tells me that she's giving us a straight story. It's also telling me that Sweet may have known more than he's willing to admit to but he wasn't complicit. I don't see him as being capable of harming anyone. He's preoccupied with getting his own masochistic needs met." There was a momentary pause. "Andy, it's going to take a while for you to stop looking over your shoulder. I know I'd feel that way if I were in your shoes. For what it's worth, I really think the ordeal is over. Only time will tell for sure. I'm just telling you how I feel."

Andy thanked the Sheriff for everything. "Otis? Brian and I went up to the island to see my boat today. They've done an outstanding job of putting it back together. While we were there Al showed me photos that were taken of the cockpit and the cabin. They were extremely grim. If I've had any doubts about how close I came to buying the farm before, I don't anymore. I'm glad that it was me who killed Stark. I feel like I have relieved the world of a monster."

"I feel the same way, Andy. I was afraid to say anything. I wasn't sure how you were handling what happened. It sounds to me like you've come down on the right side of the fence."

Andy and Cassidy went to the barn. After checking the deer carcass, they went to the studio. Andy had no sooner turned the thermostat up on the space heater when the phone rang again. It was Doc Bitner. He told Doc that he was about to try his hand at playing the saw. Doc gave him two or three tips on getting started. "My real reason for calling, Andy, is about a young female border collie. A lady brought the dog in late this morning. It looks to me like she was abandoned. No collar, looking bedraggled, practically starved to death. Sometimes people just toss critters out on some country road. The dog's pretty submissive. She may have been mistreated, but some dogs are just that way. I've checked her over. She seems healthy enough, considering." There was a brief lapse. "Oh, and I forgot to mention. She's been spayed. And did I mention she's a border collie."

"I believe you did," Andy said, "and I know what you're up to, Doc. I've been thinking lately that Cassidy is getting up there. I'm sure not up to starting from scratch with a puppy. How old do you figure this dog is?"

"Two years, maybe a little younger." Doc cleared his throat. "If you're not interested, Andy, I'll take her to the Humane Society shelter." He cleared his throat again. "Of course, you know what will probably happen to her if I do that." Andy shook his head smiling. "There's one caveat. There's the possibility that the dog may have run away, or maybe gotten lost. That happens occasionally, usually during the summer season. People traveling with their pet sometimes drive off without the creature. Fifty miles down the road it occurs to them that Fido is missing. Sounds pretty stupid I know, but it happens. What I'm saying is the owners may show up wanting their dog back. It's a remote possibility, but a possibility nonetheless. If you decide to give her a try, it may be a while before you can know for sure that she's yours to keep."

Andy asked how late Doc would be at the Clinic. Doc told him he'd be there until 5:00, later if something came up. "Sam's not here right now, Doc. I'm not up to driving just yet. If she comes in pretty soon, we'll take a run up to see the dog."

Sam came in twenty minutes later. She parked close to the side door of the house. She had groceries and parcels. Andy and Cassidy went to greet her. While Andy helped her unload he told her about Doc Bitner's call. Sam listened without comment. Once they had everything in the house she said, "Let me put the stuff that needs to be refrigerated away before we go over to the clinic." Andy asked her what she thought about the idea of another dog. Sam looked at Cassidy. She leaned down to pet him. "I don't know, Andy. I'm wondering how Cassidy is going to feel. I mean, is he going to feel like this new dog is his replacement. He's an old dog. God, he's ancient. You wouldn't know that to see him running around out there." She got to her knees and put her face next to Cassidy's. Finally she sat back and looked up at Andy. "This isn't my decision. It's yours."

"It's a shared decision, Sam. I value your input. I've thought the same thing about Cassidy. I had already decided that, if I were to ever get another dog, it wouldn't be until after he was gone. You're right. Cassidy is ancient by all standards." He paused to gather his thoughts. "If the two of us decide to give this dog a try, Cassidy's response to her will be crucial. If he doesn't seem able to handle having her around, that's it." Andy stuck his hands in his jeans pockets. "There's another consideration that we have to take into account. I go in for surgery on my face next week. I'll be in the hospital for a week, maybe longer. That means you'll be stuck with caring for two dogs by yourself. The timing isn't good." Andy turned toward the phone. "I think I'll call Doc and tell him that we can't take her."

Sam got to her feet. "Come on, Andy. Let's go take a look at her before we make any decision. We'll bring Cassidy with us, and see how he reacts to her on neutral ground."

On the way to the clinic, they talked about Sam's shopping adventure with Mike that morning. They also talked about the wounded deer that the boys had found yesterday. "Mike said that Dan was really excited about field dressing it all alone. He called his friend Steve Nelson to tell him all about it. She said he was on the phone for over half an hour. He gave Steve a complete blow-by-blow description of the process. Apparently, Steve's father doesn't think his son is ready to learn how to do that kind of thing yet. Mike thinks Steve's dad tends to be a bit overprotective."

Andy's response was, "somewhere early on, I realized that I was making a big mistake as a father. I needed to encourage my sons to do for themselves, not do it for them. The only way any of us grows is by trying ourselves at new things. It's the key to confidence building. Danny was reluctant and pretty squeamish about gutting that deer yesterday. When he finished doing it, he stood up and discovered he'd grown another foot." He looked at Sam, "I suspect that explains a lot about why you are the way you are." Sam asked him what he meant by that. "I mean you're a gutsy lady. You learned early in life that if you didn't do for yourself, you did without."

Sam looked straight at him. "What I learned was that if I didn't do for all of us, we all suffered. I think that's asking too much from any kid. There's a big difference between encouraging and expecting. What was expected of my brother and me cost both of us. I vowed that if I ever had kids of my own, I'd make damn good and sure they'd have their childhood."

Andy apologized. "You're right, Sam. You and your brother paid a terrible price. I didn't mean to sound like I thought it was a good thing."

Doc Bitner was sitting in his office reading the newspaper when they arrived at the clinic. He had his feet up on his desk and his shoes untied. His assistant escorted Sam, Andy and Cassidy to the office. Doc closed the paper. "Friday after Thanksgiving. Everybody and their uncles are out Christmas shopping today. Ask me what sense that makes." He removed his feet from his desk, but didn't bother to retie his shoes. "It's good to see you Sam, and you, too, Cassidy. Who's this you dragged in with you?" Doc tilted his head back to look at Andy through the reading glasses perched on the end of his nose. "Oh, it's you, McLeod." Doc was playing his part in the ongoing repartee that the two of them had engaged in for years.

"We just dropped by to give you another lesson in tying your shoes, Doc."

Doc led the way back to the kennel area with its stainless steel cages. There was a large cat in one of the upper cages. The border collie was in one of the bottom cages. She stood barely wagging her tail. She was smaller than Cassidy. She was black and white and looked to be a pure bred. Cassidy went over to the cage and sniffed. She raised her nose to his and reciprocated. "What a pretty face," Sam remarked. Doc agreed. He unlatched the cage door and opened it. He had to coax her out. The first thing she did was to lie on her back with her hind legs splayed.

"Remember, I told you she was submissive," Doc said.

Cassidy sniffed her. Then she got up and sniffed Cassidy's bandaged area. After that, he turned his head to hers. She sniffed his face and licked his nose a couple of times. Finally Cassidy backed up a few inches and sat down looking at her. She got to her feet and moved closer to him. She sat down in front of him and gave him two more quick licks.

Sam nudged Andy. She spoke in close to a whisper. "She's beautiful, Andy. Look at those almost sultry eyes. I think Cassidy is smitten with her."

Andy smiled, "I think you are, too." He turned to Doc. "Can we take her home now, or do we need to wait a day or so?"

"You can take her now. I'd keep her on a leash for the next few days when you go for walks. Tether her when you let her out on her own. It'll take her a while to get oriented and to hopefully accept your place as her new home. If she's a runner, she'll take off the first chance she gets. You may never see her again. Somehow, I don't figure her for that. She seems to have taken to Cassidy already. It looks like he's taken to her as well." As they were leaving, Doc said, "I hope this works out for all of our sakes. Nothing gives me greater pleasure than to see a waif like this find a good home." Andy offered to pay Doc for his services. Doc refused. "Get good on that saw, McLeod so's we can jam together." Andy told him he'd be gone for a while to have surgery on his face. Doc looked at him. "I don't know, McLeod. Personally I think you look better this way than you did before."

In the car Sam said, "you and Doc love one another, but neither of you will ever admit it." Andy told her that both of her statements were true.

He looked at his watch. "Let's stop at the hardware store. I need to get a few things for our girl. Like a collar, leash, bowl and a tether line. I never needed to tie Cassidy up. He always stuck around."

Sam asked him about a name for her. "I'll leave that up to you, Sam."

Sam frowned in concentration. "I don't know. That's a tough assignment. Do I have to come up with something right now?"

Andy smiled. "'Hey-you', will do for now."

By the time they arrived home it was time for their late afternoon walk. The sky was clearing to the west. There was a wide band of orange appearing from underneath a dark blue/gray tarp of clouds. The past two days had been warm enough that a lot of the snow had melted. There were large patches of open grass in the meadow. Cassidy stayed closer than usual as they walked. The female was constantly looking back as if to make sure she wasn't doing anything wrong and that they were still there. At no point did she strain at the retractable leash. Finally Andy reeled her in. He petted her and spoke to her gently, "it's okay, beautiful. You're safe here. This is your new home. We love you. Welcome home." He unfastened the leash despite Sam's misgivings. They continued the walk. She remained close by. After a while she began to relax a bit. The two times she stopped to take care of business, she acted like she was embarrassed to be seen. She modestly sought the privacy of some standing weeds. She never let Cassidy out of her sight. If she lost even momentary track of him, she stopped, her ears perked up and she scanned until she spotted him. For his part, Cassidy managed to conduct his usual olfactory surveillance. All the same he kept track of her, too. In that half hour walk, a pattern became established. The only thing about it that ever changed was Cassidy. He eventually resumed the wider circumference of his daily rounds. The two dogs were devoted to one another. Andy found himself with an entirely different concern. What would she do without Cassidy when his time came?

Chapter 24

Brian arrived at his father's house early Tuesday morning to take him to Milwaukee. Andy was scheduled for surgery on his forehead the next morning. Sam accompanied him out to Brian's jeep. She tried hard not to display her emotions. When Andy opened the door of Brian's jeep, she embraced him seeming not to want to let go. He finally patted her back. "See you in a few days, Sam. If all goes well, I'll return looking like a handsome prince."

She told him that she was going to miss him. Then out of nowhere she said. "Maude, I want to name her Maude."

It took a moment for Andy to realize that Maude was the name she had chosen for the dog. "I like that, Sam. It's an old fashioned, dignified name. It fits her. She'll be known as Maude from now on."

She took him completely off guard when she said. "I love you, Andy."

He wasn't sure how she meant it. He loved her, too. He wasn't sure how or in what way. He said nothing. He kissed her on the cheek and got into the jeep. He winked at her and, in his best Bogart impersonation, he said, "here's lookin' at you kid." He immediately realized that she probably didn't even know who Bogart was, plus it was a dumb thing to say. "Take care, Sam. I'll see you in a week or so." That wasn't much better. He couldn't say what he really felt.

Neither Brian nor Andy said much for the first few miles. Brian skirted the topic of Sam's display of affection. Instead he asked how the new dog was working out. *Maude,* Andy thought. *I wonder where she came up with that name.* "She's working out well. I was afraid that Cassidy was going to see her as his replacement. Instead he's more or less adopted her. He kind of watches over her. She seems to be basking in his attention."

Brian had an amused expression. Andy asked him what that was about. "Oh, I was just thinking."

"Thinking about what?" Andy had a pretty good idea about what.

"I was thinking about you and Sam." Andy asked him what he meant by that. "Come on, Pops. You and Sam are fond of one another. It probably happened within the first fifteen minutes after you met. It's kind of like Maude and Cassidy, Sam needs what you have to offer her. You encourage her and admire and respect her. You've become a good friend. You may not like my saying this, Pops, but you need her in your life. You've been alone for too long. She enjoys helping you. From what she's told me about her past, she was thrust into the role of caregiver at an early age. For a long time her sense of self-worth was based on how well she managed that role. What's nice about her relationship with you is that she's appreciated. She can give freely. She isn't expected to wait on you, and you don't take her for granted." Brian reached over and touched his father's arm. "Pops, as far as Mike and I are concerned, we see the two of you in a win-win situation. We couldn't be happier."

"Christ, Brian, it almost sounds like you see us as a couple. I'm damn near old enough to be her grandfather."

Brian thought about his comment. "Mike and I have noticed changes in both of you since you've come home, Pops. Both of us like what we see. Mike is very fond of Sam. She regards Sam as an exceptionable woman. I do too. She is one of the most creative teachers I've ever met." Brian laughed, "Have I ever told you the story about Sam's employment interview." The next several miles were devoted to Brian's accounting of how Sam came to teach at his school and some of her creative methods in the classroom. He started with a prologue story about Darien Michaels. "You should have seen her when she showed up for the interview, Pops. We almost dismissed her based on her appearance." Brian described her plethora of adornments: the nose studs, the various ring piercings in her eyebrows, and God knows where else, the ear clips, the uncountable number of rings on her fingers, her 'funky attire'. Andy asked why they had gone ahead and hired her.

"Well, aside from the fact that we were in desperate need of a replacement for Darien, her transcripts were outstanding. She seemed mature and confident. Her student teaching advisor and university supervisor gave her rave reviews. There was something about her that Gayle and I liked. Sam realized that we were turned off by her appearance. She addressed that concern on her way out the door. It was beautiful. It re-taught me a valuable lesson. He told his father what she had said. Andy had a satisfied smile. "It has proven to be one of the best decisions I've ever made."

"That's a really good story."

At the hospital Brian stayed with his father through the admitting procedure. After Andy was situated in his room he insisted that Brian leave in order to avoid the rush hour traffic. "I'll be just fine. Get going. I've already spotted a couple of nurses I want to start chasing." They hugged one another and Brian left.

Andy was wheeled into surgery at six o'clock the next morning to undergo extensive facial surgery. The procedure took close to five hours. By mid-afternoon, he was back in his room with his forehead heavily bandaged, and still groggy from the anesthetics. He dozed off and on over the next few hours. He barely touched the evening meal. At seven there was a knock on his door. To his surprise and delight the visitor was none other than Clayton McMurray. "Hey, man, nice disguise." Clayton leaned down. "It is you, McLeod, isn't it?"

"It's me, Clayton. How the hell are you?"

"I've been keeping track of you, Andy. So far you've managed not to get yourself into any more trouble. I'm proud of you, man." Clayton asked if it would be all right for him to sit on the bed. Andy gestured for him to do so. "Actually, I'm hoping that you'll wait until summer to get yourself into some new kind of trouble. I understand that Door County is the place to be in the summer."

They talked for an hour about the aftermath of the Stark shooting. "Probably the hardest emotional part for me happened last Friday," Andy told him. "Brian and I went up to Washington Island to see my boat. The owner of the marina showed me photographs taken of the boat after it was towed in. What a mess. It was like looking at the mangled wreckage of car accident, and wondering how the hell anybody could have walked away alive. It is a miracle that I survived, Clayton."

"I hear you, man," Clayton replied. "It probably also

served to erase whatever guilt you were hanging on to. That monster absolutely needed to be greased. As much as I had wanted to be the one to do it, I was pleased that it was you. It rarely happens that the victim gets to exact a righteous revenge." When it came time for Clayton to leave, he said, "our paths will cross again, McLeod. I'm positive. You take care of yourself."

By eight o'clock Andy was beginning to experience some serious pain from the surgery. To make matters worse, a headache was developing. He couldn't resort to using his old standby of Tiger Balm because of the bandaging. He asked for pain relievers and they helped to reduce the surgical pain. They barely touched the headache. By ten o'clock, he was not sure he could endure much more. He was about to ring for a nurse when a woman appeared. He'd never seen her before. The room was dimly lit. She asked him some questions about the pain. He thought he detected a British accent. She had him lean forward. She began massaging the muscles in the back of his neck and shoulders. "You're very tense," she told him. She moved from his neck to the mastoid area behind his ears applying pressure to both sides using her index fingers. "Tell me when you feel a sensitive ache." He already was and told her so. "Good," she said. She applied pressure to that area for a brief while. Then she moved up to the back of his skull and applied pressure again. She worked her way up to the top. Whenever she found a similar sensitive area she applied pressure to that area. He was beginning to experience a gradual relief. She found one more such area in the center of his skull. In a matter of minutes his head was pain free. She told him what she had just done and that by applying pressure to those sensitive areas he could treat himself. He asked how he could find the right areas. "Do what I just did. Feel around for them." He showed her his left hand and told her that he couldn't use both hands as she had done. "That's okay. You can use two or three fingers of your right hand." She demonstrated.

She wanted to look at his left hand again. She asked him to try to move his fingers. He could only move his thumb. She applied pressure to three different areas on his wrist. He still couldn't move the other fingers. She moved to an area on his upper forearm just below the elbow. She applied pressure and his fingers closed. She released the pressure and the fingers opened. "That's it," she said. She did it two more times. The same thing happened. "This can be corrected. There's a procedure that can help restore the use of your fingers. The muscles are atrophied and it will take time to regain strength in them. You won't achieve one-hundred percent use of the hand. If it's only fifty percent, that's a lot more than you have now. I'll give you the name of a doctor that can help. She asked if Andy was a veteran. He said the he was. She told him that he was probably eligible to get financial help through the VA."

She asked how his head was feeling. He reported that the headache was completely gone. "Try to get some sleep," she told him. She touched his arm. "Welcome home." He was asleep within minutes.

It was daylight when he was awakened by an energetic young nurse sporting a pony tail. She chattered incessantly while checking his vitals and entering the data into a computer. She checked her watch. "Breakfast will be here in just a few minutes. I'll bet you're hungry. It says here that you barely ate anything last evening." Andy asked who the older nurse was that had been on duty last night. She looked at him quizzically. "What older nurse? What do you mean by older?" Andy tried to describe the person who had visited him. "I'm sorry, Mr. McLeod. I came on at midnight. There were three of us on duty. None of us matches that description. You must have been dreaming. Sometimes anesthetics affect people that way." She recited a litany of examples of unusual patient reactions to anesthetics. Andy noticed a piece of paper on the bedside table. He picked it up to see the name, address, and phone number of a Doctor Eldridge Lawrence. He interrupted the nurse's ceaseless babbling to ask where this had come from. She looked at it. She scrunched her face up. "Who's Doctor Eldridge Lawrence?" She said, "I've never heard of a doctor by that name. He's not on our staff." She looked at his address. That's way up on the far north side of the city." She handed the piece of paper back to him.

He puzzled over last night's lady visitor through his breakfast. The plastic surgeon, Dr. Merkle who had performed the surgery came in to check on him at 7:30. After examining Andy he gave some instructions to one of the nurses. He asked Andy if he had any questions. "Yeah, one," Andy said. He handed the surgeon the piece of paper asking if he knew who Doctor Eldrige Lawrence was. He did not. Merkle asked what kind of doctor he was. Andy didn't know.

Brian called late in the morning. They talked for a brief while. Andy asked if Brian knew how to get a hold of Clayton McMurray. He didn't. "I've got Clayton's business card taped to one of the cabinets in my studio. I'd appreciate your getting me his number. It's not an emergency. I just have a favor to ask of him." When he wasn't napping, Andy spent part of the day manipulating the spot on his forearm that triggered his fingers to open and close. *This is not something that came to me in a dream.* He was certain of that. Neither were the pressure techniques that rid him of the terrible headache. He wondered if that same nurse, if that was what she was, would visit him again tonight. He almost wanted another headache to occur so that he could put her method to the test again. *She's not a figment of my imagination.*

The next time a nurse came in to check on him, he asked if she would bring him a Milwaukee phone directory. She offered to look up the number for him. Andy was not about to part with that piece of paper. He gave her Doctor Lawrence's name and address. Half an hour later she returned. He asked her what kind of doctor Lawrence was. "All the directory shows is the name, address and phone number. I'll see if I can find out anything more for you." She returned ten minutes later. "I called the number you gave me and spoke with Dr. Lawrence's receptionist. He's a neurologist specializing in sports medicine and kinesiology." She commented, "he has to have spent half of his adult life doing residencies to have those creds." She added, "I've never heard of him. I'd like to meet him."

Andy felt better knowing that there was an actual Doctor Eldridge Lawrence. It made sense that a man with Lawrence's medical training would know something about injuries like his. *What about that lady? What was she doing here last night?* He wondered if she was from another unit and just happened into his room. That seemed far-fetched and unlikely. Another idea popped up. *What if she's not a nurse at all, or, at least, not a nurse on staff here? What if she's another patient? The light was dim. I was dopey from pain meds. I just assumed that she was a nurse. She was-*

n't dressed in hospital scrubs. He thought about how she was dressed. She was wearing a blouse and slacks.

When another nurse came in just before the evening meal, Andy asked her if a female nurse was a patient on this unit. "Not to my knowledge," she told him. She was curious to know why he wanted to know. He told her about being visited by an older woman last night and that this woman had offered him some suggestions to help relieve him of a terrible headache he was having. The nurse asked him to describe the woman. He did. The nurse smiled. "That sounds a lot like Delores," she told him. "Delores is one of the housekeeping staff. She's an interesting person. Her parents were missionaries in China. She grew up there. She's a single mom. Her husband was killed in the first Iraq war. What surprises me is that she hung around after her shift was over at 10:00. She always leaves right on time to get home for her daughter. She's a really nice lady. None of us can figure out why she's in housekeeping. She seems far too...," the nurse couldn't think of the word she wanted, "Refined?_ Sophisticated?_ Knowledgeable? I don't know. She just doesn't seem like your average unskilled person doing that kind of work. She's well spoken. She's got real class."

That sounded like her. Andy asked, "do you know if she's on duty tonight?"

The nurse didn't know. She said she'd check and get back to him. A few minutes later she poked her head in the door. Delores will be here the next three nights. She avoids working weekends so that she can be home with her daughter."

Andy thanked her. "If you run into her, would you ask her to drop by if she gets a chance?" The nurse said that she would.

He lay back pleased to have solved that mystery. Brian called to check on him. They had a brief conversation. Shortly after that, Sam called. They both seemed awkward with one another. Andy finally said. "Sam, I don't know why it is, but this is not the same. You and I can talk for hours when we're face to face. We can sit and not say much of anything and it feels comfortable. Right now we're acting like a couple of thirteen year olds at our first dance."

"I know," she said sounding relieved. "Andy, we have some things to talk about when you get home. I really miss you. Maude and Cassidy do, too." Andy asked her what sorts of things. She sighed. "Not here, not now, when we can talk face to face." He thought she was about to hang up. She went on, "Andy, I know there are lots of different kinds of love. I meant it when I told you I love you. I loved my brother. I love my sisters," adding, "most of the time." She went on, "I was never close to my dad. I was pretty young when he died. What little I remember of him is his temper and that we all felt scared when he was around. You know how I feel about my mother. It's different with you. I've never experienced these kind of feelings before. I've never been treated the way you treat me. I keep saying to myself, 'there's this big age difference'. I've decided that I don't really care about that. I AM like that thirteen year old you just described. I've never been this confused in my life." She blew her nose. Andy supposed she was crying. "Yes damn it, and I'm not using one of your bandanas." He smiled.

"For what it's worth, Sam, I'm confused, too. I think both of us have been wandering around out there on our own for a long time. We've both had to face a lot of things by ourselves. I'd resigned myself to being alone for the rest of my life. That was just the way it was going to be for me. Hell, I'm a damaged old guy. Who'd want to hang around with the likes of me? I don't think I was even aware that I was lonely. I've got Brian and Mike and the boys. I've got a few friends. It's not like I'm stranded on some desert island. I admit I was uncomfortable about having you around at first. That changed pretty quickly. I realized how much I really missed having someone in my life full time. I enjoy your company, Sam. For the first time in years I actually look forward to the end of each day when you arrive home. I enjoy being able to visit with you. I look forward to our walks together." He could hear Sam blowing her nose. "I miss you, sweet girl. I'm glad that you decided to stay." He hesitated. "Sam, if the day comes that you decide to leave, I know that I will miss you terribly, but you will have my blessings."

"Thank you, Andy. I needed to hear you say those things. I was afraid that it was a one-way street. I love you so much." She sniffled, "I'll call you tomorrow."

At nine o'clock, Delores came into Andy's room. His eyes were closed but he sensed someone's presence. She asked if he was awake. He found the controls for his bed and raised himself to more of an upright position. There was an indirect light that was on to the right of his bed. It provided enough illumination for him to see her more clearly. She was slender, and a little taller than he had remembered her. Her gray streaked hair was cut short, for convenience, he supposed. She had sharp features. She appeared not to be wearing much, if any makeup. She was someone you would not easily forget.

She asked how he was feeling tonight. He told her he was better. "I kept pressing and releasing that place on my arm that you showed me last night. I'm just amazed at how it works." He asked her where she had learned about that as well as the methods she used to relieve his headache.

She told him that it was a long story. He invited her to sit down and tell him. "I can't right now. I'm still on duty. I have to leave as soon as my shift is over at ten. Maybe I can come in a little early tomorrow. I start work at two. I'll try to get here by one-thirty." He asked her who Doctor Lawrence was. "He's my adopted brother. My parents adopted him as an infant. I'll tell you more tomorrow." She wished him a good night before leaving.

Doctor Merkle came in again at 7:30 the next morning. He carefully removed the bandaging from Andy's forehead. He had a magnifying glass in one of his coat pockets that he used to closely examining his handiwork. "This is looking very good, Mr. McLeod. There are no signs of infection." He asked Andy to show him a smile cautioning him not to make it too broad. Then he had him frown. "Oh, you're much better at frowning." He chuckled and lightly tapped Andy's leg.

"Years of experience," Andy said.

The doctor pressed Andy's face in several places asking if it hurt there. It hurt mostly in the area closest to his left temple and above his left eye. The doctor explained that was because of how the bullet had impacted him. "It hit your forehead a little left of center tearing the skin loose here." He touched that area. "It's kind of like tearing a hole in a piece of fabric. Once the initial tear is made, then the hole is increased by ripping. The ripping requires less force and is much less stressful to the fabric, or in this case the skin. We'll need to do some additional surgery in a month or so to add skin to this smaller area. If we don't, you will experience some degree of pain whenever you smile or frown, especially when you frown." He handed Andy a mirror. Andy used it to examine his own forehead. He asked if Andy had any questions. Andy asked if it would be all right for him to dress in street clothes. That was fine. "I'll let the nurses know." He told Andy that he could plan to go home on Saturday. Before leaving, the doctor redressed the forehead, this time using a lighter amount of gauze. He also gave permission for Andy to shower. He had to wear a plastic shower cap so as to not get the dressing wet. It felt good to get back into his jeans, turtleneck and flannel shirt again. He had more of an appetite and ate a full breakfast. Over the years, he had grown accustomed to seldom eating lunch. He would snack on a piece of fruit and some sunflower nuts instead. He asked the nurses if he could have an apple or two that other patients chose not to eat. He ended up with eight or nine apples and/or oranges each day. One nurse asked him if he wanted any bowls of prunes. "You can't believe the number of bowls of prunes that end up in the garbage each day." He was afraid to say 'yes'.

Delores came in to his room at 1:30 on the dot. In the full light of day, Andy studied her. She was already dressed in her housekeeping uniform. It wasn't much different from what the nurses wore. Her name tag read 'Delores Mills'. Her eyes were a blue gray, and she had a steady gaze. Her posture was erect. She exuded an aura of almost serene confidence. Because he was dressed in street clothes, Delores asked if he was going home today. "Saturday," he told her. He invited her to be seated.

Delores took the initiative. "You asked me where I learned to relieve pain using pressure points. My parents were Anglican missionaries. They accepted an assignment in China. I was born in England, but grew up in China. I was less than two when my family moved there." She described in some detail her exposure to several healing techniques including herbal remedies, acupressure, acupuncture and meditation. Andy felt like she was reciting a résumé.

She went on to talk about her adopted brother, Dr. Lawrence, whose parents were Chinese. "He became a naturalized American citizen and went on to medical school becoming qualified as a neurologist specializing in sports medicine and kinesiology."

"And what about you?" Andy asked. "did you get formal training?"

"No, unfortunately," she told him. "I started at the university and completed two years when it was learned that my mother had Alzheimer's. I dropped out of school to take care of her. She went on at length describing the ordeal of caring for her mother. When she'd ended that narrative, she looked down at her folded hands, then back to Andy. "Mr. McLeod, do you believe in euthanasia?"

"Under certain circumstances, I do." he replied.

"I do," she said. "I have thought back and wished many times that I had had the fortitude to free my mother."

Finally, she talked about her deceased husband. "We married shortly before my mother passed. After she died, I decided that I wanted to return to school. However, I became pregnant with my daughter. My husband was in the Air Force and was deployed to Iraq during the first Gulf War. He was a fighter pilot. He was on a nighttime bombing mission when his plane experienced a mechanical malfunction. He managed to eject himself from the plane, but he was never found." They both sat in prolonged silence. Andy broke it by asking about the daughter. "Her name is Sybil. She'll be twenty years old in September." Again Delores looked down at her hands. "Sybil has Downs Syndrome. She's a sweet young lady."

Andy leaned toward her. "You've spent all of your adult life taking care of others haven't you?"

"I have," she said. "I'm not complaining. Sybil actually functions quite well.

She'll never be able to live on her own, but that's okay. She brings a great deal of joy to my life. She's an affectionate girl and extremely sensitive." She looked up at the wall clock. "I need to be getting to work. Thank you, Mr. McLeod. You're a good listener." She arose from the chair.

"What about school?" Andy asked her.

"It's a bit late for that," she said. "Please, Mr. McLeod, don't feel sorry for me. I know that you're wondering why I'm here doing what I do. It's not because I need to. I like the people that I work with. There is little, if any, stress. The hospital provides excellent benefits. I can arrange my own schedule." She smiled at him. "On top of it all, every once in a while I have the opportunity to meet someone like you."

"The pleasure has been all mine, Delores." Andy stood. They shook hands.

"Drop by when you're in the neighborhood."

She said that perhaps she would. "If I don't see you before you leave, I wish you well, Mr. McLeod." She turned and left the room.

Andy thought about her. Although she was an intelligent, rather handsome woman, he felt like he'd just spent the last twenty minutes with his stereotyped imaged of a nun. Despite her dignified demeanor and interesting background, she lacked mirth. He supposed that her life had never allowed her to 'skip and go naked'. It was probably too late for her now even if she were free to do so. He was glad to have met her and been able to hear her story.

During the course of the day as he strolled around the hospital corridors, Andy discovered an atrium area. It had three levels of water falls and a pool, with lots of tropical plants. He found a bench and sat down to enjoy this oasis.

Chapter 25

When Sam called him that evening she sounded distraught. "Andy, I found out today that Doc Bitner's wife died of a heart attack last night. One of the other teachers told me about it this morning.

"Sweet Jesus," Andy closed the book he had been reading. "Doc's going to be lost without Millie. She ran the business side of the clinic. She was Doc's right hand." He asked Sam to look up Doc's home phone number. She'd already done that and gave it to him. "You're kind of my left hand, Sam. That's a compliment."

She asked if the doctor had said anything about when he could come home. He told her that he would be released on Saturday morning. "How would you feel about my coming to pick you up?"

"I'd like that," he said. "Brian has worn ruts in the pavement going back and forth between here and there. I'm sure he'll be relieved not to have to make the trip." She told him that Shawn had a basketball game on Saturday morning. She was sure Brian would want to attend it. She asked how he was doing. He told her about his getting one of his headaches the night before, and about the woman who had come into his room and how she had relieved it. He went on to describe how this woman had revealed a way he might be able to regain more use of his left hand. As he talked about her, it occurred to him that he'd overlooked asking Delores how she had known that he needed help and how to find him.

They talked some more about last night's conversation. Sam told him how much better she'd felt afterwards. "Andy, let's always be upfront and honest with one another, no matter what."

"I agree, Sam," he paused. "After we hung up last night, I got scared." She asked about what. "We exposed a lot of our emotional selves in the course of that conversation. I said to myself, 'Whoa, McLeod. You came on pretty strong'. I meant what I said about not getting in your way if you have a change of heart."

"Oh, Andy, there are so many things I want to say to you, but not over the phone." After a moment of silence, she asked. "Andy, what is your age?"

"I like that you put it that way, rather than the standard 'how old are you'. I'm fifty-seven, almost too old to have been your father. If my daddy had gotten an earlier start, I'd be old enough to be your grandpa. I'm on the downside of the hill, Sam. Hell, there are days that I feel like I'm almost at the bottom."

Sam didn't make any comment. "We'll talk on Saturday. I know you want to call Doc before it gets too late. I'll talk to you tomorrow night. I love you, Andy. Thank you." He told her he looked forward to seeing her. He was struggling to find some perspective. *Your ego enjoys being stroked, McLeod.* He wondered if that was what it was. As good as this felt he worried that he might be flirting with disaster.

He called Doc. The phone rang several times before the answering machine clicked on. The recorded message was his wife's voice. Andy started to leave a message when Doc's voice came on the line. "McLeod, I'm here. What's up? Where the hell are you?" He sounded very tired.

"Doc, I just heard about Millie. I'm in the hospital in Milwaukee. I heard it was a heart attack."

"It happened so quickly, Andy. She sat up in bed. She reached over and shook me. Hell, I thought I'd been snoring and she just wanted me to turn on my side. So I rolled over. Then I heard her gasping. I'd no sooner turned on the lamp when she fell back dead. I called 911, and began trying to resuscitate her. I knew it was futile; she was gone." Andy asked if she had shown any signs during the day. "No, not a one, but you know Millie. She never complained about anything. Well, hardly anything. It just came out of the blue. It happened so Goddamn fast. I talked to our family doctor today. He said it's like that for a lot of women. They don't show symptoms like men do. I'm more inclined to think they're just a hell-of-a-lot more stoic than we are." Andy asked if anyone was there with him. "Naw, I invited a couple of floozies over but they turned me down."

"That's not what I meant, Doc."

"I know, I know," Doc sounded irritated. "Our daughter is going to try to break away from her busy schedule and fly in on Saturday." Now he sounded bitterly sarcastic. "Hell, we haven't seen her in the past ten years. I don't care if she shows up or not. She's probably just coming so she can pick out some of Millie's jewelry." Although Andy had known Doc for close to twenty-five years, there was a lot he didn't know about the man. He asked if the daughter was their only child. "Naw, there was a son. He died of meningitis when he was still in grade school. You know how hard that is to get over." Andy heard the tinkling of glass in the background. "I just poured the last of my whiskey. I'd go buy some more, but I'm in no condition to drive."

"Just as well, Doc. I'll be home on Saturday. You and I can get hammered together. Getting drunk by yourself only makes things worse."

"I'm considering folding up my practice, Andy. I don't want to try and hire someone else to replace Mildred. No one person can take on all of the things she did. Hell, I don't know hardly anything about how she kept track of the books and the record stuff. I just did my thing with the critters. She took care of the rest. She even became a skilled vet tech over the years. I'd have to hire two or three people to take her place. It just doesn't seem worth it."

"You don't have to decide that right away, Doc," Andy said. "Let's talk about it when I get home."

"I appreciate your calling, Andy. As I recall, you said you were having some surgery done on your face." Andy said he'd had it a couple of days ago. "Well good. Anything will be an improvement over the way you looked before."

Andy smiled. "Good night, Doc. See you soon. Incidentally, what do you drink?"

"Anything but milk or water, McLeod."

Delores did come by to see Andy the next afternoon before she started work. They chatted for a few minutes before he asked her, "Why did you come by to see me the other night after your shift ended?"

She looked away from him. She appeared to be almost

embarrassed by the question. "You're going to think I'm some kind of crack pot if I tell you." She was wringing her hands. He told her to let him be the judge of that. She took a breath. "I get these feelings sometimes. I can't explain them. I just sense when someone is in pain and they need the kind of help I can provide." She was studying his face.

"So what led you to me in particular?"

"I can't explain that either. It's not that I'm refusing to tell you. It's that I simply don't know. It's kind of like that children's game of hot potato, cold potato. Except, it's something going on inside me. I can sense when I'm getting closer to or further from the person in need." She was looking at him expectantly now. "I'm almost never wrong."

Andy smiled at her and in his finest brogue he said. "Well, Ms. Mills, it would be appearin' that ye have the gift. That's in addition ta yoor skills as a healer." He dropped the brogue. "I'm grateful to you, Delores. I hope our paths will cross again." She said that she did too. "Ya joost never know what the fates have in store for ye, now do ye?"

"Not ever," she said. They shook hands and she thanked him once again. She seemed relieved that he had been so accepting of her.

Brian still hadn't arrived by mid afternoon. To escape the tedium of his room Andy went wandering the hospital. Because of the vision loss in his left eye, he could only read in spurts before he experienced eye strain. He found his way to the cafeteria, purchased a cup of coffee and went to the atrium. He found a bench that provided a good spot for people watching. A man about Andy's age came into the atrium. He ambled over to the waterfalls. He stood before them seeming to bask in just being there. After a while, he approached Andy and asked if he could share the bench. Andy noticed that the man spoke with a British accent. He asked Andy what had happened to his head, had he been in an automobile accident? That seemed like an easy way out as opposed to explaining what had really happened. Andy said that he had. The man asked if Andy had suffered a serious concussion. Andy told him that he had. The man asked how the concussion had affected him. The man's unabashed questioning was beginning to annoy him. A satirical urge took over, "I find myself becoming much more easily irritated." The man asked how Andy's irritation manifested itself. Andy decided he's had enough. *The guy doesn't get it.* Andy started to get up to leave.

"I'm sorry," the man said. "You must think me rude. It's just that my son, who is in the military, recently suffered rather serious head injuries. He's been stationed in Afghanistan. A vehicle he was riding in was blown up by one of those, what do they call them, the acronym for those homemade bombs?" Andy supplied the initials IED, and told him what they stood for. "Yes, that's it. At any rate, because of what has happened to him, I'm curious to know how such injuries affect a person."

Andy relaxed. He felt apologetic about his impatience with the man. The two of them carried on a twenty minute conversation. Before the man left, he stood and gestured to the waterfalls. "The falling water causes the air in the room to become ionized. Breathing in ionized air is supposedly restorative. It has a tendency to boost one's energy." They shook hands before the man departed.

Andy finished his coffee and returned to his room. He was pleased with the way his afternoon had turned out. In the course of his conversation with the man, he had been tempted two or three times to bring up the subject of Corey. He hadn't. He didn't want to spark a sense of fear in the man that such a terrible thing could happen to his son. *Maybe you've turned a corner, McLeod. Maybe you're finally learning to accept Corey's death. Maybe you're even outgrowing the temptation to wallow in self-pity and self-recrimination. He's gone and with him a part of you is, too. You're not the only one who has suffered a tragic loss. He smiled to himself. 'If that guy is right, maybe you ought to go live next to a waterfall. I wonder if breathing ionized air would prevent me from having these damn headaches.*

The phone rang. It was Brian. They talked briefly. Brian seemed reluctant about not coming to Milwaukee on Saturday. Andy assured him more than once that it was okay. Andy wanted Brian to attend Shawn's basketball game on Saturday. Brian said that Dan's freshman team had a game on Friday night. "That's all the more reason for you not to come. Sam will find her way here just fine. We'll see you Saturday afternoon."

Sam called later that evening. Andy told her about his conversation with Delores Mills, and his later conversation with "the British gentlemen." Her response was, "Jeez, Andy, you're having so much fun down there. Are you sure you want to come home?"

He told her about his phone conversation with Doc last night. "Doc's talking about taking his shingle down and retiring." Sam asked him what he thought about that. "I can understand why he feels that way, but I think it would be a big mistake. The man is good at what he does. It's been his whole life. He'll end up following Millie in a short while if he quits." Sam asked Andy what he thought would happen to him if he ever retired. "I'm a whole different animal. There's a bunch of things I enjoy doing. My biggest concern is ending up not being able to do them. That's been the scariest part of this whole thing I've been through. I've had to face the possibility that I might not be able to do a lot of the things I did before. If the day comes that I can't manage my life anymore, I hope I can go like Millie. In the meantime, I want to make the most of each day."

When the plastic surgeon came in to see Andy on Saturday morning, he had one of his nurses with him. After he removed the dressing from Andy's forehead, he pointed out to the nurse what he had done surgically with Andy's forehead. "Let's schedule Mr. McLeod for an appointment in about two weeks." She reminded him that was the week before Christmas. It was decided to have him come in the week after. He explained to Andy and the nurse that it would be necessary to perform one more less extensive surgery. He prescribed an ointment that Andy was to apply at least four times each day. "This is an all-natural ointment. It's got all sorts of good stuff for the skin." He wanted Andy to also make a point of exercising his facial muscles by alternating between smiling and frowning. "You've no doubt already discovered that the skin on your forehead is temperature sensitive." Andy confirmed that. His mind jumped to Sam's creative invention using panty hose to protect his head from the cold. The doctor recommended that Andy purchase a balaclava. Finally, he told Andy, "We'll apply one more dressing this morning. Leave it on over the weekend. If your forehead looks good when you remove it on Monday, you won't need to continue redressing it. My nurse is going to transcribe these instructions and give you a copy of them to take with you. I'll fill out your discharge papers. You should be able to leave in an hour."

Sam arrived a few minutes after the doctor left. Andy noticed she had on eye makeup, which he'd never seen her wear before. In addition, she'd also had her hair styled differently. It gave her a softer look. The tight curls that she'd worn before had given her a less mature, almost funky appearance. He commented on the changes, adding quickly, "not that you didn't look good before. You just look more...," he groped for a word. "I don't know, cosmopolitan?" He tried again, "More sophisticated, more mature, all of the above." Finally he settled on, "Beautiful."

She smiled at him. "I was expecting to see you bandage free. How much longer will you have to keep your head covered?" He told her until Monday. "The dogs are in the car. Nobody was around to take care of them. I didn't want to leave them alone for the day." She dug into her large tapestry purse. "I made this for you." She pulled out a navy blue, hand-knit balaclava. "Of course, if you prefer wearing the panty hose..."

He was surprised and pleased with the gift. "I didn't know that you knew how to knit."

"There's a lot you don't know about me, McLeod." She helped him slip it over his head. He went into the bathroom to see himself in the mirror. She followed him to the door. "I thought on the way home, we could rob a couple of banks. I'll drive getaway." As he was coming out of the bathroom, she stood in his way and put her arms around him. She pulled herself close to him. "I have really missed you, Andy." He put his arms around her more loosely and rubbed her shoulders. She sensed his uneasiness and relinquished her tight hold. "Here, I'll help you take that thing off." She said slipping her hands under it to keep it from snagging the dressing.

A few minutes later the doctor's nurse came in to give Andy the discharge papers. "We'll see you on the 27th, Mr. McLeod. Have a wonderful Christmas." She turned to Sam and asked, "you must be Mr. McLeod's daughter?"

Sam didn't skip a beat, "I'm his roommate and nanny." The nurse looked at Andy, then back at Sam.

The nurse said nervously, "Well, it was nice of you to come all this way to pick Mr. McLeod up. You must have left very early this morning. How long a drive is it?"

"It took me close to four hours, but that's because I wasn't sure how to find the hospital."

The nurse wished Sam a merry Christmas, too, and fled. "And nanny?" Andy looked at her. He was on the verge of laughing.

"Sure, the dogs are the children. I help you take care of them, ergo." She helped Andy put his coat on. He picked up his musette bag with his toiletries. As they headed toward the elevators, Sam took his arm. "Relax, Andy, I could have told her I was your mistress."

"You're right, Sam. I'm wrapped pretty tight."

She gave his arm a quick squeeze. "It's not one of things I love about you, but, I understand it."

The dogs were overjoyed to see Andy. Maude sat on Andy's lap for part of the way. Once they were beyond the city traffic, Sam brought up the subject of their relationship. "Andy, I have some things I want to say to you. I want you to hear me out before you respond." He nodded. "Okay, let's start with my feelings toward you. When I tell you I love you, I mean that. I think that you love me, too, but you're scared to admit it. I think part of it is that you're hung up on the age difference between us. I think you're working overtime to try to see me as a daughter, which makes me some kind of forbidden fruit." She glanced over at him. He had his hand on Maude's back. She touched it. "Andy, one of the things I admire and love about you is that you are your own man. For the most part, you don't give a damn about what others think about you. You have some very high standards that you live by. That may be part of the problem. My guess is that you are afraid of what people will think of you if you allow yourself to love me back. You're afraid that people will see you as being..." Sam paused.

Andy interjected, "A cradle-robber." He left out 'a dirty old man, and lecherous geezer'.

"Andy, I love you as a partner. As someone I want to spend the rest of my life with. I don't care what anybody else thinks of our relationship. I don't want to be without you. I knew that you were someone very special even before we met. I've heard all sorts of things about you." She glanced over at him. "Most of it good. Your family adores you. All of the townspeople I talked to were genuinely concerned about your disappearance. I didn't know about what really happened to you until just before you came home. People don't have that kind of concern for someone they don't know and respect. I knew almost from the moment I first met you that something was happening between us. I felt drawn to you." She squeezed his hand, and then apologized remembering it was the injured one.

"It's all right, Sam. I don't have much feeling in it."

Do you remember some of the things you said to me that first evening you were home?

"We talked about a lot of things, Sam. What are you referring to specifically?"

"I felt like you were trying to warn me off. You listed several of what you regarded as your faults." He nodded. "Do you also remember how, later on that evening, we bared our souls to one another about the terrible losses we'd both experienced?" Again he nodded. "I have an opinion about what went on between us that night. I think we were telling one another about how afraid we both were to open ourselves to loving anyone ever again."

Andy agreed with her. "Sam, I have stood in awe of your perceptiveness from the very beginning. I've met very few people who are as insightful as you. Not even among people my own age who've been around the block several times. I find those qualities attractive, but I'll bet you scare the hell out of most of your male peers."

"Most people have no idea what I'm about, Andy." Sam looked at him. "Andy, I think we both knew right then, that there was no turning back. We both tried to deny what was happening because of those fears." After a period of silence Sam went on. "I think that the biggest challenge we're faced with isn't dealing with what others think. It's being able to open ourselves to sharing with one another. We've gotten a lot closer. I think it's time we turn around and face that challenge."

Andy shook his head. "I agree with you entirely, Sam. There are a couple of things that are having a big influence on me at this point." Andy hesitated. "Sam, I'm not the same man I was before all of this happened to me. I'm sure as hell not the same man I was physically a few months ago. I'm discovering, on a daily basis, that things have changed for me emotionally, and mentally as well. I do love you, much more than I have been willing to admit." He bit his lip. "I'm scared. I feel like I've aged fifty years in three months. It's one thing to lose somebody to death. It's something else to lose someone because you can't keep up with them. That's what I'm afraid of with you. I feel like I've lost a lot of the strength and vitality I had before. I'm tired, Sam. I've considered that I may be fucking depressed. I try to push myself to get myself going. I end up feeling even more frustrated. The bright spots in my day are greeting you in the morning, and when you come home in the evening. Well, and when Doc drops by to visit. I haven't had much time with Mike since returning. We've always had a special relationship. I guess what I'm trying to say is that I feel like I'm dependent on others to feel any sense of joy or purpose."

"I've watched you, Andy. I know that you're struggling. There are times when it breaks my heart to see you so frustrated. Most people would give up and just say 'screw it; this is just the way it is'. You don't. You pick yourself up and try to figure out another way."

"Maybe they're smarter than me, or at least not as stubborn."

"There's a difference between stubbornness and determination, Andy. In both cases a person refuses to give in. But with determination, they look for other options. Stubborn people just dig in their heels and continue repeating the same mistakes."

Andy relaxed a little. "I use a combination of both."

Sam smiled. "Yes, you do." She shifted the conversation. "I know that you've had some real disappointments in some of your past relationships with women. Doc told me a few things the night that Cassidy got shot. He told me about Stephanie and how hurt you were when she left. He admits that he doesn't know much about the relationship you had with that detective, Jan. He says that most of what he knows about her is via the grapevine. Apparently she had a lot of baggage from her past. He heard that she was an alcoholic, and that you tried to help her." Andy nodded. He made no comment. "He says she just disappeared one day with no explanation, or goodbye or anything."

"That's not exactly true. She had her reasons and I knew

what they were. It is true that she did disappear without saying anything to me or anybody else. I have a pretty good idea where she went when she left here. I even know where she is supposed to have ended up." Sam asked him why he hadn't gone after her. "It's been years since she left. If she had wanted me in her life, she knew where to find me. I don't think Jan will ever be able to allow herself to have an intimate relationship with any man for a number of reasons. She tried with me. It scared the hell out of her." Cassidy nudged Andy's arm from behind the passenger seat. Andy reached over to pet him. "Jan was there for me when I needed her. I was there for her on a few occasions as well. I bear her no malice. I hope she's found some peace and contentment."

"Haven't you had any relationships with any other women since Jan?" Sam asked.

"Nope, I've led a monastic life since then."

"Do you want to go back to living that way?" He stopped petting Cassidy. He rubbed his own shoulder. "Andy, I'm not interested in marriage. I'm as married to you as I could ever be. I used to think it would be nice to be married and have kids. I raised my sisters from the time I was eleven. I can't tell you how liberated I felt when they finally went to live with my aunt. I honestly don't think I ever want to be tied down like that again. Having a kid is a crap-shoot; if you're lucky enough to get one without too many problems, great." They drove in silence for a while. "What about sex?" She glanced over at him. "Is that a problem for you?"

"Christ, Sam, I'm an old guy. Getting it up and keeping it up is a problem for all of us geezers. It's apparently a problem even for younger men. Look at all those ads for pills to treat 'erectile dysfunction'," Andy scoffed.

"How do you know it's a problem if you haven't been with a woman in such a long time?" He didn't have an answer. She drove on for a while. "Okay, so let's just say that you're not always able to put on a great performance. What matters the most to me is just being able to be close to you, to snuggle up to one another, to have you touch me and to know that I am loved and that I am someone special in your life." Andy remained silent. "I can't tell you how much it meant to me and how good it felt to snuggle with you that night." She couldn't or wouldn't refer to which night. Andy knew what she meant.

He nodded, "I was glad when you came and asked to be with me. We both needed some TLC that night especially."

"Andy, I know that I'm a strong willed person. I'm not afraid to speak my mind. That's intimidating to a lot of men. How about you? Do I scare you?"

"It's one of the things I like the most about you," he told her. "Well, almost the most."

"What's the thing you like about me the very most?"

"Your smile, I'm a sucker for a great smile."

"Andy, you make me smile even when we're not together. I have never enjoyed being with anyone as much as I do being with you. Not anyone."

They were a few miles south of Green Bay. Sam saw a sign for a wayside ahead. She asked Andy if he need to make a pit stop. "Most definitely," he told her. She did, too.

Before they arrived at the wayside ramp, she asked, "do you ever think about me in a sexual way?"

"Up until now, I've tried to avoid doing so."

"Let's see what we can do to get past that."

At the rest area, she told Andy to go first while she took care of the dogs. "Bless you, girl, I don't think I could have held it much longer." He walked off briskly. After the dogs finished their business, she got out a jug of water and filled a bowl of it for them to drink. She'd also brought dog treats for them. When Andy returned to the car, he took over walking the dogs and stretching his own legs. The dogs kept interrupting their sniffing to see if Sam was returning. When they spotted her, they stopped and faced her with their tails wagging. When Andy realized that they were watching her, he turned in her direction. The feelings of fondness and admiration he had for her were almost overwhelming.

Chapter 26

For the past few years, Christmas had been something Andy McLeod had endured. The only pleasure he took in the holiday was the time he spent with Mike, Brian and his grandsons. After Corey's death, he descended into a terrible sense of grief and an almost debilitating depression. Mike and Brian made concerted efforts to include him in their lives knowing that he was miserably lost. It took him two or three years to gradually gain some control over his despair. During that period in his life, he went through the motions of living, trying hard not to dampen the spirits of those around him. As the grandsons grew to where he could begin to relate to them as people, he was able to take increasing pleasure in the time spent with them. It would have been easy for him to make them the center of his life. However, he refused to allow himself to depend on them to give his life meaning. On one occasion Brian went so far as to accuse him of being excessively and stubbornly independent. Doc accused him of being a 'Goddamn stoic martyr'. To some degree he was both of those things, but he was something more. He was a man who had suffered too many disappointments and losses. He had retreated into himself deciding not to risk any more failures. In time, he learned to ignore most of the pain of his self-imposed exile. He viewed it as the lesser of two evils.

And then Samantha Riggs came into his life. He knew from the beginning that she was special. He tried to deny his attraction to her. On those occasions when weak spots in his walls of defense were discovered, he berated himself. You damned old fool, McLeod. What ARE you thinking? What can she possibly see in you, and that's just for starters. You're on the down-side of the hill. She's still climbing up the other side. You're just setting yourself up for another major heartbreak. Do you enjoy suffering'? A part of him had wanted to tell her to leave, go find some other place to live, get a life for Chrisake. A much bigger part of him wanted her to never leave. He used up a lot of energy wrestling with his ambivalence. To risk or not to risk. For a brief while he was able to delude himself into thinking they could just be friends.

It was a futile struggle. The side of him that wanted to be with her, to risk himself at loving again was gaining control. The most compelling argument for not risking was the issue of their age difference. All of the other arguments seemed extraneous, even frivolous. He remained cautious. Not because he didn't trust her, but because he didn't trust himself. He saw himself as being so very needy at this point in his life both physically and emotionally. The last thing he wanted was to burden her. She had sacrificed herself to the needs of others for a long time. If he couldn't be strong for her, he didn't want to be a millstone around her neck. He was afraid of scaring her off. *Hold your horses, McLeod. You need to tread lightly. If you don't, and she ends up leaving, you may not survive.*

Sam knew that Andy had made a decision. She also knew that, despite his deciding in favor of her, and their relationship, he was still conflicted. She had no such reservations. She was willing to give him the time he needed. For her to try to force a resolution might ruin their chances for success. She also realized that the major burden of the risk was on him. If I can't help you, I won't hurt you, became her mantra. She knew that words were probably not going to be of much use in dealing with the challenges they faced. The two of them had embarked on an adventure. The trick was to not let it turn into a high-wire act where a single misstep could result in a disaster. They needed to be open and honest, but at the same time gentle and accepting with one another. That part was in their favor. She trusted Andy completely. She knew it would take time and patience for him to learn to regain the confidence and trust in himself that he had once had.

Christmas was less than three weeks away. As soon as Sam left for school each morning, Andy and the dogs would head for the workshop. He'd spend the day there working on Christmas gifts. Doc took to stopping by if he was in the vicinity. They'd pull up stools, have some coffee, and 'jaw-jack', as Doc put it. Doc seemed to be rebounding pretty well from the loss of his wife. He'd found a lady who was in her early thirties to apprentice as a vet tech. She had a lot of experience with horses. She'd had two part-time jobs at two different stables grooming and exercising boarded horses. Doc was able to offer her more than she was earning at those two jobs combined. Because she was a single mom, she jumped at the chance to work fewer hours and earn more. Plus, Doc allowed her to arrange her schedule so that she could see her daughter off to school each morning before coming to work. "She's working out better than I expected. She's even volunteered to take over the record keeping and bookwork. She takes stuff home with her at night. She's got a computer. She says she can knock out the paper work in an hour or two. Christ, it took Millie three or four hours doin' it by hand. I don't know what happened between her and her husband. If you ask me, he must have shit for brains to have let her slip through his fingers. I tell you, McLeod, if I were forty years younger, I'd sure have a go at trying to win her affections." That, of course, led Doc to ask about Andy's relationship with Sam. Andy said that he enjoyed having Sam around and that she was a big help to him. Doc went over to the coffee pot and poured himself half a cup of coffee. Andy refused any more. "So, are you sleepin' with her yet?"

"I wouldn't tell you if I was," Andy replied.

"You are," Doc said. "Good for you, McLeod. She's one sharp cookie and she's pretty to boot. The only thing she lacks is taste in men."

"You're relentless, Doc."

"All kiddin' aside, Andy. I'm glad to see you comin' out from underneath the rock you've been hidin' under for so long. Knowing you, you're makin' Mount Everest out of a gnat's ass over the age thing. Screw it. That little gal loves the hell out of you. I'd be willing to bet you've got some similar feelings toward her." Doc drained his cup. "If you want my opinion, and even if you don't, you shouldn't let this age thing get in the way. Hell, you've never courted public opinion in the past. Why would you start now?"

"This coming from a man who, not five minutes ago, said that he was too old to chase after a younger woman he's attracted to."

"Do as I say, McLeod, not as I do." Doc put his coat on. "Besides, it's different for me, Andy. Millie and I had a good life together. We were married for over fifty years. I loved that woman dearly, and for some strange reason she felt the same about me. You, on the other hand, have had no such luck. Life is handing you maybe, this one last opportunity. You'd be a damn fool not to take it."

"Thanks, Doc. I appreciate your advice. I mean that."

Doc patted Andy's shoulder. "Consider it an early Christmas present." He checked his watch. "I've got one more stop to make. You on top of the Christmas present thing?"

"I would be if I didn't have these constant interruptions."

"I've got some llamas to deal with up the road; nasty damn animals. They take delight in hacking up foul crap on people. I'll bring you some tomorrow."

After Doc left, Andy went back to work on a project he was working on for Sam. He felt like a huge burden had just been lifted off him. He looked outside. A few scattered snow flakes were meandering their way toward the ground. He remembered that he had been listening to a recorded book when Doc showed up. He released the pause to continue listening to it.

Sam drove in a while later. He heard the garage door opening. He and the dogs went to greet her. They always hugged when she returned home. This afternoon he held her in a prolonged embrace touching her hair. "Andy, is everything all right?"

"It is. I'm sorry, Sam. I've been a real pain. Thank you for hanging in there with me. I'm a slow learner." He kissed her forehead.

She reached up and touched his. "Your head is looking so much better, Andy." She smiled at him. "I fell in love with you the way you looked before. But I admit I like the make-over even better." Her tapestry bag was full of test papers. She had a bag of groceries in the car. Andy picked up the groceries. He needed to turn off lights and lower the thermostat on the shop's space heater. "I'll change so we can go for a walk."

During their walk, she asked Andy about his day. He told her about Doc's visit and the things Doc had said to him. "Doc's been worried about you for a long time. He wants nothing more for you than to see you happy." She took his arm. The snow was increasing. "I do, too, sweet man."

There was about four inches of snow on the ground when

Andy arose the next morning. He and Sam went through their regular week-day routine together. They usually had time for a hot breakfast but this morning they needed to move snow. Andy got the snow blower started and Sam cleared the driveway. He used a wide shovel to clear off the garage apron and the decks. The dogs, Maude especially, disliked the blower so they stayed closer to him. When Sam was ready to go, she backed out of the garage and rolled her window down. Andy went over to the car. He leaned down and they gave one another a quick embrace. "Last night was wonderful, Andy. I love making love with you." They waved to one another as she drove away.

Early that afternoon Doc came by to ask a favor. "I don't suppose you'd have time to do a special order for me this close to Christmas?" Andy said that it depended on what it was. "Well, Annie, that's the gal I recently hired, has a horse. I was wondering if you could build her a tack box." He had an equestrian magazine in hand. One of the pages was dog eared. He opened it to show Andy a picture of what a tack box looked like. "Most of the ones I've seen are made out of oak. I know that, being a wood carver you don't favor the hard woods. I was thinking it could be made out of something like ebony or sugar maple." Doc grinned at Andy who in turn raised his hands in supplication and mouthed, 'Why me'? "Naw, I was only kidding, McLeod. You like butternut. I do too. It's got a beautiful grain. Do you have any around?" Andy said that he had some and asked about the size of the box. "Here," Doc pointed to the magazine ad. "It's got the dimensions down here. You can keep the magazine. It's an old issue." Andy said that he'd do it, but he might not have it completed by Christmas. He held up his left hand as a reminder that he wasn't able to work as quickly as he once had. "Do what you can, McLeod. I'll give her a card letting her know something's on the way."

The two men visited for a while. Doc's cell phone rang. It was Annie. A mare was in labor and having trouble with the delivery. Because Annie was extremely familiar with horses she had asked all the right questions of the horse's owner. She gave Doc the information he needed. "Call her back and tell her I'm on my way, Annie. I'll be there in twenty minutes or so." Doc shrugged his coat back on. "Duty calls. See you later, McLeod."

He got in his truck, backed it up and was just starting to head down the driveway when a large luxury van came barreling up the driveway. Doc put his truck into reverse and was starting to backup when the van slammed into the front end of his truck. The force of the impact threw Doc forward causing him to hit his face on the steering wheel. The door of the van flew open and a tall, slender, wild eyed man jumped out. He was holding a pistol. He pointed it at Doc. "Are you, McLeod?" Doc raised both of his hands. He shook his head, 'No'. Blood was streaming out of his nose. The man jumped back in the van and raced toward the house. Doc leaned on his horn to try to alert Andy of the dangerous situation. Andy had heard the collision. He rushed out the service entrance of his studio seeing the van headed toward his house. Doc had his window down. He was in the process of dialing 911."The bastard's got a gun," he yelled to Andy. The man driving the van got out. He didn't bother to look back. He started running toward the front door of the house. Andy turned and went back into his studio. As soon as he opened the door, both dogs lunged past him barking and running hell-bent-for-leather toward the house and the intruder. Andy had a twenty-two semi-automatic rifle in the studio that he used mostly for shooting red squirrels. It was on a peg rack above the entrance door. He reached up and grabbed it. He clicked off the safety. The man had gone into the house. He was coming back out as the dogs came toward him running full tilt. He looked like he was scared witless of the dogs and indecisive about what to do. He turned part way back toward the house. Then he turned back toward the van. Both dogs pounced almost simultaneously. Cassidy leapt aiming for the gun hand. He hit the man's arm only catching the fabric of his jacket. The cloth tore causing Cassidy to land on his side two or three feet away. Maude came in low braking herself at the last moment. She bit into the man's calf. He yelled out more in terror than in pain. Andy had started running at an angle in the direction of the house. He needed to get closer and to where he had a clear shot. Doc yelled, "just shoot the son-of-bitch for Chrisake."

The man spotted Andy and despite his pain he yelled, "Are you, McLeod?" Cassidy had now gotten a hold of the back of the man's jacket. Andy stopped and raised the rifle. The man yelled at Andy, "You killed Melvin, didn't you?" Andy held back from shooting. The man's voice was extremely effeminate. "You killed my Melvin; I'm going to kill you."

Andy kept his aim. He yelled back, "Who the hell are you?" The dogs seemed flummoxed by what was going on. It was like they were asking themselves and one another 'should we continue to attack or not'. Maude relaxed her grip on the man's leg.

"It doesn't matter who I am. You killed my Melvin?"

Doc yelled, "Jesus H. Christ, are you going to shoot him or not?"

"What's your name?" Andy insisted.

"I'm Randall. Melvin was the joy of my life and you killed him." He was sobbing now.

"Put the gun down, Randall." Andy called to him in an almost parental tone. "You don't want to do this. Just put it down."

"I can't. I have to do this. I just have to. Don't you see?"

"No, Randall, you're the one who doesn't see. I wish I could tell you that I'm sorry for killing Melvin. I'm not. He was a very bad man. He tried to kill me twice. He's killed lots of other people. Some of them were your friends. He didn't give me a choice. It was him or me."

Randall looked like he was about to drop the pistol; then his expression suddenly changed. Andy knew what was coming next even before Randall started to raise the pistol toward his own head. Cassidy must have sensed something was about to happen too. He launched himself again grabbing Randall's gun arm. Andy squeezed off three rounds in rapid succession. The sound of a distant siren could be heard. Randall's pistol went off. He dropped it and grabbed for his backside. Andy ran forward not bothering to keep the rifle in a ready position. When he got to Randall he kicked the pistol away. Maude was slinking away. Cassidy stood ready to attack again if necessary. "Ohhh, this hurts, this really hurts." He was holding his right hand over the right side of his butt. Blood was oozing out from between his fingers. He wailed mellow-dramatically, "Why did you stop me? Why? I have nothing to live for."

Andy stooped down beside Randall, "Let me see." Randall lifted his hand wincing dramatically. "The good news is that you're going to live, Randall. The bad news is that you're probably not going to be able to sit down for quite a while."

Randall scowled, "that's not funny. You're a very mean man. I have friends. As soon as they hear about what you did to me, they're going to come and get even with you. You just watch and see." There were a number of things Andy thought about saying in response. All of them were sarcastic. He reached over and picked up the pistol. The siren was very close now. He stood up. He slapped his leg and called for the dogs to follow him. Because Andy was now holding, the pistol Maude took a circuitous route giving him a very wide birth. A Sheriff's squad car arrived racing up the driveway. The deputy brought it to an abrupt stop in front of Doc's truck.

"The shooter's over there," Doc pointed. "Andy shot him in the ass. Better call an ambulance." The deputy immediately radioed his dispatcher. She told him that an ambulance and another squad were on the way.

The deputy drew his gun and started toward the man lying on the ground. Andy was walking toward Doc's truck. "Here," Andy held out Randall's pistol. He handed it to the deputy. "It's his." He nodded toward Randall who was now loudly moaning for attention. "I'll be with you in a few minutes." Andy told the deputy. "I need to check on Doc." He went over to the driver's side of Doc's truck. "You okay, Doc?"

"Hell no, I'm not okay," he said as he took his hand away from his nose. "My goddamn nose is broken, and I cut my lip. I'm supposed to be helping to deliver a colt." Andy opened the truck's door. There was a bad smell. "And to top it all off, I shit my pants."

"Oh, no," Andy said with as much sympathy as he could muster. "Will the truck start?" Doc turned the key and the engine came to life. "Pull up to the side door. We'll get you in the house. You can take a shower. I've got a pair of bib overalls that will probably fit you. Can Annie handle delivering the colt?"

"I've already called her. She's on her way." Doc looked at Andy and grumbled. "Don't you ever say a word about this to anyone, McLeod."

"I'll be right with you, Doc. I need to put the dogs in the studio." Inside Andy moved some things out of the way on his workbench. He put the rifle on the bench. He got the dogs a couple of treats each. He left his studio and strode rapidly toward the Deputy who was stooped down next to Randall. The deputy stood as Andy approached. "Can you give me a few more minutes? I need to tend to something inside first." The deputy nodded. Doc was still sitting in his truck when Andy got to it. Andy opened the truck door. "There's no easy way for us to do this, Doc. Come on, I'll give you a hand getting up the steps. The utility room is just inside the door. The bathroom is just down the hall from there."

As they made their way from the truck to the house Doc muttered curses. "What took you so goddamn long to shoot him, McLeod?" Andy ignored the question as he helped Doc make his way awkwardly up the three steps to the side entrance. "You shot him in the ass? How come you shot him there?" They reached the landing. "That was some nice shooting, Andy. I would have just started firing and let the chips fall where they may."

"I didn't want to take the chance of hitting the dogs," Andy told him. Inside he left Doc to the task of getting his soiled pants and underwear off. He went to fetch a roll of paper towel and a waste basket. He let Doc do the preliminary cleaning before he escorted him into the bathroom. Andy had a towel draped over the shower curtain bar for him. "I'll see if I can find you a rubber ducky, Doc. I want you to feel right at home here." The old vet scoffed.

"I'll get the stuff washed out of your clothes, and throw them in the washer."

"Naw, you don't have to do that, McLeod. Just throw them in a plastic bag. I'll take care of them myself. I appreciate your help, Andy. This is Goddamn embarrassing."

While Andy had been in the house tending to Doc, the ambulance and the second deputy arrived. The paramedics had already cut the back of Randall's trousers away exposing the wound. One of them reported that there was a single bullet wound that had gone all the way through the right glut, and grazed the left one. After numbing the wounded area they applied a dressing, and strapped Randall to a stretcher in a prone position. A deputy hand cuffed him explaining that it was department policy. Before the ambulance departed Andy asked the paramedics to look at Doc's nose. Doc had taken a brief shower and had Andy's bib overalls on. The paramedic examined Doc's nose. It was swollen and bruised. When the medic removed the tissue Doc had packed his nose with, it started to bleed again. He repacked it with cotton. He started to tell Doc what he needed to do for his nose. Doc took offense. "Jesus Christ, I was setting bones and treating cuts and bruises before your daddy was even conceived. I know what to do." He turned to Andy. "These bibs fit pretty good. I'll get them back to you tomorrow."

Andy got an old towel to put on the soiled spot in Doc's truck seat. The first deputy to arrive at the scene approached Andy, "You probably don't remember me. I was here about two weeks ago when that previous shooting took place. Is what happened here today related to that incident?"

"Yeah, this guy was the other guy's lover. Sweet said he wanted revenge for what I did to Stark." The deputy took a written statement about today's 'incident' from Andy. He bagged Randall's pistol and wished Andy a good day before leaving. Andy looked at his watch. Sam would be home in a short while. He needed to wash the blood from where Randall had fallen. He first let the dogs out of the studio noticing some blood in Cassidy's bandaging. He lifted the bandages to see that a small amount of blood was seeping from Cassidy's wound. While wiping the wound clean with antiseptic towelettes he talked to the dog. "You did good, Cassidy. We're both getting too old for this kind of stuff." He applied some antibiotic salve, and a fresh gauze pad to the wound. Maude was still very spooked. On their way to the barn to get a hose, she stayed close to Andy. A small gaggle of three Canada geese honked by overhead. Andy guessed that these were hangers-on. The larger flocks had since passed over with the fall migration. He noticed that almost all of the previous evening's snow was melted. He hooked up the hose and washed Randall Sweet's blood away.

Sam drove in just as he was coiling the hose up. He and the dogs went to greet her. Sam practically tripped over Maude several times on the way to the house. The dog wanted to be as close as possible to her. "What's wrong, Maude? Why is she acting so weird?"

"Maude's had a hard day. I'll tell you all about it on our walk." When they entered the house Sam immediately noticed the strong odor of feces. She asked if Andy was sick. "Andy's had a hard day too. I'll tell you all about it." As she left to get changed Andy said, "I'll pour you a large flagon of wine."

As they strolled, Andy told Sam about what had happened. He made her promise not say anything to anyone about Doc's 'accident'. Sam felt badly for Doc. She asked what might have caused him to lose control of his bowels. "It was probably looking down the barrel of a pistol being wielded by what must have looked to him like a lunatic."

"Why didn't you shoot to kill?" Sam asked.

"If he'd shot either of the dogs, I might have," he told her. "I guess I found myself taking pity on the poor devil. He was pathetic. I'm just glad I was able to keep him from blowing his own brains out."

Sam stopped and turned to face Andy. "What about your brains, Andy? He could have killed you." She had an almost desperate expression on her face. "I love you. I don't know what I would do if anything to happened to you." Andy raised his good hand and touched Sam's cheek. She stepped closer slipping her arms around him. They stood in the forest holding one another.

"I think it's all over with, Sam. We can finally relax."

"Andy, let's go back to the house. Let's make love."

"I was thinking the very same thing, sweet lady."

Epilogue

It's been a couple of years since the 'Randall Sweet incident'. Most of the charges against him were either dropped or reduced in exchange for his guilty plea. He is currently serving a five year sentence on the remaining charges. At the sentencing hearing, he offered a sincere apology to Andy for, "my irrational and reprehensible behavior." He begged Andy's forgiveness. Andy questioned the Judge's decision to incarcerate Randall. He would have preferred seeing Sweet placed on probation and ordered to perform a liberal number of hours of community service. He didn't see prison as serving any purpose. Randall didn't pose any kind of threat to others. It was a waste of taxpayer money.

Doc Bitner is semi-retired. He sold his practice to a young woman veterinarian right out of vet school. He says that he's there, "Just until she gets her Goddamn head out of the clouds and gets in touch with reality." He decries, "All that nonsense they fill these kids' heads with in vet school these days." The fact is; they take turns mentoring one another. He won't admit it, but Doc enjoys learning about some of the new methods of veterinary medicine. She is amused by many of his quaint, antiquated but effective techniques. Annie is now a certified vet tech.

Sheriff Peterson retired last year, choosing not to run for re-election again. He and his wife sold their house and bought a motor-home. They head south for the winter months and migrate north come late spring. He sends Andy a postcard every now and then. He says that he's only sorry that he didn't retire sooner.

Brian continues to serve as the high school principal. He was named 'Principal of the Year' last year for some of his creative innovations in developing changes to the curriculum. He is well liked by the students, their parents, and his staff and even Mrs. Penelope Pitts. He and Sam run before school either on the outside track, or the school gym. There is a YMCA close to school. They work out there religiously three times-a-week.

During the warmer months Mike and Andy meet at the beach three times-a-week to go for three mile runs together. Once the lake warms up enough they often go for a swim afterward. That's followed by breakfast at a local restaurant. Mike has pretty much taken over operating the gallery. Andy comes in a couple of days each week during the season to give her time off. She has branched off from just throwing pots to sculpting in clay. A lot of her work is whimsical, but she does some extremely nice human figure pieces.

Andy had surgery on his arm to give him increased use of the fingers on his left hand. The final surgery on his face added skin so that he is able to smile and frown without the feeling of tightness. He still carves wood and does a limited number of pieces each year for display in the gallery. He and Sam sail as often as the weather permits. They've taken off in early August the last two years on extended three week cruises. They crossed the lake last summer and sailed the northwest side of Michigan.

Cassidy died in early April. He went peacefully with no suffering. He had slowed down considerably over the winter. Andy got up one morning and noticed that Cassidy was not stirring. He had died in his sleep. The ground was still too frozen to bury him. He's buried next to where Andy's two previous dogs, Lucy and Buck are.

Maude had almost as much trouble recovering from Cassidy's death as Andy and Sam did. Although she is only four years old, she's slowing down noticeably due to arthritis. Sam and Andy considered getting another dog to give her companionship. They've decided not to for the time being. Neither of them thinks Maude will be able to adapt to another dog the way Cassidy did with her. Maude will never be the same after the 'Randall Sweet incident'. She cowers and hides at the sight of a gun. Thunder storms are traumatic events for her. They cause her to shake uncontrollably.

Sam is currently working toward getting her master's degree. She is able to complete a lot of her course work online. She attends summer school at the University of Wisconsin Green Bay. During the school year she drives to Green Bay once-a-week to attend evening classes. She hopes to have all of her course requirements completed in another year.

At Andy's suggestion, Sam's two younger sisters, Marci and Becky, who are now in their late teens, have come to spend six weeks of the last two summers with them. During their stay, the girls work as waitresses earning good money. Sam strongly encourages them to put much of their earning into savings aimed at helping to pay future college expenses. Sam feels that the relationship between she and her sisters has shifted. The girls are finally able to relate to Sam as their big sister, rather as the maternal figure of the past.

There has been no word from or about Sam's mother. Sam says that she feels she can forgive her mother for running out on the family. She admits that it's easy for her to say that in the abstract. Sam's position is conditional. If her mother were to show up, a lot would depend on whether the woman had straightened herself out.

Dan is going into his senior year of high school. He stands six-foot, two inches and has developed into a talented basketball player. He's planning on attending university and majoring in pre-med. He has submitted applications to seven universities thus far. He just finished first responder training and he is the youngest member of the local volunteer fire department.

Shawn has shown a special interest in working with animals. Doc Bitner hired him to come into the clinic after school twice-a-week and on Saturdays. While he has shown some athletic ability, he has no interest in team sports. He's taking martial arts lessons in the Tae Kwon Do form of karate. It's done a lot to boost his self-confidence and self-discipline. He has a golden retriever named Angus.

Clayton McMurray stopped by to visit with Andy last summer. They went sailing for an afternoon during which time they exchanged theories and known facts about Melvin Stark. They talked some about their past war experiences. It stirred up a number of unpleasant memories for Andy. After a couple of weeks of turmoil, he told Sam that he needed to get away by himself. He sailed north. It took him a full day to reach Rock Island. He stayed there for three days. He returned home on the fifth day, vowing to himself and Sam that he wouldn't let the past mess him up like that again.

Let's see, who else? Nurse Audrey Reye recovered completely from her attempted suicide. Despite Mike's efforts to resume a friendship with Audrey, she was unable to forgive herself. She eventually resigned her position as head of the intensive care unit and left town. No one has heard from or about her since.

When it became apparent that Andy's medical bills were going to exceed the limits of coverage his health insurance provided, he sought legal counsel. He was able to get some funds from a State victim's compensation fund. A suit is pending against Melvin Stark's estate. Surprisingly Stark had a number of strong assets. Andy's attorney feels optimistic that Andy will end up not only debt free, but with a generous compensatory damage settlement. He and Sam discussed what to do with the money should it be awarded to him. Andy has suggested that a portion of the money be set aside to help pay some of the college expenses for Sam's two younger sisters. Sam insists that it only pay a portion of their expenses. She is adamant that the girls work for a good part of their education. Andy wants the remainder to be set aside to assist the families of Stark's other victims.

My friend Jim, who has helped edit this book asked me, "Did this Stark guy have an agenda, or was he just a fucking psychopath?" While I was pondering an answer, wondering if I had failed to make it clear, he came to his own conclusion. "I really identify with the Andy character."

"Me, too. He's my alter ego. He's who I wish I was. Maybe we all ought to have one."

The Andy McLeod Mystery Series:
"Starting Over"
"The Dog Who Took His Man for a Walk"

Coming Soon!
"Sometimes You Get the Bear"